ROGUE

NEW YORK TIMES BESTSELLING AUTHOR

JULIE KAGAWA

HARLEQUIN® TEEN

Recycling programs
for this product may
not exist in your area.

ISBN-13: 978-0-373-21146-3

Rogue

Copyright © 2015 by Julie Kagawa

5/15

This edition published by arrangement with Harlequin Books S.A.

For questions and comments about the quality of this book, please contact us at CustomerService@Harlequin.com.

® and TM are trademarks of Harlequin Enterprises Limited or its corporate affiliates. Trademarks indicated with ® are registered in the United States Patent and Trademark Office, the Canadian Intellectual Property Office and in other countries.

www.HarlequinTEEN.com

Printed in U.S.A.

To Laurie and Tashya

PART I

COUNTDOWN

GARRET

I stood before a silent, watchful table, six pairs of eyes on me, keen gazes ranging from suspicious to appraising as we waited for the charges to be declared. Men in uniforms of black and gray, with the emblem of the Order—a red cross on a white shield—displayed proudly on their jackets. Their harsh, lined faces reflected a lifetime of war and struggle. Some I knew only by reputation. Others I had trained under, fought for, followed commands from without a second thought. Lieutenant Gabriel Martin sat at one end of the table, his black eyes and blank expression giving nothing away. I'd known him nearly my whole life; he had molded me into what I was today. The Perfect Soldier, as my squad mates had taken to calling me. A nickname I'd picked up during the relatively short time I'd been fighting. *Prodigy* was another word that had been tossed around over the years, and *lucky son of a bitch*, if they were feeling less generous. I owed most of my success to Lieutenant Martin, for recognizing something in a quiet, somber orphan and pushing him to try harder, to do more. To rise above everyone else. So I had. I'd killed more enemies of the Order than anyone else my age, and the number would've been much higher had the unexpected not occurred this summer. Regardless of my situation, I had been one of the best, and I had Martin to thank for that.

But the man sitting across the table was a stranger, an impassive judge. He, along with the rest of the men seated there in a row, would decide my fate tonight.

The room in which I stood was small but Spartan, with tile floors, harsh overhead lights, low ceilings and walls with no windows. Normally it was used for debriefings or the occasional meeting, and the long table usually sat in the center surrounded by chairs. Except for the main headquarters in London, Order chapterhouses did not have designated courtrooms. While disorderly conduct among soldiers was expected from time to time, and desertion sometimes reared its ugly head, full-blown treason was unheard of. Loyalty to the cause was something every soldier of St. George understood. To betray the Order was to betray everything.

The man in the very center of the row straightened, eyeing me over the polished wood. His name was John Fischer, and he was a respected captain of the Order and a hero in the field. The left side of his face was a mass of burn scars and puckered flesh, and he wore them like a medal of honor. His steely expression didn't change as he folded his equally scarred hands in front of him and raised his voice.

"Garret Xavier Sebastian." He barked my full name, and the room instantly fell silent. The trial was officially under way. "For disobeying a direct order," Fischer continued, "attacking a squad mate, fraternizing with the enemy and allowing three known hostiles to escape, you are accused of high treason against the Order of St. George." His sharp blue eyes fixed on me, hard and unyielding. "Do you understand the charges brought against you?"

"I do."

"Very well." He looked at the men sitting in chairs along the far wall behind me, and nodded. "Then we will commence. Tristan St. Anthony, step forward."

There was a squeak as a body rose from a chair, then quiet footsteps clicked across the floor as my former partner came to stand a few feet from my side.

I didn't look at him. I stared straight ahead, hands behind my back, as he did the same. But I could see him in my peripheral vision, a tall, lean soldier several years older than me, his dark hair cropped close. His perpetual smirk had been replaced with a grim line, and his blue eyes were solemn as he faced the table.

"Please inform the court, to the best of your ability, of the events that led up to the night of the raid, and what conspired after."

Tristan hesitated. I wondered what was going through his head in the split second before he would give his testimony. If he had any regrets that it had come to this.

"This summer," Tristan began, his voice matter-of-fact, "Sebastian and I were sent undercover to Crescent Beach, a small town on the California coast. Our orders were specific— we were to infiltrate the town, find a sleeper planted among the population and terminate it."

The man in the center raised a hand. "So, to be clear, Talon had planted one of their operatives in Crescent Beach, and you were sent to find it."

"Yes, sir." Tristan gave a short nod. "We were there to kill a dragon."

A murmur went through the room. From the very first day the Order had been founded, soldiers of St. George had known what we fought for, what we protected, what was at stake. Our war, our holy mission, hadn't changed in hundreds of years. The Order had evolved with the times—firearms and technology had replaced swords and lances—but our purpose was still the same. We had one goal, and every soldier dedicated his entire life to that cause.

The complete annihilation of our eternal enemies, the dragons.

The general public knew nothing of our ancient war. The existence of dragons was a jealously guarded secret, on both sides. There were no real dragons in the world today, unless you counted a couple mundane lizard species that were pale shadows of their infamous namesakes. True dragons—the massive, winged, fire-breathing creatures that haunted the mythology of every culture around the world, from the treasure-loving monsters of Europe to the benevolent rain-bringers of the Orient—existed only in legend and story.

And that was exactly what they wanted you to believe.

Just as the Order of St. George had evolved through the years, so had our enemies. According to St. George doctrine, when dragons were on the verge of extinction, they'd made a pact with the devil to preserve their race, gaining the ability to Shift into human form. Whether or not the story was true, the part where they could change their form to appear human was no myth. Dragons were flawless mimics; they looked human, acted human, sounded human, to the point where it was nearly impossible to tell a dragon from a regular, everyday mortal, even if you knew what to search for. How many dragons existed in the world today was anyone's guess; they had woven seamlessly into human society, masquerading as us, hiding in plain sight. Hidden and cloaked, they strove to enslave humanity, to make humans the lesser species. It was our job to find and kill as many of the monsters as we could, in the hopes that one day, we could push their numbers over the brink and firmly into extinction where they belonged.

That was what I'd once believed. Until I met her.

"I've read your report, St. Anthony," Fischer continued. "It says you and Sebastian made contact with the suspect and began your investigation."

"Yes, sir," Tristan agreed. "We made contact with Ember Hill, and Garret began establishing a relationship, per orders, to determine if she was the sleeper."

Ember. Her name sent a little pulse through my stomach. Before the events of Crescent Beach, I'd known who I was—a soldier of St. George. My mission was to make contact with the target, determine if it was a dragon and kill it. Clear-cut. Black-and-white. Simple.

Only…it wasn't so simple. The target we'd been sent to destroy turned out to be a girl. A cheerful, daring, funny, beautiful girl. A girl who loved to surf, who taught *me* how to surf, who challenged me, made me laugh and surprised me every time I was with her. I'd been expecting a ruthless, duplicitous creature that could only imitate human emotion. But Ember was none of those things.

Fischer continued to address Tristan. "And what did you

determine?" he asked, speaking more for the benefit of the court, I suspected. "Was this girl the sleeper?"

Tristan stared straight ahead, his expression grave. "Yes, sir," he replied, and a shiver ran through me. "Ember Hill was the dragon we were sent to eliminate."

"I see." Fischer nodded. The entire room was silent; you could hear a fly buzzing around the window. "Please inform the court," Fischer said quietly, "what happened the night of the raid. When you and Sebastian tracked the sleeper to the beach after the failed strike on the hideout."

I swallowed, bracing to hear my betrayal lined out for everyone, play-by-play. The night that had brought me here, the decision that had changed everything.

"We'd found the target's hideout," Tristan began, his voice coolly professional. "A nest of at least two dragons, possibly more. It was a standard raid—go in, kill the targets, get out. But they must've had surveillance set up around the house. They were in the process of fleeing when we went in. We wounded one, but they still managed to escape."

My stomach churned. I had led that strike. The targets had "escaped" because I'd seen Ember in that house, and I'd hesitated. My orders had been to shoot on sight—anything that moved, human or dragon, I was supposed to gun down, no questions asked.

But I hadn't. I'd stared at the girl, unable to make myself pull the trigger. And that moment of indecision had cost us the raid, as Ember had Shifted to her true form and turned the room into a blazing inferno. During the fiery confusion, she and the other dragons had fled out the back and off a cliff, and the mansion had burned to the ground.

No one suspected what had happened in the room, that I'd seen Ember over the muzzle of my gun and had frozen. No one knew that the Perfect Soldier had faltered for the very first time. That in that moment, my world and everything I'd ever known had cracked.

But that was nothing compared to what had happened next.

"So the strike was a failure," Fischer said, and I winced inside at the word. "What happened after that?"

For the briefest of moments, Tristan's gaze flicked to me. Almost too fast to be seen, but it still made my heart pound. He knew. Maybe not the whole affair, but he knew something had happened to me after the failed strike. For a short time after the raid, while headquarters was deciding what to do about the escaped dragons, I'd disappeared. Tristan had found me a while later, and we'd gone after the targets together, but by that time, the damage was done.

What had happened after the raid, I'd never told anyone. Later that night, I'd called Ember, asked her to meet me on an isolated bluff, alone. I'd been wearing my helmet and mask during the raid; she hadn't known I was part of St. George. From the hurried tone of her voice, I had guessed she was planning to leave town, possibly with her brother, now that she knew St. George was in the area. But she'd agreed to meet with me one last time. Probably to say goodbye.

I'd been planning to kill her. It was my fault the mission had failed; it was my responsibility to fix it. She was a dragon, and I was St. George. Nothing else mattered. But, once again, staring at the green-eyed girl down the barrel of my gun, the girl who'd taught me to surf and dance and sometimes smiled just for me... I couldn't do it. It was more than a moment's hesitation. More than a heartbeat of surprise. I'd stood face-to-face with the target I had been sent to Crescent Beach to destroy—the girl I knew was my enemy—and I could not make myself pull the trigger.

And that was when she'd attacked. One moment I was drawing down a wide-eyed human girl, the next I was on my back, pinned by a snarling red dragon, its fangs inches from my throat. In that moment, I'd known I was going to die, torn apart by claws or incinerated with dragonfire. I had dropped my guard, left myself open, and the dragon had responded as any of its kind would when faced with St. George. Strangely enough, I'd felt no regret.

And then, as I'd lain helpless beneath a dragon and braced myself for death, the unthinkable had happened.

She'd let me go.

Nothing had driven her off. No one from St. George had arrived in the nick of time to save me. We'd been alone, miles from anything. The bluff had been dark, deserted and isolated; even if I'd screamed, there'd been nothing, no one, to hear it.

Except the dragon. The ruthless, calculating monster that was supposed to despise mankind and possess no empathy, no humanity, whatsoever. The creature that hated St. George above all else and showed us no pity, gave no quarter or forgiveness. The target I'd lied to, the girl I'd pursued with the sole intent of destroying her, who could have ended my life right then with one quick slash or breath. The dragon who had a soldier of St. George beneath its claws, completely at its mercy…had deliberately backed off and let me go.

And I had realized…the Order was wrong. St. George taught us that dragons were monsters. We killed them without question, because there was nothing *to* question. They were alien, Other. Not like us.

Only…they were. Ember had already shaken every belief the Order had instilled in me about dragons; that she'd spared my life was the final blow, the proof I couldn't ignore. Which meant that some of the dragons I'd killed in the past, gunned down without thought because the Order had told me to, might've been like her.

And if that was the case, I had a lot of innocent blood on my hands.

"After the raid," Tristan said, continuing to address the table, "Garret and I were ordered to follow Ember Hill in the hopes that she would lead us to the other targets. We tracked her to a beach on the edge of town, where she did indeed meet with two other dragons. A juvenile and an adult."

Another murmur ran through the courtroom. "An adult," Fischer confirmed, while the rest of the table looked grim. Full-grown adult dragons were rarely seen; the oldest dragons were also the most secretive, keeping to the shadows, hiding deep within their organization. The Order knew Talon's leader was an extremely old, extremely powerful dragon called the Elder Wyrm, but no one had ever laid eyes on it.

"Yes, sir," Tristan went on. "We were to observe and report if the target revealed itself as a dragon, and all three were in their true forms when we got there. I informed Commander St. Francis at once and received the order to shoot on sight." He paused, and Fischer's eyes narrowed.

"What happened then, soldier?"

"Garret stopped me, sir. He prevented me from taking the shot."

"Did he give any reason for his actions?"

"Yes, sir." Tristan took a deep breath, as if the next words were difficult to say. "He told me…that the Order was wrong."

Silence fell. A stunned, brittle silence that raised the hair on the back of my neck. To imply that the Order was mistaken was to spit on the code that the first knights had implemented centuries ago. The code that denounced dragons as soulless wyrms of the devil and their human sympathizers as corrupted, beyond hope.

"Is there anything else?" Fischer's expression was cold, mirroring the looks of everyone at the table. Tristan paused again, then nodded.

"Yes, sir. He said that he wouldn't let me kill the targets, that some dragons weren't evil and that we didn't have to slaughter them. When I tried to reason with him, he attacked me. We fought, briefly, and he knocked me out."

I winced. I hadn't meant to injure my partner. But I couldn't let him fire. Tristan's sniping skills were unmatched. He would've killed at least one dragon before they realized what was happening. I couldn't stand there and watch Ember be murdered in front of me.

"By the time I woke up," Tristan finished, "the targets had escaped. Garret surrendered to our squad leader and was taken into custody, but we were unable to find the dragons again."

"Is that all?"

"Yes, sir."

Fischer nodded. "Thank you, St. Anthony. Garret Xavier Sebastian," he went on, turning to me as Tristan stepped away. His eyes and voice remained hard. "You've heard the charges brought against you. Do you have anything to say in your defense?"

I took a quiet breath.

"I do." I raised my head, facing the men at the table. I'd been debating whether I wanted to say anything, to tell the Order to its face that they had been mistaken all this time. This would damn me even further, but I had to try. I owed it to Ember, and all the dragons I had killed.

"This summer," I began, as the flat stares of the table shifted to me, "I went to Crescent Beach expecting to find a dragon. I didn't." One of the men blinked; the rest simply continued to stare as I went on. "What I found was a girl, someone just like me in a lot of ways. But she was also her own person. There was no imitation of humanity, no artificial emotions or gestures. Everything she did was genuine. Our mission took so long because I couldn't see any differences between Ember Hill and a civilian."

The silence in the courtroom now took on a lethal stillness. Gabriel Martin's face was like stone, his stare icy. I didn't dare turn to look at Tristan, but I could feel his incredulous gaze on my back.

I swallowed the dryness in my throat. "I'm not asking for clemency," I went on. "My actions that night were inexcusable. But I beg the court to consider my suggestion that not all dragons are the same. Ember Hill could be an anomaly among her kind, but from what I saw she wanted nothing to do with the war. If there are others like her—"

"Thank you, Sebastian." Fischer's voice was clipped. His chair scraped the floor as he pushed it back and stood, gazing over the room. "Court is adjourned," he announced. "We will reconvene in an hour. Dismissed."

★ ★ ★

Back in my cell, I sat on the hard mattress with my back against the wall and one knee drawn to my chest, waiting for the court to decide my fate. I wondered if they would consider my words. If the impassioned testimony of the former Perfect Soldier would be enough to give them pause.

"Garret."

I looked up. Tristan's lean, wiry form stood in front of the cell bars. His face was stony, but I looked closer and saw that his expression was conflicted, almost tormented. He glared at me, midnight-blue eyes searing a hole through my skull, before he sighed and made an angry, hopeless gesture, shaking his head.

"What the hell were you thinking?"

I looked away. "It doesn't matter."

"Bullshit." Tristan stepped forward, looking like he might punch me in the head if there weren't iron bars between us. "Three years we've been partners. Three years we've fought together, killed together, nearly gotten ourselves eaten a couple times. I've saved your hide countless times, and yes, I know you've done the same for me. You owe me a damn explanation, partner. And don't you dare say something stupid, like I wouldn't understand. I know you better than that."

When I didn't answer, he clenched a fist around a bar, brow furrowed in confusion and anger. "What happened in Crescent Beach, Garret?" he demanded, though his voice was almost pleading. "You're the freaking Perfect Soldier. You know the code by heart. You can recite the tenets in your sleep, backward if you need to. Why would you betray everything?"

"I don't know—"

"It was the girl, wasn't it?" Tristan's voice made my stomach drop. "The dragon. She did something to you. Damn, I should've seen it. You hung out with her a lot. She could've been manipulating you that whole time."

"It wasn't like that." In the old days, it was suspected that dragons could cast spells on weak-minded humans, enslaving them through mind control and magic. Though that rumor had officially been discounted, there were still those in St. George who believed the old superstitions. Not that Tristan had been one of them; he was just as coolly pragmatic as me, one of the reasons we got along so well. But I suspected it was easier for him to accept that an evil dragon had turned his friend against his will, rather than that friend knowingly and deliberately betraying him and the Order. *You can't blame Garret; the dragon made him do it.*

But it *wasn't* anything Ember had done. It was just… everything about her. Her passion, her fearlessness, her love for life. Even in the middle of the mission, I'd forgotten that she was a potential target, that she could be a dragon, the very creature I was there to destroy. When I was around Ember, I didn't see her as an objective, or a target, or the enemy. I just saw her.

"What, then?" Tristan demanded, sounding angry again. "What, exactly, was it like, Garret? Please explain it to me. Explain to me how my partner, the soldier who has killed more dragons then anyone his age in the history of St. George, suddenly decided that he couldn't kill *this* dragon. Explain how he could turn his back on his family, on the Order that raised him, taught him everything he knows and gave him a purpose, to side with the enemy. Explain how he could stab his own partner in the back, to save one dragon bitch who..."

Tristan stopped. Stared at me. I watched the realization creep over him, watched the color drain from his face as the pieces came together.

"Oh, my God," he whispered and took one staggering step away from the bars. His jaw hung slack, and he slowly shook his head, his voice full of horrified disbelief. "You're *in love* with it."

I looked away and stared at the far wall. Tristan blew out a long breath.

"Garret." His voice was a rasp, choked with disgust and loathing. And maybe something else. Pity. "I don't... How could—"

"Don't say anything, Tristan." I didn't look at my ex-partner; I didn't have to see him to know exactly what he felt. "You don't have to tell me. I know."

"They're going to kill you, Garret," he went on, his voice low and strained. "After what you said today in the courtroom? Martin might've argued clemency if you'd admitted you were wrong, that you had a brief moment of insanity, that the dragons had tricked you, anything! You could have lied. You're one of our best—they might've let you live, even after everything. But now?" He made a hopeless sound. "You'll be executed for treason against the Order. You know that, right?"

I nodded. I'd known the outcome of the trial before I ever set foot in that courtroom. I knew I could have denounced my actions, pleaded for mercy, told them what they wanted to hear. I had been deceived, lied to, manipulated. Because that's what dragons did, and even the soldiers of St. George were not immune. It would paint me the fool, and my Perfect Soldier record would be tarnished for all time, but being duped by the enemy was not the same as knowingly betraying the Order. Tristan was right; I could have lied, and they would've believed me.

I hadn't. Because I couldn't do this anymore.

Tristan waited a moment longer, then strode away without another word. I listened to his receding footsteps and knew this was the last time I would ever talk to him. I looked up.

"Tristan."

For a second, I didn't think he would stop. But he paused in the doorway of the cell block and looked back at me.

"For what it's worth," I said, holding his gaze, "I'm sorry." He blinked, and I forced a faint smile. "Thanks...for having my back all this time."

One corner of his mouth twitched. "I always knew you'd get yourself killed by a dragon," he muttered. "I just didn't think it would be like this." He gave a tiny snort and rolled his eyes. "You realize my next partner is going to feel completely inadequate taking the Perfect Soldier's place, and will probably have a nervous breakdown that *I'm* going to have to deal with. So, thanks for that."

"At least you'll have something to remember me by."

"Yeah." The small grin faded. We watched each other for a tense, awkward moment, before Tristan St. Anthony stepped away.

"Take care, partner," he said. No other words were needed.

No goodbye, or see you later. We both knew there wouldn't
be a later.

"You, too."

He turned and walked out the door.

★ ★ ★

"The court has reached a decision."

I stood in the courtroom again as Fischer rose to his feet,
addressing us all. I spared a quick glance at Martin and found
that he was gazing at a spot over my head, his eyes blank.

"Garret Xavier Sebastian," Fischer began, his voice brisk,
"by unanimous decision, you have been found guilty of high
treason against the Order of St. George. For your crimes, you
will be executed by firing squad tomorrow at dawn. May God
have mercy on your soul."

DANTE

Fifteenth floor and counting.

The elevator box was cold. Stark. A pithy tune played somewhere overhead, tinny and faint. Mirrored walls surrounded us, blurred images staring back, showing a man in a gray suit and tie, and a teen standing at his shoulder, hands folded before him. I observed my reflection with the practiced cool detachment my trainer insisted upon. My new black suit was perfectly tailored, not a thread out of place, my crimson hair cut short and styled appropriately. A red silk tie was tucked neatly into my suit jacket, my shoes were polished to a dark sheen and the large gold Rolex was a cool, heavy band around my wrist. I didn't look like that human boy from Crescent Beach, in shorts and a tank top, his longish hair messy and windblown. I didn't look like a teen without a care in the world. No, I had completed assimilation. I'd proven myself, to Talon and the organization. I'd passed all my tests and confirmed that I could be trusted, that I cared about the survival of our race above all else.

I wished my sister had done the same. Because of her, our future was in question. Because of her, I didn't know what Talon wanted from me now.

On the thirtieth floor, the elevator stopped, and the doors slid back with barely a hiss. I stepped into a magnificent lobby tiled in red and gold, my shoes clicking against the floor and echoing into the vast space above us. I gazed around, taking it in, smiling to myself. It was everything I'd imagined, everything I'd hoped Talon would be. Which was good, because I had plans for it all.

One day, I'll be running this place.

My trainer, who'd told me to call him *Mr. Smith* at the beginning of my education, led me into the room, then turned to me with a smile. Unlike some dragons whose smiles seemed forced, his was warm and inviting and looked completely genuine, if you didn't notice the cool impassiveness in his eyes.

"Ready?"

"Of course," I said, trying not to appear nervous. Unfortunately, Mr. Smith could sense fear and tension like a shark sensed blood, for his eyes hardened even as his smile grew broader.

"Relax, Dante," he said, putting a hand on my shoulder. It was meant to be comforting, but there was no warmth in the gesture. I'd learned enough to realize that all his overtures were empty; he'd taught me that himself. You didn't have to believe what you were saying; you just had to make others believe that you cared. "You'll be fine, trust me."

"You don't have to worry about me, sir," I told him, determined to show nothing but cool confidence. A stark contrast to the twisting bundle of nerves in my stomach. "I know why I'm here. And I know what I have to do."

He squeezed my shoulder and, even though I knew better, I relaxed. We turned, and I followed him down a narrow hallway lined with office doors, around a corner and finally to a single large door at the end of the hall. A simple gold sign hung against the painted wood: A. R. Roth.

My stomach cartwheeled again. Mr. Roth was one of Talon's senior vice presidents. One of the dragons who, while not so far up the chain that he was in contact with the Elder Wyrm itself, was pretty darn close. And he wanted to talk to me. Probably about Ember and what they planned to do about her.

Ember. I felt a brief stab of anger and fear for my wayward twin; anger that she would be so stubborn, so rebellious and ungrateful, that she would turn her back on her own kind— the organization that had raised us—to run off with a known traitor, consequences be damned. Fear of what those consequences could be. Under normal circumstances, a Viper, one of Talon's fearsome assassins, would be dispatched to deal with a dragon who went rogue. It was harsh but necessary. Rogue dragons were unstable and dangerous, and they put the survival of our race in jeopardy. Without Talon's structure, a rogue could accidentally, or even purposefully, reveal our existence to the humans, and that would spell disaster for us all. The human world could never know that dragons walked among them; their instinctive fear of monsters and the unknown would overtake them, just as it had hundreds of years ago, and we'd be driven toward extinction again.

I knew the measures Talon had to take against rogues were necessary. Though the loss of any dragon was a heavy blow to us all, those who refused to align themselves with the organization had already chosen their path, proven their disloyalty. They had to be put down. I understood. I wasn't going to argue that.

But Ember wasn't a traitor. She had been misled, deceived, by that rogue dragon. She'd always been hotheaded, gullible, and he had fed her a tangle of lies, turning her against Talon, her own race…and me. *He* was at fault for her disappearance. Ember had always had…problems…with authority, but she'd been able to see reason and listen to the truth until she met the rogue.

I clenched my jaw. If she just returned to the organization, she would realize her mistake. I would make her see the truth: that the rogues were dangerous, that Talon had our best interests at heart and that the only way to survive in a world of humans was to work together. *Ut onimous sergimus.* As one, we rise. She'd believed that, once.

I had never lost sight of it.

We stepped through the door frame into a cold, stark office. One entire wall was made up of windows, and through the glass, the city of Los Angeles stretched on to the distant mountains, towers and skyscrapers glinting in the sun.

"Mr. Roth," said Mr. Smith, ushering me forward, "this is Dante Hill."

A man rose from behind a large black desk to greet us, smiling as he stepped forward with a hand outstretched. He wore a navy blue suit and a watch that was even more impressive than mine, and a gold-capped pen glinted in a breast pocket. His dark hair had been cropped into short spikes, and his even darker eyes swept over me critically, even as he took my hand in both of his, nearly crushing my fingers in a grip of steel.

"Dante Hill! Pleasure to meet you." He squeezed my hand,

and I bit down a whimper, smiling through the pain. "How was your trip up?"

"Fine, sir," I replied, relieved as he loosened his viselike grip and stepped away. Talon had sent a car to take us from Crescent Beach to Los Angeles, but the drive had been far from relaxing, with my trainer drilling me on company policies, protocol and how to act in front of the regional vice president. I was an insignificant hatchling, meeting with an elder who was likely several hundred years old. First impressions were crucial. And a terrible faux pas was, of course, to complain in the presence of Talon's executives, especially if it was about the organization. "It was so smooth, I barely noticed the drive."

"Wonderful, wonderful." He nodded and gestured to the plush leather chair sitting in front of his desk. "Please, have a seat. Can I have my assistant get you something to drink?"

"No, thank you, sir," I said, knowing the drill. "I'm all right." I sat carefully in one of the chairs, feeling myself sink into the cool leather, careful not to slouch. Mr. Smith did the same and crossed his legs as Mr. Roth returned around his desk and beamed at me.

"So, Mr. Hill. Let's not beat around the bush." Mr. Roth clasped his hands on the desk in front of him and smiled over the surface. As I'd been taught, I politely dropped my gaze so I wouldn't be staring right into his eyes. Another social gaffe, and a very dangerous one: holding the stare of another dragon, particularly a male, was a blatant challenge or threat. In ancient times, the challenge between two alpha drakes would be settled via personal combat, with the contenders ripping, biting and slashing each other, until one of them either fled in defeat or was killed. Nowadays, two rival dragons obviously couldn't throw down in the middle of the city, but there were a thousand other ways to destroy a competitor without getting your claws dirty. Which was good, because that was something I could excel at.

"Your sister," Mr. Roth said, making my insides clench, "has gone rogue." He observed my reaction carefully; I kept my face neutral, showing no anger, surprise, sorrow, shock—nothing that would be considered a weakness. After a brief pause, Mr. Roth continued, "Ember Hill is now a traitor in the eyes of Talon, something we take very seriously here. I am sure you know our policy on rogues, but I have heard the organization wishes you to be in charge of retrieving her, Mr. Hill."

"Yes, sir," I replied, careful not to sound overeager. "Whatever it takes to bring her back, whatever you need me to do, I'm your man."

Mr. Roth raised an eyebrow.

"And yet, some have called into question your own loyalty, both to Talon and our cause. As the brother of a known traitor, we worry that your motivations might be…tainted." He offered a smile, even as his eyes stayed hard and cold. "So, I fear I must ask. Can we trust you, Mr. Hill?"

I smiled. "Sir," I began, as clearly and confidently as I could. "I know my sister. Ember and I have always had… different opinions, when it came to the organization. I know she can be reckless and stubborn, and that she has a slight problem with authority." A tiny snort from Mr. Smith was the only indicator of my massive understatement.

"But Ember isn't a traitor," I went on, feeling Mr. Roth's

hard gaze on me, assessing and critical. "She's gullible and hotheaded, and I believe the rogue dragon Cobalt took advantage of this to get her to leave with him. He lied to her about the organization, and he lied to her about me, otherwise she would have never turned on us like this."

Mr. Roth's expression hadn't changed. And neither had mine. "Ember tried to get me to come with her that night," I admitted, seeing no indication of surprise from Mr. Roth. "She begged me to leave town with her and the rogue, but I knew I couldn't do it. Not because of the consequences, but because I know my place." I raised my chin slightly, not enough to challenge, just enough to state my cause. "Sir, my loyalty to Talon has never wavered. I don't know why Talon is taking a less…direct approach to dealing with my sister, why the Elder Wyrm has chosen to spare her, but I do know that I am grateful. And I'll do whatever it takes to bring Ember back so she can resume her place in Talon, where she belongs."

Mr. Roth nodded.

"Excellent, Mr. Hill," he said in a bright tone of voice. "That is exactly what we want to hear." He picked up his desk phone and pressed a button on the machine. "Please send Ms. Anderson in," he ordered into the speaker. I blinked, wondering who Ms. Anderson could be; I'd never met her before.

Abruptly, Mr. Roth stood, which prompted us to rise, too. "Your words are commendable, Mr. Hill," the VP said, walking around to stand beside us. "Therefore, Talon is prepared to give you the best possible resources to locate and bring back your sister. In a moment, you'll be shown to your new office, but for now, there is someone I want you to meet."

I gave a pleasant nod, though my mind was spinning. *New*

office? And the best resources possible to find her? I was pleased, of course. It seemed the organization had recognized my potential, but at the same time, I knew this was abnormal. Talon was huge; its reach spanned the globe, and it had countless other developments, mostly of the multimillion-dollar variety, to worry about. The disappearance of a single hatchling, rogue or not, was barely a blip on its radar. *Why? Why are they going through all this trouble to find one hatchling? Ember, what have you done?*

The office door clicked softly as it opened, and Mr. Roth raised a beckoning hand.

"Ah, Ms. Anderson. Please come in. Have you met Mr. Hill?"

"Haven't had the pleasure," said a lilting, musical voice. I turned to face the newcomer. My brows arched a bit, and I straightened quickly. Not a human; this was another dragon, and on top of that, a hatchling. Except for my sister, I'd only ever met with adult and senior dragons, but this girl looked just a year or two older than me. She was fair and slender, wearing a light blue skirt and heels and looking faintly uncomfortable in them. Like she'd rather be wearing jeans and a T-shirt. Her pale, almost silvery hair was styled atop her head, the sides pulled back to accent her high cheekbones, and the large, crystal-blue eyes stared straight ahead.

"This is Mist," Mr. Roth introduced as she regarded me in silence, her gaze coolly remote. "Ms. Anderson, this is Mr. Hill. I expect the pair of you will get along famously."

I hid my surprise. By introducing her by her first name, Roth was subtly informing her—informing all of us—that I was in charge. That, although she was slightly older and had probably been working here awhile, we were not equals. I hoped the other hatchling wouldn't challenge my position, but Mist held out her hand as if this meeting was nothing out of the ordinary. "Nice to meet you, Mr. Hill," she said, her voice as cool as her face. I took the offered hand with a wide smile.

"Mist." I smiled, holding her gaze. "The pleasure is mine."

"Ms. Anderson is one of our newer operatives," Mr. Roth continued, seemingly unaware, or uncaring, of the tension as we sized each other up. "She comes highly recommended by her trainer, and we believe her skills are adequate for this situation. She will be aiding you in the search for our wayward Ember.

"Ms. Anderson," Mr. Roth continued. "Would you please introduce Mr. Hill to the rest of his team and then have someone show him his office? I would take him myself, but I have a meeting with your trainer in a few minutes. Mr. Hill..." He turned to me. "You say you have your sister's best interests at heart? Now is your chance to prove it. Bring her back to Talon, where she belongs. We will be keeping an eye on your progress."

I nodded politely, though I knew the meaning behind those words. *We'll be watching you* was the translation of that statement. *Don't disappoint us.*

I won't, I promised silently, and turned away.

As I followed Mist out of Mr. Roth's office, I nearly ran into someone coming in, and I stepped aside with a hasty apology. The person I'd almost hit barely gave me a second glance as she passed, but my stomach dropped as I met her familiar poison-green eyes. Lilith, Talon's elite Viper assassin, gave a short nod, recognizing me as well, before continuing into Mr. Roth's office and closing the door behind her.

Apprehension flickered. *Why is Lilith here?* I thought. *Is she…?* I glanced at Mist, walking beside me with her eyes straight ahead. *Is she Mist's trainer? Is that why she's here?*

Wary now, I followed Mist into the elevator, keeping her in my side view as she pressed a button, still not looking at me. The doors slid shut, and the box began to move.

"So." Mist's voice echoed in the tiny space, startling me. I'd been expecting her to stay quiet and distant, not speaking unless absolutely necessary. I'd been about to break the silence myself and was surprised that she'd beat me to it. "You're Dante Hill."

Her voice was a challenge. It seemed we were going to butt heads after all, unless I could win her over. I could've used my position to demand obedience; Roth had put me in charge, after all, but resentful employees did not produce fast results. If I was going to find Ember quickly, I needed her on my side.

Smiling, I leaned against the wall and put my hands in my pockets, adopting a pose of easy nonchalance. "I am," I agreed pleasantly. "Though you seem surprised, Mist. Let me guess—you expected me to be taller."

Mist's expression remained neutral. "A Chameleon in training," she remarked, raising a slender eyebrow, "using humor to defuse a tense situation. Classic disarming technique."

I kept the smile on my face. "Did it work?"

She blinked, and the other corner of her mouth twitched. "No," she replied, though her eyes said differently. "But thank you for trying. I am, unfortunately, well versed in the various faction trainings and techniques. Your Chameleon charm is not going to work on me, I'm afraid."

"Give it time."

The elevator had passed the first floor. And still, we continued to descend. Past the basement, and the subbasement, going even deeper underground. "Do you have something against Chameleons?" I went on, wondering how many sublevels this place had. The glowing numbers above the door had stopped moving altogether.

"Not at all," Mist replied. "Chameleons are a vital part of Talon. We all have our place." Her piercing blue eyes remained brutally honest as she looked me over, assessing. "What I don't like is having vital information kept from me, especially if I need it to do my job."

I gave her a puzzled frown. "You think I'm hiding something from you? That's a rather hasty conclusion. We haven't known each other very long."

"It's not you, Mr. Hill." Mist's tone remained coolly polite. "But you must know that this situation with your sister is not normal. Why is Talon so interested in her? Cobalt I can understand—he's a dangerous fugitive who has caused real harm to the organization, and his actions cannot be ignored any longer. The rogue must be stopped, that is very clear." Her piercing blue gaze sharpened, cutting into me. "But why is Talon so invested in bringing *her* back? Why go through all this trouble? Ember Hill is a hatchling who has done nothing for the organization." Mist's eyes narrowed even further. "Why is she so special?"

Her words were eerily familiar, as I heard my own suspicions parroted back at me. The situation with Ember *wasn't* normal. Talon was expending considerable resources to return her to the organization when they could have sent out a Viper and been done with it. Even bringing *me* on was puzzling. Yes, I was her brother and the person who knew her best, but why bother? What made her—*our*—situation so special?

However, I wasn't going to tell Mist that I shared her concerns. If I was going to bring Ember back, if I was going to make a future for us in Talon, then I had to appear fully in control of the situation at all times. I could not appear weak, or scared, or unsure, because Talon had no use for dragons who failed. I was not going to fail.

"I'm afraid I can't give you the details," I told Mist, who gave me a cold look but didn't seem surprised. Talon shared information only if they thought it was necessary; that much at least she understood. "I would," I went on, "if I were allowed. Just know that finding Ember is our top priority. The Elder Wyrm wishes that she be returned to the organization. The reasons are irrelevant."

The elevator stopped, and the doors slid open. Mist watched me a moment longer, blue eyes appraising, then gave a tiny nod. "Of course," she said, coolly professional once more, and motioned me into the hall. "This way, Mr. Hill. I'll introduce you to the rest of the team."

"Just call me Dante," I invited, a tactic to gain her loyalty, and followed her down a long, brightly lit corridor past several offices, until we came to a door at the very end. Without hesitation, Mist pushed it back, and we went through.

I gazed around, impressed. The room beyond was enormous, a sprawling floor of desks, computers, flashing screens, and people. Aisles of long counters snaked their way across the room, each holding numerous computers with glassy-eyed humans sitting in front of them. The entire back wall was one enormous screen divided into numerous parts that projected a dozen images of maps, satellite feeds, security cams and more. The murmur of voices, ringing phones, buzzing computers and clicking keyboards all blended into a general cacophony of noise that flowed over me as I stepped through the door.

"This is our operating center," Mist explained, leading me across the floor. All around us, humans hurried by or typed feverishly at their desks, avoiding eye contact. Mist continued as if she didn't notice or care. "Talon has dozens of these centers all around the world. It's where we monitor Talon's assets, keep an eye on St. George movement and track persons of interest to the organization. We're mostly in charge of the western region of the US, which is where we think your sister is right now."

She stopped at a desk where two humans sat across from each other, a pair of large screens separating them. When Mist's shadow fell over the desk, the overweight male and small bespectacled female looked up and gave her polite, fixed smiles, which she ignored.

"Mr. Davids and Ms. Kimura have been tasked with locating your sister," Mist told me, not even looking at the two humans. "They've been trying to pinpoint her location ever since she left Crescent Beach. Unfortunately, they've been unable to find any trace of her, or Cobalt, unless something has changed in the time I've been gone?"

She looked down at the humans as she said this, and both of them went pale.

"No, ma'am," the male said quickly. "So far, there have

been no leads on Ember Hill or the rogue dragon Cobalt. We know they're still in California somewhere, but other than that, we've been unable to get a lock on them."

"Where have you been looking?" I asked, making all of them glance at me. Mist raised her eyebrows in amused—or annoyed—surprise, but I ignored her. The humans paused, obviously wondering who I was, some bossy kid in a business suit come strolling into their affairs. I kept the smile on my face and held their gazes with my own, polite but expectant, and after a moment, they looked away.

"We've been able to uncover a couple of Cobalt's nests in the past," the male informed me, quickly turning back to the screen. "His so-called 'safe houses' for rogue dragons. We've been monitoring those areas, hoping he might return to one of them to hide. Unfortunately, when one goes down, he often moves the rest, so we haven't been able to pin him down."

"What about his network?" I asked. "If he has so many safe houses, he has to be able to communicate with them somehow. Have you tried tracing messages back to his location?"

"Of course," the other human said. "We've been trying to breach his security for years. But we've never been able to crack it. Whoever's on the other side knows exactly what he's doing to keep us out."

"What about St. George?" I asked. "Do you have ways of tracking them?"

All three stared at me, varying degrees of confusion and doubt crossing their faces. "Yes," the female human said slowly. "Of course, we have extensive systems for monitoring any movement made by the Order. But we already determined that the cell in Crescent Beach returned to their chapterhouse. When Ms. Hill and Cobalt fled town, their trail went cold, and St. George abandoned the search. There hasn't been any movement from the Order for days, at least not in this region."

"Do you know where this chapterhouse is?"

More puzzled looks. "We could probably find it," the male human said, furrowing his brow. "But, like we said, St. George activity has been quiet the past few days. We believe trying to find Cobalt's underground network is more important—"

"Stop looking for the safe houses," I interrupted. "Ember won't be there. If I know my sister at all, she won't be content to sit and hide. You're wasting your time looking for them." I glanced at the huge screen on the far wall. "Find St. George," I said, feeling Mist's curious gaze on me. "Start looking for the Order. The chapterhouse is a good place to begin. Find it, and tell me when you do."

The humans gaped at me, clearly dumbfounded but too polite to say anything. Mist, however, had no such reservations. "Why?" she asked is a low, cool voice. "You're telling us to abandon the search for the rogue's network when we have clear orders from Talon's VP to locate it, and your sister. Do you know something we don't, Mr. Hill?"

"No," I said, keeping my gaze on the far wall, on one of the many maps spread across the screen. I didn't have any concrete evidence. It was just a hunch, a suspicion, that had been plaguing me since before I left Crescent Beach. But my intuition was rarely wrong, and I'd learned to trust my gut, especially when it came to my sister. I only wished I had listened to it earlier. Much, much earlier.

"But there was…a human," I went on, as they all stared at me like I'd gone insane. "One of the people I met in Crescent Beach. He was a friend of my sister's. Really, I only saw him once or twice. But…there was always something about him, something that I didn't like. I saw him fight, once—he was definitely trained. And he just showed up out of nowhere one day, always hanging around my sister."

"That is not enough reason to suspect someone, Mr. Hill," Mist said in her calm, logical voice. "You can't expect us to drop everything and switch to a new plan of action simply because you have a hunch."

"The night Ember left Crescent Beach," I continued, ignoring that last statement, "she told me she was going to meet this human, alone. She said she wanted to tell him goodbye before she went rogue." I paused, my chest tightening with the memory. "That was the last time I saw her.

"I don't know if that human was part of the Order," I went on, looking back at Mist and the Talon employees. "But I suspect that he was. And both Ember and Lilith were attacked that night by St. George. Ember was close to that human. She…might've told him things, about us. About Talon. If you can find him, track the cell he belongs to, he might lead us to Ember."

"And if he doesn't?"

I narrowed my gaze. "Then you can blame it on me. But it's worth a shot. Better than searching for places where she *might* show up or trying to crack this impossible-to-breach network."

She gave me a long, appraising look. "All right, Mr. Hill," she finally said. "It's not like we have a choice. Mr. Roth did put you in charge, after all. We'll do it your way." She turned to the humans. "You heard him, then. Find that chapterhouse. Start monitoring all St. George activity in the region. If the Order so much as sneezes, I want to know." She looked back at me, crystal-blue eyes defiant. "Did you happen to catch this special human's name, Mr. Hill?"

I nodded. "Yes," I said, feeling a slow burn of anger in the pit of my stomach. Anger at the rogue, and St. George, and the human, for taking my sister away. At jeopardizing all my plans with Talon. I would find her, and nothing would stop me from bringing her back. "His name was Garret Xavier Sebastian."

EMBER

Three hours on the back of a motorcycle, the sun beating down on your shoulders and the wind whipping through your hair, though exhilarating, reminds you why flying wins every time.

"You okay back there, Firebrand?" Riley called over his shoulder. I peeked up from his leather jacket and caught my reflection in his dark shades. My hair whipped and snapped like a flame atop my head, too short to tie back but just long enough to be horribly tangled when we stopped. Before us, the highway stretched on, an endless strip of pavement heading east. Around us, the Mojave Desert provided much the same scenery: sand, scrub, cactus, rock and the occasional hawk or turkey vulture. The air shimmered with heat, but heat never bothered me. My kind was well adapted to dealing with blistering temperatures.

"My butt has gone numb!" I called back, making him smirk. "My hair is going to take hours to untangle, and I think I've eaten like four bugs. And I swear, Riley, if you tell me I should keep my mouth closed, you're going to be riding the rest of the way sidesaddle."

He grinned. "We're about forty-five minutes out. Just hang on."

Sighing, I laid my chin against his back, watching the eternal sameness flash by around us, and let my mind wander.

It had been three days since we left Crescent Beach. Three days since my world had been turned upside down, since I'd learned Talon was hiding things from me, since I'd fought the Order of St. George and discovered that Garret wasn't who I thought he was. Three days since I'd made the decision to go rogue and leave town with Riley, abandoning my family and my old life, and branding myself a traitor in the eyes of Talon.

Three days since I'd last seen Garret. And Dante.

I clenched a fist in Riley's jacket, my emotions churning with anger, sadness and guilt toward them both. Anger that they'd lied, that I'd trusted them, only to have them betray that trust. Garret was part of St. George; he'd been sent to Crescent Beach to kill me. Dante, the brother who'd promised to have my back no matter what, had turned me in to Talon when he'd discovered I was going rogue. But at least Garret had redeemed himself somewhat, saving me and Riley from a Talon assassin, then warning us that his own people were on their way. It was because of him that I was here now, on the back of a motorcycle with Riley, flying across the Mojave Desert. I didn't know where my brother was, but I hoped he was okay. He might've abandoned me to Talon, but I knew Dante. He thought he had been doing the right thing.

Idiot twin. He still didn't know the truth about the organization, the dark secrets they kept, the lies they told us. I'd make him see, eventually. I would get him out of Talon soon.

After I took care of this other thing.

The sun was beginning to drop toward the horizon when Riley slowed and pulled off the highway into a large, nearly empty lot on the side of the road. A sign at the edge of the pavement cast a long shadow over us as we cruised by, making me squint as I gazed up at it.

"'Spanish Manor,'" I read, then looked at the "manor" in question, finding a boxy, derelict motel at the end of the nearly empty parking lot. Peeling yellow doors were placed every thirty or so feet, and ugly orange curtains hung in the darkened windows. Exactly one car, an aging white van, was parked in the spaces out front, and if not for the flickering vacancy sign in the office window, I would've thought the place completely abandoned.

Riley cruised up beside the van and killed the engine, and we both swung off the bike. Relieved to be able to move around again, I put my arms over my head and stretched until I felt my back pop. Gingerly, I tried running my fingers through my hair and found it hopelessly tangled, as I'd feared. Wincing, I tugged at the snarls and tore loose several fiery red strands while Riley looked on in amusement. I scowled at him.

"Ow. Okay, next time, I get a helmet," I said, and his grin widened even more. I rolled my eyes and continued my hopeless battle with the tangles. Of all the human beauty traditions, I found hair the most time-consuming and obnoxious. So much time was wasted washing, brushing, teasing and primping it; scales never had this problem. "Where are we, anyway?" I muttered, separating a stubborn knot with my fingers, trying to ignore the dragon beside me. It was hard.

Lean, tall and broad-shouldered, clad in leather and chains,
Riley certainly cut the figure of a perfect rebel biker boy
leaning so casually against his motorcycle, the breeze tugging at his dark hair. He took off his shades and stuck them
in a back pocket.

"We're about an hour from Vegas," he said, and nodded to
the ramshackle Spanish Manor squatting at the edge of the
lot. "Wes told me to meet him here. Come on."

I followed him over the parking lot, up a rusting flight
of stairs and down the second-story hall until we came to a
faded yellow door near the end. The curtains were drawn
over the grimy window, and the interior of the room looked
dark. Riley glanced around, then knocked on the wood, three
swift taps followed by two slower ones.

A pause, and then the door swung open to reveal a thin,
lanky human on the other side, dark eyes peering at us beneath a scruff of messy brown hair. He scowled at me by way
of greeting, then stepped back to let us in.

"About time you showed up." Wes slammed the door and
threw the locks as if we were in a superspy movie and there
could be enemy agents lurking outside, hiding in the cactus.
"I thought you'd be here hours ago. What happened?"

"Had to make a quick stop in L.A. for a few things," Riley
answered, brushing by him. He did not mention the "things"
in question, namely, a duffel bag full of ammo and firearms.
Both he and Wes ignored me, so I turned to gaze around the
room. A quick glance was all that was required; it was small,
rumpled, unremarkable, with an unmade bed against the wall
and soda cans scattered everywhere. A laptop sat open and

glowing on the corner desk, nonsensical words and formulas splayed across the screen in neat rows.

"Riley…" Wes began, a note of warning in his voice.

"Where are the hatchlings?" Riley asked, overriding whatever he was going to say. "Are they all right? Did you find the safe house?"

"They're fine," Wes answered, sounding impatient. "They're holed up near San Francisco with that Walter chap, with strict instructions not to poke one scale out of the house until they hear from you. They're bloody peachy. *We're* the ones we have to worry about now."

"Good." Riley nodded briskly and walked across the room to the desk, then bent down to the screen. "I assume this is it, then?" he muttered, narrowing his eyes. "Where we'll be going tonight? Did you get everything you needed?"

"Riley." Wes stalked after him. "Did you hear a word I just told you, mate? Do you know how crazy this is? Are you even listening to me?" The other ignored him, and with a scowl, Wes reached across the desk and slapped the laptop shut.

Riley straightened and turned to glare at the human. In the shadows, his eyes suddenly glowed a dangerous yellow, and the air went tight with the soundless, churning energy that came right before a Shift. Riley's true form hovered close to the surface, staring out at the human with angry gold eyes.

To his credit, Wes didn't back down.

"Listen to yourself, Riley." The human faced the other in the dingy light, his voice solemn. "Listen to what you're trying to do. This isn't stealing a hatchling away from Talon. This isn't walking up to a kid and saying, 'Oy, mate, your organization is corrupt as hell and if you don't leave soon you'll never be free.'" He stabbed a finger at the laptop. "This is a bloody St. George compound. With bloody St. George soldiers. One slipup, one mistake, and you'll be hanging from some corporal's wall. Think about what that means, mate." Wes leaned forward, his gaze intense. "Without you, the underground dies. Without you, all those kids you freed from Talon will be helpless when the organization comes for them. And they *will*, Riley, you bloody well know they will. Do you even care about that anymore? Do you care that everything we've worked for is about to go up in flames?" He gestured sharply at me. "Or has this sodding kid got you so wrapped around her finger that you don't know what's important anymore?"

"Hey!" I protested, scowling, but I might as well have shouted at a wall. Riley clenched his fists, nostrils flaring, as if he might punch the human or Shift into his true form and blast him to cinders. Wes continued to glare, chin raised, mouth pressed into a stubborn line. Both of them paid absolutely no attention to me.

"What are we doing, mate?" Wes asked softly, after a moment of brittle silence. "This isn't our fight. This isn't what we said we would do." Riley didn't answer, and Wes's tone became almost pleading. "Riley, this is crazy. This is suicide, you know it as well as I do."

Riley slumped, raking a hand through his messy black hair, the tension leaving his shoulders. "I know," he growled. "Trust me, I know. I've been trying to convince myself I haven't completely lost my mind since we left town."

"Then why—"

"Because if I don't, Ember will go without me and get herself killed!" Riley snapped, and finally looked in my direction. Those piercing gold eyes met mine across the room, the shadow of Riley's true form staring at me. I shivered as he held my gaze. "Because she doesn't know St. George like I do," he went on. "She hasn't seen what they're capable of. She doesn't know what they do to our kind if we're discovered. I do. And I'm not going to let that happen. Even if I have to sneak into a St. George base and rescue one of the bastards myself."

I swallowed, feeling something inside me respond, a rush of warmth spreading through my veins. My own dragon, calling to Riley's, like he was her other half.

Wes scrubbed a hand down his face. "You're both completely off your rockers," he muttered, shaking his head. "And I'm no better, since it seems I'm going along with this lunacy." He groaned and plopped into the chair, then opened the laptop. "Well, since you appear to have lost your mind, let me show you exactly what we're up against."

Riley turned from me, breaking eye contact. I knew I should go see what Wes was talking about. But I could still feel the heat of Riley's gaze, feel the caress of the dragon against my skin. I needed to get away from him to clear my head, to cool the fire surging through my veins. Leaving them to talk, I slipped into the small, only slightly disgusting bathroom and locked the door behind me.

Wes's and Riley's voices echoed through the wood, low and urgent, probably talking about the mission. Or, in Wes's case, trying to convince Riley, once and for all, not to go through with this. I sank onto the toilet seat and ran my hands through my hair, letting the words fade into jumbled background noise.

I knew Wes was right. I knew what I planned to do was stupid and risky as hell. I knew I hadn't considered all the threats, didn't realize what I was getting into. What I was planning flew in the face of everything I'd been taught, and if I voiced it out loud, it sounded insane, even to me.

Break into a compound of St. George, the ancient enemy of our race, the Order whose sole mission was to see us extinct, and rescue one of their own. Sneak into a heavily armed base full of soldiers, free a sole prisoner who could be anywhere and get out. Without getting blown to bits in the process.

It sounded crazy. It *was* crazy. It was downright suicidal, like Wes said. I didn't fault him, or Riley, for being reluctant. They had no stake in this, no reason to want to undergo a mission that could get us all killed. They had every right to be afraid. If I was being completely honest, it terrified me, too.

But I couldn't leave him behind.

I went to the sink to splash water on my face but paused when I caught sight of my reflection. A skinny, green-eyed girl stared back at me from the mirror, red hair standing on end, eyes ringed with dust and dark circles. I didn't look remotely Draconian. I looked tired, and dirty, and very mortal. Nothing fierce or primal lurked inside my gaze to indicate that I was anything more than I seemed.

Was that why he'd hesitated that night on the cliff? When he'd pointed that gun at my head, and I'd finally realized what he really was? When he'd ceased to be Garret and became the enemy, a soldier of St. George?

He could've killed me. I'd been in my human form, taken off guard, and had been too stunned to do anything at first. He'd had me at point-blank range, alone and trapped on a bluff miles from anywhere. All he'd had to do was pull the trigger.

But he hadn't. And later, he'd betrayed his own people to save me and Riley from Lilith, my sadistic trainer and Talon's best Viper assassin. Lilith had come for Riley that night, and when I'd refused to leave him and return to Talon, she'd tried to kill me, too. She'd nearly succeeded. We'd survived only because of Garret's unexpected arrival and his help in driving off the Viper. Otherwise, Lilith would've torn us apart.

But, by helping us, Garret had damned himself. To aid a dragon was treason in the eyes of his Order, and the punishment for such betrayal was death. He'd told me that himself. Garret had known the Order would kill him, and he'd still chosen to save us.

Why?

I'd tried to follow him that night, hoping to somehow get him away from the soldiers who were now his captors. But there had been no opportunity for a rescue, and Riley had finally convinced me that falling back and planning our next move was the best option. So here we were.

I turned on the sink and splashed cold water on my face, washing away the dust and grime. When that was done, I attempted to tame the snarled bird's nest atop my head, wincing as I ran my fingers through the knots and tangles, finally combing them out. I had a brush in my backpack, along with a change of clothes and other essentials, but primping seemed like a giant waste of time right now. Besides, who was around that I wanted to impress? Wes hated me, and Riley... Riley was interested in my other half.

My dragon perked at this, sending a curl of warmth through

my stomach, and I squashed it, and her, down. I didn't know
what I was going to do about Riley, but there were other
things to focus on. Hopefully, Riley and Wes had come up
with a brilliant plan, because other than knowing I couldn't
leave Garret with St. George, I didn't have a clue what to do.

When I came out of the bathroom, Riley and Wes were
bent over the laptop, talking in the same low, urgent tones.
Riley glanced up, and our eyes met once more, making my
skin flush. Then Wes snapped his name, and he turned his
attention to the computer again.

Edging up behind them, I peered over Riley's shoulder
at what looked like an aerial map on the screen. The surrounding area seemed barren—desert and dust and flat, open
ground—but in the very center of the map sat a cluster of
small buildings. No roads led to it; no other buildings or
landmarks stood nearby.

"Is that where Garret is?" I asked softly. Wes shot me a dirty
look. "That," he stated, narrowing his eyes, "is St. George's
western chapterhouse, and it took me a bloody long time to
find it, thank you very much. It's not like the Order adver-
tises where they are—technically those buildings don't exist
on any map or sightseeing brochure. But yes, the bastards that
tried to kill us in California have likely returned there, your
murderous boyfriend included." He snorted and turned away,
and I resisted the urge to slap the back of his head.

"I had no idea it was so close," Riley muttered, staring intently at the screen, his face grim. "Right on the Arizona/
Utah line. I'm going to have to relocate a couple safe houses
farther east."

"There's nowhere completely safe, mate," Wes said quietly, slumping back in his chair. "Not since they caught on that Talon moved a lot of its business to the States. They're bloody everywhere now."

"Where were they before?" I asked.

"England," Riley answered without looking at me. "St. George's main headquarters is in London, where it's been for hundreds of years. They're very traditional, and they don't like change, so it took them a while to spread out. That's why Talon does a lot of business in the US and other countries— the Order doesn't have such a strong presence here. Or it didn't for a long time." He leaned over the laptop. "This is a fairly new base," he stated, staring at the tiny white squares on the screen. "It wasn't here ten years ago." One finger rose to trace the perimeter, his face shadowed in thought. "There's the fence, and that's probably the armory, barracks and mess hall, officer housing…so this big one has to be headquarters." He tapped the screen, tightening his jaw. "That's where he'll probably be."

"Bloody fabulous," Wes muttered. "The most heavily guarded building of them all. Tell me again why we're doing this? If it was a hatchling we were all getting ourselves killed for, I'd understand. I wouldn't like it, but I'd understand. That's more your type of loony." He continued to glower at Riley and ignore me, as if I wasn't standing not three feet away. Well within singeing distance, I thought. "Even if we do get this blighter out, what makes you think he won't run straight back to St. George to tell them where we are? Or shoot us in the back himself?"

"He won't," I snapped, glaring at Wes. "I know Garret. He's not like that."

Wes turned a disgusted sneer in my direction. "Really?"

he drawled. "Then answer me this, if you know the blighter so very well—how long did it take you to figure out he was part of St. George?"

I flushed. I'd never guessed the truth, never let myself think Garret could be the enemy, not until he'd aimed a gun at my head, and even then I hadn't wanted to believe it. Wes gave me a smirk. "Yeah, that's what I figured. You only *think* you know him. But the truth of it is he was lying to you that whole time. He would've told you anything to get you to reveal yourself, anything you wanted to hear."

"He saved us from Lilith—"

"He shot at a bloody adult dragon," Wes interrupted. "Because it was clearly the bigger threat. And when it was over and his squad hadn't arrived to back him up, he told you what was necessary for him to stay alive. He told you exactly what you wanted to hear."

"That's not true!" I remembered Garret's face that night, the intense way he'd looked at me, the remorse and determination and guilt. *I'm done*, he'd told me. *No more killing. No more deaths. I'm not hunting your people anymore.*

Wes snorted. "Leopards can't change their spots," he said with maddening self-assurance. "St. George will always hate and kill dragons because that's what they do. It's the *only* thing they know how to do."

I looked to Riley, standing silently beside the desk, hoping he would back me up. To my dismay, his mouth was pressed into a grim line, his jaw set. My heart sank, even as I turned on him, frowning.

"You agree with him," I accused, and his eyebrows rose.

"You think this is a huge mistake, even though you were there. You heard what Garret said."

"Firebrand." Riley gave me a half weary, half angry look. "Yes, of course I agree with him," he said evenly. "I've seen what St. George does, not only in the war, but to all our kind, everywhere. How many safe houses do you think I've lost to their cause? How many dragons are murdered by the Order every year? Not just the Vipers or Basilisks or the ones directly involved in the war." His gaze narrowed. "I've seen them slaughter hatchlings, kids younger than you. I once watched a sniper take out an unarmed kid in cold blood. He was on his way to meet me, riding his bike through the park, and the shot came from nowhere. Because I couldn't get to him in time." Riley's eyes flashed gold, the dragon very close to the surface, angry and defiant. "So, no, Firebrand, I'm not completely thrilled with the idea of rescuing one of the Order," he finished in a near growl. "Any excuse for another of the bastards to die is a good one in my book. And don't think your human is innocent just because he fought Lilith and let us go. He has dragon blood on his hands just like the rest of them."

I cringed inside, knowing he was right. But I still raised my chin, staring him down. "I'm not leaving him to die," I said firmly. "He saved our lives, and I won't forget that, no matter what you say." He crossed his arms, and I made a helpless gesture. "But you don't have to come, Riley. I can do this alone. If you feel that strongly—"

"Firebrand, shut up," Riley snapped. I blinked, and he gave me a look of supreme exasperation. "Of course I'm coming with you," he growled. "I told you before, I won't let you take on St. George alone. I'll be with you every step of the way, and I'll do my damnedest to keep us alive, but you can't expect me to be happy about it."

I swallowed. "I'll make it up to you, Riley, I promise."

Riley sighed, running a hand through his dark hair. "I'll hold you to that," he said. "When this is over, I fully expect you to do whatever I say, no hesitation, no questions asked. But first, let's concentrate on getting through the next twenty-four hours. Come here." He motioned me forward. "You'll need to see this, if you're planning on sneaking into the base with me. You *are* planning on coming, I assume? No chance of talking you out of it?"

"You know me better than that."

"Sadly, I do."

I eased in front of him and gazed down at the screen, suddenly very aware of his presence, his hand on my arm as he peered over my shoulder, the smell of his leather jacket. Wes grumbled under his breath, something that included the words *sodding* and *bollocks*, and Riley gave a grim chuckle.

"Yeah," he muttered, his deep voice close to my ear, making my skin prickle. "Just like old times."

COBALT

Twelve years ago
1:18 a.m.

I slipped out the second-story window and dropped silently to the ground. Behind me, the office building remained dark, empty, as I leaned against the cement wall and dug my phone out of my pocket.

"It's done," I muttered into the speaker. "Everything is wired to explode. I just need confirmation that the building is empty before I detonate."

"Roger that" came the voice on the other end. "Building is empty, the only thing left is the security guard outside. You are clear to proceed when ready."

"Are you sure?" I growled, my voice hard. "I don't want a repeat of what happened in Dublin. Are you absolutely certain there are no civilians inside?"

"That's an affirmative. The building is clear. Waiting on your signal."

"All right." I stepped away from the wall. "Leaving the premises now. I'll report in again when it's done. Cobalt out."

Lowering the phone, I gazed across the empty parking lot,

thinking. It would be easy enough to slip through the fence, cross the street and vanish into the darkness without anyone knowing I was here. In fact, that was what Talon expected, what I was supposed to do. They chose me for these missions because I was damn good at my job—infiltrate a target, steal or plant whatever I was supposed to and get out again. All without being seen or leaving any evidence behind. I was probably the youngest Basilisk to infiltrate Talon's enemies, and I was here only because the last Basilisk sent out on assignment never returned. But I kept completing missions, and the organization kept sending me on more, regardless of danger, time or my personal feelings. I didn't know what this particular company had done to earn Talon's wrath, and I didn't want to know. Better not to ask questions; it was easier that way. But Talon required me to finish this assignment, and I knew what I had to do now.

Instead, I turned and headed toward the front of the building, following the wall until I found what I was looking for. A pudgy man in a blue-and-black uniform, silver flashlight dangling off his belt, sat in a chair near the front entrance. His arms were crossed, and his large chin rested on his chest as he sat there, eyes closed. I snorted.

Sleeping on the job, Mr. Rent-A-Cop? What would your employers have to say about that?

Bending down, I picked a pebble off the ground, tossed it in one hand and hurled it at the security guard. It struck his forehead and bounced off, and the human jerked up with a snort, nearly falling out of the chair. Flailing his arms, he glared around, then straightened as he spotted me, waiting in the shadows. I grinned at him and waved.

"Hey! Stop right there!"

I laughed and sprinted away as the guard scrambled after me. I jogged across the parking lot, making sure not to run too fast. Didn't want him to give up the chase just yet. Pulling out my phone, I clicked it on and began dialing a sequence of numbers, the gasping, panting voice of the guard echoing behind me.

"You there! Freeze! I'm warning you…"

Sorry, human. I reached the chain-link fence surrounding the property and leaped for the top, hitting the post and vaulting over with one hand. My thumb hovered over the final button as I walked swiftly away, hearing the guard reach the fence and pause, not bothering to pull himself up. *This is going to be a bad night for you. But at least you'll be alive. That's the most you can hope for when crossing paths with Talon.*

I pressed the button.

A massive fireball rocked the air behind me, blowing out windows, shattering walls, sending pieces of the roof flying as the building erupted in a gout of flame. I felt the blast of energy toss my hair and clothes, and didn't look back. Crossing the street, I slipped the phone into my pocket and melted into the darkness, leaving the structure burning behind me and one dazed rent-a-cop staring in dumbfounded amazement.

★ ★ ★

I reached my hotel room less than an hour later. Stripping out of my black work clothes, I changed quickly, then flipped on the news. The image showed the burned, demolished remains of the building I'd just left, surrounded by people and flashing lights. The words on the bottom of the television read: "Live: Mysterious explosion destroys office complex." I

sank onto the bed, watching grimly as a reporter's voice filtered from the TV.

"...happened around 1:00 a.m. this morning," the voice
announced, as the image flipped to a bird's-eye view of the
demolished rooftop, gaping holes crumbling into darkness.
"Thankfully, all the regular employees were gone, but we
are getting reports that the janitorial staff was in the building when it exploded. Rescue teams are on the scene now..."

No. I clenched a fist on my leg, horror and rage flooding
my body. Leaping upright, I snatched my phone from the
bed, dialed a number and stood there, shaking, until someone picked up.

"Well done, agent," the voice on the other end greeted.
"We saw the reports. Talon will be—"

"What the hell happened?" I snarled, interrupting him.
"The building was supposed to be empty! They swore to me
it was clear. No one was supposed to be inside."

A pause. "Talon weighed the information and decided that
the assignment would go forward as planned," the voice said
in a stiff, flat tone. "The loss of civilian life is...regrettable,
but necessary."

"Like hell it was! They told me the building was clear."

"It is not your place to question the organization, agent."
Now the voice sounded angry. "Nor is it your job to know the
details. Your job is to obey. You've performed as Talon wished,
and the mission was a success. This conversation is over."

The line went dead.

I lowered the phone, seething. Sinking onto the bed again,
I stared at the television, watching humans and rescue dogs
paw through the smoldering ruins, listening as a reporter in-

terviewed the guard I'd saved. He credited himself with chasing the alleged bomber through the building and across the parking lot and made the pursuit sound much closer than it actually had been. But he did describe me as a young white male with dark hair, dressed all in black, and the police were on the lookout for anyone matching that description. They wouldn't find me, of course. I didn't exist in their systems; as far as the humans could tell, I was a ghost. By the time the authorities even got close to this hotel, I'd be on the other side of the country. Back to the war they couldn't see.

Back to Talon.

I ground my teeth, tempted to hurl the phone at the wall, or maybe the television so that I wouldn't have to see the aftermath of what I'd caused. *Dammit.* This wasn't the first time something like this had happened, but it was the first time Talon had outright lied to me. Before, there had been suspicious happenstance, crossed communications, orders that could've been misinterpreted or reasoned away. Not this time. Talon had *assured* me that building was clear; I would have never pressed that button if it wasn't.

And they knew it, too.

Sickened, I switched off the TV and flopped back on the bed, dragging my hands down my face. What now? How could I go on like this, knowing Talon would lie, that they would use me and more innocent people would get caught in the cross fire?

I could hear my trainer's thin, high voice echoing in my head, mocking me. *There is no such thing as an "innocent casualty," agent,* it said. *This is a war, and people will die. That is the ugly truth of it. A few human deaths should not concern you.*

But they *did*. A lot. Maybe I was the exception; maybe no other dragon in Talon cared if a few janitors were killed because they had been at the wrong place at the wrong time. But I did. And now more people were dead because of me.

My phone vibrated beside me on the quilt. Sitting up, I grabbed it as the screen came to life, showing a new message.

Stop moping, it read, indicating no one but my trainer, the Chief Basilisk himself. Brusque and to the point as always, but somehow finding ways to insult me. A car will be at your location in five minutes. You have a new assignment.

Another mission? So soon? Dammit, I had just barely completed this one, and I was *tired*. More than tired. Sickened. Numb. Furious. Both with myself and with Talon. I didn't want to go back. I wanted to lock myself in a room and drink an insane amount of alcohol, until the scene on the news faded out of my mind. I'd be equally happy to stalk into an office and ream someone out, possibly with fire and a lot of cuss words. The last thing I wanted was to be called back for another assignment.

But what else could I do?

Methodically, I rose and began packing my things. Talon's word was law; the opinions of a juvenile Basilisk agent didn't concern them. They would send me out on another mission, and they would continue to do so, regardless of what I wanted. But I had the ominous, sneaking suspicion that I was reaching the limit of how far I could be pushed, used, lied to. One word hovered at the back of my mind, constant and terrifying, appearing in my thoughts no matter how hard I tried to shove it back.

Rogue.

GARRET

Six hours till dawn.

I lay on my cot with my hands behind my head, staring at the ceiling of my cell, watching the cracks blur and run together. Around me, the jail block was dark, quiet. The only light came from beneath the door to the guard station at the end of the hall, and I was the only prisoner in the room. I'd been given my last meal hours ago—rations and water, as the Order didn't believe in final requests—and it had been delivered by a cold-faced soldier who had spit "dragonlover" at me before tossing it to the floor. Where it still lay, untouched, near the front of the cell.

Six hours till dawn. Six hours before my cell door would open, and a pair of soldiers would step through, announcing that it was time. I'd be handcuffed, escorted across the training field and taken to the long brick wall facing the rising sun. There would be witnesses, of course. The Perfect Soldier was about to be executed for treason; there would probably be a crowd. Perhaps the entire base would turn out. I wondered if Tristan would be there, and Lieutenant Martin. I didn't know if they would come; truthfully, I wasn't certain I wanted them to witness my final moments, as a traitor to the Order. There *would* be a line of soldiers standing in front of that wall, six of them, all with loaded rifles. I would be taken before them, offered a blindfold, which I would refuse, and then I'd be left standing there alone, facing them all. The countdown would begin.

Ready…

Aim…

Fire!

I shivered, unable to stop myself. I wasn't afraid to die; I'd prepared myself for death many times before. In the field, before a strike on a nest, or facing down a single dragon—we all knew that, at any moment, we could be killed. Soldiers died; it was a fact of life, one you couldn't predict or avoid. There was no tactical reason the soldier standing just inches away would take a bullet to the temple and I would be spared. I was alive because I was good at what I did, but sometimes I'd just gotten lucky.

But there was a distinction between cheating death and knowing the exact time it would come for you, down to the last second. And there was a difference between dying in battle and standing there with your hands behind your back, waiting for your former brothers in arms—the very soldiers you had fought with, bled with—to kill you.

Five and a half hours till dawn.

I didn't regret my choice. I'd meant every word I said in the courtroom. And if it came down to it again, and I stood on that beach with the dragon I was sent to kill, knowing that if I let her go I would die instead… I would still choose to save her.

But I *had* betrayed my Order, and everything I knew, to side with the enemy. I'd seen fellow soldiers die in front of me, torn apart by claws or blasted with dragonfire. I'd watched squad mates throw themselves in front of bullets or charge into the fray alone, just to give the rest of us an advantage. I knew I deserved death. I'd turned my back on the Order that raised me, the brothers who had died for the cause, to save our greatest foes. I knew I should feel remorse, crushing guilt, for family I'd betrayed.

But lying on my cot, mere hours from my own execution, all I could think of was *her*. Where was she now? What was she doing? Did she think of me at all, or had I been long forgotten in the flight from Crescent Beach with the rest of her kind? Surely there'd be no reason for a soldier of St. George to cross her mind; she was free, she was with her own, and I was part of the Order. I was still the enemy of her people. Though it made me sick to think of it now, the number that had died by my hand. Ember should hate me. I deserved nothing less.

But I still hoped she thought of me sometimes. And as the minutes of my life continued to slip away, I found myself thinking more and more of the moments we'd shared. Wondering what would've happened…had we both been normal. I knew that wishing was wasted energy, and regret changed nothing, but for perhaps the first time in my life, I wished we'd had more time. If I'd known what would happen, I would have spent every moment I could with her. I would have done a lot of things differently, but it was too late now. Ember was gone, and in a few hours, I was going to die. Nothing would change that, but at least her face would be the last thing on my mind before I left this world.

I hope you're happy, Ember, wherever you are. I hope…you'll always be free.

Five hours till dawn.

EMBER

"Wake up, Firebrand." Riley's voice was soft and deep, and my dragon stirred to life at his touch. "It's 2:00 a.m. Fifteen minutes till go time."

I lifted my head from the pillow, fighting the grogginess pulling me down. The room was dark; only one lamp had been left on, and outside the sky was black. I hadn't thought I could sleep, but I must've been more exhausted than I'd felt. After the three of us had gone over the plan, Riley had told me once more to get some rest, and I'd drifted off almost as soon as my head touched the pillow.

The plan. I sat up as my heart began an irregular thud in my chest. It was time. This was it. Tonight we were going after Garret.

"Better get dressed," Riley said, nodding to my backpack on the bed. He had changed, too. No longer in dusty jeans and a white T-shirt beneath his jacket, he now wore a dark shirt that clung to his chest and arms, black jeans, gloves and a belt with several compartments and pouches on the side. At the desk, Wes was garbed in all black, too, a ski cap perched on his head. But he looked sullen and scared, like he'd rather be doing anything else. Riley, looming over me at the edge of the mattress, looked completely in his element, and my heart gave a weird little flip in my chest.

"Come on, Firebrand," Riley urged as I sat there, blinking at him. "We're sort of on a time schedule, here. Get your ninja suit on, and let's go."

"Right." Shaking the final cobwebs from my brain, I grabbed the backpack from the corner and hurried to the bathroom. Unzipping the top, I rummaged around until I found what I was looking for and pulled it out.

The sleek black bodysuit unfurled in my hands like a spill of ink, shaking free of wrinkles, creases, everything. It had been a final gift from my trainer when I'd "graduated" basic training and would've started my real education. The form-fitting suit was specifically tailored for me and would not rip or tear like normal clothes when I Shifted into my true form. The constantly warm, clinging fabric seemed to melt into my skin when I changed, and still covered my body when I turned back, so it was probably the coolest thing I owned.

It was, I'd discovered later, the outfit of the Vipers, Talon's deadly and notorious assassins, which was what they'd wanted me to become, too. Needless to say, I had issues with hunting down and killing my own kind simply because Talon ordered it. Talon's rule was absolute, and the Vipers were used to silence dragons who weren't loyal to the organization. Dragons like Riley who had gone rogue. I couldn't do it. And because Talon wouldn't accept no for an answer, I'd gone rogue, too. That was the main reason I'd left the organization. I would not become a Viper like my trainer, Lilith—ruthless and unmerciful, willing to kill without a second thought. I refused to turn into that.

But the suit definitely came in handy.

I slipped into the outfit, shuddering as the fabric sucked at my skin, melding to my body. Yeah, the magic ninja suit was awesome, but the way it felt almost alive was still creepy as hell. After putting on my shoes and shoving my normal clothes into my backpack, I left the bathroom and nearly bumped into Riley on the other side of the door.

He put out his hands to steady me, but quickly pulled them back with a grimace. I frowned in confusion.

"What? Do I smell or something?"

"No," he muttered, not meeting my gaze. "Sorry. It's not you, Firebrand, it's just…" He made a vague gesture at me. "That thing. Brings back fun memories, if you know what I mean."

I suddenly realized the problem. "I look like a Viper," I said, and he nodded.

"When you've been out of Talon as long as I have, the last thing you want to see is that outfit. Because it usually means you're fighting or running for your life."

"I'm a rogue now, too, Riley."

"I know." He reached out and brushed the base of my neck. A jolt of heat surged through me from that spot, as his fingers lingered on my skin. Riley's gold eyes almost glowed in the shadows. "I'm glad you're here, Firebrand," he said, his voice low and soft. "I'm glad I won't have to meet you down the road someday as a Viper. That would kill me, having to fight you." His mouth twitched in a faint smile. "You have no idea how relieved I am that you left the organization. That you saw Talon for what it really is."

I swallowed, the warmth spreading through my whole body

as the dragon rose to the surface, pushing against my frag-
ile human shell. The Viper suit tightened, flattening to my
skin until it felt like I wasn't wearing anything at all. I could
Shift, I realized. Right here in this tiny hotel room. What
did I have to lose? No one would see me but Riley and Wes.
And then, if I Shifted, Riley would probably change, too. I
wanted him to. I wanted to see his true self, his other self,
the one who called to my dragon and who peered down at
me with gleaming golden eyes.

Cobalt.

Get it together, Ember. I breathed deep to cool my lungs, to
calm the fire spreading through me, and tried to grin back.
"Yeah, well, I bet you didn't know what you were getting
into," I said lightly.

"Doesn't matter." Riley dropped his arm and stepped back
as if he couldn't bear to touch me anymore. Or perhaps, if he
kept touching me, a large blue dragon would suddenly make
a very explosive appearance in the middle of the hotel room.
"But if we live through this, you owe me, Firebrand. Big-
time." He glanced at Wes, who was packing his laptop into
a shoulder bag, his jaw set. "Everyone ready? Once we start,
there's no turning back. Wes?"

"Piss off" was the sullen answer. "Like I have any sort of
choice. When you're killed by St. George, don't expect me
to babysit two dozen bloody hatchlings the rest of my life."

Riley ignored that. "We'll take two vehicles until we're a
couple miles from the base. From there, we'll go the rest of
the way on foot. Wes, how close will you need to be to pick
up their signal?"

"Bloody too close," Wes muttered. "But it shouldn't be

hard to find, since they'll be the only ones within a hundred miles putting one out. The challenge will be jacking in without raising any kind of alarm."

"If you do have to move closer, don't go in the van. Last thing we need is for them to see headlights cruising toward them across the desert."

"Oh, really? Is that what I'll want to do, then?" Wes zipped his bag ferociously. "Silly me, here I was thinking we needed big neon signs that said Here We Are, Shoot Us Please on top of the roof."

Riley rolled his eyes but didn't comment. "ETA at the St. George perimeter will be zero three hundred. Once we're finished inside, we'll meet at the rendezvous and get the hell out of Dodge. Ember…" He turned, and his gaze met mine. "You're with me. Let's go."

★ ★ ★

The drive to the Arizona/Utah line was silent and mostly empty. Few cars passed us on the long stretch of highway across the Mojave Desert. Overhead, the moon peered down like a sleepy, half-lidded eye, surrounded by a billion stars that stretched on forever. Out here in the desert, many miles from cities or lights or civilization, the sky called to me. I thought of Shifting, of leaping off the bike, changing forms midair and soaring through the empty sky. Annoyed, I pushed all tempting thoughts to the back of my mind, willing my dragon to settle down. In a couple hours, we would be sneaking into a heavily armed base filled with soldiers whose main goal was the complete genocide of our species. There were more important things to focus on than midnight flights in the desert heat.

Garret. I hope you're okay. Hang in there, we're coming for you.

It felt like a thousand tiny snakes were writhing in my stomach, and I breathed deep to calm them down. Was the soldier going to be there when we came for him? Was he still alive? What would he say when we finally found him? I would think that a dragon showing up at a St. George base in the middle of the night wasn't something that happened often, if ever. Would Garret be happy to see me? Would he accept help from a dragon, the creature he'd been trained to kill on sight?

Or would he turn around and alert the rest of the base to our presence, having concluded that dragons were the enemy after all and needed to be destroyed? It had been days since that lonely night on the beach where I'd almost died, attacked by my own trainer. Garret had saved us, but he was also a soldier of the Order. According to Talon doctrine, St. George couldn't be reasoned with, accepted no compromise and showed no mercy to their enemies. Garret was back with his own people now. What if they'd convinced him that he'd been wrong after all, that dragons were the enemy, and the next time he saw one he'd put a bullet in the back of its skull?

Garret wouldn't do that, I told myself. *He's different than the rest of them. He saw that we weren't monsters. And he…he promised me that he was done killing. He wasn't going to hunt us anymore, that's what he said.*

I had to believe that. I had to believe Garret would keep his promise, that the soldier who'd helped fight off Lilith and let us go was the same person I'd gotten to know over the summer. The boy I'd taught to surf, who'd played arcade games with me, whose smile could make my stomach do tipsy cart-

wheels. Who had kissed me in the ocean and made all my
senses surge to life, who'd made me feel like I wasn't a dragon
or a human, but a strange, light creature somewhere in between. That person was not a soldier of St. George, a cold
ruthless killer who hated dragons and slaughtered without
mercy. No, when Garret was with me, he was just a boy who,
at times, seemed just as uncertain and confused as I was. I'd
seen a glimpse of the soldier on the bluff, when he'd pointed
a gun at my face, his eyes hard and cold. But even then, he
hadn't pulled the trigger.

Would he pull the trigger now?

I sighed and pressed my cheek to Riley's back, trying to
stop my brain from looping in endless circles. Rescue Garret
first. That was the looming issue at the moment, the thing I
had to focus on right now. We could deal with everything
else *after* we were clear of St. George.

Riley made a sharp left turn, pulled off the highway and
headed into the desert. Startled, I tightened my arms around
his waist, and we sped between rocks and cacti, following
the van ahead of us. Abruptly, Riley flipped off the lights,
as did the van, and we traveled in darkness for a while, only
the faint light of the moon guiding the way. Finally, the van
slowed and pulled behind a shallow rise, skidding to a halt in
a billowing cloud of dust. Riley swerved, cruising beside it,
and killed the engine.

Heart pounding, I sat up as the absolute silence of the desert descended on us like a glass dome. Except for my own
breathing and the soft creak of the motorcycle, the complete
absence of noise was chilling, and my dragon bristled. I didn't
like it. It reminded me of my old school in the middle of the

Great Basin, the place my brother and I had spent the majority of our lives, learning how to be human. Surrounded by desert, open sky and a whole lot of nothing. You could go outside and stand for hours in the same spot, the sun blazing down on you, and your ears would start to throb from the eternal, looming silence. I'd hated it. Sometimes, it had felt like the silence was trying to steal my voice; that if I went too long without making any noise, I'd become as still and lifeless as the desert around me. Dante had never understood why I was always so restless.

Dante. A lump rose to my throat as I clambered off the motorcycle, and I forced my thoughts away from him. One problem at a time.

"Still up for this, Firebrand?" Riley whispered, jolting me out of my dark musings. With a mental shake, I nodded as my heart resumed its painful thud against my ribs. Riley gazed at me, then turned and pointed across the desert to where a scattering of distant lights winked at us in the darkness.

"That's the base," he said quietly as I stared at the glimmers marking our objective. Garret was somewhere behind those walls, and with any luck, we'd get to him and be long gone before anyone from St. George knew we were there. "We're about two miles away," Riley went on, "but we can't risk driving any closer and having them see us. Stealth is our only chance to pull this off. From here, we walk."

Wes slipped out of the van, ski cap pulled low over his head, and stalked around the vehicle to yank open the back doors. Riley joined him and dragged a black duffel bag out from under the seat. My heart lurched as Riley casually pulled out a small black pistol, checked the chamber for rounds and holstered it to his belt with easy familiarity.

I swallowed at the sight of the gun. "Riley?" I ventured, suddenly terrified and angry about being terrified. "Tell me the truth," I said as he glanced over. "And don't think for a minute that I'm backing out, but…how dangerous is this really going to be?"

Wes snorted. "Oh, sure, *now* she asks. On bloody St. George's doorstep."

Riley sighed. "Truth, Firebrand? I wouldn't agree to do this if it was complete suicide," he said, holding my gaze. I blinked at him, surprised, and he gave a weary smile. "Wes might preach doom and gloom, but trust me when I say I know what I'm doing. We'll be going in when most of the base will be asleep. This particular chapterhouse is extremely remote and well hidden; they're using isolation to deter unwanted guests, so security should be minimal. If no one knows where you are, why bother with a ton of guards and patrols? And trust me, two dragons sneaking *into* a St. George compound doesn't happen often, if ever.

"But," he went on as I relaxed a bit, "that doesn't mean it won't be dangerous. These types of missions usually go one of two ways: without a hitch, or spectacularly wrong. Hopefully, we'll be able to sneak in, find what we want and tiptoe away without anyone knowing we were there. That's the best-case scenario. I think you can guess the worst-case scenario. So, on that note…" He held out a pistol to me. "Ever shot one of these?"

Numbly, I shook my head. I'd handled a gun before, both in my training with Lilith and then briefly when I'd disarmed the Glock aimed at my face, but I'd never fired one. Certainly not at a living creature.

Riley smiled grimly. "If it gets to the point where we're shooting at people, then the mission is FUBAR and we need to get out of there as fast as we can." He held up the weapon. "These are only to be used as the very last resort. But if the mission does go south, you're going to want something to defend yourself with. The problem with claws and teeth is that you have to get in close to attack, and that might be tricky if they're all firing M-16s at you."

"I've never fired a gun before, Riley. I don't even know if I could…shoot someone. Not for real. I've never killed anyone before."

Riley's lip curled in a hard smile. "Yeah, well, you're gonna have to get over that, Firebrand," he stated bluntly. "We might not be part of Talon anymore, but St. George doesn't give a damn about that little fact. To them, all dragons are the same. Rogue, hatchling or Viper, it makes no difference to the Order. They'll kill us regardless of faction or sympathies." He lowered the gun, his gaze almost accusing. "This is still a war, but we aren't just fighting one side anymore. Not only do we have to be on the lookout for St. George—Talon will be breathing down our necks, as well. We kind of got the shit end of both sticks, if you haven't noticed by now."

I blinked, stunned. I'd never heard Riley sound so bitter. Although, ever since we'd left Crescent Beach, he'd seemed… different. More serious and take-charge. This was not the cocky, insufferable, devil-may-care rogue I'd met before. He was not the mysterious lone rebel I'd thought he was, but the leader of an entire rogue underground, with who knew how many dragons and humans depending on him. I suspected now that the dragon I'd met in Crescent Beach had been putting on a show, a mask, the perfect identity for the current situation. I wondered, yet again, if the Riley I faced now was the real one.

At my silence, Riley gave me a weary, sympathetic look, his voice going softer.

"Sorry, Firebrand. I didn't mean to jump down your throat like that. I know you've never killed anyone, and I don't expect you to. Not tonight, anyway." He sighed and raked his hair back. "I've just…seen a lot, you understand? From Talon and St. George. I've lost friends and hatchlings to both organizations, and some days it feels like I'm pushing a boulder up a never-ending cliff, and if I let up for one second, it'll roll back and crush me." His brow furrowed and his eyes darkened as he looked away. "One day it *will* roll back and crush me."

His gaze flicked back to mine. "What I'm trying to say is, if you're going to stand against Talon, you have to do whatever it takes to stay alive. And one day, that might involve shooting someone. Or incinerating them. Or tearing them apart. Yeah, it's ugly, it's messy and it's not fair, but that's the truth of it. This is our world, Firebrand. This is the world you live in now." He held the gun out to me once more. "Unless you want to go back."

I swallowed. "No," I said, and reached out for the weapon, curling my fingers around the hard metal. "I'm not going back." Riley tossed me a holster as well, and I slipped it around my shoulder, feeling the weight of the gun, cold and deadly, against my ribs. I hoped I would never have to use it.

"All right." Riley shut the van and looked toward the distant base. I saw him take a short, furtive breath, as if steeling himself for what was to come. "I think we're about ready. Just remember…" He shot a firm glare in my direction. "We do this my way. If I tell you to do something, don't question it. Don't even think about it. Just do it, understand?"

I nodded. Riley glanced at Wes, who watched him with the grave, resigned expression of someone who thought they might never see him again. "We're going. If I give the word, get out and don't look back. Wish us luck."

"Luck?" Wes muttered, shaking his head. "You don't need luck. You need a bloody miracle."

And on that inspiring note, we started across the desert.

RILEY

One mile to the gates of hell.

I shoved the thought away as I led Ember across the dusty plains, heading closer to that ominous glow looming ahead of us. Fear and second thoughts were dangerous now. This insane rescue was officially under way, and I had to focus on what was important; namely, getting us in and out without being discovered and gunned down. When I was a Basilisk, I'd been taught never to ask questions or think too hard about what I was doing. I didn't need to know the *whys*, I just needed to complete the missions.

Of course, it was when I'd started asking questions that I'd realized I couldn't be part of Talon anymore.

Ember walked behind me, silent in her black Viper's outfit, gliding over the sand like a shadow. She made no noise, moving like a Basilisk herself, graceful and sure without even realizing it. Lilith had taught her well. The only thing she hadn't taught her was the Vipers' ruthlessness, that apathy toward killing that Vipers were known—and feared—for. I was glad of it, but at the same time, I knew it wouldn't last. Not in our world. There was too much at stake. Too many factions that wanted us dead, too many people to try to protect.

Eventually, the day would come when Ember would have to kill someone and when it did, she would have to make a choice as to what kind of dragon, and person, she really was. I just hoped it wouldn't change her too drastically.

"You're about two hundred yards from the fence." Wes's voice buzzed in my ear, courtesy of the wire I was wearing. Part of the package I'd picked up in L.A. "No security cameras as far as I can tell, but be careful."

"Got it."

We reached the perimeter fence, nothing heavy duty or unusual, just simple chain link topped with barbed wire. Signs reading Private Property and Trespassers Will Be Prosecuted hung from the links every thirty or so feet, but there was nothing to indicate that a heavily armed military compound lay beyond. St. George was nearly as good as Talon when it came to hiding in plain sight, as private armies were sort of frowned on by the United States government. The bases where the soldiers were housed used isolation and misdirection to stay off the radar of those that might take issue with a large number of armed fanatics squatting on US soil.

Good news for us: this base was counting on its remoteness to deter unwanted visitors, so the fence wasn't well patrolled. Bad news for us: if they did start shooting, no one would ever hear it.

Ember crouched beside me, peering through the barrier. We'd approached the base from the north, giving the fence a wide berth as we circled around, and I could see a cluster of squat buildings about a thousand yards beyond the fence. The space between was dark and shadowy, but terrifyingly flat and open.

No turning back now.

Pulling out my wire cutters, I began snipping through the links, silent and methodical. Oddly enough, the familiar task helped calm my nerves; how many times had I done this before? Ember pressed close, her shoulder brushing mine, and my pulse leaped at the contact, but I didn't stop until I'd cut a line just big enough for us to slip through.

"Stay close," I murmured, replacing the cutters. "Remember, don't do anything until I give the word."

She nodded. Reaching down, I peeled back the steel curtain, motioned her through, then slipped in behind her. As we passed through, the fence gave a soft, metallic slither, echoing the chill running up my spine.

Okay, here we were, on St. George soil. Still in a crouch, I scanned the layout of the base, noting buildings, lights, how far the shadows extended. Ember waited beside me, patient and motionless, green eyes shining with resolve. I sensed no fear from her, only stubborn determination, a will to see this through no matter what, and squashed the flicker of both dread and pride.

"We're in," I whispered to Wes.

"All right." I imagined furious typing on the other end. "Hang on, I'm trying to find the security system…there we go." More silence followed, as Ember and I huddled at the fence line, gazing around warily. "Okay," Wes muttered at last. "Looks like only headquarters and the armory actually have cameras. So you're going to have to get inside before I can walk you through."

"Got it," I muttered back. "I'll let you know when we're in. Riley out."

Staying low, we scurried across the open ground toward the buildings, keeping to where the shadows were thickest. It being the very dead of night, the compound was quiet; most soldiers were asleep, probably having to be up in a couple hours. I did spot a couple guards near the perimeter gate, but other than that the yard was deserted.

"It's so quiet," Ember whispered as we crouched behind a Hummer, maybe a hundred yards from the first set of buildings. "Just like you said. That's a good thing, right?"

"Yeah, but let's not get cocky." I nodded at the roof of the largest structure, straight ahead behind a clump of smaller buildings. "If this isn't exciting enough for you, wait till we get inside. All it takes is for one alarm to go off, and the entire base will swarm out like we poked a stick down an ant nest. So stay on your toes, Firebrand. We're not out of here yet."

Her eyes flashed, but she nodded. We continued across the yard in silence, even more wary for hidden dangers and sudden patrols. The base remained quiet and still, but I stayed on high alert. Ember might think this was a walk in the park, but I knew how quickly things could turn. And if they did turn, our chances of getting out were slim to zilch.

As we drew close to the first row of buildings, creeping along the outer wall, the door in front of us swung open. Biting back a curse, I dived behind a corner, pressing myself against the wall, as Ember did the same. I felt the heat of her body against mine and squashed the impatient riling of my dragon as a pair humans paused at the bottom of the steps, talking in low, rough voices.

"Damn kitchen duty," one growled, sounding sullen. "Of course, I'd have to pull it today. You going to the execution?"

"I dunno," the other replied as Ember stiffened beside me. "It seems…kinda wrong, you know? I saw him in the South American raid, when he charged that damn adult lizard by himself. Kid's completely fearless."

"He's a dragonlover." The other soldier's voice was cutting. "Did you not hear what he said at his trial? I personally can't wait to see his guts sprayed all over the ground. Better than he deserves, if you ask me."

They walked on, arguing now, their voices fading into the darkness. When they were gone, I blew out a quiet breath, slumping against the wall, then glanced at Ember.

Her face was white with horror and rage, her eyes glowing a bright, furious emerald in the shadows. Like she might Shift, here and now, and tear those two soldiers to pieces. Quickly, I put a hand on her arm, feeling it shake under my fingers, and leaned close. "Easy, Firebrand," I whispered as my dragon tried pushing its way to the surface again. I shoved it back. "This is why we're here. He's not dead yet."

Though that *was* the confirmation I needed. They were going to execute the soldier today, probably as soon as it was light outside. Not that I cared—I'd be more than happy if another St. George bastard kicked it—but that didn't give us a lot of time to work with. If we were going to get him out, it had to be now. But Ember's reaction to the news sent a flare of anger through my veins. Why did she care about this kid so much? He was just a human and, more important, he was St. George. I remembered the way she'd looked at him, the way she had danced with him, and my anger grew. Ember was a dragon; she had no business getting involved with a human. Once we rescued this bastard and were far enough from St.

George that I could breathe again, I would show her exactly
what it meant to be a dragon.

Ember took a deep breath and nodded. Carefully, we eased
around the buildings, hugging the walls and shadows, inching
steadily toward the large, two-story building near the center.
We avoided the brightly lit front, of course, sidling along the
back wall until we reached a small metal door.

Ember started forward, but I grabbed her arm, motioning
to the camera mounted over the steps. We shrank back into
the shadows again as I spoke into the mic. "Wes, we're at the
back door of the main building. No guards, but there is a
camera up top and it looks like you need a key card to get in."

"Hang on." Wes fell silent while Ember and I pressed
against the wall and waited. "Okay," he muttered after a few
seconds. "Just give me a minute to see if I can turn it off."

As he was talking, a body suddenly came around the corner. A human, wearing normal clothes, his dark hair buzzed
close. He jerked, startled, and for a split second the three of
us gaped at each other in shock, before his muscles tensed,
mouth opening to shout a warning.

And Ember lunged in, a black blur across my vision, hitting the soldier in the jaw right below the ear. The human's
head snapped to the side, and he collapsed as if all his bones
had turned into string, sprawling facedown in the sand.

I breathed in slowly, as Ember blinked and stared wide-
eyed at the fallen soldier, as if she couldn't believe what she'd
just done, either. My arms were shaking, adrenaline coursing
through my veins. It had happened so quickly; I hadn't even
had time to move before the soldier was unconscious. And
my reflexes weren't slow by any means.

"Firebrand," I breathed, and she looked at me, almost frightened. "That was…impressive. Where did you learn that?"

"I don't know." She backed away from the body, as if afraid she wouldn't be able to stop herself from doing something else. "I just… I saw him and…" Her eyes darkened, and she shook her head. "I don't even remember what I did."

Lilith's training. This was what the Vipers taught their students—how to be fast, how to be quick and lethal, and to strike without thinking. To recognize a threat and take it out. Immediately.

"Riley." Wes's voice crackled in my ear, wary and anxious. "You okay? What's going on?"

I shook myself. "Nothing," I told him, moving toward the fallen soldier. Ember had had to silence him, no question, but we still had to deal with him. Last thing we needed was for him to wake up and alert the rest of the base. "Small problem. It's been dealt with," I continued, kneeling beside the human and reaching into a compartment on my belt. "How's the unlocking the door part coming along?"

"What are you doing, Riley?" Ember asked suddenly, watching me with wary green eyes. "You…you're not going to *kill* him, are you?"

I shook my head, showing her the plastic zip ties I pulled from my belt, though I found it a little ironic. Had Ember been a full Viper, I doubted this human would be alive. And I wasn't going to snap his neck or slit his throat while he lay there, helpless. Even though I hated the bastards, and would gladly blast him to cinders if I had to, I wasn't a killer. Not like them.

Wes's voice continued to buzz in my ear. "I can get the door open," he said as I pulled the soldier's arms behind him and zip-tied his wrists together. "But if I start blacking out cameras, they might get suspicious. Best I can give you is a thirty-second feedback loop, but you'll have to get inside before the feed goes normal again. Think you can do that?"

I gagged the human with the roll of duct tape in my belt, then heaved the unconscious body over my shoulder. He hung like a sack of potatoes—a heavy, well-muscled sack of potatoes. "Do it," I grunted, staggering toward a Dumpster we'd crouched behind a moment ago. "Just give us fifteen seconds. Ember, get the cover, will you?"

She scurried to the Dumpster and pushed up the lid, releasing the stench of old milk, rotting things and decay. I probably shouldn't have felt so spitefully pleased as I dropped the body between reeking sacks of garbage and closed the top, but I did.

At the bottom of the steps, we hung back in the shadows, watching the door and the camera up top. "Gimme a moment," Wes muttered as I drummed my fingers against my knee, feeling highly exposed. Another soldier could come waltzing around the corner anytime. We might've gotten lucky once; twice would be pushing it. "All right," Wes finally said. "In ten seconds, the camera will go off and the door will unlock. Both will happen almost simultaneously, so you'll have to get up there fast. Ready?"

"Yeah," I muttered, feeling Ember tense beside me.

"Then…go! Now!"

I burst forward and raced up the steps, not daring to look at the camera peering down at me with its soulless black eye. My fingers closed on the handle just as there was a soft beep, and the light above the key-card slit turned green. Wrenching open the door, I motioned Ember inside, then ducked over the threshold myself. The door closed, shutting behind us with a soft click that seemed to echo down the long, brightly lit corridor ahead.

We were inside St. George HQ.

Now the real fun began.

EMBER

I should probably be terrified.

I *was* pretty nervous. I was inside the St. George complex, surrounded by a whole army of dragonslayers who'd kill me without a second thought if they knew I was here. We still had to find Garret and somehow sneak *him* out without being discovered. And that close call with the soldier... my nerves were still singing, my hands shaking with adrenaline. I hadn't even thought. I'd just seen him and...boom, he was on the ground. Would I do that again? *Could* I do that again, if I had to?

Was this what my trainer meant when she said I'd be an amazing Viper?

I pushed those thoughts away. *Focus, Ember. Find Garret. That's why we're here.*

"Where to now?" I whispered to Riley.

He huddled against the wall, speaking softly into his wire. "Wes, we're in." A few seconds passed with Riley listening to whatever the human was saying. Finally, he nodded. "Right," he muttered. "Heading there now."

"Did he find Garret?" I asked.

"No," Riley answered, making my heart sink. "But he's

jacked into the security system and says that there's a prison floor somewhere below us. If your human is scheduled for execution in a couple hours, that's where he's going to be." Riley cast a wary look down the corridor. "There are still guards wandering about. Be careful."

I nodded, and we started down the hall, which at this time of night was empty and deserted, but way too bright for comfort. Doors lined the corridor, most of them closed, but a few sat open, showing office-type rooms with desks and computers. I wondered what the soldiers and officers of St. George did when they weren't killing dragons. It was hard to picture them doing normal things like checking email and IMing with friends.

As I passed yet another office door, a glint of metallic red caught my eye. And, for some reason, the hairs on the back of my neck stood straight up. I paused just outside the door and peeked in, letting my eyes adjust to the dim light. At first glance, it seemed like just another office, with standard office furniture: chairs, metal cabinet, giant desk in the center. Nothing strange or out of place...until I saw where that faint glimmer was coming from. For a second, I frowned, not knowing what I was looking at.

Then it hit me like a punch to the stomach, and bile surged up my throat, burning the inside of my mouth. I was frozen, unable to look away, unable to do anything but stare at what lay through the door.

On the wall above the desk, spanning nearly corner to corner, hung the hide of a small red dragon. I could see the long elegant neck, the lighter belly scales, the curved black talons still attached to the feet. Its scales were a darker red than mine, almost rust colored, and it had thin stripes down its back and tail. From its size, it had been a hatchling at the time of its death, my age or younger. At one time, this lifeless skin had been a dragon, just like me. And now...now it was a trophy decorating someone's office.

I think I made a choked, strangled noise, because Riley was suddenly at my side, pulling me away. "Shit," I heard him growl, almost yanking me from the door. "Don't look, Firebrand. Don't look at it. Come here."

I was shaking. Riley dragged me into the hall and pulled me to him, holding me close. I buried my face in his shirt and squeezed my eyes shut, but I couldn't forget the horrible image seared into my brain. I could still see that limp, empty skin hanging on the wall, and I knew it would probably show up in my dreams.

Riley's arms were around me, a shield between me and the rest of the world, a world that slaughtered teen dragons and nailed their hides to the wall. "You okay?" he whispered, his head bent close to mine. I wasn't, but I nodded without looking up, and he blew out a breath. "Damn St. George," he muttered, and his voice was slightly choked, too. "Murdering bastards. Damn them all."

"I'm...okay," I whispered, though I really, really wasn't. It was like something out of a horror movie, seeing someone's skin nailed to the killer's wall. I wondered what they'd done with the rest of the dragon once they'd peeled its hide away, then immediately wished I hadn't. "It's all right," I managed, drawing back, though his grip didn't loosen. "Riley, I'm fine. It's..."

A door squeaked somewhere in the mazelike hallway. We

tensed as footsteps echoed down the corridor, growing louder every second. Riley jerked up with a whispered curse. As the steps drew closer, we gazed frantically around for a hiding place, but, other than the open door behind us, there was nothing.

Sorry, Firebrand, Riley mouthed, and yanked me into the room with the dead dragon. I bit my cheek, feeling tainted, as if the ghost of the murdered dragon lurked in the room with us, and I might glance up to see a pale, bloody figure watching accusingly from the wall.

Pressing into the corner beside the file cabinets, we held our breath as the footsteps came toward the room. I turned my face into Riley's arm and clenched my jaw, trying not to look at the grisly symbol of death on the wall in front of us.

The footsteps passed the room without slowing down and continued down the corridor. Riley waited a long moment after they had faded away and silence fell once more, before finally leading us from the room. I kept my face down and my eyes half closed until we were out of the office, but I could still feel the dead dragon's presence at my back.

"Damn St. George," Riley hissed again, sounding almost as sick as I felt. "Depraved, murdering… Ugh. I'm sorry you had to see that, Firebrand." He put a hand on my arm, steady and comforting. "Sure you want to keep going?" he asked. "It's not too late to turn around. Do we keep looking for the human, or get the hell out of here?"

Frowning, I pulled back to look at him. He gazed back grimly. "This is the true face of St. George, Ember," he said, and his voice was almost a challenge. "This is what they do. What they *all* do." He nodded to the room behind us. "How many times do you think your soldier saw that hide hanging on the wall and thought nothing of it? It was just a skin, a trophy, not a living creature with thoughts and fears and dreams, like everyone else." His eyes narrowed. "We're not people to them, Firebrand. They don't see us as anything but monsters. And I know you don't want to hear it, but your human was raised to think exactly like them. He saw you in the same way he did that hide on the wall."

I shuddered, remembering the skin, tacked onto the wall in plain sight, and for a moment, my resolve wavered. Was I making a mistake? Was it really possible for someone to change his entire perspective? Garret had grown up in St. George, where these awful tokens of death and murder were considered trophies. Decorations to hang in someone's office, like a stag head or a tiger pelt. Because to St. George, we were monsters. Animals. What if Garret still thought like that?

What if he doesn't?

I swallowed hard. Regardless of what Garret believed, I couldn't leave him. If I didn't get him out tonight, he would die. Even if he saw me as a monster, I wouldn't abandon him now.

"No," I told Riley, turning from the office door and the horrible trophy hanging within. "We don't stop. We keep looking. I'm not leaving him to die."

Riley shook his head. "Stubborn idiot hatchling," he muttered, though one corner of his mouth curled up. "All right, we keep going. Wes, you there?" A pause, and Riley rolled his eyes. "Yeah, she did. Of course not, have you met her? How far are we from the stairs?"

We crept through several more hallways, passing more

darkened rooms and offices that I was careful not to peek into, until we came to a door that opened onto a stairwell. Here, Riley stopped us, saying there was a camera on the other side, and we had to wait until Wes shut it down. Once he did, I darted through the frame and started down the cement stairs, feeling Riley close at my back. The steps didn't take us far; just one loop around to an identical metal door, which we pushed through and stepped into yet another hallway.

At the end of the hall stood a door, lonely and unguarded. There were no cameras or humans around, but Riley grabbed my arm when I started forward, pulling us to a stop a few feet from the end of the corridor.

"Got it," he muttered, speaking to Wes, I figured, and turned to me, his face grave.

"What's wrong?" I whispered. "Is Garret not here?"

"Oh, he's here, Firebrand," Riley said, his voice matching the look on his face. "Wes confirmed it on the security feed. But he's not the only one." He nodded to the door. "That's a guard room. You need to pass through it to get to the jail block beyond. One problem, though. Guard rooms tend to be guarded."

My skin prickled. "How many?" I asked.

"Two." His expression darkened. "Both armed. They won't be expecting us, but we're going to have to be fast if we want to take them out before they sound the alarm. Think you can pull off another crazy ninja Viper attack? We're not going to get another shot at this. Once I open that door, there's really no going back."

My stomach dropped. After a moment, I took a deep breath, steeling myself. Whatever it took, I would find Garret. Even though these new instincts freaked me out. Even though I wanted nothing more than to be done with this place, with its armed humans and dead dragons hanging on the walls. We were almost to the soldier; his life depended on us reaching him, and I wouldn't let anything stop me now.

I glanced at Riley and nodded. "I'm ready. Let's do this."

GARRET

One hundred and twenty minutes till dawn and counting.

The hardest thing about waiting to die is being torn between wanting more time and wishing they would just get it over with already. You can't sleep, of course. You can't focus on anything else. Your mind keeps tormenting you with questions and memories and what-ifs, until you wish they'd just do you a favor and knock you senseless until it was time. Maybe that was a coward's way out, but I didn't want to show up to my execution looking beaten down and exhausted. I would not beg, or cry or plead for mercy. If this was my last day on Earth, I wanted to end it well, facing Death on my feet with my head held high. That was all a soldier of St. George could hope for.

As I lay on the cot, unable to sleep, unable to stop the relentless countdown in my head, my nerves suddenly prickled, making my breath catch. It was faint, but I recognized it instantly. The same feeling I got when I was about to kick down the door to a target's residence, or when I suspected an ambush lay just ahead and we were about to walk right into it. A soldier's instincts, telling me that something was about to happen.

Carefully, I swung my legs off the mattress and walked to the front of my cell. The room on the other side of the bars remained empty and dark, but I couldn't shake the feeling that something was wrong. Were they coming for me early? No, that wasn't right. The Order was nothing if not punctual. I still had another hour and fifty minutes before I was scheduled to die. Maybe the pressure was finally getting to me. Maybe I was having a nervous breakdown.

A sudden *boom* in the absolute stillness made me jump, the familiar crash of a door being flung open or kicked down, and I instinctively went for the gun at my belt, though of course I was unarmed. Shouts and cries of alarm rang out from the guard room beyond the cell block. Helpless, I clenched my fists around the bars, listening as a battle raged just a few yards away, muffled through the wall. There was a short scuffle, the scrape of chairs and the thud of bodies hitting the floor... and then silence.

I waited, holding my breath, my whole body coiled and ready for a fight. I didn't know what to expect, but whatever was coming, I was ready.

And then the door to the guard room opened, and I met a pair of vivid green eyes across the hall. Turns out, I wasn't ready at all.

The breath caught in my throat, and for a moment, I could only stare. *Not only a nervous breakdown, I'm also hallucinating.* Because there was no way she could be here. No sane reason she would show up in the middle of a St. George base, minutes from my execution. My mind had snapped; I was seeing things that weren't there. *The Perfect Soldier, unable to face his own death, goes crazy at age seventeen.*

Numb, I gaped at her, unable to look away. Bracing for the girl silhouetted against the light to writhe into shadows and moonlight and disappear. She didn't vanish but smiled, in a way that made my heart twist, and hurried to the door of my cell.

"Ember?" Still incredulous, I couldn't move as the figure drew close, gazing up at me. A hand reached through the bars, pressing against my jaw, and I drew in a shuddering breath. It was warm, and solid, and real. Impossible as it was, this was real.

My hand closed on her wrist, and I felt her pulse, rapid and steady, under my fingers. "What are you doing here?" I whispered.

"I came to get you out, of course," Ember whispered back, her breath fanning across my cheek, further proof that she wasn't a ghost or a figment of my imagination. Her gaze met mine through the bars, flashing defiantly. "I wasn't going to leave you, Garret. Not after you saved us. I'm not going to let them kill you."

"You came here for me?"

"Ember," growled a new, impatient voice, one that was vaguely familiar. I gazed past her shoulder and saw a second figure, dark haired and dressed in black, scowl at me from the open door of the guard room. With a start, I realized it was the other dragon, the one Ember had fled with when she left Crescent Beach.

"No time for this, Firebrand," he snapped, and tossed something to her, something that glittered as she caught it. "Come on. Those guards won't stay down forever. Open the door and let's get the hell out of here."

I was still reeling from the fact that Ember was *here*, that two *dragons* had shown up in the middle of the night to save me, but the second dragon's words jolted me out of my trance. As Ember shoved the key into the lock and wrenched the door open with a rusty creak, I suddenly realized what this meant, what was really happening.

"Garret," Ember said as I paused, staring at the open door. "Come on, before someone sees us. What are you doing?"

At the edge of the hall, the other dragon gave a snort of disgust.

"I told you, Firebrand." He gestured sharply in my direction. "You can open the monkey's cage, but you can't force it to leave. He's not moving because we're the enemy, and he'd rather stay and let them put a bullet through his skull than escape with a pair of dragons. Isn't that right, St. George?" The figure turned to me, mouth curled in a sneer. "Never mind that they sold you down the river without a second thought. But you know, I don't care one way or another about your loyalty hang-ups. You have three seconds to choose before I say the hell with it and leave you here. So what's it gonna be? Come with us, or stay here and die?"

Escape. Leave St. George with two dragons. With the enemy. I'd been fully prepared to die a moment ago, but now freedom was staring me in the face. If I did this, if I stepped through that door, there was no turning back.

For just a moment, the Perfect Soldier recoiled at the idea of accepting the help of our greatest enemies, even now. But I knew the truth, and it cast an ominous shadow over my thoughts. There was something wrong within the Order, something I'd never seen before I met Ember. It was treason to speak against St. George doctrine, treason to consider that the Order could be mistaken. No one in St. George was willing to hear the other side of the story, that a dragon, a creature whose race they had hunted and killed for hundreds of years, could be more than just a monster. No one was willing to accept the idea that the Order of St. George had slaughtered those who did not deserve it.

Regardless, the Order was no longer home. I'd already been sentenced to die, at the hands of the very people who had raised me. I wouldn't be any more of a traitor if I left this place in the company of two dragons who'd risked their lives to get me out. That made a pretty good argument, right there.

"I'm with you," I said quietly, and stepped through the door. The other dragon was still watching me, gold eyes assessing, but my gaze sought Ember's, and I saw relief spread across her face as I left the cell. I heard another disgusted snort from her companion, but I ignored it. I was a soldier of St. George no longer. I had no idea how Ember and her companion were going to get us *out* but, at least for now, I was free. If I was going to die today, I would go down fighting.

"Come on," growled the second dragon, gesturing impatiently. "It's almost dawn."

We hurried from the cell block, passing through the guard station, where two soldiers lay in crumpled heaps on the floor, out cold. One of them had what looked like a broken nose and the other's forehead was a mess of blood where, I suspected, he'd been bashed against the edge of the desk. I paused, kneeling down to grab the 9 mm from one of their side holsters, trying not to look at them as I checked the chamber for rounds. I might be with the enemy now, but they were still my former brothers, men I had trained with and fought beside. That couldn't be forgotten in a single night, or even in a single act of betrayal. The male dragon glared at me as I rose with the gun, obviously not pleased with the idea that I was armed, but didn't challenge me as we continued down the hall and up the stairs to the main floor.

The building was quiet as we exited the stairwell; it was still too early for most soldiers to be up and about, though I could see the sky had turned a disquieting navy blue, no longer the pitch-black of true night. Morning formations began at oh five hundred, which was less than an hour and a half away. The base would be stirring soon. Not to mention, we still had to get past security and the patrols around the perimeter fence. I didn't know how Ember and the other dragon had managed to get this far without being seen, but I was less than optimistic that we could waltz out again without trouble. Everything was quiet. This seemed way too easy.

The other dragon—Riley, I remembered his name was— stopped us at the back door and spoke quietly into what I presumed was a wire. A moment later, he nodded and pushed open the door, confirming what I suspected; they had an outsider hacked into the security cams. He had to be good; Order security was tight. He also had to be fairly close to pick up the signal.

Outside, it was still dark. We skirted the light and stayed to the shadows, moving low and silent across the barren yard. Once, a patrol passed us, talking in low voices, and we flattened ourselves against a wall until they disappeared. The buildings provided some cover, though we had to be wary of windows and doorways where someone could spot us. But what worried me the most was the last stretch to the fence line; flat and open, with little to no cover. If we were spotted and they opened fire on us then, we'd be gunned down in seconds.

I imagined the uproar this would cause. If the Order realized two dragons had been able to walk in, free a prisoner, and walk merrily out again, there would probably be several weeks of chaos as chapterhouses around the globe scrambled to tighten security, double patrols and lock down networks. Training would intensify. I imagined heads would roll higher up the chain of command. Dragons making a mockery of the Order? Sneaking in right under their noses? A few months ago, the idea would've angered and horrified me; right now I was severely disinclined to care. St. George was done with me. I didn't know *where* I would go from here; the Order had been my whole life. I didn't know what else was out there. But one thing I was sure of: dawn would not find me standing in front of the firing wall, about to be executed for saving a dragon.

But we weren't out of here yet.

Four hundred yards to the perimeter fence...and everything exploded.

As we huddled by a wall, ready to make that final dash over open ground toward the fence line, a siren blared, shattering the quiet. Ember jumped, and the other dragon cursed, pressing back into the wall as lights erupted all around us. Spotlights flashed to life, huge white circles gliding over the ground and scouring the sky. Doors opened, and soldiers began pouring from everywhere, looking confused but alert as they gathered in loose squads, gazing around warily.

"What's going on?" Ember whispered.

"They know we're here," the other dragon spat. "Probably found the empty cell and the guards." He swore again and peered around the corner, narrowing his eyes. "Wes, we've been discovered. Can you kill the lights?" A moment passed, and he shook his head. "Fine, then get out of here! Don't worry about us—we'll catch up at the rendezvous point." He paused a moment, then snarled, "I don't care, Wes, just go!"

Soldiers were everywhere now. I raised my gun, though I cringed at the thought of firing on my former brothers. "We're not going to make it," I told the other two quietly. And for a second, I felt a stab of regret that Ember had come. I'd wanted her to be free of St. George, to not live in fear of dragonslayers trying to kill her. Now, she would die here with me.

"It's too far," I told them as they glanced back. "There are too many between us and the fence line. We'll never reach it without being seen. Ember…" I looked into her wide green eyes. She stared back without fear or regret, making my heart twist. "I'll lead them away. They'll be looking for me. You and Riley get out of here, any way you can."

Her eyes flashed defiance. "Don't you dare, Garret," she almost snarled. "I didn't come all this way to free you just to leave you behind again. That's the most pointless thing I've ever heard." She stepped away from the wall, and her eyes were glowing now, a luminous emerald green. "We're getting out of here, all of us, right now!"

A searing white light swung around, pinning us in its glare. I winced and raised my arm to shield my face, just as the girl in front of me disappeared and a fiery crimson dragon reared up to take her place. Shouts rang out over the base, as the red dragon landed on all fours, dark wings outstretched, and roared a challenge that made the air shiver.

"Shit!" There was another ripple of energy as Ember's companion shed his human form, becoming a sleek blue dragon with a fin down his neck and back. My pulse spiked as the two inhuman creatures turned on me, eyes glowing. Even now, instinct was telling me to run, that they were the enemy and I had to gun them down before they attacked and tore me to shreds.

Shots rang out behind me, sparking off the wall. Ember snarled, flinching back, and I spun, raising my weapon. A patrol of two was rushing at us, guns drawn and firing on the dragons pinned in the spotlight. They hadn't seen me, or rather, their attention was riveted to the creatures behind me. I raised my gun, silently asking forgiveness, and fired at their legs. The soldiers cried out and pitched forward, crashing to the ground, but I could see more running toward us. The whole base was alerted now and knew dragons were inside the compound.

"Garret!"

A metallic red body lunged to my side, and I had to force myself not to leap away as a narrow, reptilian face peered at me. "Get on," the dragon said, lowering her wings. "Hurry! We have to fly."

Get on? *Ride* a dragon? For a split second, I balked. Talking with dragons was one thing. Accepting their help was another. But riding one? Especially if I knew the dragon was also a slender, green-eyed girl I had kissed on more than one occasion?

With a roar, the blue dragon reared up and blasted a cone of fire at a patrol that came around the corner, guns raised. The soldiers fell back with cries and screams, and Ember snarled, baring her fangs at me.

"Garret, come *on*!"

I shook myself and vaulted onto her back. Her spines poked at me as I wrapped my arms around her neck and settled between the leathery wings. I could feel heat radiating from the scales, the muscles shifting and coiling beneath me, and I repressed a shiver. This was not the Ember I knew. The girl had vanished, any hints of humanity disappearing as the dragon moved, savage, majestic and terrifying at the same time. She craned her neck to look back at me, long muzzle close enough to show rows of fangs, the scent of ash and smoke curling from her jaws.

"Hang on."

More gunshots rang out, and the blue dragon snarled something in Draconic, the guttural, native language of dragons. Ember spun, making me tighten my grip, took three bounding leaps forward and launched herself into the air. Her wing muscles strained beneath me like steel cables pulsing beneath her skin, and we rose into the sky. The spotlight followed, keeping us brightly illuminated even as we left the base behind. Gunshots roared; I heard a howl of rage from the blue dragon, and gritted my teeth, hunched low over Ember's back. She jolted suddenly, then her wings flapped furiously as we picked up speed, racing to get away from the spotlight and out of range of the compound. Very gradually, the spotlight disappeared, and the gunshots faded away, as we fled St. George and escaped into the desert.

★ ★ ★

We were out. We'd actually escaped St. George.

The wind whipped at my hair and clothes as I shifted on

Ember's back and cautiously sat up, gazing around in amazement. The desert stretched out before me, vast and endless, looking like an ocean of sand in the predawn light. Where it met the sky, a faint smear of pink was peeking over the horizon, though the land was still dark and shadowed. From this height, I could just make out the distant highway and the tiny glimmers of cars that followed it.

I drew in a quiet breath, wondering if all dragons felt this exhilaration. I'd gone surfing with Ember before, had felt that addictive rush of excitement and adrenaline while coursing down a huge wave.

It was nothing compared to this.

On impulse, I glanced behind me, at the compound I was leaving behind, and my blood chilled. Headlights speared the darkness from several vehicles, following us across the open desert. I counted three SUVs and at least one Jeep with a spotlight fixed to the roof, all straining to close the distance. There was no place to hide out here. If those vehicles got much closer they would start shooting, and we wouldn't stand a chance.

"There's the van!"

I looked at the blue dragon, then at the ground, where a large white van was speeding across the flat plain, trailing a billow of dust. Instantly, the blue dragon folded his wings and dropped from the sky, plunging toward the ground. I felt the subtle shift of muscles beneath me as Ember did the same, though a ragged shudder went through her as she glided after the blue. She was panting hard, sides heaving, and I hoped carrying me away from the base hadn't put too much of a strain on her.

The blue dragon plunged low to skim the ground, then wheeled hard so that he passed in front of the van, in full view of the driver. Instantly, the van slammed on its brakes, coming to a skidding halt in a writhing cloud of dust. As the blue dragon landed, the front door opened and a human jumped out, wild haired and skinny, shouting something at the dragon as he hurried forward.

I realized with a start that Ember had dropped low to the ground and was gliding toward the van at top speed. Alarmed, I tensed, wondering when she would slow, but another shudder went through her, and she abruptly dropped from the air like a stone.

At the last second, she flapped her wings and pulled up enough to slow her momentum, before we crashed headfirst into the ground. I was thrown clear, striking the earth and rolling several yards, the world spinning around me, before I finally came to a halt several yards from where Ember had fallen.

Wincing, I staggered upright. My head throbbed, my arms were bloody and the world was still spinning, but nothing seemed broken. I ignored the stab of pain from a bruised or cracked rib and stumbled toward the dragon.

"Ember..."

My stomach twisted. She lay on her side a few yards away, heaving in great, shuddering gasps. One wing was crumpled beneath her, the other lay limp on the ground. Her legs moved feebly, clawing at the loose sand and rock, and her tail twitched a weak rhythm in the dirt. But in the time it took me to reach her, she slumped and went motionless. Her wing gave one final spasm and was still.

"Ember!"

A dark-haired, naked human raced up to her, dropping to his knees beside the scaly neck. "Ember," Riley said again, putting a hand on her side. "Can you hear me? What happened? Are you—?"

He stopped, his face going pale. I limped up beside him just as he pulled his hand back, the palm and fingers covered in red, and my heart stood still.

"Oh, no." His voice was a whisper, and he surged to his feet, glaring back at the van. "Wes!" he yelled. "Ember's been shot. Help me get her in the van before St. George catches up."

"Bloody hell." The shaggy-haired human raced around the van, pausing to throw open the back doors. "I knew this was a bad idea, Riley. I knew the stubborn brat was going to get us all killed."

"Shut up and help before I rip off your legs and leave you for St. George."

"I'll help," I broke in, and he turned to glare daggers at me. Without waiting for an answer, I stepped around the unconscious dragon and knelt beside her, sliding my arm beneath a scaly foreleg. Ember stirred weakly, her claws raking the sand once, but she didn't wake up. Riley hesitated, then crouched on the opposite side, taking her leg.

"Wes!" he spat as we braced ourselves to lift the dragon off the ground. "Get over here. You're going to have to help, too."

"On three," I said as the other human dropped beside me, muttering curses the whole time. Over Ember's back and wings, Riley gave me a last baleful glare, but then his attention shifted to the dragon between us. "One...two...three!"

We lifted. Ember sagged, wings and tail dragging along the ground, her neck dangling awkwardly. She wasn't as heavy as I'd expected, considering this was a very large, armored reptile who was complete dead weight at the moment. Somehow, the three of us manhandled the dragon over the ground and into the back of the vehicle, grunting as we pushed and pulled her inside. She barely fit; her wings were crumpled against the sides, her neck bent at an awkward angle, and we had to loop her tail over her back. I ended up pressed against the front seat with her neck draped over my lap, curved talons pricking my leg through my jeans. Riley glared at me over Ember's motionless body, obviously hating how close I was, but there was no room to move. Nor was there room for the both of us to be back here, with an unconscious red dragon sprawled across the floor.

"Riley!" Wes snapped as the other hesitated, reluctant to leave me alone with Ember, I guessed. "St. George is coming! Bloody hell, put some pants on, would you? Let's go!"

Riley cursed and backed away, reaching out to close the back doors. His eyes glowed yellow in the shadows of the van as he stared at me. "If she dies," he said softly, "I'm going to kill you." It was not an idle threat.

The roar of a distant engine, not our own, echoed over the hill behind us, getting steadily closer, and my stomach lurched. St. George was not about to let us go. Wes shrieked at Riley again, and the doors slammed, cutting off my view of the outside world. Ember groaned and stirred, wings fluttering, but she didn't awaken. I swallowed hard and scooted aside so that the narrow, horned skull was pillowed against my legs. Her breath was shallow and hot against my skin, and I put one tentative hand on her scaly neck, trying to ignore the rows of fangs hovering over my leg, the claws that scraped close to my body.

The blood seeping across the floor, making my insides cold.

The van lurched forward, bounced once and gained speed as it rumbled over the sand. We fled into the desert, the roar of St. George behind us, the head of a dying dragon resting in my lap.

PART II

ALL THAT GLITTERS

COBALT

Twelve years ago

"Agent Cobalt? They're ready for you now."

I stood and rolled my shoulders forward and back, trying to shake out the stiffness, then followed the assistant down the hall toward the room at the very end. I hated meetings like this: sitting in a cold office building, being polite and deferent, while the flat, appraising glare of a senior dragon bored into me from across the table. Normally, Talon didn't bother with face-to-face conferences, speaking to me directly only when they felt the assignment especially important. I'd rather the organization contact me the usual way: via an envelope or a folder left at a dead drop, where I could read through my assignment in peace. Where I didn't feel like I was being judged.

Especially now. Especially since I was still furious with the way the last assignment had gone down, the lives lost because of me. Because Talon had lied, and I'd believed them.

I strode into the meeting room, where a trio was seated around a long wooden table in the center of the floor. I recognized Adam Roth, a youngish-looking man in a perfectly tailored gray suit. One of Talon's junior VPs, though he was still older than me by at least a couple centuries. I held his gaze a split second longer than was probably safe, saw a flicker of something lethal go through that calm expression before I averted my eyes, glancing at the pair seated across from each other a few chairs down.

My stomach dropped. My trainer, the crusty old bastard himself, sat quietly with the tips of his fingers steepled against his lips, ignoring everything around him. Or appearing that he did. I knew better. Nothing in this room would have escaped his notice, not even the pigeons nesting on the sill behind his head. He was older than Roth, one of the oldest trainers in the organization; a tall, thin man with a sharp chin and even sharper black eyes that were never still. His dark hair was streaked with silver, and the jagged scar beneath his left eye only added to his mystique.

Not long ago, the sight of him would have filled me with both anticipation and dread, like a nervous schoolboy handing his report card to his parents. Now the only thing I felt was resentment. Why was he here? As if I needed someone else judging my every move, silently criticizing.

The last person in the room was barely noticeable, his presence overshadowed by the two adult dragons. A human, I realized when I finally studied him. Thin and gangly, with a mess of brown hair and a rumpled collared shirt half tucked into his pants. By human standards, I guessed he was fairly young; maybe eighteen or nineteen. I was surprised. If he was in this room with Roth and one of the oldest trainers in the organization, then he had to know what we were. Who was this human, and what did he do, to warrant such privileges? He didn't look like anything special to me.

"Ah, Agent Cobalt," Roth said, rising smoothly from his chair. "Thank you for coming. Please, have a seat." He gestured to the table, and I sat one chair down from my trainer, leaving the human on the other side by himself.

"Hello, Cobalt," the Chief Basilisk murmured without looking at me. One corner of his lip curled in that faint, amused smile I hated. It had been more than a year since I saw him last, but he could always make me feel like a bumbling hatchling again with just a look. "I hear you've been doing well."

"I'm sure you have," I muttered as Roth sat down, smoothing his tie, then folding his hands before him on the table. "I'm sure you've heard all kinds of things about me lately."

This was not smart, antagonizing my trainer in front of the VP. A few years ago, I could have expected a swat upside the head at best and a six-hour training session at worst. But the years of being cowed by him were over. I was a full-fledged Basilisk, and not only that, I was one of their best. This might be a dangerous game I was playing, but it was no more hazardous than the missions they expected me to pull off without a hitch. Let him know I wasn't happy; I couldn't do anything about Talon or my assignments, but I didn't have to be thrilled about them.

My instructor's thin mouth twitched—impossible to tell if he was angry or amused by my lack of respect—before he turned to the head of the table. The VP was watching us now, dark eyes intense.

"I have reviewed your previous assignments, Agent Cobalt," Roth began, dispensing with the pleasantries, which was a relief. I didn't have the patience for useless small talk about my trip and what I thought of my accommodations. "Your trainer speaks highly of you and, from what I can discern, with good reason. We have not had such a young Basilisk do so well in a long time. When we asked your trainer who was best suited for this assignment, you were his top pick. Congratulations."

"Thank you, sir," I said flatly, dredging up a polite nod and a stiff smile. "I do what I can for the good of the organization."

I almost gagged on the words. But it was what I was expected to say. I was not so crazy as to insult the organization itself; if I did, I probably wouldn't walk out of this room alive.

Mr. Roth smiled, though his expression was cold. Turning to the giant screen on the far wall, he pressed a remote, and an image flickered to life: a satellite feed of a snowy wilderness in the middle of nowhere. A scattering of plain gray buildings sat within a fence at the edge of the mountains.

"I am certain you know what you are looking at," Mr. Roth said, watching me across the table.

I gave a short nod. "It's a St. George facility," I replied, observing the image on the screen, committing the layout of the place to memory. "If I had to guess, one of their northern chapterhouses."

"Yes," Mr. Roth agreed. "A brand-new Order chapterhouse, in fact. We discovered this base last week and have been monitoring it heavily ever since. As their security system isn't online yet, we have decided this is a perfect opportunity to strike. Do you see this building, Agent Cobalt?" A red circle appeared on the screen, around one of the identical gray buildings in the center of the compound. "That is their data center. And your target." Roth's voice remained matter-of-fact, as if he'd just announced the time of the next conference call. "We need you to infiltrate their base, find the main computer and download a sensitive file from their network. After that, destroy the building so that no traces of us, or the information theft, can be found."

I kept my expression cool, but inside, my stomach dropped. I'd received dangerous assignments before, but this? Sneak into a St. George base? Break into a chapterhouse swarming with enemy soldiers? "What will I be looking for?" I asked. "I have some computer skills, but I'm no hacker. Even in a new base, their files are sure to be well protected, or at the very least encrypted."

Mr. Roth smiled. His cold gaze shifted to the person sitting across from me, and the human looked up from his laptop.

His eyes were sullen. As if sitting in a room with three dragons not only failed to impress him, he resented being here in the first place.

"Right. Hang on a moment." Somehow, his English accent didn't surprise me. I watched as the kid reached around his laptop, yanked something free, then slid it to me over the table.

I picked it up: a simple black USB drive rested between my fingers. Puzzled, I looked back at the human and raised an eyebrow.

"What is this?"

"A program that will let me hack into their system undetected, find the data we're looking for and download the correct file to Talon's network," the kid answered, not meeting my gaze. "Take back the drive, and the theft will be untraceable. They won't be able to follow it back to us. So don't worry about the technical stuff. I've got it covered. All you have to do is plug it in. You can do that, can't you, mate?"

Ignoring the challenge in the human's voice, I nodded, slipping the drive into a pocket. I wanted to ask what the data was for, what was so important that I was crossing enemy lines. But I understood that everything was on a need-to-know basis, and if Roth thought the information was important, he would tell me. If not, then he wouldn't answer the question regardless. I had my mission; I didn't need to know the whys.

I was, however, even more curious about the human across from me. He obviously knew what we were; Roth was making no attempt to hide it. Talon employed some of the brightest and most talented humans from around the globe, luring them with promises of wealth, power, security, whatever they desired. But most of Talon's human workforce had no idea who—or what—their employers actually were. They did their jobs, went home to their families and returned the next morning, completely unaware that the company they worked for was anything but normal. Only a few mortals were privileged with the truth, those whose silence had been bought with money, threats or blackmail. There were a few humans in Talon who were slavishly loyal to the organization, who truly believed dragons were the superior race and were proud to work for them. But every dragon knew that humans, as a whole, were gullible, weak and easily swayed. To bring one into the know, to reveal our true nature, was a massive risk and something the organization avoided unless there was a solid, undeniable reason the human would not betray us to the outside world.

So, what was *this* human's reason? I wondered. Why did he seem nearly as angry and resentful as me?

"When you are finished transferring the file," Roth continued as the kid dropped his gaze and went back to staring at his computer, "find the data storage center and destroy it. This will cripple their network and blind this particular base. They will be unable to recover quickly, making retaliation against us nearly impossible. But there is another reason we are sending you, agent."

He paused, and his gaze flicked to my trainer, who grunted and sat up in his chair before turning to me.

"The other reason," the old Basilisk said with one of his faint, evil smiles, "is to test what we hope will be a fun new toy for our side. So you're going to be a bit of a guinea pig for this assignment. We have something that we've been working on, and we believe it's nearly ready for use in the field. Congratulations, agent, you get to take it for its trial run."

I suppressed a wince. A hatchling or rookie agent might've been excited for this news, willing and eager to test out something new. I was not. I knew what kind of "toy" I'd be working with, and frankly, it scared the crap out of me. Talon had always been on the cutting edge of science and technology, knowing that keeping ahead of the times was not only profitable, it was essential for our survival. As a race, we had survived because we had evolved, and knowledge was power. Talon hoarded knowledge like they did wealth, turning everything into profit for the organization. Not only did they fund countless research centers, they had their own laboratories, where the most brilliant minds the organization could find worked tirelessly, uncovering secrets, pushing boundaries, experimenting with things best left alone.

Things like magic. Magic still existed in the world today, otherwise how could a fifteen-ton dragon shrink down into a two-hundred-pound human body? Just because nobody used it anymore didn't mean magic didn't exist. In the Elder Wyrm's time, at least according to the stories, magic was everywhere. There were witches and demons, monsters and ancient swords, wizards, the Good Neighbors and even the rare unicorn, wandering the deepest parts of the forest. But with the rise of civilization and technology, magic had been long forgotten. Even the Elder Wyrm didn't use it anymore, or maybe there wasn't a lot of the ancient power left in the world. Because we had lost the capacity for it—or perhaps because we really didn't need it anymore—Shifting into human form was the last bit of old magic we could do.

But, in recent years, the Talon laboratories had been coming out with strange, crazy, unexplainable things. Bodysuits that wouldn't tear when you Shifted, drugs that specifically targeted the dragon anatomy, weird crap like that. According to rumors, they were experimenting with blending old magic and science, mixing them together, though that should've been impossible. There were also whispers that these tests were just preliminary; that the scientists were working on something "big." Something that would change the dragon world forever. I didn't know how much of that I believed, but whenever the labs came out with a brand-new "toy," somehow my trainer was the first to get his hands on it.

I could feel the old Basilisk watching me, his gaze burning the side of my head, and stifled a sigh. "Of course, sir," I muttered, not meeting his gaze. "Whatever Talon needs me to do." Because that's what they expected me to say, even though my insides roiled with anger as I did. A pause and then, though I knew better, my curiosity got the better of me. "What kind of thing will I be testing out, exactly?"

My trainer chuckled. "Oh, I think you'll like this, Agent Cobalt," he said, his hard smile making me realize I would feel the exact opposite. And the old bastard knew it, too. "In fact, I believe it's right up your alley."

GARRET

"Bloody hell," the man beside me muttered.

I turned from the window and gave him a wary glance. We'd been traveling for nearly an hour, fleeing down dusty roads with the sun beating down on us, turning the inside of the van into an oven. Knowing St. George was still out there, we'd avoided the main strip of highway, taking back roads and constantly looking for vehicles that could belong to our pursuers. No one seemed to be giving chase, and with every mile, we drew farther and farther away from the St. George chapterhouse, but being out in the open like this made me nervous. The Order wouldn't stop hunting me, especially now that I was in the company of dragons. Dragons who had broken into their chapterhouse and escaped with a traitor. We had to find shelter soon. I hoped my rescuers had a place they could go.

The driver, Wes, I think his name was, pursed his lips at the dashboard before raising his head to call over his shoulder. "Running on fumes here, Riley," he said, his voice tight and sharp. "I'm going to need to stop for gas, or we'll be hauling a bloody dragon carcass across the desert on foot."

"Dammit," came the low voice from the back. "All right, pull off when you get the chance, but let's do this quickly."

Wes immediately made a right turn and hit the gas pedal, presumably heading toward the highway again. I turned in my seat to peer into the back. Riley crouched at Ember's side, fully clothed with a bloody rag in hand, pressing it to her ribs. We'd switched places not long after the van started moving, as I had no idea what to do with a wounded dragon, and Ember was bleeding all over the place. She now sprawled across the floor of the van, large wings brushing the windows like leathery curtains. Her scales gleamed metallic crimson in the sunlight through the glass and threw fragments of light over the walls. She was not, I realized with a chill, something small or subtle that we could easily hide. All anyone had to do was peek in the window to see a large red *dragon* curled up on the floor.

The smell of blood soaked the back of the vehicle, making my stomach turn. "How is she?" I asked, and the other dragon shot me a murderous glare.

"Not good." His voice was clipped, as if he was speaking to me only out of necessity. "She's lost a lot of blood, and that slug is still inside her somewhere. I've stopped the bleeding for now, but we have to get her somewhere safe before we can take care of the wound." He put a hand on a scaly foreleg, his forehead creasing with worry. "Probably a good thing she's unconscious, but she won't be able to Shift back until we get it out. It could tear something vital if she changes back with the round still inside her."

My stomach twisted with worry. Not only for Ember, but that we wouldn't be able to get somewhere safe without anyone noticing the large mythological creature in the backseat. As if reading my thoughts, Riley's gaze flickered to me and turned hard. "So you'd better hope no one sees her between then and now," he growled, "or we'll have the Order back on our tail faster than you can pull a trigger. And probably Talon, come to think of it." He snorted, lip curling with disgust. "It would be just like them to show up now."

I frowned, not sure I'd heard him correctly. "Why would Talon be after you? I thought all dragons—"

"Well, you thought wrong." He gave me a look of contempt. "There's a lot about us you don't know, St. George," he went on, an accusation and a challenge. "Maybe if you tried talking to us instead of blowing us to pieces, you'd realize that."

"Riley," Wes broke in before I could answer, "gas station in three miles. If we don't fill up now, we might not get another chance. And I need to visit the loo."

"All right." Reaching down, Riley grabbed the edge of the canvas Ember was sprawled on top of and began tugging it free. "Do it, but hurry up."

I turned in my seat and watched the desert flash by. Watched the pavement stretch on, until a lone gas station appeared on the side of the road, shimmering in the near distance. My apprehension grew. It was not a tiny little outpost in the middle of nowhere. It was a huge truck stop with a restaurant and mini-mart attached, and there was a crowd. I glanced back as Riley gently peeled one of Ember's wings from the wall and folded it carefully against her body before pulling the canvas over her. Her tail and the tips of her claws poked out, but at least she wasn't as blatantly noticeable as before. Still, if anyone got too close, they would immediately know something large, scaly and inhuman was sprawled on the floor of the van.

We pulled up to one of the pumps, and Wes leaped out and slammed the door behind him, leaving the keys in the ignition. I scanned the station warily, keeping an eye out for anything suspicious, but nothing seemed out of the ordinary; families wandering back to their cars, a couple large trucks sitting off to the side. No soldiers, black SUVs or anything that belonged to the Order. So far, so good.

Wes wrenched the pump off the handle, shoved it into the tank to start the flow of gas, then went hurrying into the store. I scanned the area once more before glancing at the two dragons behind me.

"You're not part of Talon," I confirmed, as Riley smoothed the canvas over Ember, covering the exposed parts as best he could. It was a strange concept. All dragons, we were told, belonged to Talon, the huge dragon organization that spanned the globe. Banded together, working together, to overthrow mankind. I'd never thought there could be discontents.

But then, I'd never thought I could befriend a dragon, either. Or that she would risk her life to save mine.

Riley, tugging a corner over Ember's front claws, gave a snort.

"No."

I waited, but he didn't offer any further explanation. But there was something there, an undercurrent of disgust that wasn't pointed entirely at me, but at Talon. Curiosity prickled. And guilt. Here was one more fact about dragons that the Order had gotten wrong. This dragon wasn't part of the organization; in fact, he seemed to despise it. How gravely was the Order mistaken when it came to our ancient enemies? And how many lives had *I* taken, because I believed we were doing the right thing?

"If you're not part of Talon," I ventured, "who are you with?"

"Myself." Again that clipped, brusque reply. Somehow, it didn't surprise me.

Something chirped close by, startling us both. Riley reached back and pulled out his phone, staring at the screen. His expression screwed up with disgust.

"Oh, for God's sake, Wes. Really?" He stuck the phone in his back pocket, shaking his head. "You and your damn nervous stomach. Perfect timing as always."

He straightened and peered out the window, scanning the surroundings just as I had a moment ago. I recognized that wariness, that caution for traps and enemies and hidden dangers. He had been a soldier, once. Or some kind of operative. We were parked at one of the farthest pumps, and no one was close by, but he still scanned the area for a good twenty seconds before glancing at me.

"I'm going inside." His glare was hard, his face taut with suspicion. "We'll need a few things if we're going to be holed up for a while, and my idiot partner is out of commission. I'll only be gone a minute, but..." His gaze flicked to the large canvas lump beside him, the tail and claws poking out from beneath. "Can I trust you with her, St. George?"

I met his glare, keeping my voice steady. "Yes."

His lips tightened like he'd swallowed something foul, but he didn't say anything as he made his way to the front door.

Snatching the keys from the ignition, he slipped out of the
van and slammed the door behind him, leaving me alone with
an unconscious dragon in the backseat.

Silence descended, throbbing in my ears, broken only by
Ember's slow, labored breaths beneath the tarp. I turned in my
seat to look at her fully. The canvas hid most of her body, but
her feet, ending in hooked black talons, stuck out of the bottom, as did the long, spade-tipped tail. I could see the points
of her horns and wings, the curve of her neck, the very tip of
her muzzle peeking from the edge of the cloth. She twisted
and curled a lip in her sleep, revealing a flash of very long,
very sharp fangs, and a cold knot formed in my stomach.

Ember... *This* was the real form of the girl I'd met in Crescent Beach. I'd seen her like this before, but only in passing.
When we were battling one another, soldier to dragon, each
of us fighting for our lives. And later, when I was urging her
to run before my team showed up to kill them all. I'd seen
her real form then, but it was a fleeting awareness, buried in
the urgency of the moment. I'd been too distracted to give
it much thought.

Now, though, it was staring me in the face, impossible to
ignore. Ember was a *dragon*. A huge lizard, with scales and
wings and claws and a tail. All my memories from Crescent
Beach, from the summer that had disappeared too quickly,
were of the girl. Surfing with her. Slow dancing at a party.
Kissing her in the ocean, feeling my blood sizzle and my
breath catch. The green-eyed girl with an infectious smile and
a fierce love for life. But Ember wasn't a girl. Ember wasn't
human. Ember was...this.

A car pulled off the highway and cruised to a stop at the

pump next to ours. The doors opened, and a family of four piled out, making me tense. But after a short squabble between two small boys and their mother, she managed to herd them toward the mini-mart. The father remained behind long enough to fill the tank and make me nervous, before he finally meandered into the store. I drummed my fingers on the armrest, wondering where Riley and Wes were.

A scraping sound jerked my attention to the back. The canvas lump was moving, shifting from side to side with confused growls. Ember tossed her head, flinging the cloth away and exposing a bright red dragon to the open air. She tried staggering upright, but lurched to one side and collapsed against the door with a loud thump, making the vehicle rock. Her tail lashed the sides of the van with metallic clanking sounds as she growled and clawed herself up again, the sunlight gleaming along her metallic crimson scales.

"Ember." Swiftly, I moved to the back, barely dodging a wingtip as it flapped against the wall. "Hey, stop. Calm down." Her head whipped toward me, and I instinctively threw up my hand, catching a horn as it smacked into my palm. "Stop!"

She froze at my touch, and I was suddenly holding the head of a groggy red dragon, her muzzle right at eye level. Her fangs gleamed as she stared at me, nostrils flaring, and for a second, I felt a jolt of fear, realizing how close she was. If she lunged or snapped or spit fire at me, I'd catch it right in the face.

Quickly, I released her. She didn't pull away but continued to stare at me, a puzzled expression in her reptilian green eyes.

"Garret?"

My muscles unclenched at the sound of her voice. It was weak, confused and in pain, but it was *her* voice, Ember's voice. Though I didn't know what I'd expected. Those slitted eyes blinked again before she sagged weakly, struggling to stay upright. "Where am I?" she asked, her words slurred. "What's going on?"

I took a careful breath. "You need to lie down," I told her gently. She stumbled and fell against the side, and I winced as the van rattled. "Ember, look at me." I reached out, catching one of her horns again, forcing her attention back to me. "You have to relax," I said as she looked up, her eyes now bright with pain and fear. Her jaws parted as she panted, showing rows of deadly fangs, and I resisted the urge to yank my hand back. "We're out in the open, and you can't be seen right now. Please. Lie down."

She stared at me a moment, and I forced myself to breathe calmly. This had to be one of the most surreal moments of my life: pleading with a near-delirious dragon to lie still so that we wouldn't be discovered. With the exception of the flight from the base, I'd never been so close to a live dragon, not for this length of time. Never close enough to feel its breath, smelling of heat and smoke. Or the bony ridges of its horns under my palm. In the past, if a dragon had been near enough to touch, it was either dead or I was fighting for my life, trying to make it so.

A tremor went through the dragon in front of me and, to my relief, she sank down again, her head touching the floor with a muffled groan. Her wings fluttered once and her tail thumped the side of the van, before her eyes closed and she went limp, asleep once more. I let out a short breath, glancing out the side window, and froze.

A boy of maybe five stood a few feet from the van, clutching a fountain drink in both hands, his eyes huge as they stared at me. I gazed back, guessing that he'd seen everything, unsure of what to do, as his parents walked around the car, his mother reaching for his arm.

"Jason, come on. What are you looking at?"

The boy pointed. "The dragon."

"A dragon?" Her gaze rose, a puzzled look crossing her face as she spotted me. Heart pounding, I offered a feeble smile and a helpless shrug, and the woman frowned.

"Okay, that's nice, dear. Come on, Daddy's waiting." Taking the boy's wrist, she quickly steered him toward the car, and I started breathing again. As they piled into the car, the little boy's face peered through the window at me, eyes huge and staring, until the car pulled onto the highway and sped off toward the horizon.

Riley and Wes came out of the store, each carrying a couple plastic bags, and hurried toward the van. I pulled the canvas over Ember again, gently covering her head and body as much as I could, before slipping quietly into the front seat.

A moment later, Wes wrenched open the front door, tossed a couple grocery bags into my lap and moved aside to let Riley in. The other dragon climbed into the back through the front seats, not wanting to open the side door and risk exposing Ember to the world, I guessed. But he paused, his gaze flickering over the sleeping dragon and the obviously disturbed tarp, before shifting to me.

"Problems, St. George?" he asked, his voice suspicious. I shook my head.

"Nothing I couldn't handle."

He continued to glare at me, but at that moment, Ember flapped a wing in her sleep, throwing back the canvas again. A line of red spattered the window, making my insides curl. Riley muttered a curse.

"She's bleeding again," he growled, kneeling swiftly at her side. "Wes, grab the first-aid kit—she can't afford to lose any more blood. St. George, get us out of here."

I waited until Wes slid into the back with Riley, then moved to the driver's seat and turned the key in the ignition. "Where am I going?" I asked as the van roared to life.

"Vegas" was the snapped reply. "It's not far, and I have a place we can hole up for a few days." Ember twitched, kicking a back leg against the wall, and Wes let out a yelp. Riley cursed. "I'll give you directions when we get close, but right now, just drive!"

Throwing the van into gear, I pulled onto the highway, passed a dusty sign that read Las Vegas 64 Miles and sped off into the sun.

DANTE

"Mr. Hill. Do you have a moment?"

I looked up from my desk. Mist stood in the doorway, manila folder in hand, looking poised and calm and expectant at the same time. Her silver hair was pulled into a ponytail today, and it made her look younger, not quite so severe. It was hard to believe Mist was my age; she acted so composed and mature, I wondered if she'd had a normal upbringing. Or whatever was considered *normal* for us, anyway.

I sighed and put down my pen, where I'd been scribbling notes on a yellow sheet of paper. "Mist," I said, smiling as I beckoned her into the office. "How many times have I asked you to call me Dante?"

"Counting today, exactly five times." As always, there was a subtle note of challenge beneath the polite tone. "And I predict you will ask me at least twice more in the future. But that is irrelevant at this point." She stepped back into the hall, looking suddenly anxious. "If you would come with me, Mr. Hill, I think you should see this."

★ ★ ★

Back in the operations room, I gazed up at one of the enormous screens, watching a satellite map blip into view, showing a swath of dusty brown, with patches of green inter-spersed throughout. Mist stood beside me, also watching the screen, while the two human workers sat at their keyboards, typing furiously.

"This," Mist explained, leaning back against a desk, "is the eastern Mojave Desert, close to the Arizona/Utah line. When you told us to look for the Order's western chapterhouse, we began directing our satellite feeds to the areas close to and around Crescent Beach."

"Hold on," I said, holding up a hand. "We have satellites?"

Mist gave a short nod. "We own one of the largest satel-lite communication networks in the world," she said coolly, "It isn't difficult to put in a few extras.

"Regardless," she continued, as if that was unimportant, "when we started searching, we found...this."

The feed zoomed in, focused and showed a bird's-eye view of a facility smack in the middle of nowhere. Even from this height, it didn't look very impressive. I could see a fence with two gates, several long rectangular buildings and the road that cut through the vast, empty desert surrounding it.

"That," Mist announced, as if she could feel my skepticism, "is St. George's western chapterhouse."

I frowned. "Are you sure? It doesn't look like much. Cer-tainly not a heavily armed military base."

She gave me a look of veiled annoyance. "That's what they want you to see, Mr. Hill," she said. "The Order uses a combination of security and complete isolation to hide their chapterhouses. Some of them, like the main headquarters in London, are too heavily armed for us to do anything about. Some of them, like this one, rely on isolation to keep them secure. Talon knows of several large Order facilities around the world, but the smaller chapterhouses are good at concealing themselves and hiding in plain sight. The only reason we found this one was because we were actively searching for St. George movement in the region. At your request, Mr. Hill, and this took us all night."

I held up my hands. "Point taken. No need to bite my head off. I believe you." She sniffed, looking mollified, and I glanced back at the screen. "So, this is their western chapterhouse," I mused, crossing my arms. "I'm sure Talon will want to know about this. Have you informed Mr. Roth?"

"No," Mist replied gravely. "I figured you deserved that honor. After all, you were the one who pointed us in the right direction. But that's not all we found," she continued, before I could feel smug that I had been right. "Look at this."

The screen went dark as the scene faded to night, only a few points of light glimmering in a sea of black. Then one of the humans clicked a key, and the image switched to a grainy green color. I could see the buildings, blurry and indistinct, through the emerald haze, and the fence surrounding the base as the camera zoomed in. The time on the bottom left of the screen read 3:26 a.m., dated two days ago.

I blinked. Two small black dots were moving across the desert from the east, looking like tiny crawling insects from this height but definitely making a beeline toward the fence. They weren't coming in from the road; in fact, it looked like they were actively avoiding the gates, heading toward the most isolated corner of the compound. As I stared, amazed, they paused at the fence a few seconds, slipped through a hole they must've cut out and began creeping across the yard toward the main headquarters.

"What in the world?" I whispered, baffled as I watched their progress. "That can't be…"

"We believe it *is* Ember, Mr. Hill," Mist finished solemnly. "And Cobalt. None of our agents have received orders to move on a St. George facility in several months. Cobalt has the knowledge and the skills for this type of work, and he is bold enough to infiltrate even an Order chapterhouse. It's one of the reasons he is so dangerous to the organization."

"But why is Ember with him?" I asked, unable to tear my gaze from the two tiny figures, darting through shadows and around corners, avoiding the light. Anger and fear caught in my throat. She was inside a St. George base! What was she thinking? If anyone spotted her, she was dead. *Get out of there*, I wanted to shout, knowing it was futile. *Ember, you stubborn idiot, why are you doing this? Get out of there before you're killed.*

Mist didn't say anything. Turning, she nodded to one of the humans, who bent over the keyboard. A moment later, the screen jumped to fast-forward, with the time in the left corner accelerating rapidly, though nothing inside the base appeared to move.

"Stop," Mist commanded, and the screen froze. "Look at the upper left corner, Mr. Hill," she went on, nodding to the blurred image above us. "Behind the vehicle, near the main headquarters. What do you see?"

I followed her gaze and drew in a sharp breath. "Three of them," I muttered, squinting to make sure I was seeing correctly. No, I wasn't mistaken. There were the two figures in black from earlier, only now there was a third party mem-

ber, huddled behind the car. "They were there to get someone out," I breathed, trying to wrap my head around what it
could mean. "But...why? St. George doesn't take prisoners,
at least not with us. Who...?"

I trailed off, a cold lump settling in my stomach. "The
soldier," I whispered, feeling the blood drain from my face.
"The human from Crescent Beach. They were there to free
the soldier of St. George."

My legs felt weak. This was not what I'd expected. I'd
hoped that, by watching the chapterhouse Sebastian belonged
to, he would lead us to Ember. Or that Ember would contact him, somehow, and we could follow when they moved
on her and the rogue. I'd never expected her to breach St.
George itself.

Mist's eyes were grave as she turned to me. "So, not only
has your sister gone rogue, she is also fraternizing with the
enemy," she said. Her voice was quiet, meant only for me
and our team members. "What do you intend to do with
this information?"

I took a deep breath. "I have to tell Mr. Roth," I said,
feeling slightly ill, but knowing there was no other choice.
"If Ember is associating with St. George, Talon must know
immediately. She could unknowingly put the organization
at risk, though I have no idea what she thinks she's doing."
Anger flickered, and I scrubbed a hand down my face, trying
to stay calm. Ember going rogue was bad enough, but to aid
one of the Order? How was I supposed to advance my cause,
convince Talon that my sister was being manipulated, if she
kept pulling stunts like this?

Straightening, I looked back at the paused screen, at the

trio of figures huddled against the car. "Did they escape?" I asked, almost dreading the answer. Surely Mist wouldn't be showing me this footage if they hadn't. But if the worst had occurred, if Ember hadn't gotten out of that compound alive, I wasn't going to stand here and watch. Even after everything, I didn't think I could handle seeing my sister gunned down right in front of me.

Surprisingly, the other dragon's lip twitched into the faintest of smiles. "Oh, you could say that," she said, and hit the pause key on the computer.

Seconds later, with my heart in my throat, I watched the two dragons flee the compound amid a flurry of lights and gunshots. If I'd had any doubts that one of the figures in black was Ember, they were long gone now.

I took a slow breath as the two dragons soared offscreen, vanishing westward and out of sight. The soldier sat astride one of them, and a flicker of rage and disgust pierced my amazement. With a brisk nod, I turned on one of the humans.

"Send a message to Mr. Roth immediately. Let him know we've found her."

EMBER

"Ember," Dante said. "Get up."

I groaned. My bed was warm and comfortable, and the air outside my nest of blankets was cold. It was a Saturday, at least I thought it was a Saturday, and I was supposed to meet up with Lexi later this afternoon to go surfing. She didn't want to go early because of *reasons,* which meant I could sleep in today. Of course, that didn't account for obnoxious brothers coming into my room to bother me.

I peeked through the covers, intending to tell said obnoxious brother to go away, only to find I was no longer in my room.

I sat up, blinking. Moonlight filtered in from a window, casting hazy light over an assortment of shadows and unrecognizable lumps. I frowned in confusion, sliding out of bed, giving a little shiver as I stood. The floor beneath my bare feet was hard and icy cold.

"Ember."

I turned. Dante stood a few feet away, watching me with eyes glowing green in the darkness. Behind him, the labyrinth of crates hovered at the edge of the light, looming and ominous, casting Dante in their jagged shadow.

"Traitor," he whispered.

I growled, curling my lips back from my fangs. I didn't know when I'd Shifted forms, but tongues of fire licked at my teeth as I snarled and half opened my wings, facing my brother down. "You're one to talk," I said, my voice echoing weirdly off the rafters. "I thought we were leaving Talon together, but you had no intention of coming with me, did you? You were going to tell Lilith where I was all along."

He didn't respond and I slumped, tail and wings drooping, while my twin watched me without expression. "You lied to me, Dante," I said, feeling the cold flood of regret douse the flames within. "I thought I could trust you, but you sold me out to Talon."

"I did no such thing." Dante's voice was calm, though his eyes narrowed to shining green slits. "*You* were the one who betrayed us, Ember. When you left with that rogue." He slipped away, his voice growing faint as he faded into the black. "You made the call. It was your choice to leave, to abandon everything we had worked for. Sixteen years of preparation, gone in an instant. You walked out on Talon, and you walked out on me."

"Dante, wait."

He didn't stop but vanished into the darkness, the echo of his footsteps fading to nothing. Calling out, I started after him, but the shadows closed in, and everything went black.

★ ★ ★

Wincing, I opened my eyes.

I lay on the floor in a room I didn't recognize, curled up on something soft. It took only a second to realize I was in dragon form, lying in a nest of blankets, and this had been a bedroom at one point, because a bed and a dresser had been shoved up against the far wall. Apart from those two pieces of furniture, the room was unnaturally empty. No clothes on the floor, no pictures or posters hanging from the walls, nothing to give the room personality. It seemed to have been empty a long time.

My thoughts swirled sluggishly, like they were trapped in glue. I blinked hard, trying to focus as I raised my head, waiting for my vision to clear. What had happened to me? The last thing I remembered was flying away from something, and a sudden jolt to my side, like I'd been hit with a hammer. I didn't remember passing out, but I must have, because everything after that was a blur. How much time had elapsed since then? I wondered.

And where am I now?

Cautiously, I looked around, trying to get a sense of where I was, and froze.

A body was slumped in a chair a few feet away, sitting against the wall with his arms crossed and his eyes closed. Even through the confusion and sleep haze, I knew it was Garret.

My stomach tightened, and memory came back in a rush. I remembered everything that had brought me here; infiltrating the St. George base with Riley, freeing Garret, fleeing across the wasteland with the soldier on my back. There was also one very hazy memory of a voice that sounded exactly like Garret's, telling me to lie down, but that might've been from a dream.

But I wasn't dreaming now, and the soldier was here, in the very same room. Sunlight slanted through the blinds over the windows, glinting off his pale hair, painting bright bars over his clothes. He wore faded jeans and a white T-shirt, and in sleep, he appeared younger than he was. Less a hardened soldier and more like a normal teen. Like the Garret I'd known in Crescent Beach. Before he became St. George, the enemy, a soldier who had killed dragons his whole life.

I rose carefully, trying to be silent as I sat up, but Garret was either just dozing or a really light sleeper, for his eyes shot open as soon as I moved. Piercing metallic-gray pupils met mine across the room.

"Ember."

His voice made me shiver, low and soft with relief. Carefully, as if trying not to make any sudden moves, he stood, his expression teetering between wary and hopeful. "You're awake," he breathed. "Are you all right?"

"I…think so." I stood slowly, bracing myself for pain. There was a dull ache in my side as I moved, but nothing sharp or stabby, which was a relief. Cautiously, I eased myself upright, craning my neck, curling and uncurling my talons, testing muscles. Except for the subtle but persistent ache in my side, everything seemed to be working fine. I took a breath and let it out slowly. "Looks like I'm all here. What happened?"

"You were shot," Garret said quietly. "When we were running from St. George. We brought you here, and Wes managed to dig the slug out, but it was touch and go for a while."

"What do you mean?"

His gaze flicked to my side, where the ache was coming from. "You nearly died, Ember," he whispered. "We didn't know how serious it was until we got here. You lost a lot of blood, and if the bullet had gone a few inches to the left…it would've struck your heart."

"Oh," I said, as the gravity of that statement sank in. "Really?"

He nodded, his face tightening. "That first night," he said in a curiously choked voice, "I didn't know if you were going to make it. You didn't move the entire time, not to eat, or Shift, or anything. Riley said that…that you had gone into hibernation, that when the dragon body takes a lot of damage, it slows to almost nothing and falls into a near coma until it can heal itself. I had no reason to doubt him, but…you were so still. You've been out for three days, and I couldn't even tell if you were breathing or not."

"Hey." I stepped toward him, slowly, knowing I was still in dragon form and not wanting to make him nervous. "It's all right. Look." I half opened my wings, casting a dark shadow over the walls and floor. "I'm okay," I said, offering a smile. "I'm still here."

He gazed at me with an expression that made my heart turn over, before his eyes narrowed and he shook his head. "You shouldn't have come," he said, sounding almost angry now. I blinked and reared back in surprise as he turned on me. "Back at St. George. You shouldn't have risked it. You don't know what you've done, what the Order will do to your kind now. St. George won't let this stand. Word of the break-in has probably reached London. Every chapterhouse in the region will be looking for you. You'll never be safe."

I lashed my tail, nearly knocking over a lamp on the dresser. "Guess next time I'll just stand back and let you be shot to death."

Garret winced and had the grace to look ashamed. "I'm sorry," he muttered, and the anger vanished as quickly as it had come. "I don't mean to sound ungrateful. I owe you my life, and I'm glad you came for me. I just..." He paused, uncertainty creeping into his voice and stance. "I'm not entirely sure *why*."

"Why?" I cocked my head, peering down at him. "What do you mean, you don't know why? The answer should be obvious."

Hope rippled across his features, so fast I might've imagined it. Though his voice remained neutral. "I'm a soldier of St. George," he insisted. "All my life, I believed what the Order believed. I followed the tenets, and I killed when they told me to, what they told me to, without question. Every single time." He looked away for a brief moment, eyes darkening. "You know what I've done," he murmured, staring at the wall. "You know what I am. Why would you risk your life to save a dragonslayer?"

A lump rose to my throat. "You weren't a soldier of St. George to me." The words came out a near whisper, and I swallowed hard. "Not in Crescent Beach. I never hated you, Garret. Even after...that night." The night he'd pointed a gun at my face, and I'd seen what he really was for the very first time. The night we'd inevitably turned on each other, because what else could we be except lifelong enemies? A soldier of St. George and a dragon. "And after what happened with Lilith, I couldn't leave you to die. Even if it was the Order, I wasn't going to let them kill you."

Garret still wasn't looking at me. He stared at the far wall as if he couldn't bear to see a huge reptile standing beside him instead of a girl, and my heart sank. "So, what now?" I asked softly. "Are we enemies, Garret? Do you hate me for being a dragon?"

"No!" He looked over quickly, his face earnest. "I could never hate you, Ember. If anything, I should be asking *you* that question. If you really knew what I've done…" He sighed, bowing his head. "But no. I'm not your enemy. You risked your life when you went into St. George, you and Riley both. I'm in your debt."

I sat down, curling my tail around my legs as I gave the former dragonslayer an exasperated snort. "Yes, well, for future reference," I said, thumping the spade-tip of my tail against the ground, "when someone decides to save your life, for whatever reason, the proper response is *thank you*. Guilt and groveling optional but highly encouraged."

A tiny chuckle escaped him then, as if he couldn't help himself. "Point taken," he murmured, the hint of a smile finally crossing his face. "Would you like the groveling done now or later?"

"Oh, later. Definitely later. When I can get comfortable and enjoy it for a few hours."

"Hours, huh? I'll keep that in mind." He shook his head, meeting my gaze. "Thank you for coming after me," he said, quite serious now. "You didn't have to, but I'm grateful you did. I wasn't…quite as ready to die as I thought."

I nodded. The haunted look had not quite left him, but it was a start. At least he was talking to me like a normal person again and not walking on eggshells around "the dragon." For now, it was enough. "So, where is everyone?" I asked, gazing around. Garret nodded out the door.

"Riley was sleeping in his room, last I saw" was the answer. "Wes left a few minutes ago for supplies. The three of us have been taking watch in turns since we got here. We've been waiting for you to wake up before we decide where to go next."

"Where are we, anyway?"

"Vegas," replied a new voice from the door.

I craned my neck around to look back. Riley stood in the frame, his gold eyes intense as they met mine. He wore ripped jeans and a black T-shirt, and looked strange without his ever-present jacket. His dark hair was mussed and shaggy, his clothes rumpled. Half circles crouched beneath his lids, as if he hadn't slept in a while.

I forced a weak grin, even as my senses flared to life, sending heat through my veins. "Hey, you. I'm up."

"Dammit, Ember." Riley entered into the room and, without hesitation, strode to my side. Garret drew back, melting into the corner as the other drew close. Riley's hand came to rest on my neck, a searing spot of warmth even through my scales. "Are you all right?" he asked, his gaze flicking to my ribs, where the bullet had pierced through. "Why didn't you tell me you were awake?"

"It was on my to-do list."

He pressed his forehead to mine, skin to scales. "Don't scare me like that, Firebrand," he whispered, as my stomach danced and my wings fluttered restlessly. "If you had died, I don't know what I'd have done, but it would probably involve eating that St. George bastard over there."

"That's not very reasonable," I whispered back, knowing that Garret could hear us, and Riley probably didn't care if he did. "Then all our scheming against St. George would've been for nothing."

He snorted and drew back, rolling his eyes. "Have you eaten yet?" he muttered, an exasperated smile crossing his face. "You were out for three days. I imagine you're probably starving right now."

Food. I was suddenly ravenous, like a bear coming out of winter hibernation: skinny, starving and cranky. Food sounded wonderful. In fact, nothing else mattered right now except food. Riley chuckled.

"Yeah, that's what I thought. There's pizza in the fridge and— Whoa, hold on, Firebrand." He put his hands out, stopping me as I pressed forward. Impatient, I glared at him, and he smirked. "No dragons in the kitchen. The neighbors would have a fit." I blinked, remembering that I was still in the form that wasn't supposed to exist in normal society. The one that would cause a panic if seen. I repressed a sigh. It felt so natural to be in my real body again; I was reluctant to Shift back.

"Your clothes are in the dresser behind you," Riley said. "Get changed, and meet us when you're human again." His smile faded, a darker note creeping into his voice. "There are things we have to discuss."

RILEY

Ember exhaled, sending tendrils of smoke curling around me, and turned away, padding toward the dresser in the corner. I watched her a moment, the sweep of her neck and wings, the way the narrow bars of sunlight glinted off her crimson scales. The urge to Shift was almost painful, burning my lungs and making the air taste like ash. I turned away before it got too tempting and jerked my head at the soldier, motioning him out of the room.

We walked into the hall and shut the door behind us. "All right," I said, keeping my voice low, so Ember wouldn't catch it. "You've seen her. She's going to be fine now. Why are you still here, St. George?"

The soldier kept his gaze on the closed door, his voice low and flat. "I have nowhere else to go."

"Well, that's not my problem, is it?" I brushed past him into the kitchen, knowing Ember would be out soon and on the hunt for food. Except for a box of leftover pizza, there wasn't much to be had, and I'd sent Wes out for supplies a couple hours ago. Hopefully he'd be back soon. This wasn't the nicest neighborhood, miles from the glitz and glamour of the Strip, the stretch of giant casinos Vegas was famous for. If you looked out the back window, you'd see a bunch of small, ugly houses and beyond them, the flat, dusty expanse of the Mojave Desert, stretching away to the distant mountains. Crime and poverty ran rampant here, but that suited me just fine. No one asked questions, no one came poking around, and no one wondered why a white van was suddenly parked in the driveway of a previously vacant abandoned house.

The soldier followed me into the kitchen, sweeping his gaze around the room, like he always did. "They'll be hunting you," he stated, making me shrug.

"Nothing new there."

"You're going to have to move soon. It's dangerous to stay here, especially with St. George looking for us."

Irritation flared, and the anger that I'd repressed during the whole ordeal surged up with a vengeance. In the three days we'd been here, we had tolerated each other's presence in the most mature way possible: pretending the other didn't exist. St. George didn't talk to me, I didn't talk to him, and things were good. Sort of an unspoken truce between us while we waited for Ember to revive.

Now, though, all bets were off. I narrowed my eyes, wondering what would happen if I Shifted forms and bit the soldier in half. Ember might've forgotten that he was part of the Order. She might have forgiven him for hunting down and slaughtering our kind without remorse, but *I* wasn't okay with it. In fact, the only reason I hadn't shoved him out of the van and left him in the middle of the desert to fend for himself was the girl who'd convinced me to rescue the murdering bastard in the first place. She was also the reason I hadn't chased him out of the house with fire and told him not to come back. Right now that was a pretty tempting option.

"Don't tell me how to do my job, St. George," I said in a low, dangerous voice. "I've been at this a lot longer than you. I've been outsmarting your kind since before you could wrap your itchy little fingers around a trigger. I don't need some murdering dragon killer telling me to be careful of the Order."

"You've never broken into a St. George chapterhouse," the human countered, as if he knew anything about me and what I used to do. "I know the Order. They're not going to let that stand. Once word of this reaches London—and it probably already has—they're going to throw everything they can at us, and they won't stop until we're all dead."

"Oh, is that why you're still here?" I challenged, crossing my arms. "You want the dragons to protect you, now that you're the hunted one?"

"No." St. George glared at me, a flicker of anger crossing his face. "I don't care what happens to me," he said, sounding so earnest I almost believed him. "But I want Ember to be safe. I owe her my life, and I can't leave knowing the Order is hunting her right now."

"They were *always* hunting her, St. George," I snapped. "Every single day. The hunt never stops. The war never ends. Or did that fact slip your mind? The only thing that's changed is now the Order has a wasp up their ass because their pride has been stomped on, and they'll be desperate to save face. Never mind that they've been kicking down our doors and blowing us to pieces for years. But don't worry about Ember."

I smirked, as his face darkened. "The Order won't ever get that close. I'll take care of her."

"Also," came a new voice from the doorway, "she's quite capable of taking care of herself."

Guiltily, we turned. Ember stood at the edge of the tile, arms crossed, looking peeved with us both. Her red hair stuck out at every angle, and she was definitely thinner than normal, making my gut squeeze tight. But her green eyes were as bright as ever, and the fire lurking below the surface hadn't dimmed. I could see the dragon peering out at me, the echo of wings hovering behind her. She shot us—well, *me*—an exasperated glare, before marching to the refrigerator door and yanking it open.

"Ember," St. George began as she emerged with a flat white box. "I—"

"Garret," Ember interrupted. Her voice was a warning as she turned around. "Not to sound rude, but I am a dragon who hasn't eaten for the past three days. Unless you're about to reveal a stash of doughnuts hidden somewhere in this room, I would steer clear right now."

He blinked, and I snickered at his shocked expression as Ember moved past us, heading toward the counter. "Number one rule when dealing with dragons, St. George," I said, as the girl hopped onto a stool and opened up the box. "Don't get between a hungry hatchling and its food. You might lose a finger."

Ember glared at me, looking like she might growl something in return, but then decided food was more important and devoured half a slice in one bite. I went to the fridge for a soda, and St. George settled quietly against the wall, as the starving dragon went through an entire pepperoni pizza by herself. Two minutes later, Ember trashed the box, dusted off her hands and finally turned to look at us.

"So." She drummed her fingers on her arm, looking back and forth at each of us. "What now?"

Good question. "I guess that depends, Firebrand."

"On what?"

"You." She frowned at me, confused. Crushing the empty can, I put it in the sink and went to the fridge for another. "Let me ask you something," I said as I closed the door. "What did *you* think was going to happen, Firebrand? After you left Talon? After you went rogue?"

She cocked her head. "I...don't know," she stammered. "Isn't that where you come in? I thought you had this whole rogue thing worked out."

"Normally, I do. But my plans don't usually involve sneaking into highly guarded St. George compounds to rescue the enemy." I didn't look at the soldier as I said this, and St. George didn't give any indication that he cared. "This whole situation is a bit abnormal for me, Firebrand. Frankly, I didn't expect to have you around this long."

Anger flashed across her face and she raised her chin. "Well, if I knew you were just going to get rid of me, I would've saved you the trouble."

"Don't be thick. That's not what I meant." I shook my head, giving her an exasperated look. She glared back, and I sighed. "What did you think I was going to do after taking you away from Crescent Beach?" I demanded. "Toss you out on the streets and say, 'Good luck, have a nice life'? Give me some credit. I'm a little more organized than that."

She frowned. "Then…what *was* going to happen to me?"

I started to answer, then paused. I didn't like talking about my network so openly, especially with the human still in the room with us. Not that I was afraid he could go running back to the Order, but I trusted him about as far as I could throw him. Hunted or not, he had dragon blood on his hands, and that would never change.

As if reading my thoughts, the soldier raised his head and met my glare. "You can tell her," he said in a low voice. "It's not like I can take your secrets back to the Order."

I smirked. "If I thought you could, you'd already be a pile of bones in the desert, St. George," I stated. "That's not what concerns me."

"Riley!" Ember scowled. "You don't have to be a jerk. He's not with the Order anymore."

"Firebrand. You don't get it." I turned on her, narrowing my eyes. "It's not about me. This isn't just my life I'm risking, it's *all* the dragons I've freed from Talon. They look to me to keep them safe, keep them off Talon's radar and away from the Vipers. Not only do I have to worry about the organization, I have to worry about St. George, too, because the bastards don't know there's a difference between rogue dragons and Talon, and they wouldn't care if they did."

I shot another piercing glare at the soldier, who didn't reply. Though by the look on his face, he knew I was right.

"So, yes, Firebrand, I'm a little paranoid that there's an ex-soldier of St. George in the same room as us," I finished. "I believe the *last* time there was a soldier of St. George in the room with us, we were being shot at." I put a fist to my chest, glaring at her. "This is *my* network, my underground.

I've spent too many years getting dragons out of Talon to put their lives in danger now."

Ember stared at me, surprise and amazement reflected in her eyes. "How many dragons are we talking about?" she asked. "How many rogues do you have?"

I sighed again, feeling my shoulders slump in defeat. Too late to hold back now. "Over twenty this year," I admitted, and her mouth fell open. "And that's just counting dragons, not the humans working for me. The hatchlings I steal from the organization are all green and starry-eyed, so they have to have a human agent looking after them until they're ready to set out on their own."

"I had no idea."

I smirked. "When I said I'd take care of you, Firebrand, I wasn't joking. I already have a place set up and waiting. A quiet little town near the mountains. You'll be living with your 'grandfather' on a couple private acres of forest that butts up against a national park. No beaches, sadly, but it's green and peaceful and isolated enough that Talon or the Order will never find you. You'll be safe there, I promise."

"And what will you do?"

"What I've always been doing. Fighting Talon. Getting hatchlings away from the organization. Helping them disappear." I shrugged, feeling suddenly tired. "Maybe if I do this long enough, there'll be enough free dragons someday to take a stand against Talon," I muttered. "That's my pipe dream, anyway." Impossible, unattainable, but I had to hope for something.

"I'll help you."

Ember's response was immediate. No hesitation or fear, just

eager determination. I straightened quickly, alarm and exhilaration rising up at the same time. Part of me had known this would happen; after Crescent Beach, how could my brash, stubborn hatchling want to do anything else? But at the same time, I knew I couldn't subject her to this life. It was dangerous, terrifying, bloody and occasionally it was just soul crushing. I'd seen so many die, had been responsible for countless deaths myself. There had been nights when I wasn't sure I'd survive till dawn, when I'd wondered if the next hour would be my last. I'd seen the worst of Talon, St. George and the whole damn world, and it had turned me into a hard, cynical bastard. I couldn't do that to her.

And of course, there was that *other* reason. The one pounding through my veins, even now. The one snarling at me to say yes, to take her with me so we could be alone, no humans or dragons or soldiers of St. George to interfere. The reason I was an exhausted, cranky mess, because I couldn't sleep while she lay there, still as death. I couldn't focus, couldn't eat or plan or do anything. If St. George had kicked in the door, I would've burned the whole place to the ground before I left her behind.

I couldn't keep going like this. It was dangerous; for me, for Ember, for everyone in my underground. She was a distraction, a fiery, tempting, intriguing distraction, and I had too many people counting on me to keep them safe. I had to get away from her, for both our sakes.

Though, convincing *her* of that was going to be a challenge.

"I'm not going to your safe house, Riley." Ember's voice was final, as if she knew what I was thinking. Her eyes flashed, and she crossed her arms, staring me down. "Don't think you can get rid of me now. I'm not going to hide away and do nothing while you're running around dodging Vipers and dragonslayers and who knows what else. I'm not blind anymore. I've seen what Talon does, how they're willing to kill anyone who doesn't conform to their standards. I'm going to help you and all the dragons who want to be free. I want to get as many of us away from Talon as we can."

"Firebrand," I began, and she set her jaw, ready for a fight. "I know you're angry with Talon," I went on, "and you want to strike back at them somehow, but think about what you're doing. This is a dangerous life. We're constantly on the run, from the organization, and St. George, and the Vipers. Hell, you just woke up because you were *shot* three days ago. That's the kind of situation you'll be facing again if you come with me."

"I know."

"You'll never have a normal life," I insisted. "I can't suddenly decide I don't want to do this anymore. There are too many who are counting on me, too many I promised I'd keep safe. I'll probably be doing this for the rest of my life, or until something—either a Viper or a St. George bullet—kills me."

"That's why you need someone watching your back."

My temper flared. "Dammit, Ember—"

The door banged open, crashing against the wall. I jumped and spun around as Wes lunged into the room, turned and slammed the door behind him. His eyes were wild in his pale face.

"St. George!" he gasped, making us all jerk up. "They're here! I think they're right behind me!"

EMBER

They're here.

Fear crawled up my spine. St. George had come. Again. It didn't seem to matter where we went, what we did; they were always one step behind, seconds from kicking in the door and spraying us with lead. And now that I had so blatantly waltzed into their territory and given the figurative finger to them all, they would be eager for retribution. It was no longer a job, I suspected, no longer a routine slaying of faceless enemies. Now, it was personal.

"What do you mean, they're right behind you?" Riley snapped, stalking toward Wes, who had already locked the door and was peering through the eyehole. "St. George doesn't know who you are, they've never seen you before. How would they know you're even a target?"

"I have no idea, mate, but *someone* was staring at me in the parking lot," Wes snapped, spinning around. "And when I was driving back, I noticed I'd picked up a tail. That's why it took me so bloody long to get here. I was trying to lose the bastards, but they could still be out there."

Riley walked to the edge of the windows and peered

through the glass, keeping his back to the wall. "I don't see anyone," he muttered. "Maybe you lost them."

"They're out there." Garret's quiet voice cut through the tension. We all glanced at him, standing against the wall with his arms crossed. His stance was weirdly calm. "If this really is St. George, the surveyors Wes saw will be narrowing the houses down right now. The assault team is probably on its way. We don't have a lot of time."

"Then we need to leave." Riley strode out of the kitchen. "Right now. While there's still daylight. Wes, get everything together."

"Where are we going?" I asked as Wes hurried out of the room, muttering curses. Riley turned to look at me, frowning slightly.

"Into the city," he said. "Downtown, where there's lots of people. The Order won't try to murder us in a crowd. At least, I hope they won't resort to that." He stabbed a glare in Garret's direction before turning back. "Hiding in plain sight has always been a good tactic for us. We disappear into the crowds, and neither Talon nor the Order can come after us without arousing suspicion. Besides, there's someone there I have to see. We just needed you to wake up before we left."

I felt a brief stab of guilt. "You were all waiting on me?"

One corner of his mouth twisted up. "Kinda hard to hide a dragon in a hotel room, Firebrand. The fire marshal would blow a gasket." He brushed my arm, a brief, light touch that sent curls of heat through my insides. "Hurry and get packed so we can get out of here. I *really* don't feel like seeing St. George again."

We gathered everything, which took only a few minutes. I

didn't have anything except my backpack with some clothes and a couple small personal things. Wes had his laptop, and Garret had the gun he'd taken from the Order and the borrowed clothes on his back. Everything else fit into a single duffel bag, which Riley swung over his shoulder. The rogue traveled light and efficient, ready to pack up and move at a word. Everything was disposable; clothes, vehicles, places to stay. In fact, the only thing I knew he kept with him at all times was that dusty leather jacket.

"All right," he muttered, staring through the peephole in the front door as we crowded behind him. At my side, Garret pressed close, making my heart skip. I could feel his presence, burning across my skin, even as I tried to focus. "I don't see anything out there," Riley went on, his gaze scanning one end of the street to the other. "Looks like we're still in the clear."

"Don't be fooled," Garret murmured. "If St. George is out there, watching us, you won't be able to see them."

Riley snorted without turning around. "Well we certainly can't sit here until they kick down the door," he growled, and turned the knob. Bloodred sunlight spilled through the crack as he pulled the door open, and dying sun shone directly into my eyes, making me squint. For a moment, he didn't move from the frame, casting one final look around the empty street. Shielding my eyes, I peered past his shoulder, searching for anything out of place. The yards and streets were empty; no suspiciously parked cars, no "electricians" or "painters" pretending to be working nearby. Everything seemed perfectly normal. The van sat inconspicuously at the edge of the driveway, but it seemed an impossible distance away.

"Okay," Riley went on, pulling the door back and stepping into the open. "All clear. So far, so—"

A muffled crack rang out from nowhere, making my heart jump to my throat. A sharp hiss followed the gunshot, and the van jerked, then sagged to one side, its back tires deflated in an instant.

"Shit!" Riley lunged back inside and slammed the door, as the rest of us backed hastily away. "Dammit, they're already here." Another crack rang out, and the front window shattered with a ringing cacophony, sending glass raining to the ground. I yelped, covering my face as splinters flew everywhere, and Garret grabbed my wrist, dragging me away from the glass.

"Stay back from the windows," he ordered, pushing me against the wall beside the window frame. I grunted at the impact and scowled at him, but he wasn't looking at me. His gaze, narrowed and grim, was on the rows of houses beyond the broken glass. "Snipers," he breathed, as Riley pressed himself to the other side of the frame, his lips curled in a silent snarl. "They've found us."

"Brilliant," Wes spat from behind the couch. "Snipers, that's bloody fabulous. I am *so* glad we risked life and limb to rescue you, St. George." He glared daggers at Garret, as if wishing the next bullet would make the soldier's head explode. "I don't suppose giving you back will make them leave us alone?"

"Over my dead body," I snarled at Wes, my stomach clenching violently at the thought. "Try it, and I'll throw *you* through that window."

"It wouldn't matter, anyway," Garret replied in a serious

voice, as if Wes's suggestion was actually legitimate. He looked down at me, his expression pained. "I would surrender to them," he said, "if I thought the Order would spare you. But they're here for all of us, and they won't bargain with dragons. I'm sorry, Ember."

I glared back at him. "I wouldn't let you go, anyway. So you can stop being so damned fatalistic. No one is giving anyone up. We're getting out of here together, or not at all."

He blinked, a raw, almost vulnerable look passing through his eyes, and we stared at each other a moment. Outside, it was eerily silent. The sunlight slanting through the broken window caught on shards of glass and glittered red, like drops of blood.

Riley's low, frustrated growl broke the silence. "Dammit, where are they?" he muttered, peeking cautiously around the frame, careful to keep his head back. "Why don't they just charge in and shoot us already?"

"This isn't the full strike force." Garret stared out the window, his expression grave. "Not yet. When the survey team followed Wes back, they had to alert headquarters to let them know they found the targets. They have the sniper guarding the house just to pin us down, make sure we don't leave until the assault team arrives."

Wes swore again, peering around the sofa. "Right, then, if that's the case, I vote we not stand here and let them pick us off. And since the van is now shot to hell, who's up for sneaking out the back door?"

"No." Garret shook his head. "That would be a bad idea. The sniper will be positioned in a spot where he has a full view of the neighborhood. If we try to leave, he'll just as easily pick us off from where he is now. It's not worth the risk."

Riley snorted. "You've got it all figured out, don't you, St. George?"

Garret's voice was flat. "It's what I would do."

"Oh, that's right. You've done this before, haven't you? Shot kids in the back while they were running away?"

"Guys," I said in exasperation, glaring at Riley. "This isn't helping. Focus, please. Garret…" I glanced at the soldier, touching his arm. "You know St. George. You know how they think. What can we do?"

Garret nodded, looking thoughtful. "We'll need to neutralize the threat first," he replied, slipping into soldier mode, logical and calculating. "Find out where the shooter is, sneak around and take him out before the rest of the team arrives."

"Oh, is that all?" Riley frowned, gesturing to the broken window. "And how are we supposed to find where this shooter is without taking a hole to the head? I don't feel like playing whack-a-mole with a trained sniper right now."

Garret edged close to the window, keeping his back pressed to the wall. For a brief moment, he closed his eyes and took a deep breath, as if preparing himself. Then, before I could stop him, he straightened and peered through the frame, leaving his whole head exposed. Almost immediately, a shot rang out, slamming into the sill and tearing away chunks of wood in an explosion of splinters as he ducked back. I flinched, pressing close to Garret with my heart thudding against my ribs, but he wasn't even breathing hard.

"Jeez, Garret!" My voice sounded shaky, unlike the soldier beside me. He straightened, looking perfectly calm, like getting shot at by snipers was routine. I scowled and smacked his arm. "Are you crazy?" I demanded. "You want to get your head exploded? Don't do that again. We'll find the shooter another way."

"One block down," he murmured, making me frown with confusion. His eyes were closed, brow furrowed, as if recalling an image from memory. "Across the street on the corner. There's a two-story house with an attic window. Foreclosed, I think. The shots are coming from that direction."

I stared at him in amazement. "You got all that just now?"

"Partly." He peered out the window, keeping his back against the wall and his head inside this time. "But I observed the area when we first arrived, made note of all the places we might be attacked, where someone could set up an ambush. The house on the corner would be Tristan's ideal…" He stopped, his jaw tightening. "It makes the most tactical sense," he finished stiffly.

"Okay," I said. I wished I could peek out the window, see the house for myself, but I also didn't want to risk a bullet between the eyes. I didn't know if I'd be fast enough, especially now that the shooter knew where we were, and maybe had his crosshairs trained right at me. "So we know where the sniper is. What now?"

Garret drew away from the window, face grim. "Wait here," he said. "Stay inside, I'll try to get close enough to take him out."

"What? You're not doing this alone." He ignored me as he sidled past, keeping close to the walls, and I grabbed the back of his shirt. "What if there's more than one?" I insisted as he turned in my grasp, his face stony. "What if he has a partner and you get hurt, or shot? There'll be no one around to help. You need someone watching your back, at least."

"Firebrand," Riley warned in a no-way-in-hell voice, and I turned to glare at him, too.

"What?" I demanded, still keeping a tight hold of Garret's shirt. "I can do this. I've been *trained* to do this. Lilith taught me herself, or did you forget that I was supposed to be a Talon assassin?" He took a breath to argue, and I raised my chin. "I seem to remember sneaking into a heavily armed St. George base a few nights ago and doing just fine."

"Until you got shot!" Riley made as if to stalk forward, then jerked back, away from the window. His eyes glowed angrily as they met mine. "This isn't a normal bullet, Firebrand," he said. "This isn't something you can recover from. You get hit in the head with a sniper round, you don't have a head anymore."

"I won't get shot."

"You can't know that!"

"Ember." A strong hand closed over mine, gently prying me loose. I turned back to meet Garret's steely eyes, gazing down at me. His face was expressionless, and for a moment, I didn't know if he would tell me to stay behind or not. Which was too bad, because I was coming with him whether he liked it or not. But then he gave a small sigh and released my hand, his gaze flicking out the window.

"We'll have to move fast," he said, scanning the street like he was planning the best route to the sniper perch. "Stay low, keep your head down and don't stop moving. A moving target is much harder to hit. We'll have to circle around, and we'll stay in cover as much as we can, but don't panic if you're shot at. And don't freeze, no matter what. The sniper will likely have a partner guarding his back, too, so we'll probably have to deal with more than one. Do you have a weapon?"

I shook my head, ignoring the fear spreading through my insides, making my stomach curl. "I won't need one."

Behind me, Riley made an impatient sound and reached for something at his back. "Dammit, Ember," he growled. "Yes, you will. Here." He tossed the pistol at me, and my heart lurched as I caught it. "Just don't get yourself killed, all right?"

His eyes stabbed at me, and I couldn't tell if he was furious, worried, or absolutely terrified, before they shifted to Garret. "We're running out of time," he said, his voice clipped and matter-of-fact. "What do you need on our end, St. George?"

"We'll never make it to the house if the sniper sees us coming," Garret replied calmly. "Can you cause a distraction? Something that will take the shooter's focus off the surrounding area for a few seconds?"

"Yeah." Riley nodded, and raked a hand through his hair. "Yeah, I can do that. Wes…" He glanced at the human, still huddled behind the couch. "Get ready to move. You're in charge of finding us another car, now that the van's been shot to hell." There was a muffled curse behind the sofa, and Riley turned back to us. "Get going. I'll make sure their attention is elsewhere."

"What are you going to do?" I asked.

"Oh, you'll know it when you see it."

"Right." I took a breath and glanced at the soldier beside me. "Okay," I whispered, resolved for what I had to do. "Ready if you are."

"Ember."

Riley's voice was almost strangled. I looked back to find those piercing gold eyes on me, his expression tormented. "Don't get hurt, Firebrand," he said in a low voice, meant only for the two of us. "I don't think I could take it this time. Come back alive, okay?"

A lump caught in my throat, and I nodded.

Garret brushed my arm, indicating for me to follow. With one last look at Riley, I turned away, trailing the soldier through the living room and out the back door, stepping into a dusty, weed-strewn yard. We sidled around the house, keeping our backs to the wall, until we came to the corner and the edge of the driveway. Garret peeked around the wall, his gaze scanning the open street and the rows of houses across from us. I braced myself against him to peek over his shoulder, feeling the tension lining his back.

"When do we move?" I whispered, thinking that the distance from one side of the road to the other had never looked so far.

"We have to wait for the distraction," Garret replied, easing back. "Right now, we're right in the shooter's line of sight. We have to get across the road and behind the houses without being seen."

I swallowed. "I wonder what Riley's going to—"

There was a roar, a sudden inrush of air, and a window above us exploded into shards of heat and flames. Glass and splinters of burning wood showered us, making me flinch and press against the wall, as a massive firestorm erupted inside the house. As Riley launched his distraction in the most dragony way possible.

Garret tapped my leg. "Now."

GARRET

I darted from the house and sprinted across the road as quickly as I could, Ember close at my heels. I knew we were exposed; even with the rogue's distraction, there was a chance the sniper would see us. But it seemed the sudden firestorm was enough of a disruption; we reached the other side without any shots fired and ducked behind another house.

The building we'd left had quickly become an inferno, tongues of fire snapping from the windows and roof, as dragonfire burned hotter and fiercer than normal flame. It hadn't gone unnoticed by the rest of the neighborhood, either. Cries of alarm were beginning to echo through the streets as civilians spilled from their own homes onto the pavement, gaping at the fire. A crowd formed rapidly in front of the burning house, talking to each other or speaking frantically into their phones. Some were even taking pictures. The police would arrive soon with the fire department, and they'd likely shut down the whole block. We didn't have much time.

"This way," I told Ember, and we crept swiftly up the street, weaving between fences and ducking behind cover when we could, moving toward the house on the corner. Ember stayed with me, never hesitating or slowing down, following my lead without fail. No more shots were fired on the house; there were far too many people out front now, watching the building burn. St. George wouldn't risk firing into the crowd and hitting a civilian. But we didn't want the soldiers following us, either. Or alerting the rest of their squad to where we'd gone. The threat had to be nullified before we could escape.

Which meant I would have to fight St. George face-to-face.

For a moment, crouched with Ember behind a parked car in a driveway, preparing for the next dash to cover, I felt a stab of guilt. What was I doing? These were my former brothers, men I'd fought beside just a few short weeks ago. What if the sniper was someone I knew? What if I got up there... and it was Tristan facing me on the other side? And if it was my former partner, staring at me down the sight of his gun, could he make himself pull the trigger? Could I?

We approached the last house, slipping through a rotting privacy fence and across an overgrown yard, moving swiftly for the door. There was no time for regret. I had made my choice. Past friendships, memories, the camaraderie I'd always been a part of—none of that mattered. The Order would kill me and my companions if I didn't do something now.

We reached the back entrance, a simple wooden door that was probably locked from the inside. There was no time to pick the lock, no time for a quiet entrance. I drove my foot into the door, aiming for the weak spot right beside the handle, and it flew open with a crash.

The interior of the house was dark and empty, littered with trash and cobwebs. The windows were boarded up, and the air was musty and stale. A flight of wooden steps sat against the wall on our left, leading to the second floor. No St. George soldiers in sight, but they would likely be upstairs.

I jerked my head at Ember and started up the staircase, muzzle of the gun leading the way. The steps opened into a small corridor with two bedrooms sitting across from each other, their doors partially open to show empty, gutted floors and walls. A flight of wooden attic stairs had been pulled down and sat open in the middle of the hall.

As I started toward it, gun drawn, a flicker of movement in the corner of my eye gave me just enough time to react. As a soldier stepped out of the adjacent bedroom with his gun raised, I spun and struck his wrist, making him drop the weapon. Immediately, he lunged, grabbed my weapon arm and slammed me into the opposite wall. He was bigger than me, stocky and broad shouldered, with a shaved head and small black eyes. I recognized his face, though I didn't recall his name. A scar twisted one side of his lip down as he snarled and smashed my wrist into the frame behind me. Pain shot through my hand, and the pistol clattered to the floor.

"Fucking dragonlover," he growled, and threw a hard right hook at my temple, thankfully letting go of my wrist. I managed to block, ducking and getting my arm up, though the blow still rocked my head to the side. I lashed out with my other fist, throwing a body shot below his unprotected ribs. He grunted and slammed me back, cracking my head against the plaster, then smashed a fist at my face. I threw out my arm, deflecting the blow to the side, and spun with the motion, using the momentum to smash him into the wall.

He whirled with a back elbow at my face. I shifted, letting it graze my cheek, then drove my foot into the side of his knee.

There was a pop, and his leg crumpled beneath him. As he hit the floor with a howl of pain, I snaked one arm around his throat and braced the back of his neck with the other. He thrashed, beating at my arms, trying to loosen the grip on his neck, but I set my jaw and didn't move, counting down the seconds. At eight and a half, with no blood carrying oxygen to his brain, he shuddered and went limp in my arms.

I held him there a few seconds longer before I relaxed and let the body slump to the floor. One soldier down. But his partner, probably the sniper himself, had to be close—

A shot rang out in front of me.

I jerked, tensing to attack, then froze. Ember, wide-eyed and pale, stood at the top of the steps, a smoking pistol pointed at the ceiling behind me. Heart in my throat, I turned as a body dropped from the attic stairs and hit the floor with a thud.

A small hole pierced his forehead, right above his eyes, a near perfect head shot. Blood trickled down his face, over the bridge of his nose toward his mouth, open in surprise. One limp hand clutched his sidearm, a gloved finger still curled around the trigger.

Ember gave a tiny gasp and lowered her weapon. "I—I saw him through the hole," she whispered, sounding dazed. Her arm trembled as she gestured weakly at the attic steps. "He had his gun out...pointed at your back. I didn't know what else to do."

She was shaking, eyes glassy as she stared at the body on the floor, as if waiting for it to move. When it didn't, she looked up at me, almost pleading. "Did I...? Is he...?"

I blew out a long breath, closing my eyes. "He's dead."

Painfully, I bent to retrieve my weapon, reluctant to glance at the fallen soldier, in case it was someone I knew. Rising, I checked the firearm out of habit, feeling aches from new bruises start to bloom along my body. My head throbbed, and my neck and back were sore from where I was slammed against the wall. But I was still alive.

Finally, inevitably, my gaze strayed to the body crumpled at the bottom of the steps, the sniper who had been firing on us from the attic window. For a split second, I tensed, wondering if I would see a familiar face with short dark hair, glazed blue eyes now staring at nothing. But the body at the foot of the steps was older than Tristan, unfamiliar to me. Through the aching guilt of what I'd just done, I felt a tiny prick of relief. I was truly the enemy of St. George now. I'd fought beside our ancient foes and had struck down my former brothers in arms but, at least for today, I wouldn't have to face the person I dreaded fighting more than anyone else.

I hoped it would never come to that.

Ember was still standing at the top of the stairs, gazing down at the fallen soldier. Her skin was ashen, her bright hair a shocking contrast to her face. "I killed him," she whispered, her voice choked and horrified. "He's really dead. I didn't… I didn't mean to…"

"Ember." I took a step toward her, and she flinched away, wide-eyed and trembling. Sympathy curled my stomach. I remembered *my* first kill, several years back, though it felt like a lifetime ago. It had been a dragon, and though I'd received nothing but praise and admiration from my brothers, I'd never forgotten the way it had stared at me as it lay there in the grass. I remembered its gaze, confused and terrified, before its eyes glazed over and it passed into death. I'd never spoken of it, but the nightmares from that day had haunted me for weeks afterward.

I knew what Ember was feeling right now, and I wished I had the words to comfort her, or the time. Sadly, we had neither. "Come on," I said, starting toward the stairs. "Hurry, before the authorities arrive. We can't be caught here."

She blinked as I brushed past her, then followed me down the steps. "What about the...body?" she asked, stumbling over the word. "The police will find it. There'll be a murder investigation at the very least. If anyone saw us enter the house, they'll be looking for us, too."

"Not likely."

She frowned at my brusqueness. "How can you know that?"

"Because St. George has ways of covering this up," I explained as we left the house, easing around the faded walls. "That soldier you killed," I went on, gesturing back to the empty building, "he's a ghost. We all are. We have no background, no past, no family except the Order. We don't register in any system. When we die, we vanish, as if we never existed."

"Oh," Ember mused, though she didn't sound reassured. "That's...kind of sad. All that fighting, and no one even remembers you when you're gone."

I didn't have an answer for that, so I stayed quiet. We slipped through the fence and huddled on the corner of the street, keeping a wary eye on the crowd surrounding the burning house. The roof was fully engulfed, clouds of black smoke billowing into the evening sky. I hoped Wes and the rogue dragon had been able to get out safely. And that they had come up with a getaway plan.

Sirens wailed in the distance. I tensed, and Ember froze, gazing down the street. The authorities were on their way. I glanced at the burning house, debating whether to search for our companions or to vacate the area and hope they caught up.

A sleek black SUV suddenly rounded a corner, barreled across the road and squealed to a stop in front of us. The driver's window buzzed down, and Riley glared out at us, jerking his head at the back. "Get in!" he barked, as the sirens grew louder. "Let's go!"

Yanking open the back door, I ducked into a black leather interior, the smell of new car surrounding me. Ember followed and slammed the door behind her, and the tires screeched as Riley stepped on the gas and roared away, leaving chaos in our wake.

COBALT

Twelve years ago

Nearly there.

I pressed back against the office wall, holding my breath, as a pair of soldiers swept down the hallway just outside the door, their boots thumping in unison. They marched around a corner and out of sight, and I exhaled slowly in relief. Getting into this place had been a huge pain in the ass, with more close calls than I was comfortable with. It had taken all my considerable skills to make it this far unnoticed, and I still had to get out again once I was done. But one problem at a time.

A large wooden desk sat against the far wall, a computer perched atop the surface. Pressing into a corner, I hit a number on my phone and held it to my ear. One ring, and someone picked up.

"I'm in," I whispered. Slipping around the desk, I jiggled the screen to life and pulled the human's thumb drive out of my pocket. "Inserting the program now," I said, and stuck the drive into the side of the computer.

For a few seconds, nothing happened. Then, a bar flashed across the top of the screen, the tiny white numbers above the strip at 0 percent. As I watched, it flicked to 1 percent, then 2 percent as the numbers started inching upward. Very, very slowly.

Oh, don't rush or anything, I thought, peering around the desk at the open door. *No life-threatening situation here. Just me, a dragon sitting in the middle of St. George. Please, take your time.*

Footsteps echoed down the hall, coming gradually closer. I winced and ducked beneath the desk, shoving myself into a corner as voices drifted into the room, talking of meetings and drills and other boring things. Two humans passed by the door and continued down the hallway without slowing. I waited until they were truly gone before popping out and glaring at the bar on the screen.

Eighty-six percent. Dammit. How long did hacking a file take? Biting back my impatience, I waited, drumming my fingers on the floor, until the strip had completely filled and the numbers finally hit 100 percent. I yanked it out and stuffed the drive into my pocket then rose, relief and a strangely grim sensation stealing over me. One thing down.

But I wasn't done yet.

The backpack felt heavy against my shoulders, reminding me of what came next. I slipped out of the room and made my way through the building, on high alert for guards, until I found the stairs. According to the Chief Basilisk, my final objective was below me, on the very last floor.

The hallways were dark as I crept across the tile, though a light glowed near the end of one of the corridors, the murmur of human voices drifting through an open door frame. Thankfully, I didn't have to go far. My objective sat behind an inconspicuous white door at the end of a lonely hall, unguarded and exposed. The door was locked, but my skills got it open fairly quickly, and I eased inside.

A cold blast of air hit my skin, and my breath billowed in front of me as I gazed warily around. The room was windowless, stark and almost freezing. The walls were bare, the floor empty except for three metal towers in the center of the tile, blinking with dozens of green and blue lights. As server rooms went, it was pretty small, unlike the vast rooms with dozens of computer towers lining the floor that I had seen in other buildings. These servers would provide only enough information for this one isolated compound. I wondered why Talon was so keen on blowing it up. Still, I had my mission, and it wasn't my job to ask questions. The sooner I was done here, the sooner I could leave.

Shrugging out of my backpack, I knelt and carefully eased the padded black case out, then clicked it open. The incendiary device sat within, and my heart pounded as I stared at it. The new "toy" I was supposed to try out was a bomb, and not just any bomb. This one was much more powerful than a normal explosive, my trainer had said. A combination of science, magic and dragonfire, packed into this small, deadly package. Dragonfire was not like normal fire; it burned hotter, fiercer, and was capable of melting steel and turning flesh to ashes in minutes. It had the tendency to cling to whatever it touched, consuming any material until it was completely gone. Even now, with all the technology and tools and firearms dragons had adapted over the centuries, our breath remained our most lethal weapon. It was the main reason St. George feared us in battle. If this thing worked the way Talon expected, it would not only destroy this room and pulverize the servers, it would spread caustic, roaring dragonfire through the whole floor, blowing out walls, weakening supports and bringing the whole building down on top of it.

And of course, anyone caught in the blast would be nothing but a smoking, blackened skeleton when they were found, an image that made my gut clench. More killing. More deaths. But at least this target was a heavily armed St. George chapterhouse, filled with active soldiers dedicated to making my race extinct. They understood their part in this war; they knew exactly who they were fighting.

Whatever you have to tell yourself, Cobalt. Let's get this over with.

As smoothly as I could, I placed the bomb on the tile floor and slid it beneath one of the towers. It glimmered dully in the shadows, silent and deadly, and for a moment, I hesitated, staring at the device. Press a button; that was all I had to do. Press a button, and get out. The most dangerous mission of my life was nearly done. I was almost home free.

I shook myself, then reached down and firmly pressed the small red button on the side of the case. There was a faint click, and glowing numbers flashed across the tiny black screen on top. They blinked for a moment, then began counting down.

15:00
14:59
14:58

Swiftly, I rose, my steps heavy as I headed toward the door. Fifteen minutes. Fifteen minutes before this place exploded in a hellish firestorm and turned everyone inside to ashes.

These are soldiers, I reminded myself again as my hand closed on the knob. *They've accepted the risks. For every one of them you kill, more dragon lives will be saved. This is for the good of us all.*

So why did I feel like I might puke if I thought too hard about it?

I opened the door, stepped out of the room…

…and came face-to-face with a girl.

I froze. The human looked up at me, green eyes appraising in a round, pale face. She wore a simple yellow dress, and curls of white-blond hair tumbled down her shoulders. She seemed completely unafraid, and for a split second, we stared at one another.

Then the girl blinked her somber green eyes. "You're not supposed to be in there," she said softly.

Instinctively, my muscles tensed, ready to spring forward, cover the human's mouth and yank her back into the room. I knew I couldn't let her run away and alert the rest of the base to my presence. But as she gazed up at me, bold yet curious, I faltered. She was a kid, no more than six or seven in human years. Not a soldier, not even an adult. If I grabbed her now…I'd probably have to kill her.

The girl cocked her head as I struggled with my decision. "What are you doing?" she whispered, her voice furtive, as if she was in on the conspiracy. "Are you hiding from someone?"

"Uh…yeah." I had no idea what the hell I would even say to her after that. If the kid screamed, my chances of survival were basically zero. But the thought of killing her, feeling her small neck snap under my fingers, made my insides curl. Even though I knew she would grow up to hate my kind and want us extinct. Because she was part of St. George, and that's what they did. Took people as normal and innocent as this girl and turned them into dragon-hating zealots.

The little human blinked again. "Why?" she asked, still keeping her voice soft. "Who's looking for you? Are you in trouble?"

Oh, definitely. "No," I whispered, giving her what I hoped was a careless grin and shrug. "I'm…uh…playing hide-and-seek with some of the soldiers." Even as I said it, I winced inside at how stupid that sounded. But I couldn't stop now. "It's…a…a new exercise," I went on, as she frowned. "They have to find me before time runs out, or I win. But if I'm caught, I have to wash everyone's dishes for a month."

The girl's frown deepened, bordering on outrage. "That's not fair!" she whispered indignantly. "There's a lot of them, and only one of you. Not fair." She put her hands on her hips, and I shrugged again, giving her a "what can you do?" look. Her nose wrinkled, lips pursing in annoyance. "Do *they* have to wash dishes if you win?"

"Um…no," I said, wondering how I had been drawn into this crazy conversation, and how I could leave it without being discovered.

"Why not?"

"Because…ah…"

"Madison?"

A new voice drifted from another hallway, and I cringed. This was it. I was going to be caught, because I'd been stupid and softhearted, and hadn't silenced this kid when I had the chance. But the girl turned her head, eyes widening, then glanced back at me.

"You better go," she whispered. "Before they see you."

I stared at her, stunned, and she made shooing motions as she backed away. "Go," she whispered again. "Hurry up and hide! I won't tell anyone where you are, I promise."

"Madison!" The voice sounded annoyed, and closer. The girl grinned and, before I could do or say anything, turned and scurried off, vanishing around a corner as quickly as she had appeared.

Just like that, I was alone.

"There you are," said the man's voice, as I pressed against the door frame, listening with a kind of numb anticipation. "I thought I might find you down here. What do I keep telling you about wandering off? Who were you talking to?"

"Nobody," Madison drawled, way too sweetly I thought. "I wanted to see if Peter was down here. He promised he'd show me the server room if I was good." My heart pounded, but the man, whoever he was, simply grunted.

"You and your computer fascination. Well, come on. I have to finish one last report, and then we'll go get breakfast."

And their footsteps faded down the hall in the opposite direction. A door slammed shut, and silence fell once more. I let out my breath in a rush and collapsed against the wall.

Waaaaay too close, Cobalt. Still a lucky SOB. Now get out of here, before that bomb goes off…

Shit. The bomb.

I started to move, to hurry back into the shadows and make a beeline for the gate as quietly as I could, hoping to somehow avoid both the soldiers and the deadly explosion *minutes* from going off.

Then…I hesitated. In the middle of a St. George chapterhouse, surrounded by enemies who would kill me on sight, with my seconds rapidly ticking away, I hesitated, unable to make myself take another step. If I left now, if I finished the mission and walked away, everyone on this floor would die.

Including that kid. Madison, the girl I'd met for only a couple minutes, would die. She was human, she was part of St. George, but she wasn't a soldier. And without even knowing it, she had saved my life.

I raked my hands through my hair. *So, what are you going to do, Cobalt? Not complete the mission? Go back to Talon and admit you failed? You know they won't accept that.*

No, they wouldn't. So that left me with exactly three options. Return to Talon having failed the mission. Accept their punishment, whatever it was, knowing they would never trust me again, knowing they would consider me tainted and incompetent and somehow corrupted. Talon had little use for dragons who failed; my future with the organization was assured only if I continued to be valuable. It was career suicide, but I could kill the bomb, return to Talon and face the consequences of my decision, whatever they might be.

Or, I could finish what I came here to do: leave the bomb and get out, knowing more people would die. Knowing that kid would burn to death like everyone around her, because she had let me go. And I might never sleep again without seeing her face, staring up at me from my dreams.

Then, of course, there was the final option.

My chest felt tight, my stomach twisting into painful knots. Everything, it seemed, had come down to this moment. Run, or stay? Continue with the organization, or take my chances on my own? Hunted. Hated. A traitor to my own kind.

A rogue.

My hands shook, and fear spread through me as I realized the truth. I couldn't do this anymore. I couldn't go back to the organization knowing some little kid had died…no, that *I'd* killed her, and Talon wouldn't think twice about it. Why should they? She was only human, and human lives meant nothing to dragons. If a few mortals died so that our race was preserved, then the sacrifice was worth it.

But they never had to see the faces of those they destroyed; the *sacrifices* they spoke of, the consequences of our war, never touched their desks. They had me. I was doing their dirty work for them.

No. No more. That ended right now.

Numbly, I went back into the server room and walked to the place the bomb sat, tiny and ominous, red numbers ticking down. Looking down at it, everything inside me went cold.

2:33
2:32
2:31

Two minutes? What the hell? Even after the conversation with Madison, there was no way that much time had elapsed. Though the reason for it was immediately clear: the timer was moving twice as fast as a normal clock, eating away the seconds at a frightening speed. Even as I stared, they seemed to go faster, until the seconds were nothing but a red blur against the screen. My head spun with the implications. I'd never make it out in time. If I hadn't come back, I would've died with the humans when the building went down.

Horror flooded me. Dropping to my knees, I pulled out

my wire cutters and stared at the tangle of wires surrounding the bomb. Red, blue and yellow. My hands shook, and I clamped down on my resolve. If I chose wrong, none of this would matter, except my death would arrive a few seconds earlier than planned.

I clenched my other fist. Without thinking too much about it, I jammed the blades around one of the red wires and, before I could second-guess myself, snapped them shut, severing the line.

The device gave an ominous beep...then stopped. Nothing exploded in a blinding cloud of dragonfire, and my heart started beating again.

Dropping the snips, I ran my hands down my face, everything inside me twisting into knots as the realization of what I'd done—what *they* had done—hit me full force. Maybe the bomb had malfunctioned, maybe there had been a glitch to make the countdown accelerate like that. But I knew better than to think this had been accidental. Talon had never intended for me to come back.

In a daze, I rose from the tile floor and stumbled toward the exit. Fear clawed at me, dark and crippling. Talon was my whole life; my entire existence had been spent serving the organization. I knew what would happen once they figured out I hadn't died like I was supposed to. I was fully aware of what they did to those who went rogue. But there was no turning back. This had been coming for a while now. I knew it, my trainer knew it...and Talon had known it, too. My days of spy missions, sabotage and blowing up buildings full of innocent humans were over.

That's it. I remembered Madison's face, the way she'd smiled up at me, and my resolve grew. *No more. Do you hear that, Chief? I'm done. This is Agent Cobalt, checking out for the last time.*

Crossing the room, I opened the door and melted into the shadows. I still had to get free of St. George, but even if I escaped, the organization would have accomplished at least one thing. A Talon operative had died in this building tonight. As of this moment, Agent Cobalt no longer existed.

EMBER

My hands wouldn't stop shaking.

I couldn't stop them. My heart was racing, and my nerves felt charged with electricity. My trembling fingers were still curled around the smooth handle of the gun in my lap. The gun I'd used to shoot someone.

My stomach heaved, and I closed my eyes, but it didn't help. I could still see him, the slack face and the sightless, staring eyes. The bullet hole in his skull, oozing blood. I didn't even remember pulling the trigger. The moment I'd seen him through the attic opening, aiming his gun at Garret, I'd reacted. Without thinking, just as I had in the St. George compound—quick and lethal, almost instinctive. Now, because of me, a man was dead. I'd become a killer, an assassin, just like Talon wanted.

Lilith would've been proud.

"Where are we going?" Garret's voice echoed beside me, calm and composed. He didn't sound remotely anxious or freaked out, as if being targeted by snipers, breaking into a house and taking out two fully armed soldiers was a perfectly normal day for him. Business as usual. For a moment, I resented his perfect composure. I'd just killed a man, one of his former brothers in arms; you would think he'd be slightly upset by that.

"Downtown," Riley answered without looking back. He sat in the front seat, both hands on the wheel, and drove like he rode a motorcycle: fast and with purpose. Beside him, Wes hunched over his laptop, not looking up when Riley took a corner without slowing down, making the wheels screech. "Near the Strip. I have a friend there who can hide us."

"And the vehicle?" Garret looked out the back window, maybe searching for flashing lights. "I assume the original owner isn't going to be happy about us hot-wiring his car."

Wes snickered. "Hot-wire a car," he scoffed. "Please. Is that how you do things, St. George? How very primitive." He tapped two fingers against his skull. "Modern cars these days have lovely computerized brains that you can turn on with a phone. Makes them fairly easy to hack into, if you know what you're doing."

Great, I thought, crossing my arms. The gun dropped onto the seat beside me. I didn't want to look at it, much less touch it anymore. *So now we're murderers and car thieves.*

A soft click made me look up. Garret had reached over and taken the pistol from where it lay between us, then smoothly flicked on the safety. He turned the weapon around and offered it to me again, his gray eyes solemn as they met mine.

"You had no choice," he said, holding my gaze. "Those soldiers would've killed us both if they could. There was no other option, you did what you had to do."

The lump in my throat got bigger, and I eyed the weapon like it was a giant venomous spider. But I made myself reach out and take it back, closing my fingers around the now warm metal. "I know," I whispered, setting the gun carefully on my leg. "But that doesn't make it all right." I shot a wary glance at the front, where Riley and Wes were talking in low voices. Wes was pointing to a map on the laptop screen, where a glowing blue dot approached an intersection. Riley swore, gunned the engine and ran an aging yellow light. Neither seemed to be listening to what was happening in the back-seat, but I lowered my voice anyway. "I don't want to be like them," I murmured. "Either of them. Talon *or* St. George. If I start killing without a thought, if it becomes instinct, why did I leave Talon at all? What makes me any different than the Viper they wanted me to become?"

The blare of a siren made us jerk up. A cop car passed us, going in the opposite direction, lights flashing blue and red, speeding toward the distant column of black smoke curling into the sky. The soldier leaned back, gazing out the window, and didn't answer my question.

★ ★ ★

The sun had set over the distant mountains, leaving only a fading orange splash on the horizon, when we reached the inner city, or the Strip, as Riley called it. My misery was tem-porarily forgotten as I pressed my nose against the car win-dow, gaping at the wonders looming overhead. I'd never seen so many cars, lights, people. The streets practically glowed; hotels, casinos, massive signs, monuments, all blazing with neon luminance against the darkening sky. An enormous car-toon cowboy waved to us as we drove past, and a miniature sultan's castle boasted a colorful rainbow of lights across its domed roof. I caught a glimpse of the Eiffel Tower, shim-mering gold against the night, rising above the streets like a beacon. Not *the* Eiffel Tower, I realized; as far as I knew, the real one was still in Paris, so this was obviously a replica. But it was still huge, and impressive, and blazing with light, like everything around us.

"Close your mouth, Firebrand," Riley remarked with a smirk in his voice as we cruised down the street, passing buildings and people and an endless string of cars. "You're fogging up the windows."

I tore my gaze from the massive buildings surrounding us, sliding back in my seat. "Are we going to stop soon?" I asked, hoping the answer was yes.

Riley snorted. "Not here," he said, and all traces of amusement fled. He shot a grim look out the window at the glittering structures lining the roads. "Definitely not on the Strip. Vegas is a huge cash flow for the organization. They have their claws in basically every vice you can imagine—gambling, drugs, strip clubs, you name it." Riley pulled a disgusted face, curling a lip. "Thankfully, there aren't many actual dragons in Vegas. Just *one*, really. But he's a temperamental bastard who makes even Talon nervous, and he owns nearly all the hotels and casinos on the Strip. We step into the wrong building, we might as well be walking around with glowing signs above our heads."

"Then why are we here?" Garret asked, voicing my own question. "If this city is so heavily influenced by Talon, why are we risking exposure by staying?"

"Because I want to know what Talon is up to," Riley snapped, glaring back at him. "I want to know why my safe houses keep disappearing, and if Talon is doing anything shady. More shady than normal, anyway. I want to know how the Order knows about me, knows who I am, when they didn't have a clue in the past. If my entire network is in danger, I want to know why, and what I can do to stop it." He turned back, gripping the steering wheel, eyes narrowed and hard.

"I have a contact here," he said at length. "One who keeps tabs on any movement between St. George and the organization for me. Nothing happens in Vegas without him finding out. If anyone knows what's going on, he will."

We turned off the Strip, leaving the mega hotels and dazzling lights behind. Several minutes later, Riley pulled the car to the side of the road and killed the engine.

"All right, let's go. The hotel we want is two blocks down, but we're ditching the car here. I'm sure it's been reported as stolen by now." He turned in his seat to look back at us and glanced at the pistol I still held. "Stash the guns," he ordered, and Garret immediately turned and pulled the duffel bag from the backseat. "Last thing we need is for someone to call the cops on us. Everyone keep your head down. We do this quick and quiet. Oh, and one more thing. Wes, you got them IDs, right?"

The human mumbled something and held up two plastic cards without taking his gaze from his computer. Riley snatched them from his fingers and held them out to us. "Cover identities for the hotel," he explained as I took my driver's license and peered at it curiously. My face smirked back at me, familiar and baffling; I had no idea where he'd gotten the photograph. According to the license, my name was Emily Gates, and I was twenty-one years old.

Curiosity and excitement flickered. What could I do with

a fake ID in Vegas? I wondered. I could definitely think of a few things.

"Those should hold up to most background checks," Riley went on, as Garret slid his own license into a pocket then continued stashing the guns. "But we don't want to draw attention to ourselves. So no ordering from the bar or wandering the casino floor. Those IDs are just to get us past the door. Firebrand…" Riley's gold eyes fixed on me, appraising. "Are you listening to this? We are here to *lie low*, understand? Shall I explain the meaning of the term?"

I wrinkled my nose at him. "I know what it means. Smart-ass."

His lip quirked. "Just keep that in mind, and try not to get distracted by the shiny."

I rolled my eyes. Garret finished zipping up the bag, swung it to his shoulder and opened the door. A dry breeze ruffled my hair as I stepped out onto the warm, crowded streets of Las Vegas.

Riley took the lead, striding purposefully down the sidewalk, with Wes, Garret and I trailing behind. And the rogue's warning was instantly forgotten. I couldn't stop staring at… well, everything really. Crescent Beach had been a small, sleepy town, with few highways and not many large buildings. Vegas was like another world. I'd never seen rows of buildings so high they were like canyon walls, or so many glowing lights that I couldn't see the sky through the haze, or an endless river of cars, red brake lights stretching on to the horizon. Unfortunately, navigating bustling sidewalks while trying to look at everything didn't really go well together. I kept bumping into passersby, muttering apologies and getting annoyed looks in return.

"On your six," a voice muttered, as I slowed to gaze at a building across the street. Confused, I turned...and someone barely swerved around me with a muffled curse. Blinking, I looked up at Garret, who shot me a half amused, half exasperated look before going back to scanning the crowds.

I offered a weak grin and fell into step beside him. "On your six?" I asked. "Is that soldier talk for 'pay the hell attention to what you're doing'?"

"We *are* in enemy territory." Garret watched a pair of thuggish-looking guys approach, relaxing only slightly when they passed. "Talon and St. George are both searching for us. They might have agents on the streets right now. A little situational awareness is probably...prudent."

Feeling chastised, I followed him, trying to stay close. Garret moved through the throngs like a fish through water, metallic-gray eyes constantly scanning, watching. I remembered his discomfort with crowds in Crescent Beach, that hyperalertness, as if a ninja could come leaping out at us from a potted plant. Back then, in the lazy little beach town, it had seemed odd. Now, I understood. That paranoia had probably saved his life more than once.

Finally, Riley took us across a huge parking lot and through the doors of a smaller, though still impressive, building. Nero's Garden Hotel and Casino, the sign read as we approached the front. A pair of marble lions guarded the entrance, though I saw someone had drawn a tiny mustache below one lion's nose. Then the doors slid back, and we stepped into a brightly lit lobby with green tile, fake marble columns lining the room and statues of half-naked Greek people in alcoves along the wall. A huge check-in desk ran the length of the back wall, and off to the side, through a fake marble arch, the casino floor buzzed, twinkled, chimed and flashed like a sprawling neon circus.

"Well, here we are," Riley said with false grandeur, and offered a sarcastic grin as he gestured to the glittering casino. "Welcome to Vegas."

DANTE

From the air, the city looked like an island of stars in the center of a black void.

"Can I get you anything before we land, sir?" the flight attendant asked, showing perfect white teeth as she smiled down at us. Or, more accurately, at me. At my side, Mr. Smith didn't look up from his phone, and across from us, Mr. Roth made a vague gesture with his hand, waving her away. I made a point of returning the smile as I shook my head.

"No. Thank you."

"Of course, sir." The human regarded me through lowered lashes. "Please, let me know if you need anything." She wandered toward the back of the jet, where a second attendant glared at her with stony eyes.

Mr. Roth chuckled.

"Do you see your protégé, Mr. Smith?" the VP said, as my trainer put his phone away and looked up. "You'll have to keep a closer eye on him. If we're not careful, we'll have humans clawing each other's eyes out for his attention."

I stayed quiet, not knowing if this was praise or a reprimand. Mr. Smith gave a small laugh that could have meant anything, but he didn't comment. I took a furtive breath and settled back in the plush leather seat, trying to calm my nerves. Normally by this time, my trainer would be going over Talon rules and protocol, grilling me on etiquette, making sure I knew what I was doing. But he couldn't now, or he wouldn't, not in front of Mr. Roth. There were no other passengers on Talon's elite private jet; it was just the three of us. My trainer, one of Talon's senior VPs and me. A sixteen-year-old hatchling who was keeping company with some of the most powerful dragons in the organization. A hatchling who, just yesterday, had been standing outside the door of an office in Los Angeles, waiting to be acknowledged.

★ ★ ★

"I believe we found them, sir," I'd announced, when Mr. Roth finally waved me into the room. I stepped through the frame, closing the door behind me. "We think they're in Vegas."

The VP arched one slim, elegant eyebrow at me over his desk. "Vegas, you say," he repeated. "That's…unexpected. One of our biggest operations is in Vegas. That Cobalt would flee there is unusual." His gaze sharpened, brows drawing together. "How did you come to this conclusion, Mr. Hill?"

I handed him the folder Mist had given me; her report and the satellite pictures of the Order chapterhouse sat inside. "We've been monitoring St. George ever since Ember and the rogue broke into their western chapterhouse, sir," I said, as Mr. Roth flipped it open. "We believe St. George is looking for them as well, and recently, we've seen a lot of Order activity in and around Las Vegas. They appear to be converging on the city. We think Ember and the rogue are hiding somewhere close, maybe near the Strip."

"I see." Mr. Roth closed the folder and laced his hands under his chin. "Reign's territory. Of course, they would have to make this complicated."

My heart beat faster. Ember was in Las Vegas, I could feel it. Just a few hours' drive away, in the middle of a huge, dangerous city with St. George closing in on all sides. "Sir," I began, "if Ember *is* in Vegas, I believe I should be the one to bring her back. If we can find her, I would like to go. She'll listen to me. I just need to talk to her."

And if I can bring her back, Talon will know how valuable I am to the organization.

"Of course, Mr. Hill." Roth glanced up at me and smiled. "Of course you are going to retrieve your sister, that was never a question. However, there are protocols that we must observe, if we want the best chance of finding Ms. Hill and Cobalt. Before we do anything in Las Vegas, there is someone we must speak to first. I'll arrange the meeting."

★ ★ ★

Mr. Roth hadn't wasted any time. I'd been driven back to my apartment with orders to pack for a few days' trip, and this morning I'd been taken to a small airport, where Mr. Smith, Mr. Roth and a private jet awaited me. Everything had happened so quickly, I hadn't had time to reflect or feel nervous, until now.

Crossing my legs, I leaned back, affecting a pose of professional nonchalance. This anxiety wasn't like me, but everything, it seemed, hinged on bringing Ember back. *Everyone is watching you, Dante*, I reminded myself. *Talon is watching you, even closer than they did in Crescent Beach. This is your chance to prove yourself. To start building a future in the organization, to do great things for Talon. You have to impress them. You have to do better than anyone expects.*

"Sir," I ventured, making Mr. Roth glance up and raise an eyebrow at me. "Our contact in Las Vegas—his name is Reign?"

"That is correct," Mr. Roth replied.

"Is there anything I should know about him?" I went on, careful to keep my tone deferent. "Anything special I should be aware of before the meeting?"

"Ah yes, our good friend Reign." Roth smiled, though his tone was brittle. "Only know that he is one of the oldest dragons in the organization," he said, making my stomach drop to my toes. "He was around when the Elder Wyrm rose to power, so that should give you an idea of who you're dealing with. He is also very, shall we say…old-fashioned? He prefers things a certain way, and the Elder Wyrm allows him his small idiosyncrasies. He is crucial to the organization, as most of Talon's assets in Las Vegas come through his casinos, but Reign himself can be…challenging to deal with." Mr. Roth gave me a scrutinizing look and leaned back in the seat. "My advice to you, Mr. Hill? Be polite. Reign is loyal to the organization and will not risk the Elder Wyrm's wrath, but he is not fond of having other dragons in what he considers his territory. It is always good to be cautious when dealing with self-proclaimed kings."

The jet landed at another private airport on the edge of town, and a limo stood waiting to drive us into the city. Once inside I leaned back against the cold leather seat and crossed my legs, deliberately not looking out the tinted windows. I was resolved to appear as cool as possible, and not like a gawking, starstruck tourist who had never seen the glamour of Las Vegas.

I nearly broke that resolve when the limo pulled up in front of the biggest hotel I'd ever seen in my life. It soared above us, blazing with millions of lights, so bright you could barely see the sky overhead. Inside, it was even more difficult not to gape at the enormous foyer tiled in gold and black, ringed with silver-threaded onyx columns, a marble fountain in the center of the opulence. A retinue of well-dressed humans greeted us in the glittering foyer, with instructions that "Mr. R." was waiting for us, and to please follow them.

We did, trailing the escorts across a crowded casino full of flashing lights, bells and, of course, people. The place was enormous. The gold tile we walked on reflected the millions of lights, and the whole casino had an air of fantasy and surrealism, where time didn't exist and you could lose hours, or even days, without knowing it. Humans sat at tables with columns of colored chips, or fed bills into the rows of flashing machines that lined every aisle. Everything screamed wealth, riches, luxury, and for a moment, I felt a glimmer of envy through the fascination.

I wanted this.

The humans led us to the elevator bay, escorted us into a box and bowed as the doors slid shut. They did not, I noticed, press any buttons, and neither did Mr. Roth or Mr. Smith. But, after a moment, the elevator shuddered and started to move. Down.

It continued down for a long, long time. No one spoke, and I concentrated on remaining still and keeping the calm, serene expression on my face. When the elevator finally stopped and

the doors opened, I saw a short cement corridor, a lone florescent light and a single door at the end of the hall.

I caught Mr. Smith's eye as we stepped out of the elevator. His gaze was a warning, cold and ominous. This was it,
I realized. The moment where all my training, everything
I'd learned about Talon and its inner circle, came together. It
was either sink or swim, impress or disappoint. Through that
door, my future with Talon hung in the balance.

I met my trainer's stare and gave a short nod. I was ready.
Today was the day I started making a name for myself. Mr.
Smith watched me a moment longer, then turned away, fol-
lowing Mr. Roth toward the end of the hall.

We stepped through the door into a massive, dimly lit cavern. A huge, yawning chamber that soared up into the darkness, hiding the ceiling from view. The floor was cement,
but the walls, as far as I could see, were of natural rock and
stone. The air in the cave was unnaturally warm, surprising
for being so far underground, and smelled faintly of smoke,
though I couldn't see any fires. There were also no overhead
lights, no florescent bulbs or lamps, or even candles. In fact,
the only light came from a group of enormous flat screens
near the back wall. Over two dozen televisions, bolted to a
network of steel frames, formed an immense, flickering semi-
circle of noise and images. Each huge screen showed something different: sports, world events, news stations in several
different languages. A few of them appeared to be casino security, cycling through different areas of the hotel. More than
one screen showed nothing but the Dow, tracking the rise and
fall of stocks. Horses sped down a track, police sirens wailed
and an attractive Asian reporter babbled at me in Japanese.

It was a chaotic flood of imagery, a hundred different things happening all at once. So I didn't immediately notice what lay beneath the circle of screens. Then Mr. Smith put a warning hand on my shoulder, stopping me from advancing any farther into the room, and I dropped my gaze from the televisions.

My mouth nearly fell open, and I bit my cheek to keep from gasping in shock. An enormous pile of gold lay sprawled on the floor beneath the screens, the light glimmering off the metallic surface. In the darkness and shadows, it was difficult to see how big it really was, but I guessed it was at least forty feet long and fifteen feet high, a virtual mountain of gold in the middle of the cavern. So *this* was why Reign was so touchy about other dragons being in his territory. He was sitting on a literal treasure hoard. Old-fashioned indeed.

And then, the mountain moved.

The bottom dropped out of my stomach, and my mouth did fall open this time, as the entire hoard shifted, unfurled two colossal leathery wings and sat up. A head rose on a long, snaking neck, and a tail uncurled to double the length, as an eighty-foot golden dragon turned with a scraping of claws and scales and fixed us with a massive yellow eye.

My legs were frozen. I couldn't move. I could only stare at the creature before me, torn between awe and utter panic. Besides my sister, I'd only ever seen one other of my kind in its real form, an adult who wasn't even half the size of this dragon. He had to be a Wyrm, one of three dragons in the world who had passed the thousand-year mark, who had survived so long that they were the size of buildings. Everyone in Talon knew of the Elder Wyrm, the oldest and most powerful of us all, but the identities and locations of the other two were a jealously guarded secret. Reign was ancient, a lesser god gazing down at three tiny insects scurrying around his feet.

I suddenly realized why Talon allowed him his…idiosyncrasies, as Mr. Roth put it. Who would dare to tell him no?

"Well." The deep voice reverberated through the cavern like thunder, making the walls tremble. "Here you are, then." Reign pulled himself to his full impressive height, dwarfing everything in the cavern as he stretched, before sinking back and curling his tail around himself. His scales, like antique coins, glittered as he lowered his head to regard me with a blood-chilling smile. "Welcome to my casino," he continued, giving me a clear, terrifying view of his fangs. "I trust the accommodations are acceptable?"

He was talking to me, I realized, not my trainer or Mr. Roth. Which struck me as very odd. Why would one of the most powerful dragons in Talon take the time to address me and not my superiors?

Be polite, Mr. Roth had said. Always a good plan when staring down an eighty-foot dragon who could swallow you in one bite. "Yes, sir," I managed, grateful that my voice didn't shake. "You've been more than accommodating. Thank you for seeing us on such short notice. Your hotel is very impressive."

Reign sniffed, but he seemed pleased. "I see they've trained you well," he rumbled, and raised his head to observe the other dragons, standing patiently to either side. "Though I wouldn't have expected anything else. But I have little time for pleasantries. Let us talk business."

His eyes glittered, and he folded his front claws before him like a cat, the curved talons lightly raking the floor. "So the other little hatchling has run away," he said, sounding amused and impatient at the same time. "And now, you think she is somewhere in my city." He snorted, sending a billow of smoke into the air. "I find that highly unlikely. Nothing happens here without my knowledge. No one comes or goes unless I know about it. I have eyes in almost every casino, every hotel on and off the Strip." He angled a horn at the bank of screens surrounding him. "If this girl has entered my territory, what makes you think she can hide from me?"

"She's not alone, Reign." Mr. Roth's voice was cool as he stepped forward, though I noted he didn't stare directly at the other dragon but kept his gaze off to the side. "We believe she is with a former Basilisk operative who went rogue several years ago. He knows about you. He would know which hotels to avoid, and in which areas you might not have as large a presence." Reign's gold eyes narrowed dangerously, showing his obvious displeasure with the contradiction, though Mr. Roth did not relent. "He'll know how to stay hidden and out of sight, even from you."

Reign growled, not loudly, but I felt the vibrations through the cement. "A rogue Basilisk," the dragon king mused, tapping his claws against the floor. "I've heard of this upstart, Cobalt." His voice took on an annoyed edge. "I suppose he is also the reason St. George has suddenly appeared in my city?"

"Yes. We believe the Order is searching for them, as well."

Reign's nostrils flared. "So why should I risk exposure when the Order is swarming around out there, thanks to your wayward agent?" he asked. "Helping you with your rogue problem could expose my operations to St. George.

I've avoided the Order for a very, very long time. I intend to keep it that way."

My stomach turned. Ember was close, I could feel it. We were in the same city, the same territory. I just had to reach her before St. George did. Or before she left town with the rogue, and we were back at square one. Determination rose up, and I took a deep breath. I could not let anyone, even the ruler of Las Vegas, put my sister or my plans in danger.

"Sir," I began, and Reign peered down at me in amused surprise. I felt Mr. Smith's incredulous gaze on me as well and knew I was probably breaking protocol, a hatchling daring to contradict an ancient Wyrm. This was a gamble, but it was too late to back out now. I faced the ancient dragon, keeping my voice calm. "Forgive me, sir, but it's in your best interests to help," I said evenly. "You have a lot of resources at your disposal, and the sooner we find Ember, the sooner you can get St. George out of your city. Surely that is enough reason to assist us."

Reign cocked his massive head, the hint of a smile crossing his muzzle. "Is that so, hatchling?" he mused in a soft, deadly voice, making a cold sweat break out on my neck. "You're awfully confident about that."

"She's my sister," I replied. "No one knows her like I do." Those primeval eyes continued to watch me, unblinking, and I stifled my fear. "I just need to find her. If I knew where she was, I could reach her. I can bring her back to Talon."

"The boy has a point, Reign," Mr. Roth broke in. I wanted to glance at him but didn't dare take my attention from the Wyrm glaring down at me. "Once we retrieve Ms. Hill and deal with the rogue, the Order will have no reason to stay in

Vegas. They will leave, we will return to the organization, and your assistance will be much appreciated once it gets back to the Elder Wyrm."

"I'm sure it will." Reign hadn't looked away from me the entire time. "But let me ask you this, little hatchling. Let us say your sister is truly lost, that she refuses to return to the organization. What then?"

I swallowed, realizing he was testing me, seeing how far I would go. "Everyone has something that they want, sir," I replied. "Everyone has a price that they are willing to pay. Ember is with the rogue dragon, Cobalt, and even he has weaknesses. If we can find them, exploit them, we'll have them both."

Reign blew out a long, rumbling breath, filling the air with the smell of sulfur. "Spoken like a true dragon of Talon. Very well," he growled, and shifted upright, making my pulse skip at how big he really was. "I have several agents who might be able to track them down. One in particular has been very helpful, keeping eyes on the parts of the city I cannot. I'll have my people contact him. If the hatchling and the rogue *are* here, he'll know where to look." The tip of his tail thumped the ground, and he blinked slowly. "Will that be sufficient enough for you, Mr. Hill?"

Again, he wasn't looking at Mr. Roth, but at me. I bowed my head, letting gratitude seep into my voice. "Yes, sir," I said. "Thank you, sir. Talon will not forget this."

"I'm sure they won't." He shook his massive head. "Though I might have to have a talk with the Elder Wyrm about too-clever hatchlings who overstep their bounds. I assume you have a plan for dealing with this girl and the rogue, once you find them?"

My mind was already spinning. Bring Ember back, and make sure the rogue could never take her away again. That was all that mattered. Talon was watching me; I would not fail them. "Yes," I answered, setting my jaw. "I do."

RILEY

Come on, you bastard, I thought, glaring at my phone. *You know we're here. Text me back already.*

The device in my hand remained obnoxiously silent. Sighing, I shoved it into my jacket pocket and tried not to pace, feeling time ticking away from me. At least the room was large, airy and luxurious, though a bit on the gaudy side. I could've done without the shiny gold curtains and bright purple carpet. And the painting of the barely clad Greek woman lounging by a pool.

I snorted in derision. *Caesar's Palace, it ain't.* This wasn't a casino the high rollers and professional gamblers would set foot in, or come within a hundred yards of, really. Which suited me fine. No one from Talon—no one important, at least—would be caught dead here. And I wouldn't have to share the queen-size bed with anyone else; Ember was in the room next door and the other two—Wes and the soldier—had their own individual quarters across the hall. Money had never been an issue; during the years I'd worked for the organization, I'd racked up quite the nest egg. When I had gone rogue, those accounts had been frozen, but not even Talon's security was a match for Wes after he joined my team. The money was now hidden in overseas accounts under false identities so that Talon couldn't trace it back to us. Not to mention, having an elite hacker around was pretty helpful for those times I needed *other* things: bank codes, fake IDs, false reservations and the like. Most times, I didn't even have to touch my own accounts.

Now, if only my other contact would be as helpful.

As if on cue, my phone finally buzzed. I yanked it out and stared at the message on-screen, short and to the point. I smiled grimly. Time to get to the bottom of things, or at least have some questions answered. Making sure I had my wallet and fake ID, I left the room and stepped into the green-and-gold corridor.

I met Wes in the hallway, bottle of Mountain Dew in hand as he headed back to his room. "Griffin finally get back to you?" he asked, lowering his voice as he paused beside me. I nodded.

"Heading down to meet him now. Where are the others?"

"In their rooms, last I saw them." Wes pointed the green bottle down the corridor. "One sulking, the other doing bugger all. Hope the blasted hatchling doesn't wander off. She looked quite put out when you told her not to leave the floor."

I groaned inwardly. Boredom and following orders were two things that Ember did not excel at. And below us was an entire casino full of flashing lights, games, shiny objects and other things that could tempt a curious dragon.

"Keep an eye on them," I said. "Make sure Ember stays put, but watch the soldier, too. He might've broken from the Order, but he's still St. George, and that will never change. If he moves or leaves the room, I want to know about it."

Wes smiled grimly. "Want me to stick a bug in his lamp when he's asleep?"

"No." I shook my head. "I doubt he's in contact with the Order. They're hunting him now, same as us. But if he goes off alone, or gets within twenty feet of Ember, let me know. If everything is too quiet, let me know. Hell, if the St. George bastard sneezes or takes a piss, let me know. I have no idea why he's still hanging around, but if he stays with us much longer, I want to know what I'm dealing with, and why."

"Fabulous," Wes muttered. "Thirteen years of being the best hacker in this circus, and now I'm a bloody babysitter." He sniffed and took a quick swig from his bottle before ducking his head and lowering his voice even further. "Where are the guns, if you don't mind my asking?"

"In my room, of course. You think I'm going to let St. George anywhere near them?" The black duffel was sitting inconspicuously beside my bed, two 9 mms and a Glock wrapped neatly in my clothes. The do-not-disturb sign already hung from my doorknob, and I intended to keep it there. The last thing I needed was a curious maid tripping over a bag full of guns, but it would be worse if I was caught wandering the casino floor with an unlicensed firearm. Even in a place like this, security was trained to look for and spot anyone concealing a deadly weapon, not to mention the thousands of cameras watching your every move from the ceiling. Which meant I wasn't going to be armed while I was here. But at least the soldier wouldn't be carrying, either.

"I'm off," I said, stepping away from Wes. "Call me if the room explodes."

"You know, that'd be funny if I wasn't terrified it could actually happen."

Smirking, I entered the elevator and descended into the madness.

As usual, the casino floor was a chaotic sea of milling people, garish lights and clanging bells. Slot machines stood in endless rows throughout the room, blue-haired old ladies and men in suits alike feeding coins or cards into the machines with glassy-eyed determination. Crowds of men and women clustered around roulette tables, cheering wildly or groaning in turns. Dealers flipped cards at blackjack tables, smoothly picking away at players' stacks of chips until there was nothing left. *Humans and their wealth*, I thought with equal amounts of pity and disdain as I maneuvered through the crowds. *You fight and kill and work so hard to get it, only to throw it away like it's nothing. I'll never understand.*

I finally spotted the person I was looking for at a blackjack table in the corner, sitting calmly with his hands resting against the lip. A dark-skinned human in a bright red suit, matching hat perched atop his head. His gaze was riveted to the pair of cards in front of him: three of spades and nine of clubs. Crossing my arms, I leaned against a nearby column to watch. The human in the red suit tapped the table edge. The dealer flipped a card, a five of clubs, bringing the total to seventeen. The human paused, then very deliberately tapped the table again. The dealer flipped one more, turning up a five of hearts. Twenty-two and bust.

The man in the suit sniffed, rose from the chair and turned to face me.

"You threw that hand," I said. "You knew perfectly well it was going to go over."

He gave me a brilliant smile. "Oh, sure, please announce it to the whole casino," he said in a low voice, holding my gaze and grinning the entire time. His gold tooth glimmered in the artificial lights. "Blackjack isn't really my thing, but since I was meeting you tonight, I figured I didn't have time for an honest game of Texas Hold'em. Funny thing about blackjack, though. Win too often, and they start watching you. Keep winning, and they'll accuse you of card counting, which is perfectly legal in the grand state of Nevada and will get you banned from every casino on and off the Strip for life. That's the number-one rule in this town. The House always wins. Always." He continued to smile, but it had an edge now, and the eyes above the teeth were hard. "So I'd be ever so grateful if some cocky lizard didn't blow my cover and force me to change identities again. Now, laugh, you son of a bitch, like I said something hilarious."

He threw back his head and bellowed with laughter. I managed a chuckle, shaking my head. "Haven't changed at all, have you, Griffin?"

"Only my name," he responded with another grin, this one genuine. "And my face. And my personality. Helping *you*, if I remember. And I'm about to do it again, aren't I?"

"Who's the guy who got you out in the first place?"

"Touché." He gave me a rueful look. "What do you need, Riley?"

I shot a brief, wary glance at the numerous black globes on the ceiling, the cameras watching our every move. "Is this a safe place to talk?"

"Not in the slightest," he replied cheerfully. "Do you need a drink? I feel like I need a drink. Come on."

And he started across the casino floor, weaving through the crowds like he'd done it all his life. I followed him, keeping a wary eye out for anyone who might be watching. No one seemed to pay us any attention, except casino security, who eyed my dusty boots and black leather jacket with the same bored suspicion as they did everyone else. Clearly, they'd seen far stranger. Or thought they had, anyway.

We left the casino floor, and ducked into a crowded restaurant with dim lighting and dozens of flat screens lining the walls, all playing sports of various kinds. Humans sat like pigeons along the bar or clustered around tables, laughing, talking and oblivious to the world around them. Griffin and I took a booth in the corner. A group of college-age guys sat behind us, but with all the noise and chaos, I wasn't worried about eavesdroppers. The waitress took our drink orders and hurried off, leaving us in peace.

Griffin eyed me over the table. "So," the human began, folding his hands together. "Here we are. What brings you to Vegas, Riley?"

I sighed. "What do you think?"

"Hmm. Well, considering all the hubbub around the city of late, I'm guessing nothing good. I assume *you're* the reason St. George has moved in recently?" Griffin went on, making my stomach tighten. "Seems like they're on the warpath, and mighty pissed about something. Word on the street is that Talon is not happy with the Order being in their territory and are scrambling over each other trying to figure out what's going on. I'm thinking you poked a stick down a wasp nest and stirred it up a bit. Then kicked it for good measure."

"You could say that." I paused as the waitress returned with our drinks, then tossed the alcohol back, finishing the Scotch in two swallows. I didn't drink very often; it was tough to get a dragon wasted, even one in human form, so I didn't see much point in it. Tonight, though, I'd make an exception. Griffin drank his bourbon slowly, watching me over the glass rim, waiting for an explanation. I gave him a faint smirk. "Someone might have…snuck into their western chapterhouse and broken a prisoner out last week."

"Holy shit, Riley." The human lowered his glass with a look of disbelief and horror. "The Order chapterhouse itself? So, what you're telling me is you've gone insane."

"Very likely," I muttered.

"One of your hatchlings?"

"No." I scrubbed a hand through my hair. "One of *them*."

He stared at me, then used both hands to point at himself. "Okay, see this face? This is my what-the-hell face. Seriously, Riley. What. The. Hell. You snuck into enemy territory, dropped a figurative wasp down their pants and then brought that mess *here*, so I have to deal with it? Are you out of your freaking mind? *Why* would you do such a thing?"

"It's…complicated." He continued to give me his what-the-hell expression, and I scowled. "Look, I don't need you to understand or approve of what I did. What I need is to know why my safe houses keep disappearing, and how St. George suddenly knows *exactly* who I am and where I'll be. If there's a mole in the network, I want to know about it. And I need to find out what Talon is up to, where they are, if they know

I'm here. Think you can grease a couple palms and dig up some dirt for me?"

"On Talon *and* the Order?" Griffin scratched his eyebrows. "Probably, but it could take some time. I'm going to have to be very, very careful about whom I talk to."

"Please. I know the kind of people you work with. I don't think you have to do too much greasing. If they need incentive, you know I'm good for it."

He sniffed and sipped his drink. "Actually," he mused, looking thoughtful, "there is this one thing that came up recently. Something I heard just this morning, in fact."

I rubbed my eyes. "That didn't take long."

"Oh, trust me. You'll want to hear this." He paused as the waitress returned, asking if we needed anything else, and waved her off with a smile. "I don't know how credible the story is," he went on, "but my contacts seemed to think it's legit. It's actually quite amusing. Apparently, some poor bastard saw *something* in an abandoned hotel that freaked him out of his mind. A 'fucking huge lizard' I believe were his exact words."

I straightened quickly. "A runaway hatchling?"

"They seemed to think so." Griffin shrugged, swirling the ice in his glass. "I can't do anything about it, of course, but this sounds like the type of thing you'd be interested in. Might be worth checking out."

"Dammit." I sighed, knowing I couldn't ignore this. "Fine, send me the info. I'll check it out when I can. It's not like I have a million other things to do, like keeping Talon *and* St. George off our backs." I glared at him over the table. "This place is still off their sights for the time being, right?"

"Of course, idiot. You think I'd be here if it wasn't?" Griffin rose, tugging his suit jacket into place. "Give me a couple days," he said. "I'll see what I can find. And for God's sake, don't try to contact me until then. I'll call you."

I smirked. "Don't keep me waiting too long. Wouldn't want some cocky lizard sitting down at your table and ruining your perfect game, would we?"

"You're a bastard, Riley." Griffin gave me his most brilliant smile yet and turned to leave. "Thanks for the drink. Tell Wes I said hello."

I paid for the drinks and wandered back upstairs, hoping nothing had exploded while I was gone. And that a certain stubborn redhead had stayed put, or at least out of trouble.

Apparently, that was too much to hope for.

As the elevator doors opened and I stepped into the hallway, I caught sight of Ember's lean, slight form slipping across the hall and into the room on the other side.

EMBER

Nice place. Too bad it was driving me nuts.

The room was too quiet, too empty and still despite the paintings of naked Greek people on the walls and the bust of some square-jawed guy staring at me from the corner. Now that we could finally slow down enough to breathe, there was nothing to keep me distracted, no life-threatening situations to divert my attention. I flipped on the television, just for the noise, but that didn't stop all the images shifting around in my head. Memories I couldn't shut out. Everything that had happened in the past two weeks flooded my brain in a rush, pounding against me like waves. I could see the red dragon hide hanging on the wall of the St. George office, a lifeless trophy that had once been a hatchling like me. I remembered the look in Garret's eyes as he'd stared at me through the bars of his cell as if I were a ghost. The memory of his skin under my palm, his fingers curled gently around my wrist. The flight across the desert with him on my back, and that red-hot blaze of pain as the bullet had slammed into my body.

The enemy soldier, crumpling to the floor of the abandoned house, glassy eyes staring back at me. And Lilith's voice, telling me I was born to become a Viper, a killer like her.

Shivering, I rose from the bed and walked to the window, gazing down at the city. Las Vegas sparkled with a million neon lights, massive hotels and casinos standing tall and glowing against the horizon. Talon's territory. Going rogue hadn't been what I'd thought it would be. Riley hadn't mentioned this part—the running, the fear, being chased and shot and having to kill to survive. If I'd known what would happen after I'd left Crescent Beach, would I still have chosen to go with him?

Of course you would. A little voice, my dragon, perhaps, sneered in my head. *You know yourself better than that. Riley made it very clear what being rogue was like—you heard exactly what you wanted to hear. And if you had to do it again, knowing what you do right now, your choice would be the same. You're too stubborn for anything else.*

Angrily, I stalked back to the bed and flopped down again, putting a pillow over my face. I wouldn't regret my decision. I'd seen the dark side of Talon, knew what they really wanted, beneath the facade of "protecting our kind." And I refused to be a part of it. I just wished I could talk to someone, sort out these crazy, unfamiliar emotions that tried to drown me whenever I was in my own head. I wished I had someone here, just so I wouldn't be alone. Not the boys. They were part of the dilemma, part of the chaotic, confusing mess inside me. I couldn't talk to them.

I wished...

I wished Dante were here.

Dante betrayed you. I didn't know which voice this was, mine or the dragon's. But it continued with ruthless logic and disdain. *He sold you out to Talon. Lilith would've killed you and Riley that night, because Dante told her where you'd be.*

"No," I growled into my pillow. My throat felt tight, and I swallowed hard. "He didn't know what she would do. Talon lied to him, just like they lied to me, and everyone. It wasn't his fault."

Great, now I was talking to myself. Nothing crazy here. Throwing off the pillow, I stood once more and gazed aimlessly around the room. Everything was unfamiliar, and even with the television babbling, the silence seemed to press down on me. A lump caught in my throat. I was homesick, I realized. I missed my friends, my town and my old life.

I missed my brother.

"Dammit," I whispered, and felt my eyes prickle. I wanted Dante back. I wanted him to be with me, on the side of the rogues and away from Talon. Talon was using him, like they did everyone in the organization. I wished I could tell him, right now. All Talon's dirty laundry, all their secrets, the true price of staying with the organization. Dante needed to hear it. If he only knew the truth, he would never stay with them.

Maybe I *could* tell him, somehow.

Hope flickered, and I paused to think. I didn't dare call him; if Talon was looking for us, they'd be watching my brother closely, maybe even tapping his phone. The same went for texting and email. The organization had eyes everywhere; normal methods of reaching my brother could put us all in danger. Me, Garret, Riley and all the rogues under his watch. I wasn't going to risk that.

But, there *was* someone who was an expert at getting past Talon's radar unseen.

I crossed my room and opened the door a crack, peeking out. The long corridor was empty. I was probably being overcautious; Riley had said this hotel was safe enough, from Talon at least. But if there were strange humans wandering about who looked like they might be armed, I wanted to see them before they saw me.

Slipping out, I took three steps across the green-and-gold carpet and knocked on the door across from mine.

A moment later, it swung back, revealing Wes's haggard, unkempt face. His shaggy hazel bangs hung in his eyes, and his jaw and mouth were lined with stubble. He scowled when he saw me, clearly expecting someone else—probably Riley.

"Oh, it's you." His gaze flicked up and down the hall before returning to me. "What do you want?"

"Hey, Wes. I have a question." I offered a smile, making an attempt to be friendly. I knew Wes didn't like me, but maybe I could change his opinion. He just stared blankly, and I sighed. "Can I come in? I don't want to talk out in the open."

"Bloody hell," Wes muttered, but he stepped back, letting me cross the threshold into his room. It was much like mine, gold curtains, queen bed, pictures of Greek people in compromising positions on the wall. His bag had been tossed on the bed and forgotten about, but his computer sat open and glowing on the desktop.

Wes shut the door and turned to watch me with wary eyes. "Well?" he demanded as I hesitated, wondering how to convince him. "Whatever this is, can you make it quick? I really don't have time to faff around with hatchlings right now."

"Faff around?"

"What's the bloody emergency?" Wes snapped. I took a

deep breath, wondering how best to put it, then decided on the direct approach.

"I want to get a message to my brother."

The human's eyebrows shot into his hair. "Your brother," he repeated in disbelief. "I'm sorry, you mean the bloke who sold us out to Talon? Are you off your rocker? You want to let Talon know exactly where we are?"

"He didn't sell us out," I snapped back. "Talon lied to him. He didn't know what would happen when he told Lilith where we were. He didn't know she would try to kill us." Wes gave me a look of supreme disbelief, and I narrowed my eyes. "I know Dante. I've known him all my life. He wouldn't willingly do anything that would put me in danger. Talon used him, like they used all of us."

"Be that as it may," Wes said, "he's still part of the organization, or have you forgotten they're the ones sending Vipers after us? Even if your brother is being manipulated, it doesn't change anything. Talon will still use him to get to us. So, sorry, can't help you there. I like our status as is—alive and breathing."

Anger and despair rose up, and my chest squeezed tight. Half of me wanted to threaten the stubborn human before me with fire and fangs, the other half knew he was right, that he was only protecting himself and the rest of us. But still, Dante was my twin, my only family. I knew Talon didn't approve of such things; the organization was our "family," and we weren't supposed to need attachments to anything, or anyone, else. But growing up, it had always been me and Dante against the world. I wouldn't abandon him, even if he had turned his back on me in favor of Talon.

"Please," I said quietly, making the human blink. "Wes, please. He's my brother. I don't know what's happened to him, if he's okay, if Talon is making him do something awful." Wes thinned his lips, looking annoyed but hesitant, and I pressed forward earnestly. "I won't tell him where we are," I promised. "Or give him any information that can be traced back to us. I just need to know if he's all right."

Wes sighed. "Even if I wanted to do this," he said in a softer voice, "which I *don't*, let's make that very clear—I'm not going to risk it without Riley's approval. You haven't really seen the blighter lose his temper yet, and as I am not fireproof, I'm not going to sneak around behind his back. You'll have to take that request up with him."

"Fine," I said, backing toward the door. "Then I'll find him and ask him myself."

"Ask me what?"

I whirled. Riley stood in the doorway, watching us, and my dragon perked at his arrival. "Everything all right?" he asked, his amber gaze flicking past me to Wes, then narrowing slightly. "What are you doing in here?"

Wes snorted before I could answer. "Bloody hatchling wanted me to send a message to her brother," he replied, already back at his computer. I scowled at him over my shoulder, but his eyes were on the screen. "I told her that before she brought the whole of Talon and St. George down on our heads, she'd have to take it up with you."

"Ember." Riley's voice, furious and horrified, made my stomach clench. I quickly moved back as he stepped through the frame and swiftly closed the door, glaring at me. "Tell me you didn't try to contact Dante," he growled, backing me

into the room. "Do you want the organization to know exactly where we are? Do you *want* to wake up surrounded by
Vipers? What were you thinking?"

"He's my brother!" I protested.

"He's part of the organization!" Riley shot back. "He was
in direct contact with Lilith herself. Did you not learn your
lesson last time? You gave him a choice—Talon or blood—
and he chose Talon. He'll do it again if given the chance."

"I don't believe that." The tightness in my throat was back,
and the corners of my eyes stung. I'd already had this argument with Wes, but it was harder with Riley. "I don't believe Dante would willingly hurt me," I said, steadying myself
under his accusing glare. "I think Talon is using him, and he
doesn't understand who they are, or what they're capable of.
If I could just reach him, make him see—"

"How?" Riley demanded, stepping forward. "What are
you going to say? How do you think you're going to convince
him?" He poked his chest, glaring at me. "I've been on the
inside, I know how the organization works. Every second he's
there, Talon's influence on him gets stronger. They'll smile
and pat his back and promise that he's doing the right thing,
that this is for the good of us all, and he'll believe them. He'll
accept everything they say without question, because *they*
believe it, too. And even if you could somehow change his
mind, how do you think you're going to get him out? He's
too deep within the organization to risk contact." Riley shook
his head, giving me an exasperated smirk. "I'm *not* storming
Talon headquarters, Firebrand, even for you."

I briefly closed my eyes against the angry stinging. "He's
my brother," I said once more, raising my chin to stare Riley

down. "I won't give up on him. There has to be a way. And if you won't help me, then I'll do it myself."

"Ember," Riley began, but I brushed past him and stalked from the room. He didn't understand. He didn't have a sibling. None of them did. Dante and I were the only pair that had been raised together, the only dragon siblings in existence. Riley couldn't understand because he didn't have one, but Dante was family. Talon couldn't have him.

"Dammit, Firebrand. Hold up."

Strong fingers grabbed my wrist just outside the door, halting my angry storm-out. Bristling, I tried yanking out of his grasp, but Riley pulled me back into the room with him and slammed the door behind us.

"Just wait a second," he snapped, but I was full-on pissed now and punched him in the arm. "Ow! Will you stop? Listen to me." Grabbing my arms, he pinned me against the door, glaring down with angry gold eyes. My instincts flared, rising to the challenge, nearly bursting through my skin as he shoved me back. I barely clamped down on the impulse to Shift right then and pounce on the dragon in front of me.

Riley took a deep breath, as if he, too, was struggling to hold his dragon down. "Look, I'm sorry about Dante," he said. "But we can't help him right now. We can barely help ourselves. If you try contacting him now and Talon finds out where we are, we'll be dead. Even if he doesn't give our location away, the organization will be monitoring his every move, because he's connected to *you*. They're watching him, Firebrand. They know Dante is their way to you, and if they find you, they find all of us. I do not want to wake up in the middle of the night surrounded by Vipers." His fingers gripped me tighter, his face intense. "It's too dangerous to send Dante any kind of message, Ember. Promise me you won't try to contact him."

Defiance rose, egged on by the dragon, the surging heat inside. Of course, he was right, but… "I'm getting him out, Riley," I said, meeting that intense gaze, almost seeing Cobalt peering out at me. "One way or another. I can't leave him there."

"I know, Firebrand. I do understand. Trust me, I would take them all away from Talon if I could." Riley straightened, sliding his hands up my arms. "But slow down for me a little. I know you want to save the world, but there are only three of us. We can't take on Talon, or St. George, by ourselves. We'd need an army for that, and they're not just lying around for the taking." One hand rose to the side of my face, brushing a curl aside with his thumb. "Just trust me a little longer, okay? Let's figure out where we're going, what we're doing next, before we go charging the organization's front door. Can you do that, without burning the hotel down in the meantime?"

I swallowed, then took a slow breath. It didn't cool the heat of the wild surging flames within. "I guess so," I muttered, relinquishing the fight for now. He exhaled in relief, and I gave him a faint smirk. "Though I can't promise not to set anything on fire, especially if St. George kicks my door down."

Riley grimaced. "At least there are extinguishers by all the exits," he said, rolling his eyes. "I can see the headlines now, though. Vegas Casino Mysteriously Ignites on Twelfth Floor. Strange Creatures Seen Flying out Window. That wouldn't catch Talon's attention at all." He shook his head. "You certainly keep my life interesting, Firebrand."

"You love it. Just think how boring life would be without me."

A grin tugged at one corner of his mouth. "My old trainer gave me a bit of advice once," he said. "Not that I listened to his ramblings most of the time, but this one stuck out. He said, 'A flame that burns twice as bright lasts half as long.' Any idea what that means?"

"Um. That you're a secret philosopher who writes poetry between car heists and jailbreaks?" I guessed.

He snorted. "Normally I don't break out the metaphorical crap, but I thought I'd make an exception." One hand rose, knuckles very lightly brushing my cheek, searing and tingly. My heart leaped, and warmth bloomed through my stomach. "You remind me of that flame, Firebrand," Riley murmured. "You burn so hot, and so bright, you set everything around you on fire. And you don't even realize what you're doing."

"I'm a dragon," I said, trying to catch my breath. He was so close; part of me wanted to pull away, though my back was still against the door and there was nowhere to go except through Riley. The other half wanted to step closer, to press my body against his until our combined heat became an inferno. "I'm supposed to set things on fire. What's the point in lighting a candle if you're going to hide it away so it doesn't help anything?" His brows arched, and I grinned. "Ha, see? I can be philosophical, too."

Riley's smile turned grim. "Just be careful that the people around you don't get singed," he said in a low voice. "Or that you don't burn too hot, too quickly. The brightest flames are usually the ones that are extinguished first." His eyes went dark for a moment. "I know what I'm talking about, Ember. I've seen it before. I don't want that to happen to you."

"It won't," I promised.

He paused, as if he wanted to say something more but thought better of it. For a moment, we stared at each other, both our dragons very close to the surface. Riley's fingers still gripped my arms; I could feel the heat of his body as he stood there, gazing down at me.

Wes cleared his throat, very loudly, from the corner.

Riley blinked, as if just realizing where he was, what he was doing, and let me go. Disappointment rose up, but what surprised me was the fact that I didn't know whose it was, mine or the dragon's.

"It's been a long day. Get some rest." Riley didn't look at me again as he turned and walked toward Wes. For a second, I had the crazy urge to grab him and pull him back, but he stepped out of my reach and the moment was lost. "Go watch TV, or download a movie or something. Order room service if you want. We're not going to be doing anything tonight."

I wrinkled my nose at his back. "How long are we going to be staying here?"

"Until I figure out what's going on with the Order." Riley reached the back of Wes's seat and peered at the screen over his shoulder. "And when I decide that it's safe to move out," he added. "Until then, we sit tight. Stay in your room. Don't go down to the casino floor. There are cameras everywhere and according to my contact, St. George is on the warpath and Talon is pretty pissed, too. It's a good idea to lie as low as we can right now. Think you can do that, Firebrand?"

"I'll try not to set the room on fire," I promised, and

walked out of the room. But as the door clicked behind me, I paused. Going back to my silent, empty room with only the television for company sounded depressing. I could stay in Wes's room, but the human didn't want me there, and besides, I wasn't sure I could face Riley again. My dragon was still writhing and coiling beneath my skin, frustrated at being contained. If I went back in there, I might really break my promise about not setting things on fire.

Spinning around, I crossed the carpet to the door right beside Wes's. Garret's room. Putting my ear to the wood, I listened for movement, voices from the television, anything to tell me he was awake, but there was only silence. I hesitated a moment, then tapped softly on the wood.

"Garret? Are you in there?"

Nothing happened. No footsteps shuffled toward me, no movement, sound, or voice came from the other side. The door stayed firmly closed. I hovered in the frame a moment, debating whether or not I should try again, louder this time. But if he was asleep, or worse, ignoring me on purpose, I really didn't want to disturb him.

Finally, I turned around and padded back to my door, feeling restless, lonely and slightly depressed. My room was quiet, and though the city twinkled and bustled outside the window, never still, the silence on this side of the glass made me feel very alone. I showered, turned up the television for noise and spent a good ten minutes figuring out how to order room service from the kitchen downstairs. When the food came I scarfed down the slightly overcooked burger in less than a minute, not having realized how ravenous I was until the first bite.

I guess gun battles and car chases work up quite the appetite. Not to mention nearly being shot to death.

My stomach turned, and my appetite vanished as quickly as it had come. Shivering, I left the fries to harden on the tray and crawled beneath the covers of the huge bed, pulling the quilt over my face. Curling into myself, I listened to the babble of the television filling the suffocating quiet, wishing I could just turn off my brain for a few hours. Garret, Dante and Riley all crowded my mind, each pulling at different emotions until I was a tangled knot of feeling inside. I finally drifted off, but kept jerking awake throughout the night as their faces, and the face of the man I'd killed, continued to chase me through my dreams.

RILEY

"You've gone mad for the girl, haven't you?" Wes remarked.

I glared at him from across the room. He sat on the bed with his computer in his lap, finishing off his bottle of soda. Lowering his arm, he raised a shaggy eyebrow at my expression.

"Don't try to deny it, mate." He gestured at me with the bottle, sending a spatter of Mountain Dew across the white bedcover. "I saw the two of you in the doorway, and you were a half second away from a full-on snog fest."

"Dragons don't 'snog,' idiot."

"Oh, sod off. You know what I mean." Wes shook his head, half closing his laptop to stare at me over the lid. "You're losing it, Riley," he said. "Ever since that bloody hatchling crashed into our affairs, your priorities have been screwed to hell and back. For Christ's sake, we have a bloody soldier of St. George following us around! I still don't know why you haven't told the blighter to shove off."

"He's useful," I argued. "Since he's here, I figured we might as well take advantage of having the enemy with us. If we can get him to give up secrets about the Order—"

"Bull. Crap." Wes glared at me. "That's not the reason

and you bloody well know it's not. Don't lie to me, Riley. I've known you too long for that." He narrowed his eyes, his scruffy jaw tightening in anger. "It's because of *her*. Everything we've done, everything that's happened to us since Crescent Beach, is because of her. And now we're holed up here, with Talon *and* St. George on our tail, and you're making promises you have no way of keeping. Dangerous promises. Promises that will get us all killed. If anyone else suggested we contact someone in the organization, you would've either laughed in their face and told them to sod off, or punched their bloody lights out."

"I have no intention of sending Ember's traitor brother any kind of message," I said, rolling my eyes. "So you can relax. I didn't promise her anything, and I'm sure as hell not giving that Talon clone another chance to turn us in. Once was enough."

"You're missing the point, mate." Wes rubbed the bridge of his nose, sounding tired. "Listen to what you just said. Once was enough?" He shook his head. "It should never have come to that. You *knew* that brother of hers was bad news. You knew he would sell us out to Talon, and you still let her go back for him. And what happened? Fucking Lilith, the organization's best Viper assassin, tracked you down and nearly killed you both. Because that hatchling has you so twisted around her little claw, you don't know which way is up anymore."

I took a breath to cool the sudden rise of heat in my lungs. "How about I worry about running this circus, and you worry about keeping enemy forces from sneaking in the back door?" I suggested in a flat voice. "What I do with Ember is none of your business."

"It's my sodding business if it gets us all killed!"

"I've protected this underground for years!" I snapped in return. "Before Ember even knew what a human was, I've been fighting to get my kind out of Talon. I've worked for it, bled for it, nearly died for it more times than I can count. I'm not going to throw that away, and I'm certainly not going to lose it now. You should know me better than that."

Wes slumped against the pillow. "I know," he murmured. "I know you'd do anything to keep those kids safe, just like I'd do anything to screw with Talon and throw a wrench into their plans for world domination, or whatever it is they're planning. But I've never seen you like this, mate. We've worked too hard to build this underground, to get dragons out of the organization, to weaken Talon however we can. I just want to be certain your priorities are still the same."

"No," I said, making him frown. "Weakening Talon, screwing with their plans, plotting to overthrow the evil empire, that's always been *your* objective. One more hatchling that I get out of Talon is one less dragon they can use in the future. *I* go after hatchlings because I want my kind to be free. *You* go after them because you have this crazy notion that someday Talon will fall because of us. Because of what we're doing right now."

"Everyone has their dreams, mate." Wes's voice was low, his eyes hard. "I know you don't believe it will happen, that Talon is too big, but I've seen giants crumble and empires brought down. It has to start somewhere. And if you don't think that what we're doing now will matter, even if it's beyond our lifetimes, then what is the bloody point of all this?"

An ominous beep from his laptop interrupted us. Wes

jumped and pushed the lid back, bending low. His fingers flew across the keyboard as he hunched forward, his nose only a few inches from the screen, brow furrowed in concentration. I moved up beside him, feeling tense and slightly sick, hoping that alarm didn't mean what I feared it would.

"What happened?"

Wes's fingers froze. His face blanched, and he slumped back against the headboard with a hollow thump. His face was blank with resignation as he looked up, and I knew what he would say before he opened his mouth.

"We've lost another nest. St. George is moving in."

GARRET

Why am I still here?

I tilted my face to the hot stream of water, letting it pound my forehead and sluice around me, trying to drown the question that had been plaguing my mind for the past three days. The water ran into my ears, muffling all sound, to no avail. I was used to long periods of inactivity, waiting for orders or for missions to begin, but I couldn't escape my own thoughts.

This afternoon had passed in silence; television had no appeal, and since I wasn't allowed to leave the floor, I'd leafed through random travel magazines or just lain on my bed, staring at the ceiling. Finally, needing to do *something*, I'd spent the rest of the afternoon working out in my room, pushing my body to the limits of its endurance, hoping that fatigue, at least, would provide a much-needed distraction. But the second I'd walked into the shower, it returned. The whisper that still haunted me, that nagging sensation of uncertainty and doubt, when before I'd always been so confident. Why was I still here? Why was I, a former soldier of St. George, choosing to remain in the company of dragons? I wasn't a prisoner; though the rogue dragon hated me—with good reason—he wouldn't try to stop me if I walked out the hotel door and vanished into the night. On more than one occasion, he'd encouraged me to do just that.

So why hadn't I?

The obvious answer—because the Order was hunting me—was a stall at best. I was resourceful enough to evade their notice for a while. And while St. George paid their soldiers only a small stipend each month, they also provided us with everything we needed, so I had a sizable amount sitting in an account I rarely touched. It wouldn't last forever, but it was enough to start over, to begin a new life.

The real question was: Could I pass for normal? I'd lived my whole life within Order walls, only venturing out when there were dragons to be slain. I had little experience of the real world beyond that brief summer in Crescent Beach and, truthfully, with no one giving me commands, telling me where to go, I felt slightly lost. My existence until now had been habit and structure and routine—the life of a soldier—and I'd welcomed that order, knowing exactly who I was. Left to my own devices, I felt I was wandering aimlessly, waiting for something to happen.

But fear, even fear of the unknown, had never stopped me before. I didn't need a command to walk away, to leave my strange new companions behind, to fade into anonymity. I was a trained soldier, and survival was one of my strong suits; even with a price on my head, I could manage the real world if I had to. What was stopping me?

With a sigh, I placed my palms against the tile wall and bowed my head, letting the water beat my shoulders and run down my skin. I knew the answer, of course, why I hadn't left. It wasn't because of St. George, or Talon. It wasn't because

I owed these dragons my life, or that I felt I could fight the Order that raised me. It wasn't even the guilt, the memories of blood and death that kept me up at night now. It wasn't any of those reasons.

It was Ember.

I shut off the water, toweled briefly and pulled on my last pair of semiclean jeans, one of two pairs to my name. I'd need new clothes soon. Wes had gotten me the essentials while we were holed up in the abandoned house, waiting for Ember to recover, but I couldn't count on him or Riley now. Especially since I suspected something had gone down with the rogue's network; last night, he and Wes had been talking in low, angry voices, and this morning, when I'd ventured out for a soda, Riley had stalked past me down the hall, his face like a thundercloud. He hadn't looked like he was inclined to share what had happened, and I'd known better than to ask.

Shirtless, I wandered to the window and stared at the glittering sea below. The sun was setting behind the distant mountains, and a haze had settled over the urban sprawl of Las Vegas. Where was St. George? I wondered. What was happening in the Order? Were they still out there, hunting for me?

And what am I supposed to do now?

A sharp rap on my door had me automatically reaching for a gun that wasn't there. With a grimace, I snatched a T-shirt from the bed and pulled it on while walking across the room. Peering through the eyehole, I felt a strange flood of both tension and relief wash over me, before I pulled back the lock and opened the door.

"Ha. There you are." Ember grinned at me, making my

stomach knot. She wore shorts and a loose tank top, and looked perfectly normal standing there in my door frame. Like any other human girl. "I was afraid you might've snuck out the window or something. Didn't you hear me knocking last night, or were you already asleep?"

My heart beat faster as I faced that familiar smile. She was a dragon, I reminded myself. Not evil or soulless as I'd once believed, but an alien creature nonetheless. Not human. I stifled the urge to touch her, to reach out and ease the worry in her eyes, the exhaustion she was trying to mask. A memory of another room, another time when it had been just the two of us, rose up to taunt me. I ruthlessly shoved it back.

I shook my head. "No, I didn't hear you. But I might've been in the bathroom." Truth was, I hadn't slept at all the night we'd arrived, and only a couple hours since. Not that I'd expected to. I'd been trained to survive on very little sleep, but more important, it was difficult to relax when there was a price on your head. And since the rogue dragon had all the weapons and I was currently unarmed, sleep was out of the question.

Ember looked at me expectantly, green eyes shining beneath her bangs. I sighed and took a step back. "Do you want to come in?"

She beamed and scurried across the threshold, gazing eagerly around as I closed the door and locked it out of habit. I heard a snort, imagined her shaking her head.

"Jeez, Garret. Two days, and your room doesn't look like it's been touched. Are you making *your own* hotel bed? You do know there's a maid service here, right?"

I managed a tired smile as I turned around. "Where I come

from," I told her, "if they ever discovered you let an old lady clean up your mess, you'd never live it down."

"Whatever. I'll take any excuse not to clean my room." She hopped onto one of the neatly made beds, rumpling it nicely. "If I can see my floor through all the clothes, I consider that a win. Besides, didn't you know, Garret? A messy room is a sign of genius."

"I've never been inside your house," I reminded her in a grave voice, "but if that's true, I have the feeling I'm talking with the smartest person on the planet."

She reached back and threw a pillow at me. I dodged, hearing her laughter ripple up, wicked and bright and cheerful. A strange lightness filled my chest, and I found myself smiling, too. Snatching the pillow from the floor, I prepared to hurl it back.

And caught myself, a cold chill driving away the amusement.

Too easy, I realized. Too easy to relax around her, to slip back into that role I'd adopted over the summer. A normal civilian, unguarded and carefree. Which was extremely dangerous, because this situation was anything but normal. I could not afford to drop my guard, even for her. Perhaps she'd come here to escape, to forget the reality of our situation. Maybe she wanted to pretend everything was normal for a while. But I couldn't be that person she wanted, that ordinary boy from Crescent Beach. I was a soldier of St. George; I'd killed too many, hunted her kind with the sole intention of driving them to extinction. My hands were stained with the blood of countless dragons. No matter what my feelings, I could never escape that.

Stone-faced, I replaced the pillow, not looking at her. "Why are you here, Ember?" I asked. "Did you need something?"

"Actually, yes." I looked up and found her watching me with a certain maniacal glee in her eyes. "You can come downstairs with me," she announced. "Right now. I swear, if I have to watch one more pay-per-view, I'm going to set something on fire."

"Downstairs?" I repeated, and she nodded eagerly. "To the casino? Why?"

"Because it's Vegas!" Ember exclaimed, throwing up her hands. "Because we're here. Because I'm literally going to start climbing the walls if I don't get out and *do* something." She raised her chin, and her eyes glinted. "And because I went to Riley's room to see if he has any new information on Talon and St. George, and he had already left."

I straightened quickly. "He's gone? Where?"

"No idea. I tried asking Wes, but he just said Riley had 'important things to do'—" she put air quotes around the phrase, rolling her eyes "—and wouldn't tell me what. Of course, he left without telling us, or leaving any hint as to where he went or when he'll be back. So much for trusting me, I guess."

With a sniff, she hopped off the bed, grinning up at me. "So, come on, Garret. We're in Vegas, the night is young and we have fake IDs. Even you must realize what we could do with those."

"We aren't supposed to leave the floor."

She actually growled at me. "If you want to stay here and mope and be boring, I can't force you to come," she said. "But *I* am going downstairs. The hotel is safe enough. Riley said so himself. Talon and St. George don't know where we are, and even if they see me, they're not going to shoot me in the middle of a crowded casino with guards and cameras and people everywhere." She bounced past me, heading toward the door. "I won't be long. I just need a change of scenery before I go completely nuts. If you see Wes, tell him I'm looking for Riley."

I grimaced. "Wait," I said, and caught up to her in the doorway. This was not a good idea, and I knew this wasn't a good idea, but I didn't want Ember to be alone down there. If something went terribly wrong, at least I would be there to help.

She grinned as I exited the room, and I shook my head. "Just for the record," I told her as the door clicked shut, "this is the exact opposite of the term 'lying low.'" She shrugged, waving it off, and I followed her down the hall. "Doesn't gambling cost money?" I asked as we neared the elevators. "How are you going to pay for anything?"

"I have a little cash," Ember replied. "Enough for penny slots, anyway. It's not like I'll be playing roulette or poker with the professionals, not unless I score really, really well. But who knows?" Her eyes sparkled as the elevator doors opened and we stepped inside. "Maybe I'll get lucky."

RILEY

I was not in the best of moods.

The taxicab reeked. Badly. Normally, I didn't mind the smell of smoke, but the patron before me had either lit three or four cigs at the same time or had been wearing a cologne called Essence of Ashtray. It smelled, it was annoying, and I was already tense enough. Of course, the irony of a dragon nearly gagging on smoke was not lost on me, but it didn't make me any less irritable, either. The memory of last night, when Wes had announced that yet another nest was gone, made me want to punch something. Dammit, what was happening? *Who* was giving us away? And could I find them before my entire underground was lost?

A guy in nothing but a Speedo, openly carrying a beer bottle, distracted me through the window and made a lewd gesture with his hips. I gritted my teeth, imagining what would happen if I set his Speedo on fire.

Clenching a fist against the door handle, I watched the lights of downtown fade in the rearview mirror and wished the cabbie would step on it. I hoped Ember was okay. I didn't like leaving her alone, especially with St. George close by, but I had no choice. This meeting was important and, like it or not, I had to follow through. Griffin had sent me the information an hour ago, saying the contact wanted to meet face-to-face, away from prying eyes, and had refused to come to the hotel. Which meant I had to go to him, and, annoying as that was, I couldn't say no. Nor did I want the other three trailing along while St. George was in town. Better for me to go alone; I was used to this type of thing, and if the Order jumped me, at least it was just my neck at risk. I'd told Wes to keep an eye on both the girl and the soldier; he was instructed to contact me immediately if he suspected there might be trouble.

I hoped it wouldn't come to that.

The taxi pulled up outside a skeevy-looking diner several blocks from the glittering brilliance of the Strip. The sidewalk wasn't well lit, and a couple thuggish-looking humans argued with each other near the entrance. Keeping an eye on them, I wrenched open the glass door and stepped inside.

The interior of the diner was dim and smelled like grease, smoke and too many humans packed into a small space. A couple Hell's Angels eyed me as I made my way across the floor, and I hoped my boots and leather jacket wouldn't offend them enough to pick a fight. I wasn't here to toss bikers through windows, amusing as that sounded. I needed to find that contact.

A dark figure in a corner booth caught my eye, and a thin hand twitched in a beckoning motion. Easing around a waitress, I walked over and slid into the seat across from him, trying not to curl a lip. The human was pale and unnaturally thin, with sallow cheeks and lank, greasy hair hanging to his shoulders. The huge sunken eyes, glazed over and unfocused, told me everything I needed to know.

"Griffin said you'd be able to hook me up." The human's voice was a raspy whisper, greedy and hopeful. He feverishly scratched at his arm, like he had spiders crawling on it. "Fifty bucks to tell you what I know, that was the deal." He scratched his other arm, leaving thin red welts down his skin. "You got the cash?"

"If the information is good," I replied, thinking I was going to kill Griffin when I got back. How in the hell was this a "reliable contact"? "Let's hear what you know, and I'll decide if it's valid."

"No way, man." The human shook his head, making his hair whip back and forth. "That wasn't the deal. Cash first, then info. Take it or leave it."

"Fine." I stood, dusting off my hands. "I don't need info this badly. Enjoy your nothing. I'm gone."

"Wait!" The human half rose from his seat, flinging out a hand. I paused, glancing back with cool disinterest. "All right, all right," he hissed. "I'll tell you what I know. But I'm not crazy, okay? I know what I saw." He squirmed, casting wary looks around the diner as if someone was listening to us. No one was; the whispered rambles of a junkie in a dark corner didn't merit a second glance here. I sat down, waiting silently, while he assured himself no one was lurking in the shadows in the next booth. Finally he hunched forward across the table, his eyes even wilder than before.

"My buddies and I, we have this squat several miles past the Strip, right? One of those big, half-finished hotels that was abandoned when the recession hit. It's been empty for years, and we don't bother no one, okay?" He sounded defensive, as if he thought I would care what he and his friends did on other people's property. I didn't say anything, and he dropped his head, his voice becoming a harsh whisper.

"So, a couple nights ago, we come back to find these two chicks in our squat, right? Pretty ones, not from around here. We thought they were runaways."

That piqued my interest. "How old were they?" I asked, making the guy flinch.

"Um." He scratched at his arms. "Fifteen? Sixteen? It was hard to tell, man. It was dark. Plus, they bolted when they saw us. We, um...*followed* them to the upper floors." He must've seen the fury in my eyes, because he jerked back, holding up his hands. "Just to talk. Hey, they were in our room, man. Two chicks show up unannounced in your squat, you wanna know why. If they in trouble with the cops, you need some sort of *insurance* to keep them hidden, you know?"

I took a furtive breath to keep from incinerating this low-life on the spot. "So what happened?"

The human blinked glazed brown eyes. "Uh, right. So, anyway, we followed them to the top floors. To talk to them." He emphasized *talk*. "You know, because it was dangerous up there, all unfinished and shit. We didn't want them stepping on a nail or falling off the edge, right? We were worried they'd get hurt."

Right, I thought furiously. *And I'm a were-newt.* "You're wasting my time," I warned, glancing at the window as if I was bored. "And not telling me anything worthwhile. You have about five seconds to make this interesting. Four. Three."

"Chill, man, chill. I'm getting to that part." The guy's

face turned the color of old glue, and he leaned forward, his voice a reedy whisper. "So, we went up there, looking for those girls," he rasped, while I contemplated how satisfying it would be to break his nose. "And we were poking around these half-finished floors. It's like a maze, right, but we knew they couldn't have gone far. But then, we looked up into the rafters and..." The human trembled. Shook violently, like he was in desperate need of a fix. The water glass on the table rattled, and the utensils clinked together until the guy took his arms from the table, putting them into his lap.

"And?" I prodded.

"And, I swear to God, man. There was this big, scaly *thing* looking back at us."

My stomach dropped, but I fixed a grimace of contempt on my face and leaned back in the booth. "This is the info Griffin promised was reliable?" I sneered. "Some user's drugged-out hallucination?"

"Man, it wasn't no hallucination!" Flecks of saliva spattered the table between us at the outburst. "I swear there was this fucking huge lizard in that room. Or maybe not a lizard, but *something*, okay? It was big, and black, and made this hissing sound when it saw us. I even think smoke came out of its nose."

"What did you do?"

"What do you think we did? We pissed our pants and ran. Haven't gone back since."

"Huh." I quirked a brow at him, though my heart was racing. "Sure you didn't see a big scary bat and think it was a monster?"

"Whatever, man." The human scratched his arm, glaring mulishly. "I know what I saw."

I slid to the edge of the booth, my thoughts whirling. Two new hatchlings in the city. Were they mine? Wes hadn't gotten any messages from our safe houses; could these two have escaped the recent Order strikes sweeping the country like the plague? I'd have to find them, and quickly, before St. George did.

Glancing at the human, who watched me with a greedy, hopeful expression, I held up a couple bills. "This was worth about twenty bucks, if that," I said, watching his face fall. "But I'll bump it to fifty if you can do two things. Stay away from that hotel, and don't tell anyone about this, ever. Think you can do that?"

"Sure, man." The junkie shrugged. "Whatever you want. No one else believed me, anyway."

Alarm flickered, and I narrowed my eyes. "No one else? How many did you already tell?"

He cringed and scratched his neck. "No one, man," he mumbled, not looking at me. "I didn't tell no one."

He was lying, but I couldn't dwell on that now. Throwing the cash on the table, I rushed out and looked around for a taxi. If there were hatchlings in this city, rogues or runaways, I had to find them. Especially with St. George on the move, looking for me. They could easily get caught in the cross fire, and then it would be on my head if more innocent kids were murdered by the Order.

I had to get to them first. But as I stood there on the corner, cursing the taxis that cruised blissfully by, my phone buzzed, making me wince. The only people who had this number were Ember and Wes, and I'd told them to call only in emergencies.

Bracing myself, I pulled the phone out of my jeans and held it to my ear. "Ember?"

"Not quite, mate." Wes's voice was taut with anger and disgust. My gut churned, and I closed my eyes.

"What happened?"

"Your bloody hatchling," was the peevish reply, "is what happened. I can't find her, or the soldier, anywhere. You'd better get back here, Riley. Before something else blows up in our faces."

EMBER

You're not supposed to be doing this.

I shoved the little voice aside as I descended the final escalator to the casino floor. It was truly another world down here: colored lights, ringing bells, an air of chaos and excitement that was lacking in my empty hotel room. Just what I needed to take my mind off...everything. I didn't want to think about Talon or St. George. I didn't want to remember Lilith's training, or Dante's betrayal. I didn't want to think about Riley, or this sudden, crazy longing for the human standing beside me. I didn't want to feel any of that. For a few hours, I wanted to turn off my mind and forget everything.

Garret, looking even less enthused as we stepped off the escalator onto the carpeted floor, did his normal crowd-scanning thing while talking to me. "Where to first?"

Good question. I'd never been to Vegas before, though I'd seen plenty of commercials and several movies that featured the famed City of Sin. They all showed Las Vegas in the same light: an almost mythical city where you could make your fortune in a few hours, or lose everything just as quickly. To our kind, that concept of instant wealth was intriguing, almost intoxicating. I might've been a hatchling, on the run from the organization and St. George, but I was still a dragon.

Spotting a row of bright slot machines along the wall, I smiled and tugged Garret's sleeve. "This way," I told him and started toward the twinkling lights. "That looks easy enough. Let's see how fast you can lose a dollar to penny slots."

★ ★ ★

Answer: about thirty seconds, the first ten spent figuring out how to make the machine work. Modern-day slot machines, I discovered, didn't require you to pull the "arm" on their side down. In fact, the arm was just for decoration now. Everything was automatic, which meant you pressed a button and watched the pictures of apples and bells and sevens spin around for a few seconds before they came to a stop—always unmatched—and the screen announced that you had lost.

"Dammit," I muttered, after I'd fed a third dollar into the side of the machine and lost it almost as quickly. "That was my last single." I looked to the soldier, standing vigilant at my side like an alert guard dog. I didn't think he'd taken his eyes off the crowds once. "Hey, Garret, you don't happen to have any loose change weighing you down, do you?"

He gave me a split-second glance, the corner of his lip curling up as he went back to surveying the floor. "I thought dragons liked to hoard their wealth," he said in a low voice. "Not throw it away at slot machines."

"I'm investing." I wrinkled my nose at him. "That last spin was almost triple sevens. I'm gonna get lucky any second now."

"Right."

I poked him in the ribs. He grunted. "Fine," I muttered,

digging in my shorts pocket. "Guess I'll have to use that five instead."

But before I could stick the money into the machine, Garret abruptly pushed away from the stool and took my hand. My pulse jumped, and a tingle shot up my arm, even as the soldier pulled me away from the aisle and into the crowds.

"Garret." I almost had to jog to keep pace with him. "What are you doing?"

"Security," he replied, and I looked back to see two men in uniforms pass the row we were just in. One of them caught my eye, frowned and angled toward us through the crowds. I squeaked.

"He's following us!"

"Don't panic." Garret's fingers tightened around mine. "And don't act nervous. Just keep walking, and don't look back."

Squeezing his palm, I faced forward and followed his lead. We "fast-ambled" through the casino, weaving through crowds, circling around roulette tables, trying to appear nonchalant and move quickly at the same time. I didn't dare look back, but Garret, without stopping or turning his head, somehow knew exactly where the guard was and what he was doing.

"Still following us," he muttered as we strolled through a slot machine aisle hand in hand. "I think he's waiting to see if we try to play a game. I believe that's illegal here, right? You have to be twenty-one to gamble?"

"I *am* twenty-one," I protested, and he shot me a quizzical glance. I raised my chin. "According to the ID of Miss Emily Gates, I turned twenty-one this January."

His lip twitched. "Do you really want them checking up on that?"

"Um. No."

"And do you really want *Riley* finding out that they checked up on that?"

I grimaced at him. "Right. Point taken. How do we ditch the rent-a-cop?"

"Just be ready to move when I do."

I nodded. Garret made a meandering left turn down a slot machine aisle, but as soon as we were out of sight of the guard, lunged forward with a burst of speed. I scrambled to keep pace. He pulled us around another aisle, and I followed, clinging to his hand and biting my lip to keep a maniacal giggle from slipping out. We wove through a couple more slot machine corridors, melted back into the crowd and circled a noisy, cheering roulette table. Abruptly, Garret pulled me to the edge of the table, somehow squeezing us between a pair of half-drunk guys and their girlfriends. They jostled us, their attention solely on the spinning roulette wheel and the little ball bouncing within, but then Garret wrapped his arms around me from behind and leaned in close, and I forgot about everything else.

"Keep your head down," he whispered, his voice low in my ear. "The guard is still following, but he's lost sight of us now. Don't make eye contact, and when he passes, we go back the other way and lose him for good."

"Got it." I held my breath, keeping my eyes on the table but hyperaware of Garret's arms around my stomach, holding me against him. I could feel his breath, the slow rise and fall of his chest, the taut coil of muscle in his arms.

After a tense, yet still far too short moment, Garret pulled away, looking back over his shoulder. "Clear," he muttered, as I risked a glance in the direction he was facing. The guard was moving away from us, following the crowds as they ambled through the casino. I couldn't see his face, but from the way he was turning his head from side to side, he was still looking for us. I let out a breath and started to relax.

But then, he turned and came back our way. With a squeak, I quickly faced forward as Garret did the same, pressing close. His heart beat crazily against my back, and I suspected he could feel mine pounding away, too. Thankfully, the guard passed us by once more, and this time continued through the casino until he was lost from view.

I exhaled, then collapsed into helpless giggles, leaning against Garret. He looked down with that amused half smile on his face, as if he didn't quite know what to do with me.

"Well." I peered down the aisle, making sure the guard was really gone, then looked back at Garret. "That was exciting, wasn't it? I think next time we should try the poker tables." He raised an eyebrow, looking alarmed, and I laughed again. "Sorry," I offered. "I suppose we should head upstairs before Riley comes back and bites our heads off. I'm sure dodging casino security wasn't exactly what you signed up for tonight."

He chuckled. "I've had to lose a couple tails in my life," he admitted. "Not all pursuers have been large angry reptiles. Tristan and I once spent the night dodging security guards in a museum warehouse. Nothing like huddling under a tarp with a family of cavemen to give you perspective."

I blinked at him. "Did you have a few drinks before we came down here?"

"No. Why?"

"You realize you just made a joke."

A cheer went up from the roulette crowd, and one of the drunk guys jostled me, knocking me into Garret. He quickly put out his hands, steadying us both, and my annoyance at Rude Guy was instantly forgotten as I glanced up and met those steely gray eyes.

Garret blinked. His hands lightly gripped my arms, rough, calloused fingertips warm on my skin. Slowly, he slid them up my shoulders, raising goose bumps and leaving a trail of heat. "Maybe you're rubbing off on me," he mused, serious again. "Or maybe…I've come to the realization that every-thing I know is wrong, and I'm starting not to care anymore."

"Is that a good or bad thing?"

"I don't know." He drew closer, looking thoughtful. His gray eyes were still intense, piercing, as his fingers brushed a strand of hair from my cheek. "But I'd be willing to find out."

My heart turned over. He was giving me that look, the look of the boy from Crescent Beach, the one who had danced and surfed and kissed me in the ocean. The boy who didn't know I was a dragon, not yet, who saw me only for me.

I swallowed hard. Ever since the night we'd faced each other on the bluff, dragon to soldier, I'd known that what-ever we had over the summer was gone. Garret was part of St. George, the Order who saw all my kind as evil, soulless monsters. He might not believe that anymore, but I was still a dragon. Very much not human, despite these crazy hu-manlike emotions urging me forward, to reach up and pull his lips down to mine. I'd never thought we would be here again, face-to-face, with Garret watching me like I was the only person in the entire world. A ripple of doubt filtered through the happy longing. If I Shifted now, if I stood here in my real form, wings, scales, talons and all, would he still look at me like that?

The crowd at the table erupted once more, this time with loud groans and gestures of disgust. I swallowed a growl as Rude Guy hit me in the ribs with an elbow, and saw a dangerous light pass through Garret's eyes as his attention shifted to the oblivious human. I didn't *think* Garret would knock Rude Guy on his ass right here, much as I'd love to see that, but it was definitely getting crowded. I suddenly didn't want to be surrounded by bright lights and mobs of humans. I wanted a nice dark corner to see this—whatever *this* was— through in peace.

"Come on," I told Garret, backing away from the table. He followed me, that same bright, intense stare making my insides dance. "Let's find someplace quieter."

GARRET

What are you doing, Garret?

I followed Ember through the casino, keeping a wary eye out for security, and one guard in particular. The soldier in me operated on instinct, scanning the floor, constantly alert for hidden threats. I knew it was unlikely that St. George was here, and even more unlikely that they would attack us in the casino, but a lifetime of war and fighting had made me paranoid; I couldn't turn that off even if I wanted to. Which was good, because my emotions had become somewhat... distracting.

You know what she is. You can't plead ignorance anymore.

I knew that. Ember was a dragon; it was impossible to forget that now. I remembered the groggy red creature staring at me from the bloody floor of a van. I remembered the way she spoke in the abandoned house, the hurt on her reptilian face when she thought I was afraid of her, that we were enemies. Even then, she'd still sounded like Ember, like the girl I'd met in Crescent Beach, though her outside form had changed. It was strange; not long ago, dragons had been monsters. Ruthless, cunning and intelligent, but monsters nonetheless. Ember wasn't human, and maybe I was being profane, but the line between girl and dragon had somehow blurred, and I didn't see either of them as monstrous anymore.

You're a soldier of St. George. A dragonslayer. She should hate you, and everything you've done to her kind.

I winced. That was true, as well; I could never erase the years I'd fought with St. George, killing dragons, driving them toward extinction. That Ember had rescued me, risked her own life to save mine, was still hard to believe. She had to realize how dangerous it was, crossing into St. George territory, just to find me. Had it been a sense of obligation, the fact that I'd helped her and the rogue escape Crescent Beach, that made her risk everything to break into the Order chapterhouse? A debt that needed to be paid? Or could it be... something else?

Could I hope for something else?

I shook myself, trying to clear my head, calm the storm of confusing thoughts and emotions that battered me from within. I was still unsure what I was going to do, what was going to happen tonight, as Ember pushed back a door and led us outside. A rooftop pool glowed in the center of the space, and a few civilians lounged in a nearby whirlpool, despite the heavy desert heat.

Ember led us across the roof to an isolated corner surrounded by planter boxes and fake trees, where the bright lights of Vegas glimmered beyond the rails. The space was empty, but the soldier in me scanned the area out of habit, making sure it was safe, that we were alone. Ember gave a low chuckle and shook her head.

"Relax, oh paranoid one. I doubt there'll be Talon agents hiding in the potted plants."

"You never know," I returned, feeling strangely light and flippant, not like myself at all. Being around Ember had that effect on me, I was discovering. "It could be a brilliant Talon plot. Instead of humans, dragons Shift into benches."

She laughed. "Oh, great. Now I'm going to be paranoid every time I sit down. I hope you're happy." She turned and rested her elbows on the railing, gazing out over the city. I mimicked her pose, leaning against the rails, our arms almost touching. I was acutely aware of her body next to mine, radiating warmth, especially when Ember let out a sigh and leaned her head on my shoulder, making my pulse spike.

"Thanks for this," she murmured, as I told myself to keep breathing. "I needed to get out, to do something, or I was going to go crazy. Staying in that room alone, there were just so many memories. I can't be in my own head right now..." She paused, giving herself a slight shake, as if to drive those memories away. I didn't move, afraid that if I did it would break the spell and she would pull back. Instead, Ember pressed closer, causing all my nerve endings to stand up, and we stared out at the city lights for several silent heartbeats.

"Does it ever get any easier?" she whispered at last.

She didn't have to explain what she meant. "Yes," I told her. "Unfortunately. You have nightmares for a few weeks, and you question yourself for a long time—did you do the right thing, was there anything you could have done differently— but after a while, if you keep at it, pulling the trigger gets easier and easier. Eventually, it becomes routine, something you do without thinking." I glanced at her, hoping she didn't think I was bragging. "It's not something to be proud of," I said softly. "And it's not something you should strive for, not if you want to be anywhere near normal. I've been a soldier all my life. St. George taught me how to kill, but that's all I can do. It's the only thing I know how to do." Ember didn't answer, her gaze far away and dark. Maybe she despised me now, a soldier who took lives so easily, who killed without thinking. I wouldn't blame her if she did. "You don't want that, Ember," I said, not adding what I really thought, my own selfish desires. *I don't want that for you. I kill when I must for survival, but I wish you didn't have to be part of this war. If I could take you away from all of it, I would.*

"I know." She shivered and pulled away, hugging her arms as if cold. "That's why I left, after all," she went on, her voice barely audible. "Because they wanted to turn me into a killer, an assassin for Talon. They wanted me to slaughter people, not only in the war with St. George, but to silence anyone who wasn't loyal to the organization. They expected me to take out my own kind, rogues like Riley, if they ordered it."

I nodded, remembering an earlier conversation with Riley, how he'd said not all dragons wanted to be a part of Talon. And while he hadn't actually come out and said what happened to the rogues who left the organization, it had been strongly implied. Suspicion rose up, mingling with the guilt. Before this summer, it had never occurred to me that there were dragons who rejected Talon's ambitions, who wanted to be free of the organization. Dragons like Riley and Ember. Rogues hunted by their own.

I wondered how much St. George really knew about their ancient enemies. Were they truly ignorant of the rogues and the dragons outside of Talon? Or did our superiors choose to hide certain things from the rest of us?

"My old trainer, she was teaching me to be just like her," Ember continued, interrupting my dark thoughts. "Ruthless and completely unmerciful. Someone who would kill a defenseless hatchling in cold blood if Talon gave the word. She wanted me to strike fast and never question why, to execute people without thinking about it. She wanted me to become a killer." A shudder racked her body, and she gripped the railing, her voice a low rasp. "And now, I am."

I moved beside her and rested an arm on the railing. She didn't look at me, continuing to gaze at the streets below. Her posture was stiff, but I saw the grief, the helpless anger, the fear that she was becoming what she hated. The Perfect Soldier scoffed in disgust; this was a war. It was either kill or be killed. Pull the trigger before your enemy did, that was the only way to survive.

Before Crescent Beach, I would've agreed. Second-guessing yourself was dangerous. I had killed because the Order told me to, and I hadn't thought twice about it. But this summer, I'd met a daring, cheerful, fiery dragon girl who had turned my world upside down. Who showed me things I'd never seen, imagined or experienced. And it might've been selfish, dangerous even, considering where we were now, but I didn't want her to ever change.

"I know about the Vipers," I said, which made Ember glance at me sharply, perhaps surprised that I knew the name of Talon's infamous assassins. "I know what they do. I've seen what they're capable of."

"You have?" She blinked rapidly, her voice surprised and a little awed. "I mean, you actually saw one? And...lived?"

I gave a solemn nod. "Yes, but everyone in the Order has

seen this particular Viper," I said. "Not firsthand," I added quickly, as her eyes got huge. "No one who was there that night survived. But we've all seen the footage. It's from a security camera the Order managed to recover from the area. They make us watch it as part of our training. To fully realize what we're dealing with."

Ember wrinkled her nose. "That's morbid."

"Yes." I paused, remembering the fuzzy, black-and-white images: a warehouse aisle, a flickering overhead light, four soldiers creeping forward with guns raised. A blur of shadow as something dropped from the ceiling, into their midst. Screams. Gunfire. The light swinging wildly back and forth.

And then silence, as the lamp swayed over a blood-streaked floor and the sprawl of blackened, shredded bodies, the killer nowhere to be found. "They didn't have a chance," I said, remembering the horror I'd felt when I first saw the footage. I was eleven years old, and for weeks afterward, I couldn't walk into a dark room without scouring the ceiling for dragons. "There was no hesitation on the Viper's part. It knew exactly what it was doing."

Ember was still watching me as if she could see the scene play out in my eyes. "That dragon from the video," I went on, my voice just a breath between us, "the assassin, the killer… you're not like that, Ember." I paused, then said, very softly, "You're not like *any* dragon I've seen before."

"What am I, then?" she whispered.

My heart was pounding again. Slowly, I reached for her arm, turning her to face me. If she stiffened or pulled back in disgust, I would let her go. But her gaze rose to mine, direct and unafraid, and my breath caught.

"You're the girl who taught me to surf," I said, holding her stare. "And shoot zombies. And dance. And to never make you angry, even in human form, or risk being kicked where the sun don't shine." She snorted, not quite smiling, but her eyes lightened a shade at the memory. I smiled and eased closer, feeling the heat pulse between us, even in the stifling Vegas air.

"You're the dragon who chose not to kill a soldier of St. George when you had the chance," I went on in a softer voice. "You risked your life to break into a compound full of enemies who would slaughter you on sight, to rescue someone you should hate." Unbidden, my other hand rose, brushing a fiery strand of hair from her eyes, and she shivered. "I don't know what that makes you, exactly, but from where I'm standing, I'd say it's pretty amazing."

Her eyes gleamed, and a smile finally tugged at the corners of her mouth. "Okay, now I *am* worried," she murmured in a teasing voice. "Who is this smooth-talking, nonuptight normal person and what did you do with the real Garret?"

I shrugged. "I've been told I need to loosen up," I said, and kissed her.

She made a tiny noise of surprise, and then her hands were in my hair, holding me close, and my arms were around her waist, pressing us together. I closed my eyes, feeling my stomach twist, feeling her lips against mine, eager and insistent, her arms wrapping around my neck. She tugged on my bottom lip, and a groan escaped me as I let her in, clutching her tighter. There was no disgust. No regret. I stood on this roof, openly kissing a girl who was really a dragon, and I wasn't sorry at all.

"Ember!"

The shout cut through the quiet, and my nerves leaped in warning. I jerked back to see the rogue dragon striding across the roof toward us, a murderous gleam in his eyes.

RILEY

I'm going to kill her.

I stood in the center of the casino floor, surrounded by surging, babbling, oblivious mortals, and tried to ignore the temptation to turn the whole place into an inferno. Where was she? I'd already gone upstairs and pounded on the door to her room but, as Wes had said, she was gone. She and the soldier both. I'd called the throwaway phone Wes had given her and had been sent to voice mail both times, which meant she had either left it in her room or was deliberately ignoring me.

The urge to blast something to a smoldering ash pile grew stronger, and I started moving again, scanning the throngs for bright red hair and green eyes. Normally, Ember was impossible to miss, even in a crowd. But a Vegas casino, with its blinking lights, aimlessly wandering humans and deliberately confusing floor plans, was one of the worst places to pick someone out of a crowd. That was why we'd come here, to hide from Talon and the Order, but now that ploy was working against me. Which was ironic, annoying as hell and doing a great job of pissing me off.

Dammit, Ember. Where are you?

With a growl, I circled the casino once more before heading upstairs. I didn't have time for this. I had to get to that abandoned hotel to look for runaway hatchlings before St. George got wind of them. For every minute I wasted here, the Order could be drawing closer. There didn't seem to be any St. George activity around the casino, so I doubted Ember and the soldier were in trouble. I suspected the defiant red hatchling had gotten bored and had either bullied or convinced the human to come with her. That she was missing annoyed me. That she was missing and alone with the soldier pushed me a little closer to murderous rage, which I knew was unreasonable. She wasn't mine. I didn't want this attachment, despite every instinct telling me otherwise. I had more important things to focus on; my hatchlings, my underground, keeping everyone in my network safe from Talon and St. George. Wes was right; ever since Ember had come into my life, I'd been distracted. There was something about the fiery red dragon that I couldn't ignore, and that was stupid and dangerous and could very well get us all killed, but I couldn't help it. Like it or not, Ember had buried her claws in deep, and I was either going to have to accept it and give in, or find a way to live with it, because I'd be damned if I pushed her away now.

After searching the casino, the restaurants and the myriad stores with no success, I finally made my way to the roof. There were a couple humans floating around a brightly lit pool, but no Ember. I circled the edge and made my way toward the far wall, where the tops of the Vegas skyscrapers loomed against the night sky.

And there they were, both of them, by the railing. I saw

Ember mutter something, her eyes downcast, saw the soldier turn her to face him. He said something that made her smile…

…and then he kissed her.

Something inside me snapped. My dragon gave a shriek of outrage and reared up, filling me with fire and hatred, tinting everything with a red haze. I felt myself moving across the roof, heard myself shout something just before I reached them. The soldier glanced up, and I threw a savage right hook at his face.

He dodged, jerking his head back, my fist missing him by inches. Ember yelped in shock. St. George swiftly backed away and raised his fists, a clear invitation to fight, and the dragon roared acceptance.

Snarling, I tensed to lunge, but before I could go for him again, something grabbed my arm from behind.

"Riley, what the hell are you doing? Stop!"

I seethed, wanting to attack, to Shift to my true form and rend the human to little pieces, then char those pieces to ash. My dragon howled, violent and enraged, wanting to set something on fire. The soldier was now too far away, and on guard for an attack. I turned my anger on Ember, instead.

"What am *I* doing?" Spinning around, I yanked my arm from her grasp and glared down furiously. "What the hell are you doing, Firebrand? I leave for an hour, *one* hour, and come back to find you…" My voice caught on the words, and I curled my lip in disgust. "He's a human," I spat. "And not only that, a soldier of St. George. A dragon killer! I thought you were done with this idiocy when we left Crescent Beach."

Her eyes flashed, and she lifted her chin to face me. "You have no right, Riley—"

"You're a *dragon*," I interrupted, making her scowl. "Have you forgotten that part? Never mind that he was part of St. George. Let's ignore the fact that he's killed who knows how many dragons before his miraculous change of heart. Let's not ask how many hatchlings he's shot in the back, while they were running away." I sneered at the human before turning on Ember again. She stared me down, defiant; I growled and turned us away from the soldier, lowering my voice.

"Listen to me, Firebrand," I said, attempting to calm my anger, though my dragon still raged up and down my veins, wanting retribution. "You're not thinking straight. He's a human, with a human life span. How long do you think he's going to stick around? Where do you think you'll be sixty years from now? A hundred years from now? Have you even thought about that?"

"Of course not!" Ember snarled. "Right now I'm still trying to keep up with the present. Right now, staying alive and getting Dante out of Talon is keeping me pretty occupied. What about you?" Ember challenged, glaring up at me. "Have *you* thought about the future at all?"

"Every single day," I retorted, making her blink. "Every day, I wake up thinking about my safe houses, if they're secure, if the hatchlings I get out of Talon will survive another year. What will happen to them if *I* bite the dust, because I don't know how long I can keep getting lucky. But this isn't about me." I shot another glance at the human, wondering if he could hear us, then deciding I didn't care if he did. "Humans and dragons aren't supposed to be together," I insisted. "Their lives are a heartbeat compared to ours. What kind of future do you think you could ever have?"

Her eyes narrowed. "Don't give me that, Riley," she growled. "That's BS. Admit it—you don't want me with Garret because he was part of St. George."

I ground my teeth at her stubbornness. "I have *no* problem admitting that, Firebrand," I snarled. "What I don't understand is how you can let that murdering dragon killer anywhere near you without wanting to rip his head off!"

"Hey." The soldier had come forward again, eyes narrowed, his body tense and ready for a fight. "Leave her alone," he said evenly, as I gave him a dangerous look. "It's not her fault. I started this. Take it up with me if you have a problem."

I would love to, St. George, I thought viciously, but Ember beat me to it.

"Don't, Garret," she snapped, and I didn't know if the anger in her voice was directed at me, the soldier or us both. "I'm not afraid of jealous rogue dragons, and you don't have to step in front of him for me." She turned from the human then, looking me right in the eye. "I can take care of myself."

Jealous? I took a deep, cooling breath and stepped back, shaking my head at them both. "I don't have time for this," I said, which was true. The runaway hatchlings were still a question, and I'd wasted enough time already. "I'm supposed to be somewhere else right now," I went on, "and I'm done talking to the pair of you. Might as well beat my head against a wall."

"You're leaving?" Ember narrowed her eyes. "Again? Where are you going this time?"

"Out," I retorted, feeling mulish and immature. "Somewhere important, if you have to know." Her expression darkened, and I knew she was on the verge of demanding to come along. I took a step back. "Come or stay," I growled, "it makes no difference to me. I'm done here."

I spun on a heel, then strode across the roof without looking back. I heard them start after me, and controlled the urge to spin back around and lay the soldier flat on his back. It was my dragon talking, but what troubled me wasn't the anger, or the disgust, that Ember had forgotten everything St. George had done. She was still young. She didn't know the Order like I did, hadn't seen the true face of St. George, not yet.

No, what bothered me most was that, even after everything, my fiery red hatchling had still chosen the human... instead of me.

DANTE

The meeting room was frigid.

I didn't like the cold. Maybe it was growing up in deserts and sunny beach communities, where much of my free time was spent outside. I liked the feel of the sun on my skin, the heat blazing down on me, seeping into my bones. I didn't know what it was with Talon's executives, but all their office buildings had the AC cranked up so high you could almost see your breath. Even in Reign's opulent hotel, where the carpets were thick and gold and the leather chairs probably cost over a thousand dollars each, it was still cold enough to make my skin prickle. It certainly wasn't my place to tell Talon how to run things, but a few degrees of warmth would make things less uncomfortable. I hoped I could get through this without my teeth clacking together. I was already nervous enough.

Beside me, Mr. Smith leaned back and rested a foot on his knee, looking perfectly comfortable and at ease. As if reading my thoughts, my trainer shot me a glance, dark eyes appraising. "Breathe, Dante," he ordered. "It's a good plan. It will work."

I smiled. "I know it will."

"Good." Mr. Smith narrowed his gaze. "Don't *hope*. Know.

Hope will not bring your sister back. Hope will not impress Mr. Roth, or anyone in the organization. You must be confident of this plan, you must believe that it will work, otherwise you have wasted everyone's time."

"I'm aware of that, sir," I replied, still smiling. "And Ember will return to the organization before the night is out, I swear it."

Mr. Smith nodded and turned away, breaking eye contact as the door opened and Mr. Roth entered, followed by two more dragons. One, a slender man with slick dark hair and a goatee, I didn't recognize. He took a seat across from me and nodded, and I ducked my head in respect, but it was the second dragon that caught my attention. Lilith seated herself beside him, crossing long legs beneath the table, and smiled at me.

"I'm looking forward to seeing your plan in action, Mr. Hill," she said.

Her words were almost a threat. As if she, too, needed this plan to succeed, and there would be terrible repercussions if it did not. My blood chilled, but at that moment, Mr. Roth took the seat at the head of the table, facing us all.

"It is almost time," he stated, glancing at his watch. "Mr. Hill, have your agents contacted you?"

I breathed deep and nodded, putting my phone on the table in front of me. "Yes, sir. Everything has been set up. They're ready to move forward with the mission."

"Excellent." Mr. Roth leaned back, watching me with those cold dark eyes. "Then all we have to do now is wait. I look forward to seeing your success, Mr. Hill. Good luck."

I swallowed, glancing at the phone lying innocently on the

table, and my heart began pounding against my will. *Ember,* I thought, staring at the device as if I could sense her on the other side. *Please, don't do anything stupid. This is your last chance to choose the right thing.*

Folding my hands on the table, I waited for the phone to ring.

PART III

Leap of Faith

EMBER

You could cut the tension in the cab with a knife and serve it on a plate.

No one, of course, wanted to sit up front. Riley refused to have me and Garret in the back by ourselves, Garret wouldn't leave me alone with Riley, and I certainly wasn't going to sit up front so the boys could murder each other in the back-seat. So we sat there, the three of us, myself in the middle, Garret and Riley flanking me on either side. And the silence was deafening.

Riley still looked murderous. He didn't look at me or Garret, but stared out the window, one arm on the sill. I could feel his anger radiating from every part of him, as if the dragon hissed and raged just below the surface. It prodded at my own dragon, riling her up, making me twitchy and restless. I felt guilty, and at the same time, I was angry about feeling guilty. Riley was way out of line; we hadn't done anything wrong. But his words still echoed in my mind, harsh and accusing, as if I'd betrayed not only him, but my entire race.

How long do you think he's going to stick around? Where do you think you'll be sixty years from now? A hundred years from now? Have you even thought about that?

He was being unreasonable. Of course I wasn't thinking about the future; what sixteen-year-old—of *any* species—did that? I hadn't been trying to piss Riley off tonight. I was just feeling bored, guilty, homesick and frankly pretty miserable, and somehow, Garret could bring me out of it. He made me forget the bad things for a while, just like he had in Crescent Beach. When I was with him, I could almost pretend I was normal.

My dragon snarled at me, disgusted. *You're not normal,* she whispered, an insidious worm in my brain. *You're not human, and the soldier won't be here forever. Riley will.*

A slight brush against my leg jolted me out of my dark thoughts. I peeked over and met Garret's eyes, worried and questioning, red neon lights washing over his face. His hand lay between us, the back of his knuckles resting against my jeans. A warm glow spread through my stomach and I gave him a furtive smile, even as my dragon recoiled with a hiss.

The cab took us away from the main flow of traffic, moving away from the Strip and the glittering behemoths on either side of the street. We drove for several more silent minutes, going deeper into the fringe neighborhoods, until the taxi pulled up to a curb seemingly in the middle of nowhere and lurched to a stop. A tall chain-link fence ran the length of the sidewalk, and beyond the metal barrier, a flat expanse of nothing stretched away into the darkness.

Riley shoved a bill into the driver's palm and exited the cab without speaking. Garret and I followed, and the taxi sped off. Leaving us on a deserted sidewalk many blocks from the lights and crowds of the Strip.

"What is this place?" I asked, peering through the fence.

There were no lights, no roads or even pavement. The ground was dusty and flat, an odd field of dirt surrounded by concrete. Though in the distance, I could see the uneven, skeletal outline of some huge structure hiding in the shadows.

"It's a hotel," Riley said brusquely, shoving his wallet into his back pocket again. "Started but never finished due to the recession, most likely. It's abandoned now."

"Why are we here?" Garret added, observing the area with a wary, practiced eye. The paranoia had returned; he was a soldier once more, and every shadow could hide a possible threat.

Riley gave him a cold look, as if debating whether to explain or not, then shrugged. "I got word of a couple runaways tonight," he said, making my stomach leap to my throat. "Possibly mine. They're supposed to be here, somewhere, hiding from Talon. I figured with all the St. George activity in the city, I'd better get to them first. Before the Order shows up and blows them to pieces."

Garret frowned. "You didn't think it important to tell us *before* we left the hotel?"

"I don't owe you any explanations, St. George," Riley said. "You're not here because I need you to be. We're going in, grabbing a couple hatchlings and getting out as fast as we can. If that flies in the face of your dragonslayer convictions, feel free to take the next cab back to the hotel. No one here is stopping you."

I bristled at Riley's assholey-ness, but Garret's voice was calm when he answered. "This could be a drug den," he said. "Or a gang hideout. At the very least, there will be homeless people and squatters wandering around. If we're going to extract two dragons without opposition, one or more of us should be armed."

Riley snorted. "Against a bunch of humans? What are they going to do, babble me to death?"

"They could have weapons."

"Then we'll be really careful and not attract attention," Riley snapped. "I didn't have time to grab anything, thanks to your and Ember's little disappearing act, and I didn't want to risk carrying a duffel bag of guns through the casino. So no, we don't have any weapons this time. Get used to the idea."

"And the Order?"

"Wes is hacked into a couple traffic cams around the block," Riley answered, making a vague gesture at the street. "He'll let me know if there's trouble. Don't worry, St. George." He gave Garret a cold smile. "I've got it all figured out."

Before either of us could protest further, he turned and leaped gracefully to the top of the fence, then dropped noiselessly to the other side. Without a word, he spun and strode away into the darkness. Garret and I exchanged a glance and then hurried after him.

It was eerie, being on this side of the fence. My shoes raised small poofs of dust as we walked. Stacks of rotting wood, iron and huge cement tubes were scattered about the barren landscape, like modern skeletons in the dirt. There were no signs of life. Even the eternal sound of traffic faded, red taillights becoming distant mirages, leaving us in a bubble of darkness.

The entrance of the hotel loomed ahead, the strangely elegant front marred by a crown of jagged beams and unfinished upper floors. Again, I was struck by the eerie silence as we approached the shattered lobby doors and stepped carefully over the threshold into the darkness of the dead hotel.

The first thing I noticed was the heat. The second was the smell. The air through the doors was hot and stale, and reeked of piss, sweat, puke and general human disgustingness. I gagged and pressed closer to Garret. Who, of course, seemed unfazed by it all. Damn soldier unflappability. Riley, clicking on a small flashlight, wrinkled his nose, then turned to us.

"Stay close." His voice, though soft, echoed in the emptiness of the lobby. "Looks like there are people here after all."

"Ya think?"

There was a shuffle in the darkness, and Riley swept the flashlight around, pinning a thin, almost skeletal figure in the glare. A woman, her shirt nearly falling off her bony shoulders, gave us a glassy, deer-in-headlights stare before shambling away. My skin crawled, and I crossed my arms to hide my fear.

"Oh, that's great," I whispered, as the shuffling footsteps faded away in the darkness. "We're in a zombie movie. I swear, if I see any walking dead, I don't care who's around—they're all getting a fireball between the eyes."

Riley gave an amused snort, as if he couldn't help himself, and eased forward, sweeping the beam around the barren lobby. "Try not to burn down the hotel, Firebrand," he warned, as the light slid over the front desk, which was covered in several layers of dust and cobwebs. "This place is a tinderbox. One spark, and it's likely to explode." Something small and furry darted across the floor and vanished into a crack in the wall. Riley shook his head. "Actually, that might not be a bad thing, but if an abandoned, multimillion-dollar hotel suddenly goes up in smoke, it'll tell Talon and the Order exactly where we are. So no fireballs."

"Oh, fine," I whispered back, as we ventured farther into the hotel, following a wall as it curved away into the dark. "That's okay. If we are attacked by zombies, I don't have to run fast. I just have to run faster than you."

Garret's hand suddenly closed on my arm in a grip of steel, pulling me to a stop. At the same time, Riley froze. I looked past the thin beam of light from Riley's hand and tensed.

We'd reached the edge of what was probably the casino floor, had the hotel been finished. The room beyond was large and open; I could see the aisles of carpet where slot machines would go, the long strips for blackjack tables. Though the space was vast, it was even hotter here than in the lobby, and the smell was so bad it nearly knocked me down. I didn't know how anyone could stand it, but the small clusters of ragged, unwashed people scattered about the room didn't seem to notice.

A few yards away, a trio of humans sat huddled on a stained, threadbare mattress, giggling as they passed something small and bright between them. The glow of a lantern washed over their slack, pale faces and staring eyes. Nearby, another human glanced up from where he sat on an ancient sofa between two human girls. The girls stared at us, expressions slack and far away, but the guy's face hardened and he rose quickly.

"This ain't a public party, friends," he said with a menace-filled smile. He was tall and lanky, his torn jeans just barely clinging to narrow hip bones. A filthy red hoodie covered his head, even in the heat, and his eyes were bulging and eager. "I think you're a little lost. That's too bad, ain't it?"

Riley crossed his arms. "You mean this isn't the Palazzo?" he said, his voice echoing through the bare beams overhead. "Well, don't I feel silly. Especially since I blew all my cash on the penny slots." His voice changed, becoming slightly more ominous. "I don't suppose we can skip the pleasantries and get to the part where we walk through unmolested?"

The human snapped his fingers, and a trio of equally thin, ragged guys uncurled from the floor and shuffled forward to flank him. A knife suddenly gleamed between long dirty fingers as he raised his arm, and I went rigid. "Gimme your wallet," the junkie demanded. Garret tensed and stepped in front of me, his body like a taut wire. "And your phone. And whatever cash you have. Put it on the ground, and step away. Them, too," he added, jerking his head at me and Garret. "Jewelry, purses, whatever. Leave everything you have on the floor, and you can walk out still breathing."

Riley sighed. Raising his hands like he was thinking it over, he took a half step back, standing next to Garret. "How many?" he murmured in a voice almost too soft to hear. I frowned in confusion, but apparently, the query wasn't directed at me.

"Three here, another two on the wall behind us," Garret replied in an equally quiet voice.

"Armed?"

"No."

"Good. I'll let you take care of them. Firebrand, watch your back."

"Hey." The junkie leader stepped forward, raising the knife. "Didn't you hear me? Gimme your stuff, man, or I'll start cutting off body parts."

"I told you, I don't have anything," Riley insisted, lifting his arms in a placating gesture. "We came for the weekend and are now completely broke. I'm sure you hear that a lot here."

"Phones, then." The human turned and brandished the knife at Garret. "Gimme your phones."

"Sorry." Garret gave a helpless shrug. "Dropped it in the pool."

The junkie's gaze shifted to me, and I smirked at him. "Left mine in the cab."

"Rotten luck, huh?" Riley added.

"Man, do not fuck with me!" The junkie stepped forward, jabbing the blade at Riley's face. "Do you *want* me to gut you like a pig? Is that—"

Garret's hand shot out, grabbed the hand with the knife and wrenched it sideways, making the junkie yelp with shock and pain. His cry was cut short as the soldier moved in with a savage elbow to his temple, dropping him like a sack of stones. Before the others even registered what was happening, Riley lunged and drove a fist into one's jaw, snapping his head to the side. The junkie reeled away, toppled over the sofa to the shrieks of the two girls and lay still.

Something moved in the corner of my eye. I spun, dodged the arm grabbing for me and kicked the human's knee out as he passed, making the junkie crash to the floor. Garret blocked a fist from the second one and responded with a nasty right hook that rocked his opponent sideways. A third charged in, swinging a length of rebar, and my heart leaped to my throat. Garret ducked under the first swing and got out of the way, as Riley whirled around and smashed a fist into the human's jaw. He reeled back into Garret, who grabbed his wrist, twisted the rebar from his hand and swept his feet out from under him. As the human hit the ground on his back, Garret tossed the rebar to Riley, who turned and whacked a junkie across the temple, sending him crashing into a pillar.

As I grinned, watching the unconscious display of team-work, something grabbed me from behind and pinned my arms to my sides. Another junkie, reeking of smoke and body odor, tried to lift me off my feet and drag me away. I snarled and jerked my head back, cracking my skull into his nose. He yelped and released me, but threw a hard backhand at my face as I spun to face him. I dodged, but it clipped my cheek all the same. Pain flared across my eyes, and the dragon surged up with a roar of outrage. As the human groped for me again, I brought my foot up and kicked him between the legs as hard as I could.

His eyes bulged, and he staggered, mouth gaping. I kicked him once more for good measure, then shoved him back. He collapsed in a groaning heap on the floor, knees drawn to his chest, and didn't get up.

I curled a lip at him, then turned to find Riley and Garret. They stood back-to-back, surrounded by cringing, writhing junkies, while the rest of the den looked on from a safe dis-tance away. Riley held the length of pipe casually at his side as he gazed around the room, grinning. Garret hovered be-hind him in a ready stance, protecting his flank, scanning the area for threats.

"Anyone else?" he asked calmly.

No one came forward. The junkies on the floor crawled to their feet and staggered away, and the remaining humans suddenly seemed very interested in other things. Riley snorted, tossed the rebar away with a clank and looked around for me.

"Hey, Firebrand," he said as I walked up. "Sorry I couldn't get over to help. You okay?"

I shrugged. "Don't worry about me. Feel sorry for the guy who tried to slap me."

Garret, stepping out from behind Riley, gave me a faint smile. "I notice you managed to kick him in your favorite spot," he observed.

"Twice."

Riley winced, then looked at Garret. The other boy regarded him coolly, and Riley smirked. "See, St. George? We don't need guns. You're actually fairly competent at disabling people without them."

"I'll keep that in mind," Garret said drily, "the next time we face a dozen soldiers with assault rifles."

Riley shook his head. "Hopefully not tonight," he muttered, and turned away, observing the room once more. "So now the question is, how do we find two scared runaways in this mess?"

Soft footsteps interrupted us. I glanced over to see a skinny, zombielike figure shambling toward us from the shadows.

RILEY

The human edged into the light, shoulders hunched, watching us like a stray dog who wasn't certain if you would toss it food or kick it. A woman, I saw as she got close. As humans went, she might have been pretty once, maybe even gorgeous. But her blond hair was lank and stringy now, her skin pale and wasted, glassy blue eyes sunk into her face. She looked like a bony marionette as she eased forward and stopped just out of reach, the hollow expression and thousand-yard stare making my dragon stir restlessly.

"Angels," she whispered.

I frowned. My adrenaline was up; the fight had made me edgy and restless. I was not in the mood for this. "What?"

"The angels," she murmured again, and I saw she had only a few teeth left in her head. "The ones you want. The one's you're looking for. The pretty ones." One hand rose like a limp fish and pointed behind her. I squinted across the floor. A door sat against the far wall, barely visible in the shadows, looking like the entrance to a stairwell. "Near the sky," she whispered, as if in a daze. "The angels. They have to be near the sky."

"Upstairs?" Ember asked, but the human turned and shuffled back into the darkness, muttering to herself. I listened to her footsteps fade away, listened to her babble softly to herself, until the sounds were swallowed by the blackness, leaving us alone.

"Crazy humans," I muttered, and resisted the urge to brush imaginary loony off my jacket. "Well, at least we know where we're going."

Sick-looking, emaciated people gave us blank stares as we crossed the open floor, giggling uncontrollably, or talking to themselves in hushed voices. No one tried to stop or harass us again, except for some crazy old guy who grinned and made a lewd comment to Ember. She whirled on him, bristling. The soldier quickly grabbed her, stopping her midlunge and halting whatever she was planning to do, which was probably kick the old codger in his withered jewels. I snickered, almost sorry he'd stopped her, but by that time, we had reached the other side of the room and I pushed open the door.

A wave of dry, stale heat billowed through the opening, and a rusted metal staircase ascended into utter darkness.

"How far do you think we should go?" Ember asked once we had all stepped through the door, crowding the bottom of the stairs. It was even hotter here than the casino. My hair stuck to my neck, and even though I didn't mind the heat, I could feel sweat running down my back through my shirt.

"All the way," I answered, shining the light up the tube. "As far as we can."

So we climbed. Up several flights in blistering, oven-like temperatures, Ember and the soldier trailing behind me. We met no one else; it was just our footsteps echoing up the shaft. I assumed the heat and utter darkness kept most junkies out of the stairwell at night, though the tube still reeked of piss and garbage and other things.

And then, quite suddenly, we couldn't go any farther. The stairwell ended at another simple metal door that creaked as I pushed it back, shining the light through the opening.

We'd reached the end of the hotel's construction. Beyond the door, half walls and rotting wooden frames created a labyrinth of metal and iron. Carefully, we eased inside, brushing aside ragged plastic sheets that hung everywhere, fluttering in the hot wind. I glanced up, and saw that the roof was open to the sky, though it was impossible to see the stars through the haze of the city. I could breathe easier, though, just being this close without the stink of human filth and craziness clogging my nose. If I were two runaway hatchlings, this was where I would go.

"What are we looking for?" St. George asked as we maneuvered our way across the floor. The wood groaned under our feet, and I stepped lightly over beams and rusty metal screws. Hopefully nothing would give way beneath us; the floor looked pretty rotten.

"Two kids," I told him. "Hatchlings. Probably no older than either of you." I brushed aside a sheet and ducked under a low-hanging beam, poking the light into dark corners. "If you find either of them, let me handle it. They're going to be terrified of strangers, of anyone who could be from Talon. I don't want them running off before I—"

Something lunged from around the corner, swinging a metal pipe at my face.

I jerked back. The pipe missed crushing my skull by about an inch but hit my arm instead, knocking the flashlight from my grasp. It went spinning across the floor in dizzying circles, as the attacker raised the weapon and came at me again.

"Wait!" I dodged and backed swiftly away, ducking around a beam. The pipe smacked into the wood a microsecond later, raising a hollow thud and a billow of dust. "Wait just a second," I said as my attacker followed me around the beam, holding the pipe like a baseball bat. It swung at me again, and I dodged out of the way. "Will you relax? I'm not here to hurt you. Just listen to me."

The others started forward, and I gave them a sharp look. "Don't move!" I snapped, and thankfully, they froze. "Stay right there, both of you," I insisted, holding out an arm, the universal gesture of *let's all calm the fuck down*. "Everyone relax."

The person with the pipe hesitated, shooting fearful looks between the three of us. A girl, I realized. Lithe and graceful, even as dirty as she was, with big blue eyes and silver-blond hair to the middle of her back. She wore a ratty T-shirt and baggy cargo jeans, and looked like she had slept in them for a while.

And she was definitely a hatchling, a teenager in human form. A little older than the ones I normally saw, wide-eyed and fresh out of training, but a hatchling nonetheless. The tightness in my chest eased a little, and I let out a furtive breath of relief. We'd found her before the Order did. That was all that mattered.

Panting, the girl backed up, still holding the pipe out in front of her. "Who are you?" she asked in a trembling voice. "What do you want?" Her voice, though it shook with fear, was low and cool, her words clear. Raising the pipe again, she gave us a fierce look. "I swear, I am not going back."

"Easy." I edged forward with one hand still outstretched, keeping my movements slow and unthreatening. "Take it easy," I said again. "You're safe. We're not from Talon."

She eyed me warily but visibly relaxed. The weapon hovered between us, dropping a few inches, but didn't lower completely. "If you're not from Talon, who are you?" the girl demanded. "How did you know about this place?"

"My name is Cobalt." I offered my real name without hesitation. More people knew Cobalt, who he was and what he'd done. And even if this girl didn't, Cobalt was a dragon name, subtly reminding her that we were alike. "And I'm sort of in the business of finding people like you. People who want out. I can help," I went on, easing forward again. "I can take you somewhere safe, someplace Talon won't be able to find you. But you have to trust me."

This time, the weapon dropped swiftly, and the girl stared at me with wide, stunned eyes. "You're Cobalt," she whispered, and all the tension left her, replaced with relief. The pipe fell from her fingers with a clank and rolled across the floor, but she didn't give it a second glance. "You're really here," she whispered, grabbing a beam as if to steady herself. "We heard you might be in the city, but we had no way to contact you."

I stared at her in surprise. "You were looking for me?"

She nodded. Taking a deep breath, she seemed to regain her composure. "Sorry about before. I'm Ava. A friend and I escaped the organization maybe two weeks ago. There were rumors that you were in Las Vegas, and we heard that you could help those who got out of Talon, so we came here to find you. But we had to hide as soon as we arrived in the city. St. George…"

I nodded. "You mentioned a friend," I said, hoping the worst had not happened, that St. George had not already found them. "Are they still alive?"

Ava nodded. "Yes, she's here. One moment." She walked a few steps to peer around a wall. "It's okay," she called into the shadows. "You can come out. They're not from Talon." She gave a short, breathless laugh, as if she couldn't believe what she was saying. "It's actually *Cobalt*, of all the lucky breaks."

"Cobalt?"

Another hatchling emerged around the corner, edging shyly into view. She was shorter than Ava by several inches and looked even younger than Ember. Her skin was pale, almost porcelain colored, and a mass of jet-black curls tumbled down her back and shoulders. Enormous dark eyes peered out at us with a mix of curiosity and fear.

"This is Faith," Ava introduced, holding out her hand to the other girl. Faith blinked as she came forward, pressing close to the other hatchling. Ava put a protective arm around her, though she still spoke to me. "The day before she completed assimilation, she discovered that Talon was going to send her to 'the facility,' because she was unsuitable to be a Chameleon, which is what they had originally planned for her."

I clenched my jaw, trying not to let the rage show. "The facility" was Talon's term for the place they sent dragonells to become breeder females, whose only job was to produce eggs for the rest of their life. Talon liked to start their breeder females young, because, like everything else in a dragon's life, producing offspring took a long time. Nearly two years to lay the egg after the dragonell had been mated, and another year for the egg to hatch. When I'd still been part of Talon, there had been dark rumors circling the organization that the number of fertile eggs was in sharp decline. An alarming one in three eggs simply never hatched, and no one could figure out why. What happened to the "dud" eggs was also a mystery; they disappeared, sent off to places unknown. I didn't know what the real story was, or where the eggs vanished to, but one of my bigger goals was to find the facility, free all the dragonells there and burn the place to the ground.

Later, I told myself, as rage heated my lungs, making the air taste like smoke. *Someday, you'll be able to save them all, but not tonight. Don't get distracted.*

"How did you know about me?" I asked the hatchlings.

"Everyone in the organization knows about you," Ava said. "The executives try to deny it, but we've all heard rumors of a rogue dragon who helps those wanting to leave Talon. You just have to find him—or hope that he finds you—before the Vipers catch up."

Ember blinked. "Wow, look at that," she said, grinning at me. "You're famous, or at least infamous. A real-life Robin Hood."

I stifled the urge to rub my eyes. My defiant little Firebrand might think it was great news, sticking it to the organization, but I did not want that much attention from Talon. That they talked about me meant they were thinking about me, which was never a good thing. I'd always been careful to lie low, especially after getting a hatchling out. We'd survived this long because I knew how to disappear, to vanish into obscurity without a trace. Talon was far too big to challenge head-on. As much as I hated them and would love to see them brought down, I knew that my tiny, ragtag underground could never stand against the massive force that was Talon. Right now, I was an annoyance at best. I did not want to reach the point where the organization brought its full might against me and my network, because we likely would not survive.

Faith's dark gaze abruptly shifted to my companions. "Who are they?" she whispered.

"I'm Ember." Ember stepped forward before I could say anything. "I just got out of Talon, too. You can trust Riley, uh...Cobalt. He knows what he's doing. He'll keep you away from them."

Faith blinked. "What about him?" she asked, glancing at the soldier standing a little behind us. "He's not a dragon. Why is he here?"

Ember stiffened, and I quickly jumped in. "He's all right," I said smoothly, and ignored Ember's raised eyebrow. "You can trust him. He's here to help." I nearly choked on the words, but getting the hatchlings to trust us was more important than the truth now. I couldn't have them freaking out if they discovered what he really was. The soldier's expression remained neutral in the face of such blatant lies, and Faith finally seemed to relax.

I turned to Ava. "Are you two ready to go?" I asked. The night was fading quickly, and I was uncomfortable standing out in the open like this. Once we got back to the safety of the hotel, I'd figure out what we were going to do. "You'll have to stay with us for a bit, until we can leave the city. But after that, I'll find a safe place for you both."

She nodded tiredly. "Yes, please. Anywhere is better than here, waiting for Talon or St. George to catch up."

"No arguments there."

The phone buzzed in my jeans pocket, making me jump, then whisper a curse. There was only one person would call me now. For one reason.

No. Not now. With dread blooming through my stomach, I put the phone to my ear and snapped, "Wes. Tell me you're not going to say what I think you're—"

His hissed words interrupted me. I listened to the frantic voice on the other end, lowered the phone and turned to Ember and the soldier.

"They're here."

GARRET

"The Order?"

The rogue glared at me, anger and loathing crossing his face, as if I had summoned my former brothers here with my presence alone. "What do you think?" he spat. "Of course it's the Order. They always seem to appear these days, like magic, wherever we are." He shoved the phone in his jacket and raked both hands through his hair. "Dammit, of all the crappy timing. How the hell do they keep finding us?"

It was immature and vindictive, but I couldn't help it. "*Now* do we need guns?"

"St. George?" The dark-haired girl, Faith, shrank back, her eyes huge and terrified. "The Order is here?" Her gaze darted to the entrance of the stairwell, as if armed soldiers could burst through at any time, then flickered to the edge of the building. "We have to fly," she whispered, edging away from the other girl, toward the sudden sheer drop at the end of the floor. "They'll kill us if we don't—"

"No!" Riley whirled around. "No flying. We don't know where St. George is, or what they have out there. They could be watching the building right now, waiting for us."

"I'll risk it." The girl stopped, but looked on the verge of panic. "It's the Order! We have to fly. It's better than dying."

"Faith, stop." I didn't dare step forward, lest I scare her into plunging off the roof right then. "Listen to me. That's what they want. This is one of their tactics, send in the ground team to force the targets into the air. Like hunting quail." She blinked at me, glassy-eyed with fear. I wondered if any of this was getting through to her. "There's probably a team of snipers scanning the roof right now," I continued, gesturing to the buildings around us. "If you fly, they'll shoot you down—"

The whirl of helicopter blades interrupted me, a guttural whine in the silence. Faith flinched, her gaze going to the sky, but Ember darted forward, grabbed her around the waist and yanked her back...just as a spotlight beam sliced over the floor, passing inches from where they'd been standing. The rest of us ducked down and pressed against the walls, melting into shadow, as an unmarked black chopper circled the building once, then wheeled lazily away.

Ember glared after the helicopter, eyes flashing, as Faith whimpered and huddled close to her. "Well, there are the snipers," she said. "What now, Riley?"

Shoved against a wall with Ava, Riley growled a curse and looked at me. "Any brilliant thoughts on getting out of this?"

"Back through the building," I said. "It's a big hotel. They'll probably have more than one unit sweeping the floors, coming in from different angles. If we can get past the ground teams, we'll have a chance of making it out unnoticed."

"And if we can't?"

"Then we go through them."

Riley swore again. "All right," he growled. "Go, then. We'll be right behind you."

The helicopter swung around again, and we held our breath as it went by, spotlight crawling over the walls and floor. I waited until it passed, watched it glide around a corner, then darted for the stairwell entrance. I heard the others scramble after me, and hit the door handle without slowing down, bursting through the frame into the building.

We quickly descended the stairs, myself in the lead, Ember close behind me. Ava and Faith followed, and Riley brought up the rear, watching our backs. Our footsteps echoed throughout the stairwell, unnaturally loud in the stillness. Each time we passed the entrances to other floors, my nerves jangled, wondering if this time the door would burst open and a squad of soldiers would step in to kill us.

A body suddenly rounded the corner and lunged up the stairs, making Faith shriek. Not a soldier, but a civilian in a white tank top, a baseball cap perched sideways on his head. He stumbled, nearly running into me, and I barely stopped myself from driving a fist into his throat.

"Shit, man!" The civilian glared at me wide-eyed, then shoved past, lurching up the steps. "Move, a–holes! Fucking SWAT team is everywhere." He scrambled past Riley, who gave him a disgusted look, then continued up the stairs, his footsteps fading into the darkness.

Ember took a deep breath and let it out slowly. "They're in the building," she breathed as we started down the steps again. "How close do you think they are, Garret?"

Two floors beneath us, a door opened.

I jerked to a stop and whirled around as flashlight beams

pierced the darkness below. "Go back!" I ordered, hearing booted feet ascending the steps behind me. "Everyone, get back! They're here."

Shots rang out, sparking off the walls and railing, and Faith screamed. We fled back up the steps, hearing the soldiers give chase, spatters of gunfire echoing up the stairwell.

"This way!" Ahead of us, Riley paused at the entrance to the twelfth floor and wrenched the door back. "We're sitting ducks in here. Everyone get out. Go, go!" Ava and Faith quickly ducked through the open door, and the rest of us followed, emerging into a narrow, unfinished corridor with empty rooms lining the walls. A maze of hallways, dark and empty, stretched out to either side.

The soldiers were still coming. Without hesitation, we ran, rounding a corner just as the door behind us opened and our pursuers followed us into the labyrinth. I heard a soldier calling for backup, informing the rest of the squads where we were, and knew the entire strike force would be swarming the floor in a matter of minutes. The rest of them would be sent to guard doors, exits, stairwells; anywhere we might try to escape, they would be waiting for us. A cold lump settled in my stomach. Getting out of here was going to be difficult, if not impossible.

After a minute or two of running, when it appeared the soldiers weren't right on our tail, Riley ducked into an open room, and the rest of us followed. "Okay," he panted, leaning against a wall, "this whole thing has gone completely FUBAR. We need a new strategy, quick." He looked at me. "Suggestions, St. George? What are they doing out there?"

"Right now, all squads will be converging on this floor,"

I answered, peering into the hall to make sure the soldiers were not close by. My mind raced, trying to think of a plan, to counter whatever they were going to do. "They're going to try to cover all the exits," I went on, ducking back inside, "but if we find another stairwell before they have a chance to get here, we could possibly slip past them and get to another floor. It'll buy us some time while they're searching for us up here. The challenge will be finding an exit that isn't guarded."

"One problem at a time," Riley muttered tiredly, and pushed himself off the wall. "First thing, let's try to get off this floor before the rest of the bastards arrive. Any ideas?"

"There's another stairwell at the west end of the building," Ava said, surprising us. She stood beside Faith, looking pale but calm in the face of approaching death. Unlike the other hatchling, who was frozen in absolute terror, her eyes huge and staring. "I saw it when we first came here. We could try to reach it before St. George does."

A hollow boom echoed from an adjacent hallway, followed by a gruff "Clear!" The soldiers behind us were kicking in doors, systematically checking each room before moving on. Riley winced.

"Stairwell it is," he whispered, beckoning Ava to the front with him. "Let's go."

We raced for the end of the hall, Riley and Ava leading this time, me bringing up the rear. I didn't know if the soldiers heard us and were giving chase, and I didn't pause to look back. We fled down narrow concrete hallways, ducking beams and scrambling over rubble, praying we wouldn't turn a corner and find the way blocked by soldiers and guns.

As we approached an intersection where two hallways

crossed, the hairs on the back of my neck stood up. Four
armored, masked men rounded the corner at the far end of
the corridor we'd been moving down. Hissing a warning to
Riley, I grabbed the two closest bodies—Ember and Faith—
and yanked them into the cross section of hall, just as the
scream of M-4s filled the corridor.

Faith wailed, hands flying up to cover her ears, as the roar
of gunfire tore through the air and bullets ripped chunks of
wood and plaster from the walls. Pulling her back from the
edge, I looked up to see Ava and Riley on the other side of
the corridor of death, streams of bullets zipping between us.
The soldiers were advancing, firing short, continuous bursts
as they marched forward in unison. From the sound of the
guns, they would reach our position in a few seconds.

I met Riley's gaze, and he gestured at us frantically. "Split
up!" he shouted over the howl of carbines. "Take them and
get out of here, St. George. We'll meet back at the hotel. Go!"

I nodded and turned to the girls. "Come on," I said, and
Ember stepped toward Faith, still huddled against the wall.

"Faith." She pried the girl's arms away from her head. "Hey,
we have to go."

"No!" Faith looked up, gaze frantically searching for the
other hatchling. "What about Ava? We can't leave them."

"We can't help them now!" Ember growled and pulled the
other girl off the wall. The chatter of gunfire was getting
closer, as were the footsteps of the squad. "She's with Riley,
she'll be fine. But we have to get out of here, right now."
Faith took a breath to argue, and Ember snarled at her with
the fury of a fire-breathing dragon. "Move!"

Faith gave a desperate sob and stumbled past me down the

hall. I started after her but Ember paused, shooting one final glance at Riley and Ava, who were already sprinting in the opposite direction.

"Be careful, Riley," she whispered, before spinning and catching up to me and Faith. We rounded a corner just as the squad reached the intersection, sending a storm of bullets after us, and whatever feelings I had about Ember and the rogue were quickly replaced by thoughts of survival.

RILEY

I might not get out of this one.

Angrily, I banished the thought as I led Ava through the maze of corridors, the echo of gunfire and soldiers' voices ringing behind us. I couldn't start thinking like that. I'd survived worse than this, and besides, I had too many who counted on me; I couldn't die now.

"Riley, wait," Ava said, bringing me to a halt in the middle of the hall. The pale-haired hatchling shot a quick look around, blue eyes searching, then jerked her head at an open doorway. "This way," she announced, and darted into the room. Frowning, I followed, hearing the soldiers close behind us, wondering what she was planning. We couldn't afford to be trapped.

"What are we doing?" I hissed, as the hatchling hurried to a pair of balcony doors. "We can't fly, Ava. They've got snipers out there—"

"We're not going to fly." Ava unlocked the frame and pried back the glass doors, glancing over her shoulder at me. "I know what I'm doing," she said to my dubious look. "Trust me, Cobalt."

Shouts echoed from the hallway, making my skin crawl.

"Looks like I don't have a choice," I growled, and followed her onto the balcony. She didn't launch herself into the air but hurried to the railing and swung over, making my heart jump to my throat. For a half second, she dangled over a lethal drop, feet swinging out over nothing. Then she pumped her legs twice and let go of the rails. My heart gave another violent lurch as I leaned over and watched her drop onto the balcony directly below us, landing in a graceful crouch.

Straightening, she looked up at me, as I told my heart it could start beating again. "Hurry!" she urged, just as the glass behind me shattered. Bullets sparked off the railing, and I scrambled over the edge, taking a half second to swing my legs forward as I released my grip.

I hit the concrete and rolled, distributing some of the impact, though it still clacked my teeth together and sent a flare of pain up my arm. Ava pulled me to my feet and dragged me away from the balcony railing just as the soldiers stuck their guns over the edge and fired down on us. We fled the room into another series of darkened corridors. This one without the swarms of soldiers, at least for now.

I leaned against a wall to catch my breath, and Ava did the same. Panting, I looked at her, at the slender body and the calm, young face. "How many times have you done this before?" I asked. She shrugged, pushing long pale hair behind her shoulder.

"I was trained for this," she said as I wondered what Talon had her pegged for before she ran. Basilisk, Gila and Viper were the operatives that received special combat training. "My final exam was supposed to be this month," Ava went on, staring at the wall, her eyes dark with memory. "But I knew I couldn't do what they asked. The new management was especially unbearable." An unexpected look of disgust broke through her composure. "Hiding what I felt was getting harder and harder. I'd been planning to leave for a long time, ever since I heard about you." Her gaze flicked to mine, then away just as quickly. "I'm not usually this disorganized," she admitted, hunching her shoulders as if embarrassed. "I was going to run when my test came around, but then I heard about Faith and…things happened a little faster than I originally planned." She sighed, squeezing her eyes shut. "I hope she's all right," she whispered. "I promised I'd keep her safe."

I brushed her arm. "She'll be okay," I said, allowing a small grin to tug at my mouth. "You don't know Ember. She'll burn the building down before she'll let anyone hurt her. And the soldier…is a bastard, but he knows what he's doing. Trust me, she'll be fine."

Ava regarded me with solemn blue eyes. "You have a lot of faith in them," she said. "It's been so long since I've been able to trust anyone but myself."

"Hopefully that'll change." I pushed myself off the wall. "But right now, we have to worry about ourselves. Come on, we're not out of here yet."

We slipped through the empty corridors, keeping a close ear out for voices or footsteps, until we reached the elevator hall. Ava frowned as I walked up to a pair of metal doors and forced my fingers between the tightly sealed crack. "What are you doing?"

"Forget the stairwell." I grunted, gritting my teeth as I pried the doors back. They resisted, stubborn with rust and disuse. "The Order probably has them all guarded. Or are

using them right now. I don't want to run into any more soldiers on the stairs, so we're going the unconventional route."
She watched as I wedged my shoulder between the crack and
looked back at her. "You're not claustrophobic, are you?"

A door slammed somewhere in the maze of corridors, and
my blood froze. Claustrophobic or not, we were out of time.
With a growl, I shoved the doors as hard as I could, ram-
ming them with my shoulder. They gave a last rusty groan
and reluctantly slid back a few inches. A gust of hot, stale air
billowed out of the opening, and a long, pitch-black tube
plunged down into darkness.

I eyed the distance from the edge to the maintenance ladder on the wall, then looked back at Ava. "After you."

Flashlight beams scuttled along the wall, and the sound of
booted feet echoed through the hallways. Without hesitation,
Ava leaped into the shaft and grabbed the ladder's rungs with
easy grace, then started down the tube. I followed, gritting my
teeth as the ladder trembled under my weight. If it snapped,
we were in trouble; a fall here would kill us as surely as if the
soldiers stuck their guns through the opening and filled the
shaft with lead.

Let's hope my luck holds.

Together, we descended into the pitch blackness.

EMBER

A hail of bullets erupted behind us as we turned another corner, and Faith screamed.

"Garret!" I panted, as flashlight beams scuttled over the walls ahead of us, and the soldier stopped abruptly in the center of the corridor. I stopped behind him, shivering as harsh voices drew closer from different directions. "They've surrounded the floor," I whispered, feeling my heart pound in my ears. "We're trapped."

Garret scanned the hall, his gaze falling on a pair of open doors at the end of the corridor. "This way," he ordered, and we sprinted through the doors into a large conference-type room. It was only half-finished; scaffolding stood everywhere, and large iron beams marched down the center of an aisle, creating a tangled web of iron and steel. It was very dark in here, and the air was thick with the smell of dust and mold.

Garret pulled us behind a cage of scaffolding and iron beams. "Faith," he said softly, bringing the girl's attention to him. "Look at me." Faith's eyes were huge and liquid, and tear tracks stained her dusty cheeks as she glanced up. "Listen to me. I want you to climb to the top of the scaffolding tower, lie flat and don't move. Don't look up or make a sound, no matter what you hear. Can you do that?"

She stared at him. "What...what are you going do?" she whispered, looking between us fearfully. "You won't leave me here, will you?"

He shook his head. "We're not going to leave you," he said, with that quiet intensity that made my skin prickle. "But you have to get out of sight. I can't worry about you if I'm going to do this." She blinked in confusion, but he didn't explain. "Get up there," he said gently, nodding toward the scaffolding. "If the worst happens, wait until they're gone, then get out any way you can. Go."

With a final sniffle, Faith turned and scuttled up the ladder, vanishing from sight.

Voices echoed outside, and flashlight beams pierced the blackness beyond the doors. The soldiers were converging on the room. Garret took my wrist and pulled me farther back into the shadows.

I stepped close, resting my palms on his chest, feeling his heart race. "What's the plan?" I whispered, surprised that my own voice was so steady.

He took a deep, furtive breath. "There'll be two teams," he murmured, glancing at the entrance and the lights getting closer. "Possibly more, if they called for backup. Six soldiers at the very least, with M-4s, a sidearm and a pair of stun grenades. That's standard procedure for this type of strike." His voice was cool, unruffled, as he calmly analyzed our odds of survival. "We should split up," he said gravely. "I'll get in close, take one or two out, then you hit the others from a different angle when they respond. Try to surprise them. If they see us coming, it'll be over."

I shivered, closing my eyes. "All right," I muttered, clenching my fists in his shirt. "No problem. It's just like training back with Scary Talon Lady." *Just with real soldiers, and real guns. No paintball bullets this time, Ember.*

Garret gazed down at me, and for the first time, a shadow of fear crossed his face. Not for himself, I realized, but for me. "Ember…"

"Don't you dare tell me to stay up top and hide, Garret," I warned, narrowing my eyes at him. "That's something Riley would say, and I'll tell you exactly what I'd tell him. I'm not letting you fight them by yourself."

"I know. I mean… I wasn't going to." His hands rose and gripped my arms as he stepped close. "But…be careful, Ember," he said, his intense gaze searing into me. "They'll be searching for a dragon. They know how dangerous one is when it's cornered and trapped. Remember, this is the type of scenario they train for, what we've *all* trained for. Do what you have to do…" One hand pressed to my cheek. "Just stay alive," he whispered.

I swallowed the lump in my throat. "You, too."

Figures appeared in the doorway, freezing us in place, as six soldiers stepped through the frame, guns held in front of them. Fanning out, they advanced cautiously into the room, sweeping their weapons in tight arcs, the tactical lights on the bottom of their guns piercing the darkness.

Garret drew back. His eyes were hard, that blank soldier's mask slipping into place as he melted into the shadows and out of sight. I darted behind a scaffold, then hunkered down as thin beams of light swept the opposite wall, making my heart pound.

Okay, how was I going to do this? I took a deep breath to slow my heartbeat, and gazed around the room. Despite its vastness, it was quite cluttered. There were a lot of tight quarters and places to hide, where the soldiers would be at a disadvantage if I could get close. In fact, this was *a lot* like my training with Lilith, having men with guns chase me around a crowded warehouse while I figured out how to "kill" them. Of course, I'd "died" most of those times, too, shot down with paintball guns, as the soldiers had become increasingly aware of attacks from up top.

Up top...

Crouching down, I stripped out of my clothes and left my shorts, top and underwear at the base of a pillar. Any modesty or embarrassment I might've felt was swallowed by the need to stay alive, and besides, no one could see me in this darkness, not even Garret. In another circumstance, I might not have worried about ruining my clothes, but I didn't have my Viper suit on, and if we did make it out of here, I did not want to run through the streets of Las Vegas stark naked.

The soldiers were halfway into the room now, their lights creeping ever closer as they eased forward. Hurrying to the nearest scaffolding tower, I began to climb, feeling cold iron, rust and cobwebs under my fingers and the soles of my feet. When I reached the top, I crept silently along the wooden planks, keeping my head low, until I was almost directly above a pair of soldiers and could peer down at the tops of their heads. I couldn't see Garret, but I knew he was close, waiting for the perfect moment to strike. I would be ready when he did.

As I held my breath, muscles coiling and tingly with the energy right before a Shift, my foot brushed a loose nail on the edge of the wood. It fell and pinged off the cement, a tiny sound that might as well have been a gong in the silent room. The soldiers below immediately swept their beams straight up the scaffolding. My heart lurched, and I ducked down, pressing my cheek to the boards, as my perch was illuminated in light.

"Did you hear…?"

"Yeah." The flashlight swept back and forth along the plank. I took shallow breaths and thought invisible thoughts. "I think it might be up there—"

A muffled shout rang out from another corner of the room, followed by the sound of a scuffle, a body being slammed against a wall, a burst of gunfire. The light vanished as the two soldiers whirled their guns in the direction of the noise, and I leaped to my feet.

Here we go, I thought, and plunged off the scaffold, feeling my body explode midpounce. I landed on one of the soldiers in full dragon form, driving him into the concrete, and turned on the other with a roar, blasting him with fire as he spun around. He cringed back, tongues of flame snapping around him, but apparently his armor was fire resistant because the flames didn't stop him from raising his gun and firing. I ducked behind a pillar, sparks erupting around me, and bounded into the shadows. The soldier backed away, firing short bursts and shouting to his companions, his light sweeping wildly back and forth. His armor still burned, though the flames were slowly dying, and he looked like a torch in the darkness.

Something emerged from the shadows behind him, a pistol pointed at his back. My heart jumped as Garret deliberately paused, then lowered the gun and fired once, at the soldier's legs. The man shrieked and whirled around as he fell, raising his weapon, but Garret darted forward, smashed the butt of the pistol into his face and wrenched the rifle away as he collapsed to the cement.

More shots boomed out, the deafening roar of assault rifles making my ears ring as the rest of the squad converged on his location. Garret dived behind cover as they approached, not seeing me in the shadows.

I snarled and lunged, pouncing on one from behind, clamping my jaws around his leg and dragging him across the floor. He shouted, clawing at the ground, and his friends immediately aimed their rifles at me.

A blur of motion, and Garret hit them from behind, striking one behind the ear with the pistol and grabbing the other's weapon as he turned. The soldier beneath me tried flipping onto his back to shoot, but I pinned him down and slammed his head into the floor. He shuddered and went limp, the gun clattering to the cement. Tensing, I looked up just as the second soldier swung wildly at Garret and clipped him in the jaw with an elbow. Garret staggered, and the human immediately struck him in the head with the assault rifle, driving him to a knee, then raised the gun to fire.

I leaped with a roar, slamming into the soldier just as he pulled the trigger. He recovered, swinging the muzzle around at me, and I blasted him in the face with fire. Screaming, he reached up, tearing away the flaming helmet and mask…as Garret surged to his feet and punched him in the jaw as hard as he could.

The human reeled back, fell into a pillar and slid to the ground, his head dropping to his chest as he went limp. Silence fell, the echoes of screams and gunfire fading into the black. Still shaking with fury and adrenaline, I looked at Garret, wondering if we had really won. If it was really over.

He stood cradling his hand, gazing at the soldier slumped against the beam, his expression torn between relief and guilt. A trickle of blood ran down his face from his temple, crawling down his cheek, and my stomach knotted. "You're bleeding!" I exclaimed, jumping over the body of one of the soldiers. My claws clicked anxiously over the floor as I trotted up. "Are you all right?"

He nodded painfully. "Just a cut," he said, lowering his arm as I reached him. "It's not serious." Wincing, he looked down at his hand, clenching and unclenching a fist. "Think I burned myself when I punched the last soldier, though."

"Let me see," I said, reaching for his arm. He stiffened, and I froze when I saw my scaly foreleg, curved black talons hovering close to his skin. Claws that could easily rend and tear and rip right through him. His eyes rose to mine, and I saw my reflection in his steely pupils: a huge horned lizard with claws and wings outstretched, looming over him. For half a heartbeat, we stared at each other, dragon and soldier, surrounded by the bodies of his former brethren.

Garret moved first. In the moment before I would've pulled back, he raised his arm and held it out to me, placing the back of his hand gently in mine. Heart lurching, I very cautiously curled my talons around his wrist. He didn't move, didn't flinch or tense up, though a patch of his skin was red with the telltale shininess of a burn. I swallowed hard.

"Sorry about that."

"I've had worse." He held my gaze, gray eyes intense. "Besides, it's hard to be angry at something that saved your life."

"Garret? Ember?"

Faith edged into view. She held a length of rebar in both hands, and it shook as she gazed around at the fallen soldiers. "The shooting...stopped," she whispered, her body poised for flight, as if the bodies might leap up and attack again. "I didn't know if you were still alive, or if they had...had..." Her voice trembled, and she trailed off. I huffed a cloud of smoke at her.

"So you decided to come look for us? You're supposed to be hiding—"

One of the soldiers from earlier, the first one I'd taken down, suddenly lunged out of the shadows, gun held before him. Faith shrieked, swinging the rebar wildly as he appeared, catching him right in the face. He crashed to the floor again and lay still, while Faith scuttled behind Garret, breathing hard.

"Is he dead?" she squeaked, as I forced myself to exhale and relax my muscles, releasing the air that I'd sucked in slowly, and not in a violent explosion of fire. Garret walked to the fallen soldier, knelt and rolled him onto his back. His head flopped, blood streaming from his nose and mouth, and I couldn't tell if he was breathing or not.

"The others will be on their way," Garret muttered, not looking up from the body. He started rummaging through the soldier's stuff, checking for guns and ammo, most likely, anything to help us get out of here. "We need to hurry. Ember..." He glanced at me, narrowing his eyes. "Can you Shift back before we leave the hotel?"

I cringed. *Not without my clothes.* "Gimme two seconds," I said, and hurried to where I'd left my belongings, then changed back and slipped into them as quickly as I could. When I returned, Garret stood waiting for me, gun in hand, the soldier's belt now looped around his waist. Faith hovered beside him, watching his every move with starry eyes. All her fear of the former St. George soldier seemed to have vanished, and I bit down a snort of disgust.

Garret tossed me a pistol as I came up, and I caught it grimly. "Let's go," he ordered, and we fled the room, knowing the rest of the force was still out there, swarming the building. I suspected we weren't safe yet, and I was right.

As we turned down one last corridor, two soldiers looked up from where they guarded the stairwell at the end of the hall. The carbines blared, and we ducked back around the corner as bullets peppered the walls and floor. One of the soldiers called for backup, alerting the rest of them, and I snarled in frustration. So close; if we could just get past these guards, we were home free.

Raising the gun, I tensed to dart out of cover and fire, when Garret grabbed my arm.

"Wait." Drawing me back, he crept to the edge of the hallway and pulled something from the stolen belt at his waist. A small metal cylinder with a ring at the top. Glancing at me and Faith, he narrowed his eyes. "Look away," he ordered. "Close your eyes and cover your ears. Both of you." And he hurled what was in his hand around the corner, toward the soldiers.

The boom rocked the corridor, and even through my closed lids, I saw the brilliant flash of light, as if a star had exploded in the hall. The gunfire ceased, and Garret took my hand, pulling me to my feet with a brisk "Let's go!" We sprinted past the stunned, gaping soldiers, hit the stairwell at top speed and didn't stop running until we reached the very last door and burst through it into the hot Vegas night.

RILEY

We finally reached the end of the elevator shaft.

I heard Ava hit the bottom, the quiet thump of her feet on solid ground echoing faintly up the tube. Relieved, anxious to be done with tight spaces and lethal falls in utter darkness, I descended the last few rungs and hopped off the ladder, before realizing we weren't home free just yet.

The floor under my boots swayed slightly, as if hovering a few inches off the ground. Clicking on my flashlight, I saw we'd hit the metal roof of the elevator box, thick cables coming out of the center and rising up the tube. A small square hatch sat in one corner, and Ava crouched next to it, her hair a ghostly silver in the pale light.

"It's stuck," she whispered.

Putting the flashlight on the floor, I knelt across from her and grasped the handle at the top. "On three," I muttered, as her fingers wrapped around mine, slender and cool, and I tightened my grip. "One…two…three!"

Together we tugged. The hatch, like the elevator doors, resisted a moment, then opened with a rusty screech that made my teeth vibrate. I poked my head through the opening, shining the flashlight around, then pulled back with a nod.

"Clear."

We dropped into the elevator box, Ava landing as lightly as a cat. The doors were partially open, and I could see an empty hall beyond, dark and silent for now.

"First floor," Ava whispered, gazing at the brass number in the door frame. She sounded relieved. "We're almost out."

"Not quite." I eased into the hall, gazing around warily. "The doors will be guarded for sure, and there's no telling how many snipers they've got watching the exits. And of course, that damn chopper will be circling around, making things difficult."

"So we can't go through the doors." Ava followed me, pragmatic and as cool as ever. "How will we get out, then?"

"Easy." I grinned at her. "We use a window."

Voices echoed down another hallway, making us both tense. A moment later, the sound of boots started toward us, marching ominously closer. I switched off the flashlight, and we ran.

Ducking into an office, Ava closed and locked the door while I raced to the window and peered cautiously through the glass. The empty construction zone stretched away into the black, but past the barren lot I could see the lights of civilization in the distance, tantalizingly close. Question was, could we get across that flat, open plain without taking a bullet to the forehead?

"Cobalt!" Ava hurried to my side, her voice a warning growl. "They're coming."

Shit. Out of time. "Stand back," I told her, and grabbed an abandoned fire extinguisher from the floor. Raising it over my head, I smashed it against the window, feeling the impact jar my teeth together. Cracks appeared on the first hit, spread out on the second, and on the third, the glass finally shattered. I bashed the window a few times more, making a large enough hole, then threw the extinguisher down and beckoned to Ava. "Go!"

A heavy blow rattled the door behind us. Ava sprinted three steps and dived gracefully through the glass, then rolled to her feet like an acrobat. I followed, hunching my shoulders as I plunged through, feeling shards catch on my leather jacket. But then I was on the other side, scrambling upright, and we were running across the empty lot, hearing shots fired as we fled into the concealing night. Nothing hit us, but we didn't stop running until we reached the edge of the pavement, scrambled over the fence and darted across an empty street. Into the safety of civilization and away from the Order at last.

Taking refuge behind an auto-repair shop, I slumped against the brick wall, sucking in deep, gasping breaths while I waited for my heart to slow down. Ava leaned beside me, head back, silver hair spilling over her shoulders.

Damn, we made it. Edging to the corner of the building, I peered back at the hotel, making sure we weren't being followed. Past the streetlights and the fence, I could just make out the helicopter, still circling the empty lot, and smiled grimly. *Still a lucky SOB. Now, if only Ember and the others made it out.*

"Okay," I muttered, hearing Ava step up behind me. "Looks like we're in the clear. We'll lie low for a bit, see if the others got out okay. If we don't hear from them in ten minutes, you go on to the hotel. I might have to go back for Ember and Faith."

"No, Cobalt," Ava said, her voice low and grave. "I don't think you will."

There was a sharp pain in the side of my neck, like a hornet's sting, hot and piercing. Alarmed, I started to turn, but the ground swayed, tilted beneath me, and everything went dark.

COBALT

Twelve years ago

The door swung open without a sound, and the figure in black eased into the room. On noiseless feet, it stole over the carpet, the long, straight knife glimmering in the shadows as it drew alongside the bed. The lump beneath the covers didn't stir, as a slender gloved hand reached down to grasp the corner of the quilt. In one smooth motion, the shadow flung back the covers and plunged the knife into what lay beneath.

The pillow gave a muffled thump as the blade stabbed into it, but otherwise made no sound.

"Nice try."

The assassin spun, raising her knife as I stepped out of the closet, my pistol already trained on her. She froze at the sight of the gun, and I gave a sad smile.

"Hello, Stealth," I greeted softly, moving around the other side of bed, keeping a large obstacle between us. It would at least slow her down if she decided to lunge. She watched me with dark, impassive eyes, and a lump caught in my throat. "I knew Talon had to send someone eventually," I said, my voice tight. "I wish it didn't have to be you."

The Viper continued to regard me without expression. I stayed where I was, every ounce of my attention focused on the other dragon. I could not let it waver, even for a millisecond. Because that was how long it would take the Viper to leap across the bed and put a knife in my throat.

Stealth blinked, seemingly unconcerned with the gun pointed in her direction. She was lithe and slender, and the black Viper suit looked like a spill of ink across her skin. Straight black hair had been pulled into a tail, and her pale, slightly rounded face seemed to float in the darkness of the room. "They were going to send Lilith," she stated quietly, making my skin crawl at the name. "I convinced them that it should be me. It's the least I could do…for old time's sake."

"Yeah." I sighed, feeling an ache begin in my chest. "I could see how you would think that. You did save my life once. Only fitting that you should correct that mistake."

Her eyes narrowed a bit, but that was all. "How did you know I was coming?"

I gave a small snort. "You know me better than that," I said, grateful that, for all their lethality, Vipers did not have the same skill set I did. Or the paranoia that came with being a Basilisk. The hidden camera pointed down the hallway was synced to my phone, set to alert me whenever there was movement outside. It was annoying to be woken up by every drunk shambling down the hall at three in the morning, but a few hours' sleep was a small price to pay when it came to this.

Stealth didn't press the question, standing calmly with her hands at her sides, still gripping the dagger. "Are you going to shoot me, Agent Cobalt?"

"Not unless I have to."

Her jaw tightened. "If you don't," she warned, "I'm only going to come after you again. You know that, right? We were colleagues at one point, and I respected you, Cobalt. I still do, so consider this your only warning. Next time, there will be no words."

I nodded tiredly. "I know." This was a courtesy call. A formality between two agents who had fought on the same team. Once I left the room, that civility ended. The next time I saw Stealth, one of us had to die.

The Viper's lips thinned and, for the first time, a hint of anger crossed her cool face. "Why did you do it, Cobalt?" she asked in a harsh whisper. "You had just succeeded Blackscale. You were on your way up. There were even rumors that the Chief Basilisk wanted to make you his second. Why did you throw all that away?"

"You wouldn't understand," I told her, and she wouldn't. The Vipers were trained for ruthlessness, to take lives without question. I knew Stealth; if Talon told her to slit the throat of a seven-year-old human girl, she wouldn't even blink. "And it doesn't matter now, does it?"

Stealth shook her head. "No," she whispered, and I heard the resolve in her voice, the knowledge that when we did meet again, she was going to kill me. "I guess it doesn't."

I swallowed hard and gestured at her with the gun. "The knife," I ordered, my voice firm. "Toss it to me, now." This might be a courtesy call, but there was no way I was letting an armed assassin follow me out of the room. I might not make it to the parking lot.

Without argument, Stealth flipped the blade in her hand and arced it toward me over the bed. It hit the edge of the mattress right in front of me, hilt up, and I grabbed the blade without taking my eyes from her.

"You'll never escape us." The Viper's voice was quiet, matter-of-fact. "Even if you kill me, someone else will take my place. Talon will never let you go, and sooner or later, we're going to catch up. You're living on borrowed time, Cobalt."

Ice settled in my gut, but I sheathed the knife at my belt and gave her a half smile. "You don't have to parrot the monologue at me, Stealth," I said. "I was part of Talon just as long as you. You're not telling me anything I don't already know."

"Go, then." The Viper eased a few steps aside, away from the door. "Run, traitor. I won't be far behind."

Keeping the pistol trained on her, I slid around the bed and edged toward the exit. Stealth didn't move, only watched me with flat, expressionless eyes, as I pushed back the door and left the room.

The second I stepped through the frame, I began to run.

EMBER

Made it.

The taxi pulled up to the curb, and I scrambled to the sidewalk and raised my head to bask in the artificial glow. I'd never been so relieved to see the bright neon lights of the Strip and the crowds wandering the streets in the middle of the night. Light meant visibility, and crowds meant lots of witnesses, and no matter how much they hated us, the Order of St. George was just as secretive and paranoid of discovery as Talon. They preferred to do their killing in dark alleys and abandoned buildings, where they could murder us in peace without having to worry about silly things like questions or the law. They would not risk gunning us down in the middle of a busy street.

At least, I hoped they wouldn't.

"Stay alert," Garret warned as the taxi cruised off after leaving us on the curb. Every bit of him was tense, gray eyes sweeping the crowds and sidewalks, constantly on edge. "The Order could still be here." Faith whimpered and edged close to him, clutching his shirtsleeve. Annoyance flared, sudden and unreasonable, but Garret didn't react to the girl's pawing.

"Keep calm," he said without looking at her. "If you're scared, you'll be easy to notice. Try to act like nothing is wrong."

"Easy for him to say," Faith whispered to me. In the glow of the street lamps, she was pale and thin, with dark smudges beneath her eyes, and my irritation faded somewhat. Poor kid wasn't trying to be overly clingy; she really was terrified.

"You'll be fine," I told her, as Garret motioned us toward the hotel. "We won't let anything happen to you. Just stay close to us."

Cautiously, we ambled toward the entrance. Okay, so maybe *ambled* wasn't the right word; Faith was way too frightened to act normal, and her casual walk was more of a rigid march, eyes glued straight ahead. As we neared the doors, Garret casually reached down and took my hand, lacing our fingers together and making a knot form in my stomach. I stared up at him, and he offered a smile, squeezing my palm. I relaxed, even managing to smile at the bellboy who opened the door for us, like we were just three ordinary humans here for a good time. Faith, having relinquished her grip on Garret's shirt, glued herself to my other side and clung to my arm as we swept through the doors into the relative safety of the hotel.

Once we were past the lobby, Faith relaxed a bit, uncoiling from my arm and staring at the casino floor in awe. Before, I'd been entranced by all the lights, bells, crowds and movement; now I understood Garret's suspicion. There were so many people; any one of them could be an enemy, a soldier of St. George or a Talon agent in disguise. How many were watching us right now, gauging our movements, waiting for the perfect moment to strike?

I'd never accuse Garret of being paranoid again.

"Come on," Garret murmured, and gently tugged my hand, leading us across the floor toward the elevators. Faith trailed us doggedly, trying to look at everything, until we reached the elevator hall. Garret hit the button, then stepped aside, back to the wall, keeping his eye on the crowd behind us.

I edged close, leaning against the wall and lowering my voice. "Did you see Riley anywhere?" I whispered. Now that we'd escaped the hotel and could finally breathe, my thoughts went to the two companions we'd left behind. I'd texted Riley once when we were in the taxi, but hadn't heard anything back. Of course, that could mean any number of things, and I was trying not to assume the worst, but the hollow feeling in my gut continued to grow with every minute that passed with no word from the rogue.

Garret shook his head, not taking his eyes from the crowds. "No, but I wouldn't expect him to be on the floor," he murmured back. "If he's here, he'll be upstairs with Wes."

I nodded, trying to ignore the knot of dread uncoiling in my stomach. *He'll be all right*, I told myself. *He probably got out long before we did, and hasn't contacted us because he's afraid we're busy running from the Order. Or he's been too busy to check his phone. Of course, he should have texted one of us, just to let us know he made it out. We should have heard something by now. Dammit, Riley, you'd better be all right. You can't have gotten yourself killed by St. George.*

The elevator dinged, and I pushed myself off the wall to move toward the doors. They slid back just as I reached them, and a man in a bright red suit stepped out, nearly running into me. I dodged back with a scowl, barely catching myself from snapping something rude. Much as I wanted to tell him to watch where he put his feet, now was not the time to draw attention to ourselves.

But the human caught me looking at him and his eyes widened, like he was seeing a ghost. Ducking his head, he sped past me and vanished into the crowds.

Huh. That was weird. For a second, I hesitated, wondering if I shouldn't go after him. They way he'd looked at me…it was like he knew what I was.

"Did you know that man?" Garret asked at my shoulder, making me jump. Of course, his suspicious hawk eyes had caught everything. I shook my head as we entered the elevator, Faith close at our backs.

"No, I've never seen him before," I said, relieved as the doors closed and the elevator began to move. Had anyone else gotten on, I would have half expected them to pull a gun or a knife as soon as the doors shut. The soldier had made me completely paranoid. "Should we follow him?" I asked, as the numbers climbed steadily toward our floor. "Do you think he's with Talon or the Order?"

"If he is, there's nothing we can do about it now," Garret answered, far too calmly. "We have to get to Wes, see if he's heard anything from Riley or Ava. Maybe they're already here."

I clung to that small flicker of hope as the elevator doors finally opened and we stepped onto our floor. I made myself walk, not run, to Wes's door and rap on the wood.

It swung back almost instantly, and Wes peered out with wild hazel eyes, making my heart sink. "About bloody time you got here!" he hissed, stepping back to let us in. His room was disheveled, torn apart...and empty, as I'd feared. "Where the hell is Riley?"

"Not here," I answered, as the hollow feeling in my stomach opened into a dark, yawning pit, swallowing me whole. Garret locked the door and stood against it, gazing through the peephole, and Faith hovered anxiously, looking confused and lost.

Wes shot me a glare full of venom. "I bloody well see that! That's not what I asked," he snarled. "*Where* is Riley? I've been trying to contact him for hours. Is he all right? Is he dead? Where is he?"

"I don't know!"

"What do you mean, you don't know?"

"We were separated." Garret eased back from the door, apparently satisfied that we weren't followed and that no one lurked in the halls. "The Order swarmed the building. We had to take different routes back to the hotel."

"Well, that's bloody fantastic," Wes snapped, throwing up his arms. "So the Order is out there, hunting him down, and you two blighters went and left him to die."

At that, Faith burst into tears. Wes jumped and looked at her strangely, as if just realizing she was there. Covering her face with her hands, the girl turned into the corner and shook violently with sobs.

"My fault," she gasped, her voice muffled. "This is my fault. Ava knew I was unhappy in Talon. She convinced me to run with her. We wouldn't be here if it wasn't for me." Her voice trailed off into more muted sobbing, and Wes ran a hand down his face.

"Bollocks," he muttered, sounding both annoyed and sympathetic, which surprised me. "I didn't even see her there. I suppose this is one of the hatchlings you went to rescue?"

"Her name is Faith," I said, as Faith didn't look like she could introduce herself at that point. "There's another one out there, too, with Riley."

"Ava," Faith supplied, her voice small and choked with tears. "Her n-name is Ava. And if she dies, it'll be my fault." Turning into the corner, she collapsed into helpless sobs again.

Garret watched the crying girl for a moment, then looked at me, clearly lost. Sighing, I stepped forward, put an arm around her shoulders and drew her away from the wall. She sniffled and turned into me, hiding her face, her whole body shaking against mine.

"There was a man in the hotel," Garret went on, looking at Wes, while I rubbed Faith's back and waited for her to calm down. "We saw him at the bottom of the elevators. Dark, tall, wearing a red suit. He looked suspicious. Any reason we should be concerned?"

"Red suit?" Wes rubbed the bridge of his nose. "That's just Griffin, one of Riley's contacts. And yes, the blighter is shady as hell, but I don't think we have to worry about him. I'm more concerned about Riley at the moment." He looked at Garret, narrowing his eyes. "Did you say the Order was waiting for you?"

"They ambushed us at the hotel," Garret replied. "We had to split up."

"That's bloody suspicious," Wes muttered, crossing his arms. "No one knew where you were going. The only ones with that information were me and..." He trailed off, the

color draining from his face. "Bloody bastard," he whispered.
"I'll kill him. If Riley doesn't, I'll shoot the blighter myself."

"Can you get a lock on Riley's phone?" Garret asked, before I could ask who Wes meant. Apparently, that information
was obvious to everyone but me. The human shook his head.

"What do you think I've been doing the past hour, mate?"
he snapped. "No, I can't get a signal. It's either turned off or
dead. Which could mean all sorts of things, but I don't like
the implications of any of them, do you?"

Faith hiccupped, still shaking, possibly from the effort not
to burst into tears again. I grimaced, feeling sick and tense
and frayed myself. I wanted to know what had happened to
Riley, too, but the amount of stress and tension in the room
wasn't helping Faith and was driving my own dragon crazy.
If I didn't step away soon, I was going to snap.

"I'm taking her to my room," I told the boys, pushing back
the lock and pulling the door open. "You two stay here, girl
talk only." Garret watched anxiously from the room, then
followed us into the corridor. "Garret, we'll be all right," I
said as he frowned in protest. "Keep waiting for Riley. I'll be
right across the hall if anything happens."

He shook his head. "No, we're not separating anymore tonight. Take care of Faith, or whatever you have to do. I'll be
right outside the door. If St. George or Talon does show up,
I'll see them coming."

I nodded, too exhausted to argue. We crossed the hall,
and I slid the key card into the slot then pushed the door
open, letting Faith into the room before looking at Garret.
He leaned beside the door frame with his back to the wall,

his eyes scanning the corridor in both directions before fixing on me. I gave him a tired smile.

"Thanks," I whispered. "I won't be long."

"I'll be here."

My stomach fluttered. He was so close, gunmetal eyes intense, watching me with that protective stare. I wanted to lean up and kiss him, but Faith waited for me in the room, and now really wasn't the time. I reached out and squeezed his arm instead, before ducking through the frame.

Faith stood in the center of the floor with her arms around herself and a dazed look on her face. "Sorry about Wes," I told her as the door clicked behind me. "He's a little uptight, if you couldn't tell. Wish I could say that he's not usually such a bastard, but...well, he is."

The other hatchling didn't answer. Or even look at me. Her face was streaked with tears, her eyes huge and glassy beneath the tangle of curls. She looked very young, barely a teenager, though I knew she had to be at least sixteen.

Or maybe not. Maybe she hadn't even started assimilation, that period when hatchlings were placed with guardians in the mortal world, to learn to "blend in" with humans. It was after assimilation that Talon decided where you fit within the organization. Maybe Faith hadn't even gotten that far, and Talon was all she'd ever known.

I hoped she hadn't gone into shock and shut down completely. I didn't know what I was going to do if she'd hit zombie mode.

"Are you hungry?" I asked, figuring that was a good place to start. I knew *I'd* be hungry if I'd gone through what she had. Come to think of it, I *was*. Faith blinked at me, still looking dazed, and I tried again. "Hey, are you hungry? I don't know about you, but I'm starving. There's snacks below the television stand, or we could order room service."

She shook her head. "I'm not hungry," she whispered. Well, at least she was talking. "But thank you."

"Not hungry?" The idea was unthinkable. "Are you sure? Check this out." I opened the cupboard to display the wealth of snacks. No hatchling I'd ever heard of could resist chocolate. After a moment's hesitation, Faith edged forward and plucked a Snickers bar from the shelf, making me sigh in relief.

Grabbing a bag of peanut M&M's for myself, I hopped onto the bed and crossed my legs, motioning Faith to the other side of the mattress. She sat carefully, like she was afraid of wrinkling the covers. I leaned against the headboard and watched her, feeling a weird prickle of déjà vu. It was strange, having another dragon in my room, especially another female. It reminded me a bit of the sleepovers at Lexi's house in Crescent Beach, where the two of us would stay up all night, eating junk food and talking about various human things, usually surfing and boys. I'd missed that, and her.

I missed a lot of things, actually.

"So, how do you know Ava?" I asked, before those memories got too painful. Faith gave me a wary look, and I shrugged. "You can tell me. It's not like I'm gonna report you for treason or anything. If you want to know why I left, it's because they had me slotted to be a Viper." Faith's eyes widened; she knew what a Viper was, apparently. "Yeah. And I had a small problem with hunting down and killing my own kind. So I ran. Left town with Riley, and I haven't looked back since."

"Just like that?" Faith asked, as if she couldn't quite believe it. "No hesitation? Nothing you regretted leaving behind?"

"Well, yeah, of course there was. I had friends, and family, and…" A lump caught in my throat, and I looked down at my fingers. "Dante," I muttered. "My brother. I miss him the most. When I left, he decided to stay with the organization. He doesn't know…what they're really like." I squeezed the M&M's bag, clenching my jaw. "I'll get him out, soon," I whispered, more of a promise to myself than Faith. "Stupid twin. I'll make him see, even if I have to tear down Talon's walls to reach him."

"You're braver than I am," Faith whispered, picking at the wrapper on her candy bar. "If it wasn't for Ava, I'd still be there, even though I hated it."

I shook myself from my sudden dark mood. "How'd you get out?"

She hesitated a moment longer, then sighed, as if she was tired of holding back. "I knew Ava from way back," Faith said, nibbling at the bar. "We were in a clutch that grew up together, until they separated us for Human Training. I didn't see her face-to-face afterward, but somehow we always kept in touch. Even though it was frowned upon. Talon didn't want us to have any previous attachments once we entered Human Training."

My insides curled, remembering the long years of schooling out in the desert, and how it was just barely tolerable only because I had Dante. Growing up, he was my best friend; we had each other's backs, and no matter how miserable things got, Dante was always there. I couldn't imagine going through that by myself, how lonely it had to be. Maybe that's why I didn't fit into the organization. Maybe I'd formed too many "attachments," when my only loyalty was supposed to be to Talon.

"Ava…had been planning to run for months," Faith went on, unaware of my musings. "She'd heard rumors about Cobalt, that there was a dragon who would help those wanting to leave the organization. Her first real assignment was coming up, and she told me she was planning to go rogue then. I was too scared to tell her I wanted to leave, too."

"Was that before you found out what Talon had planned for you?"

"Yes." Faith nodded. "And when Ava found out, she offered to take me with her, even though that would make her escape even more dangerous. I almost backed out, but she convinced me to run. That it was better to be hunted and free than a slave the rest of my life." She sniffed, curling into herself on the bed. "She was the brave one, the one who was trained for anything. I was only going to slow her down. And now she's out there, being hunted by St. George and Talon, maybe dead, and it's all my fault."

"Hey." I crumpled the empty M&M's bag, making her startle and look at me. "Beating yourself up isn't going to help her," I said firmly. "She made the choice to go rogue. She had to know the dangers. Besides—" I shrugged, feigning a confidence I didn't feel "—she's with Riley, and he's been doing this for a long time. If anyone can get away from St. George, it'll be him. Don't give up on them just yet."

She cocked her head. "You think so?"

"Yeah. So try not to worry. We don't know anything yet." I felt like a hypocrite, telling her not to worry when there was a yawning hole in the pit my stomach, threatening to devour me.

I slid from the bed, managing a smile as I headed toward the bathroom. "Be right back," I told Faith as she looked up. "Feel free to grab more food, or use the bed, or whatever. I don't know what we'll end up doing after this. You should rest while you have the chance."

She nodded but didn't say anything, fiddling with the wrapper of her candy bar, and I slipped into the bathroom.

Alone, I sat on the edge of the tub and dropped my head into my hands, breathing deep to keep the fear from swallowing me whole. Riley was out there, with Talon and St. George. What if he *wasn't* all right? What if he was dead? I didn't know what I'd do if the cocky, infuriating rogue was really gone, but my dragon was torn between curling into a ball and keening her loss and ripping something's head off.

Pushing myself upright, I splashed cold water on my face and ran wet fingers through my hair, making it stand on end. I was hot, sticky, and I desperately wanted a shower. But there was no time, and besides, if Garret or Wes burst into the room, I did not want either of them to catch me naked. I did, however, find my Viper suit where I'd tossed it on the floor. I pulled it on, then yanked my regular clothes over it. The outfit sucked greedily at my skin like it was eager to have me back, making me squirm. But if we were going to head back out for Riley and face St. George, at least, this time, I'd be prepared.

Faith had fallen asleep on the bed when I emerged from the bathroom, her breathing deep and steady. I smiled, tiptoed around the bed and shut off the lamp, plunging the room

into shadow. The girl didn't even stir, soft snores coming from
her open mouth. I watched her sadly for a moment, wondering if she would be all right. If anyone needed to get out of
Talon, it was her, but I hoped she could handle being a rogue.
It wasn't the easiest life, that was for certain. Come to think
of it, *I* wasn't doing such a stellar job, myself.

I drew back, slipped quietly across the room and cracked
open the door.

Garret stood there, leaning with his back against the wall
and his arms crossed, vigilantly scanning the hallway. When
the door squeaked open, he immediately pushed himself off
the frame and turned to me, eyes questioning.

"Any word from Riley?" I whispered.

He shook his head. "Wes still hasn't been able to get a lock
on his phone. How is Faith?"

"Sleeping," I replied, and took a step back. "Come on in,
just be quiet. I don't want to leave her, and who knows when
she'll get another chance to rest."

He eased through the frame, glancing warily around the
room to make sure we were still alone, that no one had
climbed in the windows or from under the bed when my back
was turned. When he was sure the shadows were empty, he
relaxed and followed me to the sitting area, where the huge
curtained window showed off the glittering Vegas cityscape.
I peered through the crack at the glowing carpet of lights,
and my insides churned with worry. Riley was somewhere
down in that mess, dodging St. George, fighting his way back
to us. *Still alive*, my dragon insisted. He had to be. I wouldn't
let myself think that he wasn't.

"Where are you, Riley?" I whispered to the haze of neon

lights. "Don't you dare die on me." A lump caught in my throat, and I clenched my fists. "Dammit, I hate this," I growled, feeling my dragon raging inside. "I feel so helpless. I wish I knew what to do." Garret watched me, silent and grave, and I slumped against the window. Las Vegas stretched out below me, dazzling and bright, but I couldn't see the luminance anymore. Now all I could see was a war zone.

"People are dying, Garret," I whispered. "Riley's out there. Ava is out there. And I'm just…" *Scared. Lost. Completely unprepared for what being a rogue actually means.* I leaned my forehead against the cool glass, staring at the streets until they blurred and ran together. "I don't know what I'm doing," I admitted. "I thought I did, but I was wrong. I have no idea what to do now. I…" *I don't want to lose anyone else. Especially him.*

Garret moved close, and then two strong arms enfolded me from behind, drawing me close. My pulse skipped, and my heartbeat sped up, echoing his own. I felt his quiet presence at my back as he leaned in, lips close to my ear.

"Riley's a pro at survival," Garret said in his soft, low voice, making my insides flutter. No reassurances, no empty promises, just simple facts. "He's been doing this a long time, longer than either of us. I know St. George. I know how they work." He paused then, his voice becoming just a little lighter. "I'm not too proud to say that he's smarter than most everyone in the Order. If anyone can get through this, he can."

I turned and slid my arms around his waist, hugging him to me. My fingers brushed the smooth metal of the gun beneath his shirt, and I wasn't afraid. He was a soldier, a former dragonslayer, but I felt safe with him. I trusted him completely. It wasn't the fierce, fiery longing my dragon had for

Cobalt. It was…simple. Easy. When I was with Garret, it was like we just clicked.

Riley's voice echoed in my head, angry and accusing. *Humans and dragons aren't supposed to be together! Their lives are a heartbeat compared to ours. What kind of future do you think you could ever have?*

I tried to shove it down, even as part of me agreed. I was a dragon; what was I doing with this human? My instincts raged at me, edgy and restless. I shouldn't be here; I should be with Riley right now. Why did I keep resisting? Cobalt and I were the same, split down the middle. Not only in species, but in everything that mattered. His dragon called to mine, and I knew he felt the same about me. If Garret wasn't here, it wouldn't even be a question.

But, Garret is here, I thought rebelliously. *He chose to be here. We gave him the chance to leave, and he chose to stay.*

For how long? the dragon whispered back. How long did I think a former soldier of St. George would remain in the company of his enemies? How long before he realized we had no future, that a dragon and a human were two vastly different creatures, and had no business being together?

"Garret?" I asked, making him shift to look down at me. In the face of those solemn gray eyes, my throat went dry, and I swallowed to clear it. "Is this…? Are we…?" I exhaled and pressed my face to his shirt in embarrassment. Garret waited patiently for me to go on, his arms still looped around my waist. I ducked my head, closing my eyes so I wouldn't have to look at him. "Us," I whispered. "What we're doing… Is this wrong?"

Garret went very still. I counted his heartbeats, listened to the rise and fall of his breath. "I don't know," he finally said, his voice just a whisper between us.

I gave a bitter chuckle, stifling my disappointment. "That's not exactly the rousing assurance I was hoping for."

"I know," he murmured, sounding resigned, though he still didn't let me go. "But I'm probably the last person you should ask." He rested his chin gently atop my head, his voice thoughtful. "All my life, I was taught that dragons were evil, that they had no souls or emotions or real feelings, that they were just imitating humans in order to blend in." His hand traced my back, making my skin prickle. "And then, I met you. And discovered that everything I had learned, everything I thought I knew, my entire way of life, was wrong."

The pain in his voice, the underlying bitterness, clawed at me. "I'm sorry," I told him. "I never wanted you to regret this."

"I don't." Garret pulled back to look at me, his metallic gaze intense. "Maybe I would've been happier if I'd never come to Crescent Beach," he went on, making my stomach knot painfully. "If I was still with St. George, I'd still be killing dragons, because that's what they expected of me, and I wouldn't know any better. Maybe ignorance is bliss, but that doesn't make it *right*." His face tightened, eyes going dark. "I think back to who I was, what I did, before we met, and it sickens me. I'd rather die right now than return to the Order. I'd rather be hunted like the very ones I used to kill than revert to the ignorant soldier I was. That life is done. I want no part of it anymore. All because I met a dragon on a beach, and she refused to be what I expected." One hand rose, pressing against the side of my face, stroking with his thumb.

"Ember, meeting you is the most important thing that's ever happened to me," he said in a quiet voice. "I wouldn't change it for anything."

"Really?" I smiled, feeling my chest squeeze tight. His words made my heart soar, but the intensity of his gaze was too much. "Even after everything? Being shot at and chased and followed around the casino by a security guard for underage gambling?" I asked, trying to ease the tension.

"Even then," Garret replied, his eyes shining silver in the darkness. "I think…I'm in love with you, Ember."

GARRET

Did I really just say that?

Time had frozen around us, the echo of my confession hanging in the air, impossible to retract. Ember blinked at me, looking as stunned, and almost as panicked, as I felt. What had come over me? Was I losing my mind? I had absolutely no experience to draw on. Nothing like this had ever happened to me before. Tristan would've laughed at my idiocy. I had been a soldier of the Order; our love affairs involved weapons—machine guns, pistols, sniper rifles. Instruments of death, not people. The Order itself cautioned about divided loyalties, saying our hearts should belong to St. George and the mission before all else. Marriage was infrequent among soldiers; most of us died young, and dedication to the cause had to take precedent over everything else, even family. The bond we shared with our brothers, our comrades in arms, was stronger and far purer than the weak desires of the flesh. I'd known that, believed it wholeheartedly, once. I was what they made me: a weapon. The Perfect Soldier. What did I know about love?

For a second, I balked, my heart going cold in my chest. Why *had* I said anything? I knew she wasn't human. Though she looked and acted and sounded like a normal girl, Ember was, at her core, a dragon. A creature that, according to the Order, could only imitate emotion. I no longer even remotely believed that, but I barely understood human emotion; I knew nothing about the hearts of dragons.

The soldier pressed forward, blank and emotionless, ready to numb all feeling. To shield me from pain and humiliation and fear. This had been a mistake. I'd left myself open, vulnerable, but there was still time to withdraw, to retreat behind a wall of indifference and—

No. I hardened myself, steeling my emotions in a different way. No illusions this time. No doubts. I knew exactly what was happening, that the girl in my arms wasn't human. The Order would call me profane, a blasphemer, a demon lover. I was selling myself to evil. I was joining the devil's own and damning my soul to hell. Ember might not return my feelings, not in the human sense. I didn't know if dragons were even capable of love.

All of this went through my head in a heartbeat, and between one pulse and the next I decided, once and for all, that I didn't care. Ember was a dragon. She was also beautiful, fearless, kind and ironically more human than the very people who wanted her whole race extinct. I didn't know if most dragons were as the Order said they were—ruthless, conniving, power hungry—but I did know not *all* dragons were like that. Ember was different. Riley was different. I'd seen it firsthand. And the hatchlings I'd met, Ava and Faith, they weren't the savage monsters St. George claimed them to be, either. The Order had lied. Talon had lied. I didn't know what to think anymore, or who to believe. I was aware of only one thing: I was done fighting this. I no longer cared what anyone thought.

I was in love with a dragon.

Let the Order condemn me, I mused, perhaps my first truly rebellious thought in a lifetime. *Let them call me a traitor and hunt me down.* For thirteen years, I had followed commands, lived by the rigid code of St. George, become their perfect soldier, only to discover the Order I'd dedicated my life to was wrong. Everything I'd thought I knew was a lie. The only real thing was the girl in my arms.

"Garret," Ember whispered, her eyes huge in her face as she stared at me. I felt the acceleration of her heartbeat, thudding rapidly against mine, felt a tremor go through her, and held my breath. And I waited, everything frozen inside, to see if the dragon I loved would leave me unscathed, or shred my heart to ribbons in front of me. "I… I don't…"

A phone rang loudly in the darkness.

EMBER

I jumped, leaping away from Garret, as a tinny melody shattered the quiet, coming from the bed. He let me go, turning toward the sound as well, his expression shutting into that remote blankness. My heart raced, thrilled, relieved, absolutely terrified. I didn't know what to feel; I didn't know what I wanted. I only knew that the tangle of confusion, worry and dragony rage inside was threatening to pull me apart.

Later, I decided, between one muffled ring and the next. I would sort through everything later. I couldn't think about... what Garret had said right now. First, we had to find our missing dragons.

Faith stirred. Rising groggily from the mattress, she fumbled in her pocket and brought the phone to her ear with a mumbled "Hello?"

Instantly, she bolted upright, eyes going wide. Gazing across the room, she spotted me and swung her legs off the bed, holding out the phone. "It's Ava!"

I lunged and snatched the device from her hand. "Ava, are you all right?" I asked, putting it to my ear. "Is Riley with you?"

"Ember?" The voice on the end was a gasp, and cold fingers clutched my insides. "We couldn't...make it back," Ava panted, sounding frantic and breathless. "St. George followed us from the building and have spread out. They're not letting us leave the area." She took two deep, ragged breaths, her next words laced with fear. "You have to come quick. Riley's been hurt—"

The blood froze in my veins. "Where are you?"

"Some old rail yard a few blocks from the hotel. Please, hurry. We don't..." She trailed off, and in the distance, I thought I heard the sounds of gunshots.

"Ava?"

"They're coming," the other dragon whispered.

The line went dead.

"Ava! Dammit!" I yanked the phone from my ear and stood there, trying to calm the fiery urge to Shift and crash through the window after them. What did I do now? Riley was out there, wounded, maybe dying, and St. George was closing in. Panic raged inside, the dragon flaring up and down my veins, screaming at me to do something.

"What happened?" Faith asked, her eyes bright with terror. "Are they all right?"

"Riley's been hurt," I said, clenching the phone so that the edges bit into my palm. My skin felt tight, the air in my lungs simmering with heat. "They've been trapped, and can't get back to the hotel. We have to help them."

"Where are they?"

Garret's cool, steady voice broke through the rising panic. My dragon snarled at him, impatient and wanting action, not this sitting around to chat. *Stop it*, I told her. *We can't just charge through the window and wing off to find Riley. We need a plan.* I took a deep breath to calm us both and forced myself to think.

"Ava said something about a rail yard a few blocks from the abandoned hotel," I told the soldier. "But she didn't give me any street signs or numbers. And I didn't see any railroads when we were running from the building, did you?" Frustration reared up again, and I rubbed a hand across my face. "They could be anywhere, and we don't have time to guess. St. George is almost there."

"We won't have to guess. Come on." And Garret strode purposefully from the room, leaving me and Faith to scramble after him. We crossed the nearly empty hall, not pausing to look for would-be enemies, and Garret banged twice on Wes's door.

It swung back, and the gangly human glared out at us, looking exhausted. Dark circles crouched under his eyes, and his hair stuck out in every direction. "What do you—"

"Ava contacted us," Garret interrupted, making the human's brows shoot up. "St. George has them cornered in a rail yard a few blocks from the building we left. Can you pull up a map of the city?"

"Shite," Wes muttered, and ducked back into the room, hurrying to his laptop. We followed, crowding around the chair, as his fingers flew across the keyboard and his shoulders hunched in concentration.

"All right," Wes muttered, his nose very close to the computer screen, making it hard to see around him. "A rail yard, you said? That shouldn't be terribly hard to find." He typed a few more things, and the screen flipped to a large map of Las Vegas. "Okay," Wes mumbled, zooming in until street names

appeared on-screen, "this is where we are now. And here—"
he scrolled over the map "—is the site of that abandoned hotel.
So, now we're looking for a railroad… Wait, that must be
it." The mouse arrow circled a confusing jumble of lines and
squares on the map. "About five blocks east from the hotel
site," he said. "Right on the edge of town. Bollocks, Riley,
what were you thinking? You don't run *away* from the lights
and crowds if the Order is chasing you. Certainly not to an
isolated warehouse in the middle of nowhere." Sitting back,
he eyed us over the chair back. "If they're down there, that
place will be crawling with dragonslayers. You'll be walking
into a death trap."

"We don't have a choice," I said. "Riley's in there, and he's
hurt. Besides," I went on, glaring at him, "I thought this was
what you wanted. It's my fault he's in trouble, isn't that what
you implied?"

"That doesn't bloody mean I want you to rush into a trap
and get your stupid head blown off," Wes snarled back. His
eyes flashed, staring me down, before he sighed and scrubbed
a hand through his hair. "What do you think Riley will do
if you get yourself killed?" he went on in a softer voice. "He
nearly lost his mind the last time you were hurt. If anything
happens to you now, he'll never be the same. Riley is the
beating heart of this underground, but if you die, the resistance might very well die with you. Because he might not
have the will to care anymore."

I blinked in shock. Wes sighed, rubbing the bridge of his
nose, his face taut with pain. "I just want you to *think*, hatchling." He sighed. "To come up with some sort of plan, otherwise you'll *all* be killed."

"Don't worry about that," Garret broke in, and Wes turned to eye him wearily. "I know St. George," he added. "I know their tactics, and what they'll be doing. We're not going in blind. I'll get them out."

"I'm coming, too," Faith said.

Surprised, I looked at her. She stood a little ways behind us, pale and terrified but resolved. "Ava saved me," she insisted. "I wouldn't have gotten out of Talon if it wasn't for her. I want to help, however I can."

Garret shook his head. "You're not trained for this," he stated. "I can't effectively search for the others if I'm worried about protecting you, Faith. It's better if you stay here."

"Please," Faith whispered, and turned to me. "Don't leave me here," she pleaded. "I can't stay behind, doing nothing, not knowing if you'll come back. I swear I won't get in your way or slow you down. And I'll do whatever you tell me to do." Her eyes went glassy, even as she took a deep breath, composing herself. "Ava is like a sister to me," she said, making my stomach knot. "I won't abandon her. I might not be trained for this, but two dragons stand a better chance against St. George than one. Please, I have to come."

I looked helplessly at Garret, who nodded. "All right," he agreed, sounding reluctant. "Just stay close, and try to hide if things get dangerous." He turned to Wes, his voice cool. "They'll need weapons," he said. "Both of them. If St. George is down there, we can't take any chances."

Wes nodded, rising from the chair. "I suppose there's really no other way to do this," he said, pulling a duffel bag from the corner and setting it on the bed. Unzipping it, he stepped back as Garret rummaged inside and pulled out a handgun.

Turning, he offered it to me. I took it without hesitation this time, checking the chamber for rounds before shoving it into the waistband of my jeans and pulling my shirt over it, as I'd seen Garret do. No being squeamish now. I was a soldier, and this was a war. If we were going to save Riley and Ava, I had to accept that.

Faith paled when Garret held a pistol out to her, but she took it without hesitation. Wes watched the soldier with hooded eyes, his expression torn between dislike and cautious hope. "Get Riley out," he told him, as Garret checked his own gun for rounds, then snapped the cartridge back into place. "Nothing else matters. You're not just saving him, you're saving everyone in his underground. I can't do what Riley does. If he dies, all the dragons and humans he rescued from Talon are as good as dead."

"We'll bring him back," I told Wes, feeling a fiery determination spread through me. There was no way I was going to let him die. He was my other half; without him, I felt incomplete. I wasn't sure if this was my dragon talking or me, but I couldn't imagine a world without Riley. I looked to Garret, meeting those solemn gray eyes, and took a deep breath. "Ready?"

He nodded once. Together, we walked through the casino, out the doors and into the hot Vegas streets.

Back into the war zone.

GARRET

This place was a tactical nightmare.

The rail yard was separated from the rest of the city by a rusty chain-link fence and a strip of industrial desert that marked the end of civilization. Tracks stretched across the open, dusty ground, and aisles of freight containers created a labyrinth of cover and tight quarters. If I were to stage an ambush, this would be the perfect spot.

"Stay alert," I told Ember as we crouched behind a metal container on the edge of the yard. The place looked deserted, but that meant nothing. St. George knew how to stay hidden. "Watch the aisles, they'll be the most dangerous. If you see anyone, don't try to take them out. The Order never does single patrols. If there's one, there'll be more nearby. Just get out of sight."

She nodded, eyes determined. "I'll follow your lead," she whispered, raising the gun. "Tell me when to go."

Behind her, Faith trembled and pressed close, her gaze darting around the yard like a trapped deer. I felt a stab of apprehension; Ember could take care of herself. Or at least, she had faced St. George before, and she wasn't afraid to fight. Faith, despite her insistence on coming along, was not prepared for this. If we ran into the Order and had to fight our way free, I hoped I could protect us all.

I motioned us forward, and together we darted across the open yard, staying low and keeping to the shadows, until we reached the first train sitting idle on the tracks. Hugging the walls, I edged toward the front, peeking between cars for any hints of movement on the other side. Ember stayed close; I could feel her heat at my back, her steady breathing whenever we paused. For a moment, I had a distracting sense of how surreal this situation was. Again. Here I was, a former soldier of St. George, on the other side of the war with two dragons at my back, trying to rescue one of their own from the Order. It was a fleeting thought; I couldn't let myself be distracted now. I had to stay focused on the mission and our surroundings, the tactics that would keep us alive. But it crept in all the same, dark and taunting. Would this ever feel normal? And who was I? I didn't even recognize myself anymore.

"Where are they?" Ember whispered as we crept into an open boxcar after making certain it was empty. "This place feels completely deserted. Where could they be hiding?"

"I don't know," I murmured, peering out the other side of the car. The space between the narrow aisles was dark and still. Too still. No bullet holes, no footprints, no signs of a fight or struggle. I hadn't seen any telltale spatters on the ground, either, which made me both relieved and nervous. The Order was trained to strike hard and fast and to vanish without a trace when the job was done, but they would at least leave *some* signs of passing. There was nothing here. Ember was right; this place felt completely deserted.

"What about that building?" Faith said, pointing to a large

rectangular structure beyond the maze of tracks and containers. From this angle, it looked like the freight warehouse. "Do you think they could've gone in there, to hide at least?"

I shook my head. "That would be one of the first places the Order would search. If they are in there, they're either trapped, or..." I didn't voice what I was thinking, but Ember went rigid at my back, drawing in a short breath. She knew what I was going to say.

"We have to check it out," Ember said, her voice tight with anger and fear. Not fear for herself; I recognized that steely look on her face, and knew nothing would frighten her away now. It was for Ava and Riley, and what would happen if we didn't find them. Or worse, if we *did*. I remembered the aftermath of a successful raid; the smoldering ruins, the charred, blackened husks that were once people, the lifeless dragons lying in pools of blood. My stomach turned. I didn't want Ember to see that, to really see what St. George did to her kind. What I used to do.

"Let's go," Ember told me, rising swiftly. "If St. George is here, we have to help them. They could still be alive. And if they're not, if the Order killed him..." Her eyes flashed, and I caught a split-second glimpse of an angry red dragon below her skin. Her lip curled, and the air around her shimmered with heat. "If St. George wants to fight a dragon, I'll give them one."

"Ember, wait." I caught her arm, felt the faint outline of scales rising to the surface before they vanished. She turned on me, and I met the furious glare of the dragon. "Stay calm," I murmured. "Don't go charging off by yourself, not with St. George. This is *not* a good place to fight the Order." I nodded toward the warehouse. "There'll be a lot of narrow aisles and tight quarters, places where it's easy to become cornered or trapped or lost, and St. George is trained to take full advantage of that confusion. If we're separated, they'll pick us off one by one. We can't help Riley if we become hunted ourselves." She stubbornly set her jaw, and I raised my other hand, pressing it to her cheek. "Do you trust me?" I asked.

"Yes," she whispered. No hesitation. Not even a heartbeat of silence. It made my heart turn over, that blind faith in a former dragonslayer, but I shoved it down. We had to stay focused.

"I promise," I began, even as a part of me cringed inside. I never made promises to anyone; it was impossible to know if you could keep them. But the way Ember was looking at me, I wanted to give her some kind of assurance. "We'll get Riley out," I continued. "And Ava. I'll do everything I can to keep them safe, but I also know what can happen if we're not careful. The Order has us at a disadvantage. This is their ideal location for a strike, and if they surprise us we don't stand a chance."

"You seem to have forgotten that I've done this before."

"I know." I almost smiled at her indignant look. As if I could forget what she really was, what she had done. "But this is still the Order, and they'll still do their best to kill us. I can't help Riley and be worried about you and Faith at the same time."

Ember was stiff for a moment, then nodded. "All right," she said quietly. "I trust you, Garret. What do you need me to do?"

"Just follow my lead," I replied. "We stay together at all

times. And don't Shift unless it's a matter of life and death. Faith?" I glanced over my shoulder at the other girl. "Are you all right? Can you do this?"

"I'm…good," Faith whispered, though a tremor went through her voice at the end. She took a deep breath and straightened grimly. "I'm okay. Lead on. We're right behind you."

We crept silently across the deserted train yard, weaving between cars and hugging the shadows, always on guard for the Order. I kept my eyes trained for movement, footprints in the dust, spent bullet casings or drops of blood. Nothing.

"Are you sure Ava said they were here?" I asked, glancing at Ember as we crouched behind a row of shipping containers a few yards from the warehouse. She nodded vigorously.

"I'm sure. Old rail yard a few blocks from the abandoned hotel." Ember scanned the open space between the tracks and the warehouse, frowning. "She said Riley was hurt and they had to hide because the Order was coming."

Unease gnawed at me. It didn't make sense. If I wasn't sure that this was the only rail yard this side of the city, I would think we were in the wrong place. Still, we couldn't go back, not until we were certain. If Ava and Riley were here, we had to find them.

There was no movement or sound as we approached the warehouse and sidled along the outer wall, looking for a way in. Several windowpanes were out, the glass shattered and broken, but they were filthy and covered in grime and cobwebs. Nothing had gone through them in a while. Beyond the filmy glass, the interior of the warehouse was dark, with aisles of freight stacked nearly to the ceiling. Again, my sol-

dier's instincts recoiled. Another maze of narrow halls and
tight quarters; I was liking this situation less and less. The
large metal doors, where freight was presumably taken and
dropped off, were closed and locked tight, and nothing short
of a blowtorch or a pack of C-4 was going to force them open.
My hope that Ava and Riley were here was fading fast, when
Faith gave a sudden gasp and surged forward.

"Ava!" she cried, making me jerk up. "Wait!"

Before I could stop her, she sprinted forward, toward an
open door I hadn't noticed, and vanished through the frame.

"Dammit," Ember growled, and started forward, as well.
"Come on, Garret, before she gets herself killed."

I gave a silent curse and hurried after her, ducking through
the opening into the enormous shipping room. The shadows
of the warehouse closed around us, smelling of dust, wood and
iron, and the maze of crates and shipping containers loomed
overhead. Faith was nowhere to be seen.

Grimly, I raised my weapon and motioned Ember behind
me. Hugging the walls, we edged around the stacks of crates,
searching for the girl while staying on high alert. Light footsteps pattered across the floor, fading into the darkness, but it
was impossible to tell which direction they were coming from.

"Dammit, where did she go?" Ember muttered.

A scream cut through the darkness, turning my blood cold.
It was followed by a crash and the sound of a scuffle somewhere in the maze. Ember snarled something in Draconic and
rushed past me, her eyes flaring green in the darkness. Gripping my weapon, I followed. The aisles of freight abruptly
ended in a large open area, cement floor bare but for a few
stacked pallets and a forklift.

"Faith!" Ember hissed, creeping forward with the gun raised. "Where are..."

A figure melted out of the shadows, dragging something into the light, and my stomach dropped. Faith met my gaze, her eyes huge with fear, as a man in a black suit yanked her forward, one arm around her neck, the other pressing a gun to her temple.

The lights came on, driving away the shadows, and a half dozen armed men stepped into view, muzzles of their M-16s pointed right at us.

RILEY

"Comfortable, Cobalt?"

Ava lowered the phone and turned, smiling at me across the table. Without waiting for an answer, she reached over and flipped on the spotlight, beaming it right in my face. I squinted but refused to turn my head. "Anything you want to say before we get started?"

"I'm good, thanks." I tried to shrug, which was harder than it looked, being tied to a chair with my arms behind the metal back. The plastic cuffs dug into my wrists as I turned, pretending to look around the room. "Though the service in this place sucks. I ordered a glass of 'Screw you, Talon bitch' an hour ago."

Ava smiled.

"Vulgar bravado will not save you, I'm afraid." The girl walked around the table, regarding me like she might a particularly tricky math problem. Plucking a needle and syringe from the table, she held it up and turned back to me. "I assume you already know what I stuck you with."

"I'm guessing Dractylpromazine," I replied. Developed in Talon labs using a mix of science and old magic, "Dractyl" was a powerful tranquilizer that essentially put the dragon side of us to sleep, preventing Shifting and locking us into a human form for a short time. One of Talon's more terrifying weapons against their own kind, it was a jealously guarded secret, given to agents only in rare, special circumstances. I'd attempted to Shift earlier, as soon as I'd woken up and realized where I was. But the dragon had barely stirred, sluggish and groggy, as if coming out of a long hibernation. That was when I'd known this wasn't an ordinary kidnapping, that whoever had captured me knew exactly what I was and how to counter my most potent weapon. Which meant only one thing.

Talon had finally caught up. I was in trouble.

"Yes," Ava agreed, putting the syringe back on the table. "So you know escape is impossible. That dose is good for at least three hours, and I have several more where that came from. None of your friends know where you are, and I disabled your phone so that your human hacker friend won't be able to track it. No one is coming for you." She stepped in front of the table and faced me head-on. "This doesn't have to be hard, Cobalt. You know I'm going to get what I want, sooner or later. How quick, and how painful, this is going to be depends on you."

I smirked. "Is that your best opening? Take away all hope, make the victim think he has no options left, that you're always one step ahead of him. If he has nothing left to cling to, nothing will matter to him, and he'll be much more pliable to suggestion." She blinked, and my smirk grew wider. "Psychological Warfare 101, hatchling. I've *forgotten* more about Talon mind games than you'll ever know. If you think you're going to out-psyche me, give it your best shot. I can do this all night."

"Insightful," Ava said, sounding reluctantly impressed. "You do remember your Basilisk training, after all. When we first met, I thought you were just a thug who kept getting lucky. I'd forgotten you were one of Talon's best."

"I was," I agreed. "Though I must not rate *too* high on Talon's threat meter, if they're sending hatchlings to do a Viper's job. So, what's your *real* name? If we're going to go through the dance tonight, you can give me that much, at least."

The girl regarded me for a moment, then shrugged. "I suppose it doesn't matter now," she mused. "My real name is Mist."

"Mist, huh? You're awfully young to be doing this with no backup." I curled my lips into a sneer. "Is this your exam, hatchling, or are all the real agents off murdering defenseless kids in their sleep?"

She offered another faint smile. "Trying to anger me into letting information slip is not going to work, either, Cobalt. Besides, you know the answer to that as well as I do."

I did know, which made the organization's interest in me all the more insidious. Talon couldn't send one of their real agents after me because I knew them all. If someone like Lilith or another Viper showed up in town, I'd be gone the instant I got word of it—unless I was trying to convince a stubborn, red-haired hatchling to leave with me, that is. It didn't even have to be a Viper; *any* dragon from my old life, be they Viper, Basilisk, Chameleon or Gila, I was instantly wary of. Talon knew I'd never trust one of their agents. They had to send a hatchling, someone I'd never seen before and would want to help, to lower my guard.

I should've seen this coming. I knew Talon was getting irritated with my high jinks; losing even one or two hatchlings a year was a big thing when your numbers were small. I'd thought I could handle whatever big nasty Viper they sent to take me out. But Talon was also devious as hell, a master of manipulation, of finding your weaknesses and using them against you. They'd baited me with the one thing I couldn't ignore: a couple hatchlings in trouble, and I'd fallen for it like a moron. I'd been overconfident and was paying for it now.

Fortunately, I had a couple tricks up my sleeve, as well.

"Pretty clever," I admitted, looking at Ava, or *Mist* now, I supposed. "The soldiers of St. George were a nice touch. That ambush felt completely real." Mist didn't answer, and I sighed. "We can play these games all night," I said, subtly reaching my fingers into one of my jacket sleeves, feeling around the cuff. "But I'm tired and sore and kind of cranky, so can we get on with it? What do you want from me? Or, rather, what does Talon want from me?" Mist raised her brows, and I rolled my eyes. "Don't act so surprised. If the organization just wanted me dead, I wouldn't be here now. They wouldn't go through all this trouble to set me up. What does Talon want?"

Mist pushed off the table, serious now, her eyes hard and cold. "The location of your safe houses," she said, making my stomach lurch. "All of them. Where they are, how many dragons live there and the number of humans you have working for you. Give us the information, and we promise that most of the hatchlings will survive."

I barked a laugh. "Really?" I sneered. "That's all Talon wants? Me to betray every dragon and human I spent years protecting from the organization? That's not completely insane at all."

"Think of what you're doing to them, Cobalt." Her voice changed, becoming low and soothing. "Think of what their existence means for us all. All Talon wants is for their hatchlings to return to the organization, where they belong. Where we can protect them. You can't really believe they're better off with you. Constantly in hiding, always on the run? Living in fear that the Order will come for them in the middle of the night? What kind of life is that?"

"A free one," I returned, curling my lip in disgust. "One that isn't dictated by the organization's demands, or what Talon wants them to be. One where they can actually breathe without Talon looming over their heads, ready to pounce if they set one claw out of line. Where they can actually have thoughts of their own, and choose their own future, instead of being forced into the role that would benefit the organization." I gave her a grim smile. "I'm sure *you* didn't have a choice tonight. If Talon gives the order to betray, capture and interrogate your own kind, you don't get to question why."

Mist cocked her head, looking truly baffled. As if she couldn't imagine how this was a bad thing. I sighed. "Not all of us want our lives run by Talon," I finished, knowing I was wasting my time. Mist was too deep in the organization, fully indoctrinated to Talon's way of thinking. She wouldn't understand. "Some of us would rather be free. To at least be afforded that choice."

"Free?" Mist gave me an incredulous look. "At what cost? Our extinction? Is this so-called freedom so important that you would risk the existence of our entire race? How many have you lost to St. George? How many hatchlings have died because you took them from the organization and threw them into the world with no experience, no knowledge of what they were doing? Without Talon and its resources, they're exposed not only to the Order, but to all of humanity. Even you realize that we cannot let the humans know about us. Your rebellion is endangering us all. Something had to be done."

"Why now?" I asked. "I've been doing this for years, and Talon didn't seem to care much, other than a couple half-hearted Viper assassination attempts. Why are they so interested in me now?"

"I'm afraid you don't get to know that."

"Well, we're at an impasse, then," I said, leaning back in my seat as best I could. "Because I'm not giving up my nests to Talon, no matter what you say. Especially since I know you're going to kill me right after. Doesn't give me a lot of incentive to cooperate."

Mist shook her head.

"I was hoping it wouldn't come to this," she said, turning to the table behind her. "I was hoping you would see reason, and realize this is for the survival of us all." Leaning forward, she dragged a rolling cart out from under the table. It had been draped with a towel, and a shiver went through me as she pulled it into the light.

Mist walked around the cart and faced me over the toweled surface. "This is your last chance," she said, fingering the corner of the cloth. "No one is coming for you. No one will hear you. I *will* get what I want, make no mistake about it. How long it will take depends on you." She reached beneath the towel, drew forth another syringe and set it next to the Dractyl on the table, where it glimmered wickedly. My blood chilled at the sight of it. "This can be quick and painless," Mist went on, "or we can drag it out, all night if we must. It's up to you. What is your answer, Cobalt?"

I took a deep, steadying breath, feeling my heart pound through my veins. "I don't think you have the stomach for this," I said, looking her right in the eye. "What's more, I don't think you *want* to do this. It takes a certain mind-set for this kind of work, and you're not like that. Not the girl I've seen tonight, anyway." Her brow furrowed just slightly, and I pressed forward. "You can walk away, Mist," I said earnestly. "This doesn't have to be your life. Talon doesn't have to control it. Come with us, and I can show you how to be free."

For just a moment, she hesitated, a flicker of uncertainty crossing her face. I leaned forward, ignoring the cuffs digging into my skin. "You know you don't want to do this," I cajoled, my voice gentle, and she scowled. "Mist, listen to me. You don't belong with them. You're resourceful, quickthinking and one of the most intelligent dragons I've ever seen, hatchling or otherwise. Your talents are being wasted. Think of what we could do for our kind if Talon wasn't in the picture. Cut me loose, and we can leave together."

"You're wrong," Mist answered, and a steely note had entered her voice. Straightening, she narrowed her eyes to icy blue slits and pushed the cart back. "I am what Talon requires," she said, all hesitation gone. "The organization entrusted me with this task, and I will not fail them. I need that information, but if you refuse to cooperate, then you leave me no choice."

She grabbed the second needle from where it lay on the

table, turned and plunged it into my neck. I jerked, clenching my jaw as my fingers fumbled further with the cuff of my
sleeve and the thing I was trying to get at slid away. Mist in-
jected the syringe's contents into my veins and stepped back,
replacing the needle on the table.

"What was that?" I growled.

"Sodium thiopental," Mist said, wiping her hands on the
towel. "Only, this is a special version, produced in Talon labs,
specifically for our kind. Our scientists have been mixing
science and magic to great effect lately. It's still in its experi-
mentation phase, but the results have been very encouraging."

Sodium thiopental. Truth serum. Dammit. As a rule, dragons
were fairly resistant to modern drugs and their effects. Much
like alcohol, the amount required to get any kind of reaction from a dragon would kill a normal man. But we weren't
immune. Pump us full of enough shit, and we'd feel the effects, same as a human. "You're very forthcoming suddenly,"
I said, renewing my efforts with my sleeve cuff. Where was
that stupid slit? I had to find it again before I got too loopy
to do anything. "Sure *you're* not the one who got stuck with
the needle?"

Mist regarded me with a practiced blank expression. "I'm
telling you this because I want you to know that fighting
is useless," she said, "and it would be better in the long run
to give me the answers quickly. Holding out is only going
to make it worse. I *was* going to interrogate you the old-
fashioned way, but I suspect you have a fairly high pain threshold, and Talon wants the information as soon as possible. We'll
give that a few minutes to work, and then we'll see how you
feel about cooperating."

"I didn't think Vipers did this sort of thing," I said, buying time as Mist leaned back, regarding me blankly. "Isn't your shtick more murder and assassination? Is Lilith finally deciding to branch out?"

Mist paused, the hint of a smile tugging at her lips, turning my insides cold. "What makes you think *I'm* a Viper?" she asked. "I was trained to be a Basilisk, just like you. Don't worry, though," she went on, and settled back against the table, crossing her arms. "I'm not the only agent Talon sent. The Viper should be finishing up shortly."

EMBER

"Drop your weapons."

The human's voice echoed in the empty space, low and commanding. I tensed, eyeing the men surrounding us. Not soldiers of St. George; they wore black business suits and no armor, looking more like bodyguards or FBI agents than military people. Their guns, however, were all too real, pointed unerringly at me and Garret. My heart seized with the realization.

Not St. George. Talon.

The man holding Faith cocked the hammer of his weapon and shoved it harder against her temple, making her gasp. "I won't ask again," he warned. "Put your weapons on the ground and your hands on your head. Now."

"Dammit." I glanced at Garret, who lowered his gun, looking resigned. Bending down, he set the pistol on the cement and rose, clasping his hands behind his skull. With a growl, I did the same, tossing the weapon to the floor and lacing my fingers behind my head. The half circle of men closed in, motioning us forward, keeping their guns trained on us. They also kept a safe distance away, I saw as we were herded toward the front. Wary and alert, offering no opportunity to be pounced on by a dragon. They knew what they were dealing with.

The man in the suit didn't smile as we were brought before him, didn't move a muscle. His grip on Faith didn't lessen, though he kept his gaze trained on us. My mind raced. Talon was here for me. Not Faith or Garret. Just me. I didn't know how I knew this, but I did.

Faith met my gaze, pale and terrified, her eyes pleading for me to do something. Setting my jaw, I took a step forward.

"Let her go," I said, as all the guns came up, pointed at me. I stopped, keeping my hands raised, meeting the impassive stare of the human in front of us. "Leave both of them out of this," I insisted. "They're not important. Just a runaway and a human nobody. You're here for me, right? I'm the one you want."

The agent didn't reply. He continued to stare at me, expressionless, and my desperation grew. "Please," I continued, taking one more step toward him. "You don't need them. Let them walk out, and I…I'll come quietly. I'll go back with you to Talon. Just let them go."

And Faith started to laugh.

"Oh, Ember." She chuckled and slid easily from the human's grip, smiling at me. "You *are* naive, aren't you?"

RILEY

I slumped forward, feeling sweat run down my face into my eyes, my jaws aching from clenching them so hard. I knew if I relaxed an inch, I would start babbling like an idiot, but at the same time, my inclination to care was getting smaller and smaller. I knew the drug was working its way through my brain, suppressing inhibition and my ability to think straight. I had been completely, utterly trashed exactly once in my lifetime, having consumed enough alcohol to drown a football team. This felt very much the same.

"It doesn't have to be like this," Mist said in a gentle voice. "Tell us what we want, and this can be over. You know you're going to break sooner or later."

"Probably." The word slipped out before I could stop it. *Damn. Stop talking, Riley.* "Though I don't see why I shouldn't drag this out as long as I can," I went on, as my mouth refused to cooperate. "You're going to kill me as soon as this is over."

Mist didn't answer, which told me everything I needed on that front. Deliberately, I jabbed myself with the item between my fingers, and the instant flare of pain cleared my head for a moment. "Just tell me one thing," I gritted out, meeting the other dragon's cool gaze. Hoping she wouldn't notice the blood dripping from my hand to the floor. "Since I'm going to be spilling my guts here shortly, I think I deserve at least one straight answer. How much was Griffin paid to sell us out?"

Mist's slender eyebrows rose. "Enough," she replied, her gaze almost impressed. "Mr. Walker's deal with the respective parties is not important right now, but I am surprised you know about him."

"I didn't," I said, making her blink. "I was guessing a second ago. You just confirmed it."

Mist's gaze hardened. Crossing her arms, she leaned back and watched me, saying nothing more. My vision grew blurry, and everything became dreamlike and surreal. I felt like I was floating, and strange images filled my head, hazy and fragmented. Where was I? How did I even get here?

"Are we ready?" A clear, quiet voice cut through the drunken fog. I didn't know what it meant by that, but another question followed before I could wonder about it. "What is your full name?"

"Depends on who you ask," I heard myself saying, though my voice sounded slurred and detached, like it belonged to someone else. "I've had a lot of names."

"Your real name, then. The one given to you when you were hatched."

"Cobalt," I replied. That was an easy answer; no use in trying to hide it.

"And how many humans do you have in your network right now, Cobalt?"

"I don't know, exactly." I shrugged. "I've lost count. Maybe a few dozen?"

"All from Talon?"

"Yeah."

"Excellent." The girl looked pleased. She placed a chair in front of me and sat down, then leaned forward to peer into my face. I stared blankly at the floor between us and felt cool fingers against my sweaty cheek.

"Cobalt, listen to me," the voice cajoled, and I raised my head to meet those intense blue eyes. The rest of her face blurred in and out, and I blinked hard to clear my vision. "Where are your safe houses located?" she asked in a firm, direct voice. "Your resistance has been admirable, but you will answer me, now. Where are Talon's hatchlings? Tell me where you hide your rogues."

EMBER

"Faith?"

I stared in disbelief as the other girl smiled and stepped away from the man in the suit, brushing at her sleeves like she was trying to wipe away filth. The human didn't even glance at her, keeping his gun pointed directly at me. The six men behind us didn't move, either.

"What's going on?" I asked, my voice sounding small and weak in the vast chamber. Faith dusted off her hands, tossed back her curls and shot me a look of supreme disdain.

"Oh, I think you know the answer to that," she replied, with a smile that was completely different from the shy, terrified girl of a moment ago. "You're smart enough to figure it out. You wouldn't be one of *her* students if you weren't. By the way, do you like where I staged this little encounter?" She raised her arms, as if showing off the room around us. "I thought it would bring back memories."

And everything hit me with a jolt. The warehouse. The maze of crates and shipping containers. The armed men surrounding us. I stared at Faith, horror and rage creeping over me. "Lilith," I growled, making her smile widen. "You're one of her students, aren't you? You're a Viper."

Faith chuckled. "Her *only* other student. Before you came along, anyway." For a second, her eyes glittered, a flash of hatred crossing her expression, before she shook it off and smiled again. "She told me to tell you hello, and that she fully expected you and Cobalt to fall for such an obvious trap. A beginner's mistake, if you ask me. If you had only completed your training, this never would have happened."

"Where's Riley?" I snarled, making the men surrounding us raise their weapons higher. "You know where he is, don't you? Tell me!"

"He's dead," Faith replied offhandedly. "Or he will be soon. Mist should be nearly done."

"Mist?"

"Oh, sorry. That's Ava to you."

The floor dropped out from under me, and for a moment, I couldn't breathe. Not only was Faith a Talon operative, Ava was one, too. This whole thing was an elaborate plot by the organization. If they had sent a Viper, Lilith's other student, of all people, I must have really pissed them off. And Riley... might already be gone.

I clenched my fists as my dragon snarled in defiance. "No," I said, as Faith's eyebrows rose. "You're wrong. You don't know Riley. He's more than a match for any Talon agent." He had to be; I refused to believe anything else. If he was dead...I would know. My dragon would know. "It's Mist you should be worried about," I told Faith.

Faith shrugged. "Regardless," she said, seemingly unconcerned about her partner, "he's not here. And he isn't the one *you* should be worried about right now."

Her gaze shifted away from me, turning calculating and

cruel as it fixed on Garret. "A soldier of St. George," she mused, and my blood chilled. "How very...interesting. You *have* fallen quite far, haven't you?" She shook her head and glanced at me with obvious contempt. "Consorting with the enemy? Allying yourself with a soldier of St. George?" She *tsked*, a mock-sorrowful look crossing her face. "For shame, really. What would Lilith say? What would *Talon* say?"

My throat felt tight with panic. I didn't know what was happening with Riley, what Mist was doing to him, but I did know what would happen to Garret. Talon would kill him, right now, for no other reason than he had been part of St. George. It didn't matter that he was on our side now. It didn't matter that the Order itself was hunting him. They would show a soldier of St. George no mercy, unless I could somehow change their mind. Fighting right now would be suicide. With half a dozen guns trained on us, even if I survived, that first volley would kill the soldier.

We were trapped. Riley was gone, we were outnumbered and outgunned, and the Viper had us right where she wanted. This was checkmate for us, but I had to save Garret, at least. I could endure going back if I knew the soldier was still alive out there. And then, when I had returned to Talon and discovered who was responsible for this, I would take my revenge. For Riley, Dante, Garret and all the rogues Talon had crushed. If I couldn't be free, I would make them suffer for it.

But keeping Faith from putting a bullet through Garret's skull was the important thing right now.

"Let him go," I told Faith, who raised her eyebrows. "He's not part of the Order anymore. You've been around us. You know he's not one of them." Her lip twisted nastily, and my voice hardened. "He saved your life from St. George, remember that? They would've killed us all if he hadn't been there."

"Ember," Garret said quietly, a motionless presence at my back. "You don't have to do this."

I ignored that, continuing to stare at Faith. "Let him go," I said once more. "I'm the one you want, right? Trust me, you don't want to kill him."

"And why is that, exactly?" Faith smiled, eyes gleaming. I wondered how I'd ever thought of her as some innocent kid. "I've seen the war," she continued. "I know what St. George does to our kind. Who cares if the human doesn't hunt dragons now? He was still part of the Order, which means he's killed before. As a loyal member of Talon, I'm not only expected but required to take out their enemies whenever I get the opportunity. Why should I let him go?"

I swallowed hard. "Because," I whispered. "If you let him go, I'll come back to Talon willingly. I'll become a Viper, or whatever they want from me. Let him live and I...I won't try to leave again, I swear."

"No," Garret said, stepping forward. "Ember, don't—"

Two men closed on him, weapons raised. Garret stopped, lifting his arms again, but his gaze sought mine. "Don't bargain for me," he said in a low voice. "Not with Talon. They don't accept compromise. It's either all or nothing...and my life isn't worth your freedom."

I met his gaze. "Yes, it is."

"Ember—"

"Don't argue with me, Garret," I almost hissed, feeling my throat tighten. "There is no way I'm going to stand here and watch them shoot you. Just shut up and let me do this, okay?"

My voice was starting to tremble; I swallowed hard and took a quick breath to steady it. "I already lost Riley," I whispered. "If I have to go back, at least I'll know you're still alive."

"Well, this is all very interesting." Faith's cool, amused voice made me bristle. I turned back to find her watching me, that chilling smile on her face. "You are correct," she told me. "We *do* want you to return to Talon, that's why they sent me, of course. But there is a small problem with your proposal. You see, you've already confirmed your disloyalty to the organization, and they are somewhat reluctant to take you at your word. If you want to come back, you're going to have to prove that we can trust you again."

I clenched my jaw. The thought of having to prove anything to Talon rankled. But if it would save Garret's life... "How?" I asked through gritted teeth.

Faith nodded to the men behind me. As I spun, two agents stepped forward, one on either side of Garret, and forced him to his knees. The others formed a line behind the soldier, keeping their guns trained on the back of his head. I started toward them, but Faith grabbed my arm in a grip of steel.

"You want to prove your loyalty to Talon?" she asked, and pressed a cold black pistol into my hands, making me freeze in horror. Faith didn't smile as she let me go, nodding toward the kneeling soldier.

"Kill him."

My heart stood still. I stared at the weapon in my hands, torn between hurling it away and shoving the muzzle in the Viper's face. Not that it would do any good; Faith could probably disarm a person fairly quickly, and neither choice would help Garret, kneeling in front of what I knew was an execution line. Any aggressive move on my part might trigger them to blow his head off. Gripping the handle of the gun, I looked up at Faith, shaking my head in disbelief.

"You're crazy," I told her. "Did you not hear me at all? I said I'd come back to Talon if you let him go, not murder him in cold blood. You can't possibly expect me to do this."

"I don't think you understand the situation you're in," Faith replied, and made a vague gesture at Garret. "The soldier is dead," she said flatly, making my heart drop. "Either way, no matter what you decide, we're going to kill him. There is no argument that will convince me to spare an agent of St. George. I am not here to make bargains. I'm here to bring you back to Talon, and this is the final test to see if you can be trusted. If you refuse, then you will share the soldier's fate."

"Then you'll have to kill us both," I said, feeling my lungs heat, the dragon rising up for a final, desperate battle. *I'm sorry, Garret. I wanted us to be free of Talon. But if they won't let us go, I'll fight as hard as I can.*

"Really?" Faith gave me an evil, knowing smile. "So, you would sacrifice not only the human, but Dante, as well?"

RILEY

"Phoenix."

Mist cocked her head, regarding me intently, as if trying to determine whether or not I was lying. I growled a curse and hunched forward, panting, feeling the other dragon's gaze on the top of my skull.

"Phoenix," she repeated in a slow, clear voice. "That's where your safe houses are located?"

"One of the locations," I replied.

"There are others? Where?"

"All over the place. Austin, Phoenix, San Francisco. There was even one in Mexico for a little while." I listened to myself ramble on, unable to stop. "I thought about moving some of them overseas, but that would require me to travel more. I can't be on two continents at once."

"No, you cannot." I heard the triumph in her voice. "And how many hatchlings are you hiding, right now?"

"Twenty-three."

She blinked, the only outward sign of surprise. "You *have* been busy, haven't you?"

"I've been doing this awhile."

"Indeed." Mist leaned farther forward, her gaze intense.

"Where can we find them, Cobalt? Tell me exactly where they are."

"You'll never find them," I slurred, smiling up at her with the knowledge. "If I disappear, Wes will give the signal for everyone to move. They'll be gone before Talon ever gets there."

"It doesn't matter," Mist said. "Once we have them on the run, they'll be easy to track down. You're only delaying the inevitable." Her voice dropped, became soothing again. "Stop fighting, Cobalt. Where are they? Tell me the closest safe house from here."

Fighting. Why was I fighting? That seemed hard right now, too much work. "The closest safe house from here?" I shrugged. "That's easy. I have one right in the city."

Mist frowned. "Here?" she asked. "In Las Vegas?"

"Yep." I nodded, tilting my head back. The inside of my skull felt full of cotton; a weird sensation. "We were just there a few days ago, in fact."

"Who was there?"

"All of us. Me, Wes, the soldier of St. George, Ember…"

Ember.

Deep inside, the dragon stirred, rousing sluggishly at her name. It struggled into consciousness, growling defiantly, before sleep overcame it and it sank into the void again. But that brief rush of heat and fire burned away the fog and, for just a moment, my thoughts were clear.

"Was there anyone else in that safe house?" Mist went on, her voice closer now, not seeming to come from a great distance away. "Any hatchlings that could still be there, right now?"

I clenched my fist, curling my fingers around the item in

my palm. It bit into my skin, and I exhaled in relief. Still there. I hadn't dropped it. "No," I muttered, almost before I knew what I was saying, and winced. The damn truth serum was still in full effect. "There was no one else. Just us."

"All right." Mist slid off the table, coming to stand in front of me. "Enough of this," she said, and a note of impatience had crept into her voice. "You know what we want, Cobalt. You know you cannot hide them from Talon any longer. I will make this as clear as I possibly can. Where—"

"Before you ask," I interrupted, making her frown in surprise, "there's something you should probably know. Well, a couple things, really. One, you're either very inexperienced at this, or overconfident. Or both. You realize you left that second dose of Dractylpromazine sitting on the table there, right?"

"Yes," Mist said, glancing at the syringe. Her brow furrowed in wary confusion as she turned back. "But I'm in no danger. The dose I gave you is good for another hour, at least. Why?"

"No reason." I shrugged. "Only, you forgot one of the prime rules of interrogation training. Never leave possible weapons like that lying within the prisoner's reach. Because if they ever escape their plastic cuffs, that's the first thing they'll go for."

Mist jerked back, eyes widening...as I surged to my feet, snapping the weakened plastic restraints, and lunged for the syringe.

EMBER

"Dante?"

The flames within sputtered and died as I sucked in a horrified breath. Faith smiled, looking pleased, and I clenched my fist, glaring at the other hatchling. "Where is he?" I demanded. "What have they done to him?"

"He's safe with Talon," Faith went on. "For the moment, at least." She paused to let that sink in, before continuing, "You don't quite realize what's at stake here, do you? This isn't only *your* final exam. It's also Dante's. The organization is testing him, making sure they can trust him, the brother of a rogue and a traitor. This plan, well, most of it anyway, was his idea. If you fail and refuse to return to the organization, *he* fails, as well." Faith smiled evilly. "And you know how Talon feels about failures."

I felt like I'd been punched in the stomach. Dante was in charge of this. He'd sent Mist and Faith after us. He was responsible for Riley's disappearance and, if things continued down this road, Garret's death. Did he know what he was doing? Was Talon coercing him, forcing my brother to go along with their plans? If I didn't return to the organization tonight, Dante would fail. I might never see him again. But to go back, to make sure my brother would be safe…Garret had to die.

"So, you have to ask yourself—" Faith's voice was a croon, low and dangerous "—who is more important to you? Who are you going to save? The soldier of St. George? The greatest enemy of our kind? The human whose pitiful life span will be over in the blink of an eye?" She glanced at the kneeling soldier, a look of contempt crossing her face, before turning to me again. "Or will you choose Dante, the twin you've known all your life? The dragon whose only concern, from the moment you ran away from Talon, has been your safety? He's waiting for you, Ember. Everyone is. We all want you to come home."

I was suffocating, struggling to breathe, to make an impossible choice that wasn't really a choice at all. I couldn't shoot Garret—there was no way I could do that. But if I didn't, they would kill us both anyway. And who knew what Talon would do to Dante.

I looked down at the weapon in my hand, then back to Garret, kneeling on the floor in front of the firing squad. His expression was blank, carefully guarded, though his eyes were bleak as they met mine.

Faith eased closer, her dark gaze burning the side of my face, as her voice dropped to a soothing murmur. "You can start over," she said. "Everything you've done will be erased, all your crimes against Talon will be forgiven. You belong with your own kind. But, if you don't pass this test, you will die. And Dante will suffer for your failure." She leaned back, her expression confident, as if everything had already been decided. "I think you know what you have to do."

And suddenly, I did.

I shivered and closed my eyes, willing my hands to stop shaking. "If...if I do this," I whispered, "can you promise that Dante will be safe? That none of this will impact his place in the organization? And that we'll be able to see each other again, without consequence?"

Faith's voice was full of triumph. "You have our word."

"Okay." My voice came out choked. Raising my head, I met the gaze of the soldier in front of me, knowing he hadn't glanced away from us the whole time. Garret watched me, gray eyes resigned, the look of someone who expected to die.

"I'm sorry," I told him in a shaking voice, and felt my stomach wrench sideways at the look on his face. Betrayal and disbelief glimmered from his eyes, a split-second reaction, before his expression shut down and became a blank mask. Taking a deep breath, I stepped forward. "This is my brother," I went on, my voice pleading and defiant at the same time. "My twin. Dante has always been my first priority. I'll do anything to keep him safe, even this."

Garret didn't answer. I spared a glance at the men behind him and found they were watching me, not the soldier. Clearly, the dragon girl with the gun was the bigger threat, though they still kept their weapons trained on the back of his head.

My heart was pounding in my ears as I stopped a few feet from the kneeling soldier. I could feel Faith's eyes on my back, the hawk-like stares of the men behind him, but my gaze was only for Garret. He was still watching me, though his eyes were distant now, almost glassy. Like he was staring right through me, at something I couldn't detect. A lump caught in my throat, and my stomach twisted so hard I felt sick.

With trembling hands, I raised the gun, aiming it at his forehead. Garret closed his eyes, bracing himself. For a split second, with my finger curled around the trigger, everything held its breath.

"Look at me," I whispered. He didn't move, and I hardened my voice. "Look at me, Garret. I want to see your face when I do this. Open your eyes."

For a heartbeat, the soldier remained motionless. For an agonizing moment, I thought he would refuse. But then he opened his eyes and his dark, tormented gaze met mine. I stared into those gray eyes and mouthed a single phrase, hoping he would understand.

Trust me.

He blinked…and I opened my fingers, dropping the weapon at my feet.

The second the gun left my hands, I Shifted, exploding into dragon form with a roar, my wings snapping behind me as I reared onto my hind legs. The Talon agents instantly raised their weapons, sighting down the much bigger threat, but I sucked in a breath and blasted them with fire, sending two of them reeling back. Still, I couldn't catch all of them, and the chatter of assault rifle fire echoed through the room. Bullets whizzed by me, sparking off my horns and chest plates, and at least two punched through my wing membranes, making me shriek with pain.

A gun barked and two men fell. Garret had lunged forward, snatched the fallen pistol and fired with deadly accuracy into the line of Talon agents. The rest of them scattered, diving behind cover, as Garret leaped upright, still firing his weapon, and I tensed to attack.

Something slammed into me from the side, knocking me away from Garret and sending me tumbling across the floor. I caught myself, looking up just in time to see a lithe dragon, its scales a dark indigo, lunge at me with the speed of a cobra. I managed to scramble back, and Garret raised his gun to shoot it, but a hailstorm of bullets caused him to duck behind a stack of crates, hunkering down as the shots tore into the wood and peppered the wall behind him.

Ignoring the preoccupied soldier, the purple dragon turned to me, eyes gleaming yellow in the dim light. She was a little smaller than I was, with an elegant tapered head and a long, graceful neck and tail. Her scales were so dark they were nearly black, her chest and belly plates a lighter indigo, as were the wing membranes. A mane of curved black spines ran down her back from a narrow, hornless skull as she raised her head and hissed a challenge, needlelike fangs flashing viciously in my direction.

"Come on then, *Viper*," she called, raising her voice to be heard over the cacophony of shouts and gunfire around us. "Let's see who's the better student. Just you and me, no friends, no interference." She half spread her wings, giving me an evil smile. "Of course, if you want to know about your brother, you'll have to beat me first."

She launched herself into the air, soaring over my head, to land somewhere in the maze behind us. I tensed to spring after her but paused, looking back at Garret. He was still crouched behind the stack of crates, pistol in hand, bursts of gunfire tearing splinters from the barrier in front of him. Our gazes met across the room.

"Garret—"

"Go," he called, motioning with his free hand. "I'll cover you, and I'll catch up when I'm done. Go!"

He turned, firing twice at a cluster of pallets. There was a cry, and a Talon agent fell into the open, his gun clattering to the cement. I winced, then spun and bounded into the maze.

RILEY

Mist hit me hard, side-kicking me in the ribs just as I reached the table, knocking me back. Grunting, I staggered, and she followed with a nasty roundhouse kick to the temple that, had it connected, might've knocked my lights out. But she'd taken the bait, left herself open, and I caught the foot as it came in, spinning and throwing her into the corner. She crashed into the wall and slumped to the floor, dazed, though not for long. I snatched the syringe and bolted out the door.

Bursting through the frame, I hit the railing of a flight of stairs and stared into the dark, open expanse of a warehouse, aisles of containers and crates spread out below. Of course, it was the perfect place to stage this little encounter. Silent, empty and isolated—no one around to see an interrogation, a murder or a huge mythological creature chasing someone through the aisles.

Speaking of which…

There was a low growl behind me, raising the hairs on the back of my neck. I leaped over the railing, dropped the eight or so feet to the ground and sprinted behind a stack of crates as the door burst open and the roar of a pissed-off dragon echoed through the room. Ducking into the nearest aisle, I pressed back into a corner and tried to Shift, hoping that the tranquilizer had worn off.

Nope. Couldn't do it. My body stayed locked in human form, the dragon barely responding. Cursing, I looked around frantically, searching for anything that would help me even out this fight. Crates, containers, random boxes. Unless I found a hidden stash of guns, or maybe a couple grenades, this was going to go poorly for me.

My hand throbbed, and I clenched my fist, gritting my teeth. Thank God Mist hadn't removed my jacket before the interrogation; she might've discovered a few other precautions hidden within the lining, as well. A lifetime of close calls had taught me to be ready for anything: capture, imprisonment, being abandoned behind enemy lines. I'd learned to rely on myself and to always have a backup plan. Case in point: having to cut myself free with the razor blade hidden in my jacket cuff. The thin lacerations across my wrists were shallow and would heal quickly, but they still stung like the world's most obnoxious paper cut.

A large, ghostly shadow soared overhead, landing atop a nearby crate, and I froze. In her true form, Mist was as slender and poised as her human counterpart, her scales a glittering blue-white, her ivory horns curling back from her skull. Sinking to her haunches, the pale dragon folded her wings, curled a long, diamond-tipped tail around herself and peered into the darkness with slitted blue eyes.

I didn't move, holding my breath as that piercing gaze swept the warehouse. This was bad. The white hatchling was graceful, elegant and probably one of the prettier dragons I'd seen in my long existence, but I was still human, and she could turn me inside out with one claw.

Abruptly, Mist raised her hair, nostrils flaring, to sniff the air. And I winced, realizing my mistake.

She can smell your blood, idiot. Move!

I bolted from the corner just as Mist turned her head sharply, blue eyes narrowed in my direction. With a hiss, she leaped gracefully atop another aisle, then another, following me as I sprinted through the labyrinth of crates. I could hear her talons scraping over metal and wood, and didn't dare look back as I fled through the aisles, searching for anything that would save my hide.

As I hurried down a dark, narrow corridor, stacks of plywood on either side, there was a blur of motion from above. I skidded to a halt, tensing to run back the way I'd come, as the white dragon landed in front of me with a snarl. Raising her head, she drew in a breath, the fire gland below her jaw swelling, and my pulse spiked. I dived aside, toward a narrow gap between piles of wood, and squeezed through as a massive firestorm erupted behind me, setting everything ablaze. Wrenching myself through the space, I scrambled upright, feeling the immense heat at my back, searing through my clothes. Panting, I tensed to run again, when I spotted a gleam of yellow in the corner of the aisle, half-hidden in shadow, and my heart jumped.

Oh, please let that work.

An angry roar echoed behind me. Without looking back, I bolted to the corner, swung into the forklift seat and grabbed for the key, praying it would be there. It was still in the ignition, and the engine sputtered to life as I wrenched the key up and threw the machine into Drive.

A white dragon landed in the aisle with a snarl, hellish firelight playing across her scales. She had just enough time to glance up and hiss in alarm…as the forklift slammed into her, the metal prongs catching her on either side. Shrieking, she was dragged across the cement floor, ripping and tearing at the forklift, until I drove full speed into the opposite wall. The impact rocked me forward, nearly throwing me out of the vehicle, and several large crates tumbled free and crashed around us, spilling their contents everywhere.

Mist slumped against the prongs, trapped between the fork-lift and the wall. Her legs moved weakly, and she raised her head, dazed, as I dropped from the seat and stepped around to her side. Crystal-blue eyes opened, trying to focus as I fished in my jacket and pulled out the syringe.

"Wait," she muttered, trying to struggle free. Her wings fluttered, pinned against the wall, and she clawed feebly at the metal prongs. "Cobalt, stop. You don't know what you're doing."

"Sorry, kid," I muttered, and drove the needle into her neck, angling up to slide it between the scales. She snapped at me, and I dodged back, watching as her struggles grew weaker and weaker. Eventually, her eyes rolled up, and she collapsed against the forklift. I sighed, stepping away, as the white hatchling gave a final twitch and lapsed into a drugged sleep.

"I do know what I'm doing," I told the unconscious dragon. "I've always known. I just wish you could have seen it, too. I wish you could see what Talon is doing, to all of us." Shaking my head, I watched her for another moment, then took a step back. "I would have shown you everything, if you had let me."

Raking a hand through my hair, I turned and sprinted out of the aisle, back to the office to search for my phone. I had to contact the others, let them know I was okay. Let them know they were probably walking into an ambush. Alone.

With a Viper.

EMBER

Well, isn't this déjà vu?

I crept through the shadowy labyrinth of metal containers, all senses alert, searching for any hint of the other dragon. Of course, it reminded me of my training sessions with Lilith, stalking through a warehouse maze just like this one, hunting those who were hunting me. I was sure that was exactly Faith's intention; she seemed to emulate her trainer flawlessly, taking sadistic pleasure in my pain. But she wasn't going to win this time.

There was a ripple of movement above me, a shadow darting from other shadows. I tensed, craning my neck up, wary for an attack from above. For the indigo dragon to suddenly pounce from the ceiling. I had used that tactic many times my—

A blur of motion from the side, and something hit my front leg, tearing through scales and skin to the muscle beneath. I snarled, fangs bared, but all I caught was a brief glimpse of a long, slinky tail vanishing around a corner. Already gone.

Wincing, I glanced at my shoulder. Four straight, narrow gashes cut through my scales, already starting to well with blood. They weren't very deep; my armor had absorbed a good bit of the attack, but they still hurt like hell.

A scraping sound came from the corner Faith had vanished around and I whirled, ready for the attack. It came from a different direction altogether, talons ripping into my flank. Roaring, I loosed a blast of flame that seared the container behind me, leaving a black spot in the metal, but Faith had already vanished.

Growling, I turned in a slow circle, trying to watch every angle at once. "Is this what Lilith taught you?" I challenged, feeling hot blood trickle down my shoulder and back leg, dripping to the cement. Both wounds throbbed, but I refused to show pain. "How to hit someone in the back? What's the matter, scared I'll kick your ass if you face me head-on?"

A sibilant chuckle echoed from the darkness around me. "I don't know what they saw in you," the disembodied voice stated. Impossible to pinpoint which direction it came from. "For the life of me, I can't imagine why Talon chose Lilith to be your instructor. What a terrible waste of her time and talent. It's certainly not her fault you were completely un-suited to be a Viper. No discipline, no killer instinct at all." A disgusted sniff followed, though I still had no idea from where. "I heard the Elder Wyrm was hoping to ingrain some of Lilith's ruthlessness into you, that's why she was chosen as your teacher," Faith continued, "but then you went rogue and disappointed everyone. Your brother is much more sal-vageable, I hear."

"Where's Dante?" I snarled, my voice echoing through the warehouse. "I don't believe he set this up, he wouldn't do that do me. You're lying."

Another soft laugh. "I suppose the hatchling in the meeting with Mr. Roth—the one who looked just like you—was just there to discuss politics," the voice said, finally resolving itself in a direction, directly in front of me. "Of course, you could always ask him yourself. If you survive tonight!"

I spun around with fangs and claws bared to face the dragon charging in from behind. With a triumphant snarl, I lunged, thinking I had her. Quick as a snake, she changed direction, leaped over my head and soared up to land on the container aisle behind me.

Dammit, she's fast. Hold still already.

Growling, I sprang after her, using a shove from my wings to launch myself off the ground. This time, the other dragon didn't run away but smiled as I landed on the edge of the container. Somewhere in the labyrinth, a flurry of gunshots rang off the rafters; Garret and the remaining Talon agents still going at it. I hoped he was okay, but I couldn't help him now.

"No more games," I said, glaring at Faith, who watched me with her tail curled around herself, that insufferably smug grin still plastered across her muzzle. She was faster than me, and she knew it, but I wasn't going to let her get the upper hand. "That's twice now that someone has mentioned the Elder Wyrm," I went on. "What does the CEO of Talon, the most powerful dragon in existence, want with us? And how does Dante fit into all of this?"

Faith sneered. "You think they'd tell me? If you're so very curious, go back to Talon and ask him yourself. Or better yet, I can call him right now and ask him." She jerked her slender muzzle at the ground, smiling. "I left my phone right over there when I changed. There's only one number on it. Call him yourself and see what your precious twin has been doing."

Without thinking, I glanced in the direction she pointed. And Faith lunged.

I jerked up, realizing what she was doing at the last second, and the other dragon slammed into me, knocking me off the edge. I tumbled to the floor, hitting the cement on my side, the impact driving the breath from me. Gasping, I struggled upright as Faith hit the ground a few yards away, landing as lightly as a cat. Her grin was cruel as she turned to face me, lashing a slinky tail against her flanks.

"You wanted me out in the open, *Viper*," she taunted, as I growled and staggered forward, trying to ignore the dull ache in my side. "You wanted to face me one-on-one. Well, here I am. Are you ready?" She gave a weird little sidestep, her lithe body rippling like ink across the cement. "Here I come."

And she surged forward, a dark blur over the floor. I barely had time to register she had moved when something hit my shoulder and sent a flare of pain up my leg. I snarled and lashed out with my claws, but Faith was already gone, skipping back out of reach, then darting in again. I managed to dodge the blow to my neck, feeling the tips of her claws rake along my scales, and sprang forward to sink my fangs into her throat. She sidled away, quick as a shadow, and slashed me across the face, rocking my head to the side. I stumbled, disoriented, felt something hook my front leg and yank it sideways. I lost my footing and crashed to the floor again, a breathless grunt escaping me as my chin struck the unforgiving concrete.

Ow. Crap, I'm getting my ass kicked here. Panting, I clawed myself upright, searching for the other dragon. She stood a few yards away, watching me with that amused smile across her narrow face, making my temper spike. She was toying with me, just like Lilith had.

"What's the matter, Ember?" Faith asked, cocking her head like a curious dog. "I thought this was what you wanted. Are you saying you expected to be able to take on a Viper without finishing your training? If you had only stayed with Lilith, you might actually have had a chance." She shook her head, narrowing her yellow eyes at me. "Are you ready to stop this, kill the soldier and return to Talon? Or am I going to have to tear you apart bit by bit?"

Dammit, she's so fast. How do I counter it? Angrily, I thought back to the fight with Lilith, trying to think of anything that I could use. *She's quick, but she's relying on speed to keep her out of danger. If I could get close, I might have a shot.* I took a deep breath, bracing myself. *Okay, then. Let's do it. This is gonna hurt.*

Raising my head, I met the other dragon's smug grin with one of my own. "You're making the same mistake she did," I told her, making her blink. "She thought I was beaten, too. Overconfidence must run in the family." Faith's smile faded, and I bared my fangs defiantly. "Talon's best Viper did her best to drag me back to the organization, and I'm still here. What makes you think her slimy little apprentice will do any better?"

Faith slitted her eyes. "You know what?" she said, gliding closer, her body nearly invisible in the shadows. "I think I'm done playing with you. It was fun, seeing you and the soldier stumble about, completely oblivious. It was *highly* amusing, watching the pair of you dance around each other like skittish goats." Her muzzle curled back, showing rows of needle-sharp teeth. "But you crossed the line. You have feelings for that human, that soldier of St. George, and that's something no true dragon would ever allow." She sank into a crouch, her lean body coiled like a snake, ready to strike. "You're a disgrace to Talon," Faith spat, lashing her tail. "An embarrassment to us all. And I think Lilith would congratulate me for getting rid of you!"

She lunged, a streak of darkness over the cement. I snarled and leaped forward to meet her, lashing out with my claws as she got close. Like quicksilver, she sidled away, leaving a stinging gash along my neck as she did. I turned, lowered my head and plowed forward, pursuing her across the floor. She dodged and twisted away, slashing me with her talons, trying to fall back. I took the blows, gritting my teeth with every gash and cut ripped across my scales, and slammed into her like a bull.

My horns struck her chest, bowling her over with a startled gasp. She hit the floor on her back and instantly kicked out with her back legs, catching me in the stomach and ribs with her back claws as I pounced, tearing me open. I ignored the pain and went for her throat. Snarling, we rolled across the floor, tails and wings lashing, trying to pin the other down.

Shrieking with fury, we rolled into a pair of steel drums in the corner, tipping them over with a crash. Liquid spilled everywhere, sharp and acrid, stinging my nose and burning my eyes. I was instantly drenched, choking on the fumes that rose around us, but I couldn't take my eyes off the Viper beneath me. As the drums clanged to the concrete, there was a split-second hiss...

...and a firestorm erupted around us. Flames shot into the

air, running up my back, spreading over my wings. It engulfed the Viper, surrounding her with fire, until she looked like a snarling, bat-winged demon from the pits of hell. Shrieking, she raked her claws down my neck, then slapped me across the muzzle with a flame-wreathed talon. Before, the gashes had merely stung; now it felt like a hot poker was being jammed up beneath my scales, then doused with acid. Pain exploded behind my eyes, snapping the final threads of clear thought, and I roared.

Pinning the Viper to the floor, ignoring the claws that slashed at me, I bared my teeth and aimed for that slender neck. My jaws clamped shut on the dragon's throat, right below her chin, and Faith screamed, thrashing wildly. All four talons beat and slashed at me, back legs kicking my stomach, front claws trying to shove me off. I closed my eyes, braced myself and began to squeeze.

"Stop!"

I paused, jaws still clamped around the slender throat, as the dragon's frenzied cry rang out, echoing off the rafters. "Wait, please!" Faith went on, her voice strangled. "Don't kill me! Stop!"

Relief, swift and sudden, spread through me, making my legs tremble. I hadn't really been planning to kill her, not like this. Viper or no, I couldn't stand here and ever-so-casually tear someone's throat out. No matter what Talon said, I was not Lilith, and I never would be.

I eased up a bit, though not enough to let go. "Why not?" I growled through my teeth. "Why should I trust anything you say?"

She writhed helplessly, tail beating frantically against my

legs. "Because I'll tell you about Dante," she wheezed. "I'll tell you whatever you want to know, just let me live." She swallowed hard, wings trembling. "Let me Shift back to human form," she offered. "I can't hurt you like that, right? And I won't be able to run. I'll Shift, and then I'll tell you whatever you want. Your brother, Mist, Riley. Anything."

I thumped my tail, as if I was considering a moment longer, then sighed. "All right," I muttered, and carefully opened my jaws, letting her slump to the concrete. I needed that information on Riley and my brother, and I didn't have the will for any more fighting. Not that I would've killed her anyway, but it was getting hard to move without sharp stabs of pain shooting all up my body. Turned out fire in open wounds was a bad idea. If she ran now, I didn't think I could catch her, even as a human.

Faith crawled out from under me and, as the flames around us burned low, started to shrink. Tail and neck retracted, scales disappeared and wings pulled into her body, until only a human in a black Viper suit remained sitting on the floor. She hugged herself and gazed up at me, looking like that scared, innocent girl I'd first met, though I knew better now. I folded my wings and sat down, clenching my jaw to keep from hissing in pain. No showing weakness in front of the trained Viper assassin. The last of the flames had finally flickered out, burning off with whatever flammable goo was in those drums, and now that the adrenaline was gone, I ached. Badly. The outside of a dragon might've been fireproof, but the numerous gashes I'd taken blazed with agony, burned and seared around the edges.

Great. I'm probably the only dragon in history who will ever suffer from third-degree burns.

"Riley," I said, my voice a low, dangerous growl. "Where is he? Why were you sent for us? Tell me everything you know."

Faith took a deep, shaky breath and exhaled slowly. "Mist and I were commissioned by Talon to find you and the rogue," she began. "My orders were to bring you back alive and kill anyone else involved. Mist was to go after Cobalt, extract certain information from him and then dispose of him. Divide and conquer, then return to Talon with our objectives, that was the plan."

I felt ill, but tried not to show it. "What information do they want from Riley?"

"I wasn't privy to that part of the assignment," Faith replied, and shrank back as I curled a lip at her. "Mist was the only one with that information," she added quickly. "I had my orders. That's all I was required to know."

"So you have no idea where Riley is right now. Or what Mist is doing to him."

"No."

I growled in frustration, scraping my talons across the cement. The girl flinched, but I ignored her. Still no information on Riley, where he was, if he was still alive. We were no closer to finding him than we were when we left the hotel. Mist and Faith had set us up perfectly.

And then, I remembered something else.

"Where is Dante?" I asked, narrowing my eyes at the other dragon. "You said you had his number on your phone. Or was that another lie?"

"It wasn't." Faith rubbed her arm. "Dante...is the one in

charge of this operation. He and the rest of the board are standing by. I'm supposed to check in with him as soon as I take care of you, one way or another."

My stomach dropped to the pads of my toes. "I don't believe you."

"Believe what you want." Faith's gaze didn't waver. "But Dante was the one who set this whole thing up. This was part of his test, coming up with the plan to bring you back to the organization."

My throat was suddenly dry. "And if I refused to come?"

"Then I had orders to kill you."

Reeling, I shook my head, still unwilling to believe. Dante had truly done this? My own brother had sent a Viper after us, with orders to kill me if I didn't return? That couldn't be right. He wouldn't do that to me. We might've argued, fought, disagreed on a lot of things, but Dante wouldn't give the order to take me out if I refused to cooperate.

Or would he? Was he so invested in Talon's doctrine that he'd really believe he was doing the right thing? I remembered something Riley had told me once, and it made my stomach twist. *Talon has him now. He'll betray his own blood if they give the order.*

Faith curled an arm around her side, her face creasing with pain. "What are you going to do with me?" she asked in a tight voice.

I stood up, wincing as the movement pulled at the charred, blackened cuts on my body. The Viper flinched, as if expecting a sudden attack, but I was just about done with this. My mind was spinning, I ached and I felt nauseous in more ways than one. "Take a message back to Talon," I growled at the

Viper. "And Dante. Tell them to stop sending people after me. They're just wasting their time. I'm not coming back." Faith still eyed me warily, like I might pounce on her as soon as she moved, and I bared my fangs. "Get out of here!"

She scrambled to her feet, holding her side, and staggered into the darkness. I watched until she slipped down an aisle and vanished, then I slumped to the cool cement.

"Ow," I whimpered, wishing I could just lie here and not move for a few minutes. I hurt all over, but at least I had won. I'd actually won a fight with a trained Viper. A small Viper, but a Viper nonetheless. I guess I should be thankful I was alive; Lilith's prize student certainly wouldn't have spared me if the situation were reversed. She didn't know how close she'd come to beating me, that I wouldn't have been able to kill her if she hadn't surrendered. *I guess I'll never be a proper Viper after all*, I thought, and felt nothing but relief at that notion. *And if Faith had realized that, I don't think I would've won.* But I didn't have to worry about her now. My bluff had worked. She was gone.

Though Mist was still out there. And Riley.

My stomach turned over. Setting my jaw, I pushed myself upright and started to limp back down the aisle. Find Garret, find Riley, deal with Dante. Those were the items I had to focus on now, in that order. And not passing out before we could leave; that was on the list, too.

A sibilant chuckle behind me froze me in my tracks.

"Oh, Ember," Faith crooned, as the ripple of a Shift went through the air. "Haven't you learned anything? What did Lilith teach you about showing mercy to your enemies?"

I spun painfully, knowing I wouldn't be fast enough. The

Viper was already in midleap, jaws gaping, talons fully extended to tear me apart.

A shot rang out, slamming the dragon aside. The Viper collapsed to the cement and rolled into a pile of crates, screeching in pain as she came to a halt. Heart pounding, I looked over to see Garret, pistol raised, step out of the shadows between aisles, keeping the dragon in his sights. His eyes were hard and dangerous, his expression a flinty mask as he aimed the gun at the fallen Viper.

Faith screamed in rage and defiance. Tail thrashing, she tried clawing herself upright, but a second shot followed the first, jerking her to the side. The Viper struck the crates and crumpled to the floor, leaving a bright crimson smear across the wood. Her wings twitched, frantically at first, then growing slower and slower, as a trickle of red seeped over the floor from her body. Her jaws gaped, gasping for breath. Her eyes glazed over in pain and fear.

"No," I heard her whisper. "Not yet. Not like this. I can't die...like this."

I felt sick. My legs wobbled, and it was uncertain whether they could hold me up much longer, but I gritted my teeth and staggered toward the dying dragon. She was a Viper, she'd been sent to kill us, but she was still part of my race, someone who had been just like me, once.

The Viper stared vacantly as I stepped up beside her, trying not to glance at her heaving sides. At the two round holes seeping blood right behind her foreleg. A perfect shot to the heart, from someone who knew exactly how to kill a dragon. Faith blinked, and I caught my reflection in one golden eye that was slowly turning to glass.

"I wanted…to be her best student," she whispered, as a thin line of red trickled from her nostril. "Her…only…student. I wanted to make her proud. To prove…I could be like her."

A lump rose to my throat, and I swallowed hard. "You are," I told her, my voice a ragged whisper. "You were a true Viper. Lilith would've been proud."

Faith didn't answer. Her wings had stopped moving, and her gold eyes stared up at me, fixed and unseeing. She was dead.

And the soldier who had killed her was standing right behind me.

GARRET

I lowered the gun, watching as Ember stepped away from the body, feeling some of the tension leave me as I gazed at the dead dragon. It was over. She was the last; the others, the Talon agents, were scattered behind me in the warehouse. They had fought stubbornly and persistently, down to the last man. As if they had nothing to lose. Maybe they didn't. Perhaps Talon's policy was return victorious or don't return at all. Regardless, it didn't matter. No one would be returning to Talon tonight.

Abruptly, Ember staggered, catching herself with a grunt, and my alarm flared up again. Holstering the pistol, I hurried toward her, scanning the lithe, scaly body for wounds. Her crimson scales made it difficult to see if there was any blood, though by the stiff way she was moving, I suspected she'd been hurt. I'd never witnessed a full-on dragon fight, but I had seen firsthand what their claws and teeth were capable of, able to crunch through bone and rip doors off vehicles. Their scales might be fireproof, but I imagined two warring dragons could still do a lot of damage to each other.

My hunch was confirmed when I drew close and saw the glimmer of open wounds on her back, four long claw marks that had been raked across her scales. But the edges around the narrow cuts looked *burned*, blackened around the edges, the flesh inside a raw, painful pink.

"Ember," I said, lightly brushing a wingtip as I circled around. More wounds came to light, all in the same condition, claw marks scored by flame. The faint scent of smoke and chemicals lingered in the air, seeming to come off the limping dragon, and I frowned. "What happened?"

"Bad decision that seemed a good idea at the time." Her voice was tight, and she turned to face me fully. Four thin, seeping gashes scarred her muzzle, red and painful looking, and my stomach clenched. "You killed her," she whispered, not quite accusing, but her eyes gleamed angrily. "You didn't have to kill her."

"Yes, I did." I met the dragon's gaze, saw my reflection in those slitted green eyes. They narrowed sharply, but I didn't feel one inkling of fear. Strange now, that I could stand this close to a furious, wounded dragon and know, beyond any doubt, that she would never hurt me. "I had to use lethal force," I told her. "You know that. She wouldn't have stopped until you were dead."

"I know. Dammit." Ember slumped, glancing at the lifeless body against the wall. A pained expression crossed her face, and she let out a gusty sigh, smoke curling from her jaws. "She was still one of us," Ember murmured. "She was like me, once. Who knows what she might've been if Lilith and Talon hadn't gotten their claws into her." A shudder went through her, and she turned her head, closing her eyes. "I wish it didn't have to be this way."

I reached out and put a tentative hand on her neck, feeling

warm scales under my palm. My heart jumped, still thrilled by the idea of touching a dragon. "We need to take care of those," I said, mentally assessing her wounds, wondering how serious they would be in human form. "Can you Shift back?"

"No." Ember shook her head, staggering away from me. "I mean, yes, I can, and I will, but...what about Riley? He's still out there. We have to find him."

"Ember, you're hurt. Badly, by the looks of it." I sidled around to face her, blocking her path. "We need to get you back to the hotel and let Wes know what's going on. Maybe he's heard from Riley by now."

"He would've called us if he had!" Her tail lashed, and she raised her head in defiance. "I'm fine, Garret. We have to keep looking."

"Where? We still don't know his location. He could be anywhere in the city by now. Where are you planning to search?" Ember slitted her eyes, and I kept my voice calm, knowing that if a five-hundred-pound reptile wanted to walk right through me, there was little I could do to stop it. The strangeness of standing in a dark warehouse arguing with a dragon did not escape me, either.

"We have to regroup," I said, hoping she would listen to reason, that her worry and eagerness to find Riley would not override logic. Some dark little part of me bristled with anger at the thought, but I shoved it down. "Let's go back to the hotel, get you taken care of, and see if Wes has heard any-thing. That's the most reasonable course of action right now."

Ember lashed her tail, taking a breath to argue, then frowned. "Wait," she muttered, cocking her head. "Did you hear that?"

I fell silent, pulling the gun from my belt and stepping around to her flank. For a moment, we stood there, a soldier of St. George and a dragon, guarding each other's backs. Strangely, it felt no different than the hundreds of times I'd done this with Tristan.

A faint, familiar jingle sounded, somewhere in the maze. Ember gasped.

"My phone!"

She started forward, stumbled and nearly fell, hissing in pain. Hurrying to her side, I gently caught a wing joint, making her pause and look back at me. "Hold on a second," I said, wishing I knew a trick to get a dragon to lie down, especially *this* dragon. "Ember, wait. You're going to hurt yourself." She snorted and glared at me, and I sighed. "Stay here and don't move," I said, holding out an arm as I backed away. "Lie down if you have to. I'll find it. I'll be right back." And I jogged into the maze without waiting for a reply.

I sprinted back to the place we'd first been ambushed, passing the bodies of several Talon agents, slumped in corners or behind crates. The majority of the group lay sprawled on the cement where the line had been, torched with dragonfire or shot with the gun Ember had tossed me.

The weapon she was supposed to kill me with.

My jaw clenched. For a bleak moment, I'd really thought she would. I knew she and Dante were close, that they shared a bond unheard of between their kind. Dante was a dragon, her brother and her only family; I was a human soldier she had known only a few weeks. She'd told me herself, she would do anything to get him out of Talon.

Why had she chosen me over her twin?

The ringing had stopped by the time I reached the area, but after only a few seconds of searching, it sounded again. I discovered the phone lying beside a pallet and snatched it up, bringing it to my ear.

"Wes?"

"Oh, goodie." The voice on the other end, though heavy with sarcasm, was not Wes. "You're still alive."

"Riley." I felt a strange mix of both relief and disappointment. Relief because, no matter what his feelings toward me, the rogue dragon was a competent leader and strategist, a soldier in his own right. And he obviously cared about the rogues in his underground, the hatchlings he got out of Talon, something I hadn't thought dragons capable of a month ago. I hadn't wanted him dead; I was glad he survived.

But at the same time, I'd seen how Ember looked at him sometimes, and I'd caught the protectiveness on his face whenever they were close. He was a dragon; long-lived, intelligent, and able to understand Ember in a way I never would. Jealousy was not something I'd experienced before. I despised how it made me feel. But it was there all the same.

"Where's Ember?" Riley asked, making resentment flare up again, stronger than ever. I stifled my anger, knowing it was unreasonable right now, and answered calmly.

"She's fine. She's wounded, but she'll be okay. We...ran into some trouble with Talon."

"Yeah, no shit." Riley sighed, sounding angry and weary all at once. "I guess you know by now that Faith is a Viper," he continued, sounding like he really didn't want to know the answer.

"Yes," I answered simply.

"Is she…?"

"She's dead," I replied, making him sigh again.

"I figured. Fucking Talon." The pain in his voice surprised me. "They were just kids. Sending Vipers after us is one thing, but they weren't even juveniles yet. Dammit." There was a muffled thud, as if he'd slammed his fist into something. "Sending dragons to kill dragons. It makes no sense."

"Where are you?" I asked.

"Heading your way now. Old rail yard, right? I was there when Mist gave you that false information." Riley paused, then asked in a quieter voice, "How is she?"

Of course, he could mean only one person. "She sustained a few surface injuries when she was fighting the Viper," I answered, making him mutter another curse. "The wounds themselves don't look too deep, but the edges are burned fairly severely. Third-degree if I had to guess." I stifled a wince, knowing from personal experience just how painful third-degree burns were. Though I continued to hear myself speak with clinical detachment. "Other than that, from what I can tell, her injuries are minor."

"Dammit, Ember," Riley growled. "Taking on a Viper yourself, you idiot hatchling. Where is Faith now?" he went on, sounding faintly hesitant now. "Did Ember…kill her?"

"No. I did."

"Good." He hesitated again, longer this time, as if struggling to make himself speak. "Look, let's make one thing clear," he finally muttered. "I don't like you. I think you're a murdering bastard, and the fact that you've recently had a change of heart doesn't erase all the blood on your hands, and it never will. I also think you're an idiot for believing

Ember would ever choose a human over her own kind. She's a dragon, and even if she hasn't figured it out yet, dragons and humans don't belong together. You should know that, St. George. And if you truly care for her, you'll let her be with her own kind. For both your sakes.

"But," he went on, as my insides twisted painfully at his words, "I know what Talon is capable of. I know what the Vipers are capable of, even their hatchlings. Ember might be too softhearted to destroy one of her own, but I know that Faith wouldn't have hesitated to kill her. If you put that Viper down, much as I hate you for it, then you probably saved Ember's life. And for that…" He sighed. "You're not as much of a bastard as I thought."

"Thanks," I said drily, knowing that was the closest to gratitude I'd ever get from the rogue.

He snorted. "Don't get me wrong. If the Viper had ripped your throat out instead, I wouldn't lose any sleep tonight. Where is Ember now?"

Soft footsteps made me whirl around, just as a slight figure in a black suit emerged from the maze. Ember had, of course, followed me, her jaw clenched in pain and determination as she limped doggedly across the floor.

"Riley?" she asked as I hurried over, catching her by the arm just as she staggered. Four angry red gashes scored her cheek, making me grimace. But her eyes shone with hope, even through the pain. "Is that Riley?"

For just a moment, I considered lying, turning off the phone and claiming it was Wes. For a moment, I hated the fact that Riley had lived, that he could make her face light up like that. It cast a dark uncertainty over my thoughts, and all the confusion and doubt I had pushed down rose to the surface once more. Was I just fooling myself? Would Ember ever see me in the same way as the rogue dragon?

"Garret?" She looked up at me, eager and confused, her eyes searching. "Did you hang up? Who were you talking to?"

Wordlessly, I handed her the phone.

RILEY

"Riley?"

Heat flared through me at the sound of her voice, nearly making my breath catch. The dragon rose up, shaking off the grogginess, burning away the tranquilizer. And maybe I was still under the influence of the truth drug, but suddenly everything became a lot clearer. Ember was mine. I needed her. She was impulsive, reckless, infuriating...and I couldn't imagine my life without her.

"Hey, Firebrand." I sighed. "Good to hear your voice. You okay?"

"Oh, you know." I heard the tremor that went through her, the breathless relief. "A little burned, a little sore. Nearly died a couple times. The usual. You?"

"The same." I staggered through a metal door and paused outside the building to get my bearings. Some old warehouse district on the edge of town, isolated and unremarkable, as I expected. Still, I scanned the area carefully, not putting it past Talon to be watching this place, via satellite or something else. I had to get out of the area quickly. Now that my phone was back on, Wes would be able to find me; he was supposedly on his way now. "Though I am a tad confused by one part," I went on, hurrying across the dusty yard toward a chain-link fence surrounding it. "Did you just say you were burned? You're a *dragon*. How does that happen?"

"Um, I might've set myself on fire."

I closed my eyes. "Ember..."

"But look on the bright side, I managed to avoid being shot this time."

"I need you."

A very long silence followed. Long enough for me to slip through the fence and step onto the sidewalk. Gazing up and down the street, I picked a direction and started walking, toward the glow of distant lights that, hopefully, marked the edge of the city. A warm breeze blew against my face, smelling of dust and pavement; I breathed it in and smiled to myself. It was good to be free.

"Riley." Ember's voice trembled slightly, though I couldn't tell what she was feeling. "What...what are you talking about?"

"I think you know what I'm talking about." I raked a hand through my hair, feeling dangerously light and uncaring. "However, I'm probably still under the effects of a truth drug," I went on, with the same easy nonchalance I'd felt while talking to Mist. "And it made me realize something, about us. But, if you don't want to hear what I'm really thinking, I'd hang up right now."

"Do you want me to?"

Yes. Say yes, Riley. "No."

Ember took a deep, shaky breath. "Tell me, then."

No turning back now. Ah, screw it. I officially don't care anymore. "I realized something while I was in that session with Mist,"

I began, hoping to tell her everything before Wes showed up. "She's a Basilisk, you know. Talon wanted the locations of my safe houses, and they sent her to retrieve them. She was supposed to kill me after she got the information."

"Bitch," Ember growled.

"Wasn't her fault," I said, feeling a small twinge of regret that I couldn't save her, too. "You know what Talon is like. You know what they're capable of. I would've brought her with us if I could."

"Is...is she...?"

"No," I murmured. "I didn't kill her. She's sleeping off a tranquilizer that would put down an elephant, so she won't bat an eyelash for at least a couple hours. But that's not the point." I paused as a taxi cruised toward my corner but then sped by without slowing.

"I would've told her everything," I continued, feeling my stomach twist at how close I'd actually come to revealing my entire network. "I almost betrayed my entire underground. All my hatchlings, all the humans I got out. But something stopped me, kept me from spilling my guts and telling Mist everything she wanted to know."

"What was it?"

"You, Firebrand." I stopped at an intersection and leaned against a crosswalk sign. "I saw your face, and I knew I had to keep it together." A human passed by, giving me a smirk as he crossed the street, and I didn't even care. "You kept me grounded, Ember," I said quietly, resting my head against the metal pole. "You're the reason I was able to resist. I just kept thinking about you.

"I don't know what you want from me," I hurried on,

knowing this would be the only time I'd have the guts to actually say it, "or what you feel for the soldier, but I'm letting you know right now... I'm done fighting this. From now on, I'll be fighting for both of us."

"Riley," Ember said again, her voice almost a whisper, "I can't... I mean. This isn't..." She broke off, and her voice dropped even further, becoming nearly inaudible. "I can't promise anything," she whispered. "I don't know what I feel."

"That's fine, Firebrand." I looked up as headlights pierced the darkness, and a taxi pulled to the curb. "But when you figure it out, when you remember that you're still a dragon, I'll be right here. I'm not going anywhere, that's *my* promise."

The cab window lowered, and Wes's shaggy head poked out, thin arms gesturing frantically. I grinned and started toward the cab, surprised at how relieved I was to see him. "I'm heading your way now," I told Ember, sliding into the backseat, ignoring Wes's I-told-you-so glare. "Hang tight, we'll be there in a few minutes."

"Riley?"

I paused, stopping myself from clicking off the phone. "Yeah?"

"I'm glad you're all right." The voice on the other end sounded defiantly embarrassed. "You scared us there for a while. Don't do that again."

"You mean don't get captured and interrogated by Talon's double agents? No promises, but I'll do my best." I smiled, hearing her snort into the phone. "See you soon."

"Well," Wes commented as I hung up. "Don't you look like hell."

COBALT

Twelve years ago

I don't know how he tracked me down, but he did.

A human was waiting for me in the latest dump I'd rented for the night, sitting at the desk in the corner, watching as I came through the door. I tensed, going for the gun I always carried now, and he quickly held up his hands.

"Relax, mate! I'm not here for trouble. Just hear me out."

I recognized him then. The kid who had been in that meeting with Roth and the Chief Basilisk, so long ago, it seemed. His brown hair stuck out in every direction, hanging in his eyes, and his clothes looked rumpled and dirty, like he'd spent a few days in them. I racked my memory for his name, then realized it had never been given.

"Okay." I did not lower the gun, keeping it aimed at the kid's scrawny middle. He might've been human, and unarmed as far as I could tell, but I'd had a hell of a week and wasn't going to be taking any chances. "You have my attention. What do you want?"

"Uh, could you maybe put the gun down? I told you before, mate, I don't want any trouble. I'm here to help you."

I smirked. "Really? I find that a little hard to believe. One, you're human. What can you possibly do that would help me? And two, more importantly, I saw you in that meeting with Roth. You're part of Talon."

"Not anymore."

I faltered and gave him an incredulous look. "Not anymore? What do you mean?"

"I mean, I left, mate. I'm out. Went rogue, dropped off the grid, gone AWOL, whatever you want to call it."

"How?"

"I've been planning this a long time," the kid explained, a flash of anger and resentment crossing his narrow face. "If you wanna lower the gun, and not make me so bloody nervous, I'll tell you everything. Including some things about *you* that you might not know."

Sighing, I dropped my arm. "Fine," I muttered, and he relaxed. I did not need this right now, having some strange human show up on my doorstep like a lost cat, but if the kid really had gotten out of Talon, it could be worth listening to him. He might know what Talon was up to, if they had any more plans involving me and another Viper. I'd managed to avoid Stealth so far, but that wouldn't last. She was still out there, looking for me. The least I could do was hear him out. "Although," I warned, with one last jab of the pistol, "if Talon unexpectedly shows up while we're talking, you're going to be the first one I shoot. Just so you know."

He paled, but nodded. "Fair enough. Though if the bastards do show, it might be better to shoot me." Resting bony elbows on his knees, he sighed, sounding suddenly tired, and far older than I first took him for. "I think…I might actually rather be dead than go back."

Shoving the gun into the waistband of my jeans, I stepped farther into the room. "Who are you?" I asked, pausing at the foot of the bed, watching him. "How'd you find me?"

"My name is Wesley," the human said, leaning back in the chair. "Wesley Higgins, or just Wes, if you like. Not that it matters, I officially don't exist in any system anymore. And there's no need to introduce yourself, Agent Cobalt. I already know who you are. I know a lot of things about you, actually."

"Do you, now?" I said in a flat, dangerous voice. "And what exactly do you want for this information? Is the deal I give you everything I have, or you go back to Talon to turn me in?"

"That's not it at all! Look, I'm not trying to blackmail you or anything. I just…ugh." Wes scrubbed both hands through his hair. "Bloody hell, I don't want a fight. I'm on your side, okay? Let me start from the beginning. Can I do that, without you blowing my head off?"

I shrugged. Maybe I was being paranoid, but again, hell of a week. "No promises," I growled. "Get on with it."

"Right," Wes muttered, and took a deep breath. I leaned against the wall, crossing my arms, and waited.

"I've been in Talon nearly five years," the human began, eyeing me warily. "Before that, I lived in London, with my folks. I didn't have any siblings, and both my parents worked long shifts, so I was alone most of the time."

"What does this have to do with Talon?"

"I'm getting there, mate." Wes paused to gather his thoughts before continuing. "Like I said, my folks were absent most of the time. They didn't know what I did. They weren't aware that I was an…um…anonymous independent computer specialist."

"You were a hacker," I said.

"And a bloody good one, too. Still am." Wes looked faintly smug, then his eyes darkened. "Of course, that's what got me into this mess. I was home alone one day, minding my own business, when there was a knock at the door. I opened it, and two uniformed policemen were standing there on the stoop. Said I was under arrest, and that I already knew why they were taking me in. I was terrified. I was fourteen, alone and being dragged from my home in handcuffs." He smiled grimly, completely without humor. "Of course, it wasn't the police. It wasn't anyone in law enforcement. But you already know that, don't you?"

It was my turn to sigh. "Talon."

"Bloody Talon," Wes repeated. "Though I didn't know that at the time. They took me to a room, sat me in front of a computer and said that if I didn't do what they wanted, not only would they expose me, they would ruin my family, as well." Wes shook his head. "I was a stupid bloody teenager. I believed them. So I did what I was told. For three years, I worked for Talon, wondering about my parents, wondering when the organization would let me go home. And you know what I finally realized?"

"They wouldn't," I muttered.

Wes nodded slowly. "When I was sixteen, I attended my first meeting with Adam Roth. They brought me into a secure room, no windows, no other humans around. And they showed me Talon's secret. They showed me who I was working for." Wes gave a short, bitter laugh. "A gift, they said. A reward for my brilliant service and talents. Bloody bastards. I realized then they would never let me go. I was in for life."

"That's when you decided to get out?"

"They bloody kidnapped me." Wes's lip curled in a snarl. "Took away my freedom, my family, everything. I was a bloody slave to the lizards for five years. I'd be damned if I was going to stay there."

"Getting away must've taken some work," I said, amazed that the kid had pulled off something so risky, and that he'd avoided Talon even this long.

"Yeah, well, like I said, I've been planning this awhile," Wes repeated. "I had to set everything up so that when I did leave, I'd be out of their systems forever. And I had to scrape together enough secrets and blackmail to keep my family safe. When I ran, I made it very clear that if they ever threatened my folks in an attempt to get to me, there are some very interesting files on Talon's businesses that would go public."

I smirked. "Playing dirty with Talon. I'm impressed."

The human snorted. "Right. There's just one small snag," he said, lowering his brows. "I can't do this on my own. I can hack my way through just about anything, but I don't have the survival skills you do, the ones that will keep me alive and away from the organization. If I run, eventually, they'll send someone to kill me, or drag me back. Some Viper will slit my throat in the middle of the night." He shuddered, giving me a grave look. "Honestly, I've been waiting for someone like you for a long time now. When I heard that you went rogue, I knew it was my chance. I'd probably never get another one."

"So you tracked me down hoping I'd protect you from Talon?" I shook my head. "I don't need a human tagging along, slowing me down. I work alone, that's how it's always been." His face fell, making me feel like an ass, but I hardened my voice. "Do you even know what you're asking? What going rogue means to the organization? They'll never stop looking for you. They will never give up, or forgive, or accept any compromise. And they'll never forget, because dragons have insanely long memories and will hold a grudge forever. You go back now, sure, Talon will lock you away and you'll live a very sheltered existence until you die of old age or boredom. But at least you'll be alive. You come with me, and your life is going to be uncertain, violent and probably very short."

His eyes narrowed. "I don't think you quite realize the opportunity here, mate," he said, making me frown. "I'm not just some stupid kid in need of protection. I can help you, too."

"How?"

He smirked. "For starters...you know all those accounts frozen by Talon when you went rogue? I can open them again, and make it so they'll never be traced back to you."

"What?" I stared at him, and his smirk widened.

"I told you, I'm one of the best, mate. You need something, some file stolen or code decrypted, I can do that. In fact..." He reached into his pocket and pulled out a strip of black plastic. "A goodwill offering," he announced, tossing it to me.

"What is this?" I asked as I caught it.

"All of Talon's files on you. Everything you've done for the organization, all their information on where you've been, where you've stayed, your case files, your assignments, your hatching date, everything. Congratulations. You are now truly a ghost to them." I gazed up at him, stunned, and his smile turned hard. "You know you were never supposed to come back from that mission, right? According to your file, you were becoming a 'liability' and 'suspect to corruption.' Which is Talon's way of saying they couldn't control you any-more. So they decided to stage an accident, have you killed in the line of duty." He shrugged. "But, since you're here and not buried under a ton of bricks and mortar, I guess you al-ready knew that."

"Yeah," I muttered, glancing at the thumb drive in amaze-ment. My whole life, on this tiny strip of plastic. And now, it was mine alone. Thanks to this human, tracking me down had just become that much harder. "I guess that 'file' they had me steal from St. George was bogus, too," I said, slip-ping the drive into my jacket. "Just an excuse to get me into the compound."

"Oh, no, mate. That was very real." Wes grinned again as I looked up. "Talon took a very important file from St. George that day. They already had an agent inside the base, why not use him one last time? Only problem? It seems to be missing now. Like it was never there. Funny how that works."

"You have the file," I said, and he shrugged. "So what is it?"

"You're asking me? I thought you worked alone."

I glowered, but it was a mostly empty gesture. The human was right; he was far too useful not to keep around. Still, something nagged at me. "Let's say I accept your offer," I began, making his brows rise. "Why do this? What do you get out of it?"

"Besides staying alive? I would think that's a sodding good

reason right there, but…there is something else." Wes leaned back in the chair, his face suddenly hard. "The bloody lizards stole my life," he muttered. "I'll never be normal. I'll never be able to see my family, get married, have kids, anything like that. Because of Talon."

"So this is revenge?" I asked, and shook my head. "And you think you'll…what…bring them down? This isn't a single company you can infect with a virus. This is a worldwide corporation, an empire. We're only two people."

"What if there were more like us?"

"Even if there were," I said, "how would we find them?"

The human's eyes gleamed. "How indeed," he said, and opened his laptop, bending over the keys. "You want to know what that file you took from St. George was?" he said, as I edged forward and peered over his shoulder. "Check this out."

I squinted at the image that popped onto the screen, frowning in confusion. It was…a list. There was no title, no header, nothing to indicate what it was actually for. But the first line read: "Carson City, NV. Talon activity: Moderate. Sleeper agents discovered: 1."

Sleeper agents? *Sleeper* was the Order's word for the hatchlings ready to complete assimilation, when they were sent to human towns to blend in with humanity. I scanned the list, amazement and awe growing with each line. Each row held the name of a town, the level of Talon activity discovered there and one or two possible sleepers. My heart beat faster in excitement.

"This is…" I muttered, and Wes nodded.

"All the places St. George thinks Talon will send their hatchlings," he finished, and shrugged. "It's probably not accurate, some of those places might not be in use anymore, especially with Talon's paranoia. But…"

But it was something. And now that we had a list of possible sleeper locations, the wisp of an idea began to creep into my head. A crazy, impossible, terrifying idea. If we could find these hatchlings, be there when Talon planted them into a town, I could show them the truth about the organization. They needed to know, before Talon sank their claws in too deep, before they were brainwashed completely. They needed to see what Talon was really like. And, if they decided they could no longer be a part of the organization, they needed someone to help them escape, to show them how to be free.

I could show them how.

Wes noticed the change, and a slow smile crossed his face. "So, what'd'ya say, mate?" he said softly. "Partners?"

"You realize this is going to take a long time," I warned. "The type of network we're talking about, it will take years to build, decades even. We'll constantly be on the run, from Talon *and* St. George. Our lives are never going to be safe, or anything close to normal. Sure you're up for it, human?"

"Hey." Wesley Higgins leaned back with a shrug. "I'm being hunted by a bloody dragon empire that won't stop unless it's completely destroyed or taken down. What else am I going to do?"

"All right." I looked down at the screen, at the first place on the list, and nodded. Carson City, Nevada, was our first stop. "Let's get this resistance started."

EMBER

I lowered my arm, feeling my heart pound, my emotions raging everywhere all at once. Riley was okay; I couldn't express how relieved I was to hear his voice, to know he was alive. The past few hours had been a nightmare; I hadn't even realized how much Riley meant to me until he was gone.

And my dragon, surging like molten lava through my veins, was acutely aware of Riley's promise, was relishing it, even. She couldn't wait to see him again. She recognized her other half, had always recognized it. Cobalt called to her. She felt the other dragon's pull as surely as I felt the need to fly or sleep or breathe. And Riley wasn't holding back anymore.

So what was holding *me* back?

"We should move." Garret's voice echoed at my side. I glanced up and found him watching me, his face shut into that blank, expressionless mask that made my insides shrink. "Talon is probably aware by now that their ambush failed," he went on, gesturing to the carnage around us. "If they aren't, they'll find out very shortly. We should leave the premises before they send in the cleanup crew."

"Right." I nodded and pushed myself off the crate stack,

but pain shot up my leg and I nearly fell, barely catching myself on the edge. "Ow. Dammit. Ow."

"Are you all right?" Garret hovered at my side, his remote expression cracking a little with worry. I waved him off.

"I'm fine." I took another step, clenching my teeth as my leg, back, ribs and shoulder throbbed. I didn't know if it was from dragon claws, or just general aches and bruises from my fight with the Viper, but dammit I was sore. Of course, the stupid magic Viper suit didn't show rips or tears, so I couldn't even see how bad the wounds were. "Right behind you," I gritted out, wishing I could Shift to my real form again. The human body didn't deal with pain as well as a dragon's. "Just moving…a little slower than normal. Keep going."

Garret hesitated, then stepped beside me, putting a hand on my back. Surprised, I glanced at him as he bent, scooped an arm under my knees and lifted me off my feet. I gasped, wincing as the motion tore at the open wounds beneath my suit, but then he shifted me gently in his arms, and the pain receded.

"Garret." My heart pounded, my stomach tying itself into knots at being so close. I put a hand on his chest, feeling his own heart thudding beneath my palm. "You don't have to do this," I said, torn between exhilaration and embarrassment. "I'll be okay…"

I trailed off at the look he gave me. Sorrow, regret and longing glimmered in his eyes for just a moment, before they blinked and became remote once more. "Let me do this one last thing," Garret said quietly, and offered a faint smile when I frowned in confusion. "You carried me to safety once. Now it's my turn."

He sounded sad for some reason. Like this was the last thing he would do for me. Wanting to ease the tension, I looped an arm around his neck and smiled. "You know, if you really wanted to impress, I could Shift right now and you could carry me out like that."

The corner of his mouth twitched. "Somehow, I don't think I'd get very far. Riley would walk in and see a dragon lying on top of a crushed soldier. He'd probably take a picture to remember it, always."

I chuckled, feeling some of the awkwardness subside. A soldier of St. George carrying a dragon to safety—what was next? Sighing, I leaned my head on his chest, as Garret walked easily through the maze with me in his arms. His heart beat steady and sure against my ear, and I relaxed. We were okay, all of us. St. George had come for us, and we'd survived. Talon had sent two deadly double agents to force me back to the organization, and I was still here. Riley was alive. Garret was alive. We'd taken the worst Talon and the Order could throw at us and had come out on top.

But the casualties were high, even if they weren't on our side. I didn't have to look up to see the dozen or so Talon agents, sprawled throughout the warehouse. More dead humans than I'd seen in a lifetime. Dead humans that would probably show up in my dreams for weeks to come. And of course, somewhere in that mess of blood and darkness was the lifeless body of a purple dragon. A girl who, at one time, had been just like me.

Anger burned, and shockingly, I felt my eyes stinging. It was a waste. Such an awful, stupid waste, and for what? Faith didn't have to die. Talon didn't have to send her. Why couldn't they just leave us alone? Why was it so important that I return to the organization? Now a hatchling and a dozen humans were dead, because someone in Talon had ordered my assassination...

"Garret," I whispered, clenching a fist in his shirt, "wait!"

He stopped and gave me a puzzled look. We were almost to the exit; I could see the open door to the rail yard dead ahead. Riley and Wes would be here soon, and we had to get out of here before Talon, the Order or the authorities showed up. But something still nagged at me, and if I didn't resolve it now, I'd drive myself crazy wondering.

"I have to go back," I told Garret, whose puzzled look deepened to a frown. "You don't have to come. Put me down and go wait for Riley if you want. But I have to go back. There's something important I forgot to do."

DANTE

She should have called by now.

The clock on the wall was too loud, every ticking second like a miniature drill in my brain. The senior dragons did nothing, said nothing, sitting around the table with the patience of mountains, their blank eyes on me. Occasionally, they would speak to me, or each other, their voices cool and remote, but for the most part, they waited, silent and unmoving. I mimicked their positions, trying to remain calm and patient, staring at my folded hands until the image was seared into my retinas.

The phone buzzed on the table.

I jolted in my seat like I'd been stung. Without waiting for Roth's approval, I snatched it up and put it to my ear, my voice low and grave.

"Faith? Is it done?"

"It's not Faith."

I froze. The room froze. I sat rigid in my chair, the eyes of four senior dragons on me, as *her* voice echoed in my ear, low and unmistakable. They couldn't hear the conversation, but from the looks I was getting, it was clear they knew something wasn't right. Heart pounding, I closed my eyes, knowing it was useless to hide it.

"Ember," I said, and felt the attention in the room sharpen to a razor's edge. I swallowed hard and forced myself to speak calmly. Maybe I could salvage what was left of this assignment. "Where are you?"

"I think you already know that, Dante." Ember's voice was icy. She'd spoken to me that way only a couple times in her life, and I had painful memories of one, and a tiny scar from the other. "Considering you were the one who set this up."

The weight of the combined stares was becoming unbearable, four senior dragons pinning me with hard, intense eyes. "Where is Faith?" I asked.

A heartbeat of silence. "She's dead."

The ground dropped out from under me. I sat there, unable to believe what I'd just heard. I'd always known Ember was rebellious, reckless and stubborn, but I'd never thought her capable of this. "She's dead?" I choked in disbelief. "You killed her?"

"I didn't kill her."

"The soldier, then," I guessed. "St. George. You're with him now, aren't you? And you let him kill her." There was no answer on the other side, and my voice hardened. "How could you let him do that?"

"You've got some nerve asking me that," Ember hissed. And though she sounded furious, her voice cracked on the last word. "Don't play innocent with me, Dante. You were the one who sent her, after all. You set this whole thing up, didn't you?"

"Yes," I admitted, not knowing where this absolute rage

was coming from. "I did. To bring you back. You belong here, Ember. You belong with Talon." There was a squeak, as someone in the room rose from their chair, but I barely heard it. "I'm trying to keep you safe," I said, suddenly furious myself. "I'm trying to make a future for both of us, but you insist on tearing it down! I can't believe you let that human kill Faith, just because you didn't want to come back. What is wrong with you!"

I was almost shouting into the phone now, and a second later, it was smoothly plucked from my grasp by Mr. Roth, who gave me a blank, chilling smile before putting it to his ear.

"Ms. Hill," he said cordially, "this is Adam Roth, senior vice president of Talon's western operations. How are you tonight?" He paused, smiling faintly, his sharp face giving nothing away. "Well, I'm sure you don't mean that literally."

I buried my head in my hands, raking my fingers through my hair, not caring how it made me look. I could only imagine what Ember was saying to Talon's senior vice president. My stomach turned, shocked at how badly this had turned out. Faith was dead. Where was Mist? I wondered. Had she been killed, too? The two hatchlings had been our best bet to find Ember and the rogue; as the newest agents of Talon, they wouldn't be recognized by Cobalt or his network, so they'd be able to get close without arousing suspicion. Originally, I'd wanted Mist to talk to Ember, convince her to come back, but she'd later informed me that Talon had other plans for her. I'd been annoyed—this was my operation, after all, and Mr. Roth had put me in charge. But then I'd spoken to the second agent, Faith, who'd assured me that she would bring Ember safely back to the fold. Before talking to her, I'd had serious doubts that the quiet, delicate-looking girl was a good fit for this assignment. Cobalt was a dangerous rogue, and calling Ember stubborn was putting it mildly. But it took only a few minutes of discussion to know that Faith was more than she seemed. And when she'd told me she would get the job done, I believed her, though I had made it clear that she was not to harm my sister in any way.

"Bring Ember back to Talon," I'd told her. "Use everything at your disposal to convince her to return, but do *not* hurt her. If she refuses to come back, do what you must. But I want my sister returned alive and safe. Do you understand?"

"Of course, sir." Faith had smiled at me, confident and professional. "Your sister will not be harmed in any way. I will make certain of it."

And now she was dead. Faith was *dead*. Because I had sent her after my wayward twin, and Ember had let her be killed rather than return to the organization. How had this happened? How could she have resorted to that, after everything we'd gone through together? Apparently, I didn't know my sister at all.

And now, because of her, I had failed. I had failed Talon.

My hands shook, and I flattened them on the tabletop, trying to steady myself. Above me, Mr. Roth continued with polite coolness. "I'm afraid I cannot tell you that, Ms. Hill," he said evenly. "If you wish that information, you must return to the organization." Pause. "No, Mr. Hill is in no danger. He is a valued member of Talon, and we appreciate his cooperation." Pause. "No, our policy on rogues is very clear. Cobalt is a criminal who has caused irreversible harm to the organization. We must protect ourselves from his extremist views." One last, lengthy pause, and Mr. Roth's voice grew hard. "I'm sorry you feel that way. But if you would only agree to return and speak with us, you would see that…"

He trailed off, lowering his arm. "Well. It appears Ms. Hill will not be joining us tonight." Turning, he rested his fingertips against the table and spoke to the rest of the room. "We will adjourn for now, until we can come up with a new strategy to retrieve Ms. Hill and deal with Cobalt. As Ms. Anderson has not yet reported in, perhaps she will give us better news. But it can wait until tomorrow." He looked over the table with cold black eyes. "Dismissed."

Everyone rose at once, keeping their eyes downcast as they began to exit the room. I stood as well, but suddenly Mr. Roth's long steely fingers gripped my shoulder, making me freeze.

"Mr. Hill. You will come with me."

EMBER

"Only you, Firebrand." Riley sighed.

I grimaced at him over the table, where an open first-aid kit, bandages, burn cream and disinfectant wipes sat scattered between us. My Viper suit lay discarded on the bathroom floor of the hotel room, replaced with shorts and a loose top that didn't rub against my skin. Riley leaned forward in his chair, winding the last of the gauze around my arm. His long fingers occasionally brushed my hand, sending a pulse of heat up my arm every single time. Garret had left the room a few minutes ago, saying nothing as he slipped out the door, presumably to stand guard or check the parking lot for "suspicious people," leaving me and Riley alone.

Well, alone except for Wes.

"There." Fastening the gauze, Riley looked up with a rueful smile, shaking his head. A bandage square covered my left cheek, right below my eye, and it felt weird and tight against my skin. "Don't pick at the bandages, Firebrand," Riley ordered. "Hopefully those will heal in a day or two, though this is the first time I've had to treat another dragon for burns. Like I said, you are one of a kind."

"Thank God," Wes muttered from the bed, laptop perched

on his knees. I ignored him, which was getting harder to do in the tiny room. After meeting Riley and Wes in front of the rail yard, we'd fled downtown Vegas and the Strip, putting as much distance between us and the massive glittering casinos as we could. This tiny hotel on the outskirts of town had more roaches than slot machines, and the four of us were currently packed into one room like sardines in a can, but Riley wasn't planning to stay long. According to Wes, there was a used-car lot two blocks down that would sell you anything, no credit history, no questions asked, and Riley planned to be there as soon as it opened in a few hours. I had no idea where we were going, but I knew Riley was in a hurry to leave Vegas. And after tonight, I was more than happy to say goodbye, too. Goodbye to the City of Sin. Goodbye to Talon and the Order...and Dante.

A lump caught in my throat, and I swallowed it with a growl. I refused to mourn my traitor brother, no matter how sick it made me feel. Dante was part of Talon now. Part of the organization that wanted me dead. He'd sent a Viper after me and a Basilisk after Riley, with orders to kill us both. I didn't know him anymore. Riley had been right all along.

"There." Wes tapped a final key and looked up. "I've sent instructions to all our nests, telling them to relocate immediately and not contact anyone until they've heard from you. They're on emergency evacuation until further notice."

"Good." Riley stood up, wiping his hands. "Hopefully that will buy us, and them, some time until we can figure this out. See if we can't find who the hell is leaking information to the organization and shut them up for good. If Talon wants to kill us, I'm not going to make it easy for them."

I was only half listening, still brooding over Talon and Dante and the whole screwed-up situation, so a gentle touch on my shoulder surprised me. I glanced up into Riley's intense golden eyes.

"Firebrand? You okay? Are you in any pain?"

"No," I whispered, as the now-familiar heat surged up again, pushing me toward him. Gingerly, I stood, testing my range of motion. My various cuts and burns throbbed, but they were slowly going numb with salve and painkillers. The real hurt wasn't physical, and no amount of aspirin would make it go away. "Just...thinking about Talon," I told Riley, who hadn't taken his eyes from me, "and St. George and what a bastard my brother is. You can go ahead and say *I told you so*—"

Riley stepped close and very carefully pulled me into his arms, making me freeze in shock.

"I'm sorry about Dante," he murmured, keeping one hand on my waist, the other in my hair, avoiding my many bandages. My cheek was pressed to his shirt; I could feel the heat of his skin through the fabric, his voice rumbling in my ear. "I wish we could have taken him, too. But he made his choice, Firebrand. And now you have to make yours. Are you still going to stand with me, against Talon? Even though you might be fighting your brother again one day?"

Putting my hands on his arms, I pulled back to face not Riley but Cobalt peering down at me. The human veneer was still there, still in place, but the dark blue dragon stared out through human eyes, ghostly wings outstretched, casting us both in their shadow. I swallowed hard to keep my own wings from breaking free. "Why now?" I whispered.

"I told you, I'm done fighting this," Cobalt rumbled, and one hand was suddenly against my cheek, hot and searing. "I almost lost you today. I won't make that mistake again." His fingers traced my skin, brushing my hair back, and I shivered. "You don't have to make a decision tonight," Cobalt said. "I have time." The corner of his mouth quirked, and he stepped back, looking more like Riley. "I'm a dragon, after all."

"Bloody hell." Wes's disgusted voice rose up from the corner. "Will the pair of you please stop before I yark all over the room? Riley, you might want to come see this."

Rolling his eyes, Riley pulled away. I stood there, watching them for a moment, my heart thudding in my chest and my dragon surging beneath my skin. The temperature in the room was suddenly too hot, stifling, and the walls seemed too close. I had to get some air.

With one last look at Wes and Riley, still deep in conversation, I slipped out the door into the warmth of the night. I told myself I needed to be alone, to clear my head, but that was a lie. And I didn't have to search far. A lean, pale form stood in the outdoor hall with his elbows against the railing, gazing out over the parking lot. I started toward him, but as I did, my steps faltered and I hesitated, suddenly torn between saying something and going back inside. Why was I afraid? This was Garret.

Swallowing, I forced myself to move, knowing he'd heard me come out. "Hey, you," I greeted as the door clicked behind me. I kept my voice light, a stark contrast to the uncertainty within. "Spot any ninjas yet? Maybe a secret agent hiding in the cactus?"

"No," he said quietly, still watching the pink glow over the horizon. "But there is a suspicious-looking bench near the parking lot that I'm keeping an eye on. Just in case."

Smiling, I joined him at the railing and mimicked his pose, and we stared at the distant mountains for several heartbeats. In this quiet moment before dawn, the world was silent, peaceful. I wished I could feel the same, but the raging storm of questions inside made that impossible. I wondered where we would go next. I wondered where Dante was, what he was doing, what he was planning now. I wondered if there would come a time when I could stop running. If someday Talon and St. George would just stop killing each other, if the war would ever cease.

"Ember."

Garret's voice, soft and hesitant, broke the predawn stillness. He kept his gaze on the horizon, but his whole posture was stiff, tense. "You never answered me last night."

My stomach turned inside out, and everything around us froze. Garret straightened and turned, keeping one hand on the railing, to face me, metallic gaze burning the side of my head. A little flutter of panic bloomed inside. I kept my gaze on a distant street lamp, watching it flicker against the coming dawn, and felt the silence stretch between us, brittle and terrifying. My heart pounded, screaming at me to say something, to give him the words he was waiting for. But I didn't know if I could...feel like that. When I was with him, I was happy. When we touched, my heart beat faster and my stomach did crazy cartwheels. When we were apart, I thought of him constantly, and when we were together, I was content. But I didn't know if that was love.

And how could I love him, when a part of me longed for Cobalt, standing in the very next room?

"What do you want me to say, Garret?" I whispered at last.

Garret didn't answer for a moment, then took a quiet breath, as if bracing himself. "I just want the truth," he said, and his voice wasn't angry or cold or demanding, just resigned. Sad. "I have never felt…anything like this. And I know that I'm the last person in the world that deserves it, but…I meant it when I said that I'm in love with you." His voice wavered on the last sentence, then grew stronger, almost defiant. "I love you, Ember," he said again, and I closed my eyes. "I'm not ashamed, and I'm not afraid of what it means. But I…I need to know if you feel the same."

He was putting all his cards on the table, leaving himself wide-open, and I was probably going to rip his heart out. I wanted to tell him. I wanted to say I felt the same, but at the same time, I didn't want to lie to him. My emotions were a chaotic swirl of confusion and doubt. Garret. Cobalt. Longing. Love. Which was stronger? How did people even know if they were in love?

"Garret," I stammered miserably, "I…I don't know. I'm not human. I don't even know if we're capable of…those kinds of feelings."

"I don't believe that," Garret said. "I might have once, but not anymore. I've seen you, Ember. From the very first day we met in Crescent Beach, I've watched you. You've made friends and formed attachments, and you miss them, even now. You're angry at your brother because he chose Talon over you. You refused to be what your trainer wanted, a Viper that kills without emotion. You're the one who taught me that dragons aren't really that different than us, and I abandoned everything I believed in because of you." He paused then, his voice becoming quietly desperate. "Don't tell me you're not capable of it," he almost whispered. "What's really holding you back?"

I sighed and looked up at him, finally admitting the truth to us both. "Riley."

He didn't look surprised. He just nodded once, slowly, as if I'd confirmed what he'd always suspected. I finally turned to face him head-on, needing him to understand. "Garret…I like you. I really do. When I'm with you…I feel more human than I have in my entire life. I don't know if I'm supposed to feel that way, and I don't know if that's a good or a bad thing, but at this point, I really don't care. I want to be with you. Sometimes…sometimes I wish that I wasn't a dragon, so we could be normal together." I gave a tiny, bitter chuckle. "Of course, if I was human, we would've never met, so it's kind of a catch-22, isn't it?"

Garret didn't reply. He still watched me, those solemn gray eyes making me want to drop my gaze and hide. I stifled the impulse and continued to face him.

"But," I went on, "I can't ignore what I feel for Riley. And I don't want to lie, to either of you. I honestly don't know what's going on between the three of us, and until I'm sure… I can't give you a real answer. I'm sorry, Garret." I couldn't take the way he was looking at me any longer, and I turned away. "I think…I need some time to figure this out."

"All right." His voice surprised me. I was expecting anger, contempt, accusations for leading him on, not this quiet resolve. "Then I guess that makes this easy."

I looked back at him quickly. "Makes what easy?"

This time he turned away. Only then did I notice the backpack, propped beside the door, already packed, and everything went cold inside me. "You're leaving?"

"There's no reason for me to stay." Garret's voice was calm as he swung the pack to his shoulder. "I've paid my debt, to you and Riley at least. And it's not safe for me to stick around. Sooner or later, St. George will come after me again. Better if I'm far away when that happens."

"Where will you go?"

"I don't know yet." He glanced back at me, eyes shadowed. "England, maybe, if I can get there. Something is wrong in the Order—that ambush with Mist and Faith wasn't a coincidence. St. George knew we were coming, and I don't like what that implies." His gaze narrowed, expression going dark. "If there is a connection between Talon and the Order, it will change everything St. George has believed for hundreds of years. Everything we thought we knew will be a deception. Now that I've seen both sides, I need to know if there's something more to this war than either faction is letting on." He sighed, and for the first time a shadow of doubt crossed his face. "I hope I'm wrong," he murmured. "But I have to be sure." One last pause, barely a heartbeat, one last chance to tell him to stay, before he stepped back. "Goodbye, Ember," he said, as something shattered inside me. "Thank you…for everything." And he walked away.

"Garret, wait."

He turned around, eyes widening with surprise, as I flung myself against him, wrapped my arms around his neck and kissed him. His arms circled my waist, pressing us together,

as I buried my fingers in his hair. He groaned, backing me
into a pillar, his mouth at my jaw, my neck, searing a path
down my skin. Our lips met again, hungry and eager, sending the pit of my stomach into a wild swirl. A low growl escaped me as I locked my body to his, wanting to feel him
with my entire being.

Abruptly, Garret pulled back, breaking the kiss, and set me
gently on my feet. I glanced into his eyes and saw the confusion, the uncertainty and the wary hope shining through,
and my heart stuttered. The soldier watched me a moment
longer, then closed his eyes.

"Tell me to stay," he whispered, his voice a low, husky
rasp, "and I will."

Cold flooded my body. I took a breath to answer…and
nothing came out. I knew the words that would convince
him…but I couldn't say them, even now. Especially now.
That would be even more cruel on my part, telling him what
he needed to hear, just to get him to stay with me, when I
wasn't certain myself.

Sickened, I drew back, sliding from Garret's arms. He
opened his eyes but didn't move, watching as I backed away
from him. The look on his face was devastating, but only for
a moment. Then that blank, remote soldier's mask slipped
into place, his eyes turning cold and flat.

Spinning on a heel, he walked away again, and this time his
stride was confident and sure. I watched, heart in my throat,
until he hit the stairs on the other side and started down, not
looking back once.

And then he was gone.

I swallowed, blinked rapidly until the stinging in my eyes went away and went back into the room.

Riley and Wes were still at the computer, but they had moved to the table now, with Riley standing behind the chair as the human hunched over the screen. Wes didn't move, but Riley looked up as I came in and leaned against the door, still coming to grips with the fact that Garret was really gone forever.

"Firebrand? You okay?" Riley stepped toward me, frowning in concern. "Where's St. George?"

"He…left," I answered, making Riley's brows shoot up. "Just now. He said he was going to check up on the Order or something. He's…not coming back."

"Huh." As expected, Riley didn't seem terribly heartbroken at the news. "Well, I'd say that's too bad, but then I'd just be lying. Don't glare at me, Firebrand," he went on, crossing the room. "You knew this was coming as much as I did. He's a human and a soldier of St. George. Did you really expect him to stick around a bunch of dragons for the rest of his life?"

"No," I whispered, my voice breaking a little bit. Of course not. Garret was human. He belonged out there, with the rest of humanity. Maybe now he could finally live a normal life. "I knew he had to leave sooner or later," I admitted. "I just… I'll miss him, that's all."

Riley stepped forward and, without hesitation, pulled me close. My pulse skipped, and warmth bloomed through my stomach, burning away the grief, at least for now.

"Forget him," Cobalt murmured, bending his head to mine. "You don't need the human. You have me. And when you're ready, when we reach a spot where we can both be ourselves, I'll show you exactly what that means."

Yes, my dragon agreed, as I closed my eyes, basking in the warmth. This was right. This was what I wanted. I didn't need humans or their tangle of confusing emotions. I was a dragon; it was time I finally accepted that.

Pulling back, I looked up at Riley, saw myself in that bright gold gaze and tried to smile. "So," I asked, as Cobalt peered back at me, eyes glimmering, "where to now?"

"Now?" Riley said, his voice full of dark promise as he turned away. "Now we're going to hunt down a traitor."

EPILOGUE

DANTE

I stood in another small, cold elevator, Mr. Smith and another Talon agent flanking me, as the tiny box descended into what felt like the bowels of the earth. Gazing at my blurry reflection in the metal door, I thought back to the past two days and allowed myself a small smile.

After the disastrous meeting and phone call with Ember, Mr. Roth had escorted me into his office and closed the door, inviting me to take a seat. I had obeyed with a numb sense of dread, knowing I had failed, both the organization and my sister. Sinking into the seat before the desk, I waited for the ax to fall, to be reamed out for my failure.

"First off, Mr. Hill, I'd like to congratulate you."

I had stared, unsure I'd heard him right. Why was he congratulating me? Surely this was a joke, though I hadn't known any of the senior executives to kid around. "Sir?"

Mr. Roth smiled. "This operation with your sister was a test, Mr. Hill. It was the reason we put you in charge of returning Ember Hill to Talon. We wanted to gauge your loyalty to the organization, as well as your ingenuity and commitment to doing the right thing."

"But...I failed, sir. I didn't bring Ember back."

"No, that failure was not yours, Mr. Hill." Roth's eyes glittered, though it wasn't directed at me. "You performed exactly as we hoped, and suffice to say the company is pleased with the results. There will be...repercussions. Reign is not going to be happy with the loss of his people, but that is Talon's concern, not yours. You've proven you can be trusted, that your ideals are in line with Talon's, that you value the safety of the organization above all else." He leaned back in his leather chair. "So again, I offer my congratulations, Mr. Hill. You have passed your final exam.

"Now," he continued as I sat there, reeling from the announcement. "We have business to discuss. As a full-fledged member of the organization, you now know how serious the rogue threat is. Your own sister committed a heinous act against one of her own kind, allowing her to be slain by a soldier of St. George. Such is often the case with dragons that go rogue. Without structure, they become violent and unpredictable, a danger to themselves and to the organization. Your sister has started down a very dark path, but we believe it is actually the rogue dragon Cobalt who is influencing her. He is an extremist whose hatred of Talon is well-known, and his tactics against the organization border on terrorism. Cobalt and his network of criminals must be stopped at all costs. How dedicated are you to bringing this about, Mr. Hill?"

Rage burned, and I clenched a fist on my leg, careful not to let Mr. Roth see. *Cobalt.* The rogue dragon who had lured my sister away, turned her against me, was my personal enemy now. He had almost cost me everything and would pay for what he had done. "Whatever it takes, sir," I said evenly. "Whatever Talon needs me to do."

"Even if it means working against your sister?"

I took a deep breath. "Ember made her choice," I said. "She has to live with the consequences of her actions. My hope is that she'll realize her mistake and return to the organization willingly, but if she doesn't, I will bring her back by force if I have to." Mr. Roth raised an eyebrow, appraising, and I spoke firmly, confidently. "The rogue movement must be eliminated, for the good of us all. I'm fully committed to seeing that happen, sir."

"Excellent." Mr. Roth beamed. "Then I do believe you are ready." He stood, extending a hand to lead me out of his office. "Rest up, Mr. Hill," he announced as he escorted me to where Mr. Smith stood waiting in the hall. "Tomorrow morning, you have a plane to catch."

★ ★ ★

The elevator slowed, and finally stopped with a faint ding. As the doors slid back, revealing a sterile white hallway and a pair of guarded metal doors at the end, Mr. Smith turned to me.

"Keep in mind, Dante," he warned as we stepped into the hall, passing humans in white lab coats scurrying from room to room. "This is one of Talon's greatest secrets. That you are even allowed to be here shows the amount of faith and trust the organization has in you. Do not abuse that."

"I won't," I promised, and meant it.

We came to the doors, and the Talon agent flashed a badge at one of the armed guards, who nodded briskly and waved us through. We stepped into an even smaller room, barely larger than the elevator box, where the guard pressed his hand to a small sensory pad by the door. It lit up, green lines scanning his palm and fingers, before it beeped once, and the light above the metal door turned green.

"Remember, Dante," Mr. Smith warned again, and pushed back the door.

My eyes widened. I stumbled forward in a daze, hardly believing what I saw. Steam billowed through the frame, and the air was hot and humid, as if I'd stepped into a rain forest. I was almost instantly drenched in sweat, but I barely felt it. I couldn't tear my gaze from the wonders of the scene before me.

Dragons. Hundreds of them. In rows of huge cylindrical vats marching down the aisles. They floated in translucent green liquid, eyes closed, wings and legs folded neatly to their bodies. Tubes jutted from their necks and stomachs, snaking to the tops of the canisters, where they disappeared in a tangle of machinery. From their size, most of them were hatchlings, some barely out of the egg, but there were a few near the end that were larger, older.

And they all looked the same. Through the glass and the green-tinted murk, their scales were a dull metallic gray, with no hint or spark of color at all. They all had the same ridge of ivory horns over their eyes and along their jaw. The same bony spikes jutting from their backs, shoulders and forelegs. The similarities were more than coincidence, more than sharing the same bloodline or parents. They were identical. Down to the same crooked horn on the left side of their head.

I smiled, as I realized what Talon had been planning, all this time.

"Behold, Dante Hill," Mr. Smith said, walking up behind me, his deep voice full of triumph. "Welcome to the future."

★ ★ ★ ★ ★

Thank you for reading ROGUE,
book two of THE TALON SAGA.
Look for book three, SOLDIER, coming soon.
Only from Julie Kagawa and Harlequin TEEN.

ACKNOWLEDGMENTS

Thank you to my parents for your prayers and guidance, and for encouraging me to go after my dreams, no matter how crazy they were. To the people at Harlequin TEEN for your continued hard work, amazing support, jaw-dropping covers and so on. A massive thank-you to my wonderful editor, Natashya Wilson, who continues to be Superwoman in everything that she does. To my agent, Laurie McLean, who asks the questions I cannot, without whom I would be completely lost. Also to Brandy Rivers, for championing my books and making the impossible happen.

And, of course, to Nick, my other half. My love for you burns hotter than dragonfire.

QUESTIONS FOR DISCUSSION

1. Two dragon lifestyles are contrasted in *Rogue*; that of the dragons in Talon and that of Riley's rogues. What are the advantages of each and which does Ember seem best suited for? Why does Dante want to stay with Talon? Point to evidence in the story.

2. Ember and Riley have different ways of seeing Las Vegas. How does each of them describe the city, and how do you account for the differences in their points of view?

3. Garret has spent most of his life in the military-esque Order of St. George. In what ways is he equipped to live on his own, and what challenges might he face as he learns to survive outside the Order?

4. Cobalt had become disillusioned with Talon prior to his mission to break into the St. George chapterhouse and blow it up. What experiences pushed him to leave, and what might have happened if Talon had not tried to kill

him back then? Where might Cobalt/Riley be now if Wes had not joined him?

5. In *Rogue*, Ember begins to feel a greater split between her dragon and human selves, mainly caused by her different reactions to Garret and Riley. Why does each character appeal to a different side of her, and what does that show about a dragon's ability to feel emotions?

6. Garret does not understand why Ember saved him from being executed. Ember has learned that Garret has killed many of her kind. Why is Ember so determined to save Garret, despite knowing what he is? Point to evidence about her character in the book to inform your answer.

7. Dante believes he has failed his mission to bring back Ember and is shocked when Mr. Roth congratulates him and welcomes him as a full member of Talon. Why, in Talon's view, did Dante succeed, and who do you think will take the fall for the failure of the mission?

8. Exploiting your enemy's weakness is a running theme in *Rogue*. What makes each entity—the rogues, Talon, the Order of St. George—weak, and in what ways might those weaknesses also be strengths? In what ways is the author hinting at a potential future solution to this ancient conflict?

9. Madison and Stealth both have minor parts in *Rogue* but each has a big impact on Cobalt. How is he changed by his encounter with each of these characters? How might

his actions toward each of them impact those characters in the future?

10. Dante is trusted with an incredible secret at the end of *Rogue*. What do you think Talon is planning? Discuss.

For your reading pleasure
Julie Kagawa and Harlequin TEEN
are proud to present
this exclusive excerpt from the final novel
of THE IRON FEY *series*
THE IRON WARRIOR.

The rulers of Summer and Winter stood at the head of the table, watching us as we came in. I'd never seen either of them before, but they were instantly recognizable. Oberon, the King of Summer, stood tall and proud at the table edge, silver hair falling down his back, his antlered crown casting jagged shadows over the surface. A pale, beautiful woman stood a few feet away, dark hair cascading around her shoulders, a high-collared cloak draping her armor of red and black. Piercing dark eyes stabbed me over the table, and my insides curled with fear. Mab, Queen of Winter, was just as dangerous and terrifying as I had imagined she would be. The only good thing was that Titania, the Queen of Summer, appeared to be absent today. The queens' hatred for each other was well-known, and the situation was volatile enough without two immortal faery rulers throwing down in the middle of the war council.

"Iron Queen," Mab stated in a cold, flat voice as Meghan and Ash stepped forward. "How good of you to join us. Perhaps you would like to hear the reports of what your son has been doing of late?"

"I am aware that Keirran is with the Forgotten," Meghan

replied, far more calmly than I would have expected. "I know they have been scouting the borders of Arcadia and Tir Na Nog. They have not, to my knowledge, harmed anyone or made any hostile overtures toward the courts."

"Yet," Mab hissed. "It is obvious they plan to attack, and I refuse to be besieged in my own kingdom. I propose we take the fight to the Forgotten now, before they and their mysterious Lady set upon us en masse."

"And how do you plan to do that, Lady Mab?" Oberon asked, his voice like a mountain spring, quiet yet frigid. "We do not know where the Forgotten *are*, where the rest of this army is hiding. Whenever anyone tries to follow them, they disappear, both from the mortal realm and the Nevernever. How do you propose we find something that does not exist?"

Mab glared at him. "They cannot simply vanish into thin air," she snapped. "An entire race of fey cannot simply will themselves into nothingness. They have to be somewhere."

"They are," I answered. "They're in the Between."

All eyes turned to me. My heart stuttered, but I took a deep breath and stepped forward, meeting the cold, inhuman stares of a couple dozen fey.

"King Oberon is right," I said, moving beside Meghan, feeling the chill of a Winter knight to my left. "The Forgotten can't be found in the mortal world or the Nevernever because they're *not* here anymore. They're slipping in and out of both worlds, from a place called the Between. It's—"

"I know what the Between is, Ethan Chase," Mab stated coolly, narrowing her eyes. "Most call it the Veil, the curtain between Faery and the mortal realm, the barrier that keeps our world hidden from mortal sight. But the ability for fey to go Between has been lost for centuries. I know of only one who has accomplished it in the past hundred years, and she has not seen fit to share her knowledge with the rest of Faery."

Leanansidhe. I nodded. "Well, it might've been lost to the courts, but the Lady—the Forgotten Queen—remembers how," I said. "And she taught the rest of the Forgotten, too. You haven't been able to find them because they're all hanging out in the Between."

Mab's icy black gaze lingered on my face, seeing far too much. "And the Iron Prince?" she asked in a soft, lethal voice, making Meghan stiffen beside me. "Does he have this special talent? Has the Lady taught him to go Between, as well?"

I swallowed.

"Yes," Meghan confirmed before I could say anything. "Whatever old knowledge the Lady brought with her when she awoke has passed to her followers. Keirran can move through the Between like the rest of the Forgotten."

Oberon raised his head. "Then it seems the Lady has chosen her champion," he stated in a low, grave voice. "And so the prophecy comes to pass. Keirran will destroy the courts unless we stop him. Iron Queen…" He gave Meghan an almost sympathetic look. "You know what you must do. Declare Keirran a traitor and cast him from your court. Only then may we stand united against the Forgotten and the Lady."

"What? Whoa, wait a second." I leaned forward, feeling the frigid edge of the table bite into my hands. "You don't know what they want. Keirran is only trying to help the Forgotten survive. Yeah, he did it in the most ass-backward way possible, but maybe you should try talking to them first before declaring all-out war."

"And what do you know of war, Ethan Chase?" Mab inquired, as her cold, scary gaze settled on me again. "You are the reason we are here, the reason the prophecy has come to pass. It was your presence that allowed the Forgotten to invade, your blood that tore away the Veil, even if it was for but a moment. You and the Iron Prince have brought nothing but chaos to Faery, and now you dare to tell us that we should be merciful?" Her lips curled in a terrifying smile. "I have not forgotten your hand in the destruction of my Frozen Wood," she said, making my blood chill at the memory. I tried to draw back, but I suddenly couldn't move. My hands burned on the edge of the table, and I looked down to see ice had crept up and sealed my fingers to the surface. "You are lucky that the impending war demands my attention for now," Mab hissed, "but do not think for a moment that I will let that slide. You and the Iron Prince have much to answer for."

"Lady Mab." Meghan's cool, steady voice broke through the rising fury. "Please stop terrorizing my brother before I take offence." My hands were suddenly free, and I yanked them back, rubbing them furiously to start circulation. "I am aware of the prophecy," Meghan went on, as I stuck my frozen fingers under my arms. "I am aware that, misguided or not, Keirran has done terrible things. But I beg you all to consider what we are really dealing with. This is my son and your kin. Both of yours," she added, looking to the Summer King and the Winter Queen in turn. "Are we going to declare war on our own blood without knowing the details? We are still uncertain as to what the Forgotten and the Lady really want."

"I can tell you what she wants," said a new, familiar voice behind us.

The blood froze in my veins. I spun, as did the rest of the table, to face the entrance of the room. The double doors had been pushed back, and a figure stood in the entryway with a pair of shadowy sidhe knights flanking him.

Keirran.